MURDER IS BLISS

ELLEN ANTHONY

LN Books Limited

The characters and events portrayed in this book are fictitious.
Any similarity to real persons, living or dead, is coincidental
and not intended by the author.

First published in 2013. Revised edition 2023

Published by LN Books Limited
4500 Cannon Avenue #63
Klamath Falls, OR 97603

Paperback ISBN-13: 978-1-948168-19-9

Dedication

To my friends, past and present, in all worlds, and for the Seanchai Library and AOL Writers club denizens the world round.

To my growing legion of fans. There is more to come.

Contents

Chapter 1 - Monday,

12 July 2179

Rising from the North Platte River, a flock of geese skimmed over treetops and past the spire of the Plains cathedral. Their wings surged as they flew higher, oblivious to the city buried beneath them. Settling into their vee, they turned their backs on Laramie Peak and flew northeast, their honkings fading away.

Below them the cathedral jutted up out of miles of trees, the tallest building in Plains, Wyoming. Its height was misleading for it only stood forty-two feet above the forest floor. Below ground it extended deep into the city, almost three floors of it buried in its depths.

The spire wasn't alone. Beneath the trees there were paved walkways leading to red brick schools and gardens scattered here and three. The tan brick of the public exits and the dark gray of the police buildings were also there. There were even a handful of privately owned homes scattered among the trees but they were rare leftovers from the city's beginning. No one built above ground any more.

Here and there lay ventilation shafts too with their sleek forms rising sixteen feet into the sky. To a student of a more ancient time, they would look like sleek-sided missiles standing guard over the fruit trees. Necessary structures, they brought clean air into the city and vented air that had become too stale. Together they serviced a city of four hundred thousand people.

In Southland Mall, a floor below ground level, people were shopping, eating, or sunning beneath the great domed skylight. Groups walked around the great track on the upper level in their skimpy sunning outfits while a few, those who could afford it, sunned on private balconies over the stores. On the lower level, beneath the transparent floor, were the luxury shops. The busiest of these was the import store and today it was of great interest to Lieutenant Jasper Stone.

"Everyone hold position," he said into his com unit. "Our mark should be along soon." Striding past the mirrored front of a beauty salon, he barely noticed the lean dark-haired man in the mirror. Clad in the standard suit of all police detectives with his white shirt and black single-breasted jacket, he had none of the radical embellishments currently in fashion. His hair, still thick at thirty-eight, was dark brown and well trimmed. His chin, long ago defoliated, was firm and his lips thin. People recognized him as a police detective but one that exuded an air of confidence. Jasper Stone knew his job and did it well.

Inside the import store he walked past rows of terminals where customers were searching for their next big order. His sharp brown eyes took in how many there were and a tiny frown creased his brow. Too many. He didn't expect this situation to get ugly but each person in the store added a complication. Their quarry wouldn't come in though if the store looked deserted.

The counter bisected the store, separating terminals from the shelves of boxes, big and small, that lined the back half of the store. The packages came in a variety of colors and shapes and each box sported a red inspection sticker to show they contained no contraband.

Seeing his partner, Jasper moved over to where Brown stood. With her coffee-colored skin and black hair swept back into a tight braid, Detective Lori Brown had the looks of a model when she chose to. Today though she was dressed in the same brown shirt and khaki pants of a store employee. Lacking only a nametag to make her disguise complete, Brown simply blended into the store's background. That was her skill.

"Anything?" Jasper asked, his eyes sliding over the personnel behind the counter and the customers they waited on.

"He's been notified the package is here," she said. "He said he'd be here at two forty."

He glanced at his watch. "Pretty precise."

"Some people are like that," she said. "It fits with what I found out."

"Give me a report later," Jasper said, his thoughts already flying to other things he had to check. He had more than fifteen people stationed outside ready to snatch the professor and the box of drugs he was picking up--illegal drugs shipped in a box that was supposed to contain a book.

He still didn't know how the inspections system missed the drugs and they'd had no opportunity to find out. The box was sealed and stamped and his department was prohibited from re-opening it without a warrant. They had to wait for the receiver--and they wanted him.

He'd be here soon. He didn't know how Professor Andrew Nugent tied into the illegal blissex trade. The history professor was a department head at the city college and he had no priors, nothing at all.

Stepping outside, Jasper quietly eyed the mall. He could see uniformed officers at every elevator but one. Good. They wanted their mark to take that one if he got past them. It was set to take him up to a surface customs station where regular duty officers waited.

The mall was huge, nearly a half kilometer long, with two levels of stores. Overhead sunlight poured down from the massive skylight. He could see the upper level was packed with sunbathers. He wasn't concerned with them.

This level was where the luxury shops were. The import store, clothing stores, the little spice shop he favored, and the specialty shops were all here. The largest of the city's theaters was at the end of the mall, its columned portico bringing a taste of the world's past to the futuristic city.

Only people with money to spend came to this level. There were a few subbies, their pastel and gray clothing proclaiming their subsistence status but even they had a few hard-earned dollars to spend. One woman, looking embarrassed to be here in her pink tunic and gray pants, strode purposely past him to the spice store.

Jasper didn't look directly at her. The woman was like his mother, forced to go on to subsistence due to a job loss or ill health but still proud. She wasn't likely to be on it long. His parents had made it out in a little over two years.

It was humiliating having to go on city charity when you'd always worked for a living and most people didn't stay on it. They found a job or created one or did something to get off the rolls. It was not enough to have clothing, housing, and food provided. They needed their pride.

He wrenched his thoughts back to the present, speaking into his com unit. "He'll be here at two forty. You have his picture. Do not detain him until I say. Confirm."

The green confirmation list popped up his screen with each station registering receipt of his order. Station six was slow in responding. He glanced over that way to see the guard, a temporary he'd had to pull off cargo screening, messing with his com unit. The confirmation blinked on.

His lips tightened. Apparently they didn't use com units much. This operation was big enough that he had six such people. The neighboring sections hadn't been able to give him trained field officers because it was payday for a large percentage of the city. Their people were either on duty or getting ready to go on duty. He hadn't even been able to use trained officers from his own department who were scheduled for evening shifts and night shifts. Instead he'd had to pull people from the least critical assignments. At least three were cargo screeners and there would be a backup because of it.

"Bird spotted." The message was audible as well as on his screen. He glanced at it, saw it was elevator two and looked that way. It took him only a few seconds to spot the professor in his tweed suit--itself an antiquarian affectation in their climate-controlled city.

As the professor came closer he could see the man's neatly trimmed beard, his spectacles, and briefly admired the image he portrayed. The man could have stepped out of a vid about mid-twentieth century New York. He looked bookish.

Briefly wondering if the spectacles were real, Jasper moved back toward the import store. Stopping at the display outside it, he looked at the goods displayed on the screen. An image of a toy antique car was replaced by a set of fine dishes as the professor walked by.

Keying his com unit's screen to show the interior view of the store, he watched him go straight to the counter. Just as promptly, a store employee greeted him by name and went to fetch the package. The pastel blue box was laid on the counter between them but the professor made no attempt to open it. Instead he pulled out a little notebook and started conversing with the employee.

Jasper saw Detective Brown moving closer but then a man in maintenance overalls blocked his view. Brown's attention was on the professor. It wasn't until the professor himself turned with a cry that Jasper knew something had happened.

"All units stop the maintenance man!"

Jasper caught Brown's audio. He stepped into the store, saw no maintenance man, and hurried out, followed by his partner.

"He came out and turned left. He has the package."

"You're sure?"

"I'm sure."

"Stay here. Grey coveralls?"

"Yes. Brown carry-all."

"Damn." Jasper pulled his trank gun off his belt and hurried down a maintenance hall right to the left of the import store. The hallway was narrow and led to receiving rooms, cleaning closets, and..... a freight elevator!

One man was in the hall but not in gray.

Shoving his badge in his face, Jasper snapped "Where?"

The man gestured at the elevator. "He didn't have his key. I opened it," he said before it registered what he'd done. "God, I'm sorry."

"Maintenance level," he snapped into his com unit after a glance at the elevator controls. "Brown, get the professor. All others go to maintenance level. Looking for a man with gray coveralls but a brown carryall. He doesn't have a maintenance key."

Turning to the inadvertent helper, he snapped. "ID."

The man handed it over, still apologizing. "Sorry, detective, it never occurred to me..."

Jasper slapped the ID on his com unit and it registered. Handing it back, he cut the man off. "We'll talk later."

The elevator was back. He moved in quickly, hitting the button for the only level it serviced below this one. Thank the designers this elevator didn't go to residential areas. If he made it into those, they'd never find him.

Jasper blinked rapidly to adjust his eyes to the dimmer maintenance level. He could see splashes of light near routinely maintained equipment and in between glow strips furnished a minimum of light for navigation. Pipes, electrical conduits, and pneumatic tubes lined the walls, broken here and there by storerooms for the stores in the mall and maintenance closets. Those should be locked. He tried the first one and it was.

The alley was wide enough for the city trucks that delivered goods to the mall but there were no carts in the parking spots he passed. He slapped a logger and it confirmed none were supposed to be there. The operator would order one for him if he liked.

"Where's the closest cart?"

"There are no carts available closer than section four," the female voice answered.

"Has one just left from here?"

"Define."

"This section in the last ten minutes."

"One left station five gamma two minutes ago, detective."

"Shut bulkheads to section four maintenance," he snapped.

"Authorization?"

"Ten eighteen alpha tango, Lieutenant Jasper Stone."

"Shutting bulkheads section four maintenance."

He heard the warning siren as he rushed toward it. Section five ran half the length of the mall and section four completed it. If they could trap him at the bulkhead doors-- His stride broke when he saw a carryall tossed against the wall. Guessing it was brown and the package wasn't in it, he kept going.

"Got him!" His com unit burst out with a touch of glee. He didn't recognize the voice. "On a cart at the section doors. Grey coverall not armed. No carry-all."

He could see the cart's headlights at the end of the passage as he ground to a halt, gasping for breath. "That's him. Get his ID and look for the package."

"He's blissed out," another voice said in disgust. "Lieutenant, he's barely with us."

Jasper swore as he walked quickly down the maintenance alley. Blissed out? He couldn't even be questioned until three hours after the bliss wore off. Holstering his trank, he strode on.

He was the third man there. One of the cargo inspectors was standing over the man they'd been hunting. The snatcher's hands were secured in binders but one look at his slack-jawed expression and half-closed eyes told him the man wasn't going anywhere. He was having a good bliss high, probably far better than the legal dose would give him.

The other man, Officer Hunter, was just closing the maintenance compartments of the cart. "No ID," he reported, "And no package. I found one bliss wrapper and this." He held up a maintenance key.

"He had one?"

"Had to if he wanted to use a cart," Ed said. "They're locked. Too many kids joy riding."

"Right." Jasper knew he should have remembered that but it had been years since he last caught a joy rider. "I saw the carry-all, I think. Let's get our people down here and start looking."

"And him?"

"He can wait." The sandy-haired miscreant was totally relaxed against the wall. He might go to sleep but he wouldn't be moving any time soon.

"This is Lieutenant Stone, authorization ten eighteen alpha tango. Unlock section four maintenance doors."

"Yes, lieutenant."

He waited till he heard the bolts grind then spoke again. "Dispatch."

"Dispatch here."

"We need a sweep of section five maintenance. Notify my squad then have the maintenance supervisor section five call me."

"Yes sir."

As soon as he shut it off, his com unit buzzed again.

"Brown here. I have the professor. He's really upset."

"Upset? Because of us?"

"No sir," Lori Brown said with a touch of asperity. "He wants his book."

Chapter 2 – New Assignment

Two bloody hours and they still hadn't found the package. Jasper scowled and rubbed his smooth jaw then straightened up as the door opened and his captain came in. He glanced at Brown as they both rose to their feet. He wasn't sure why they'd been recalled to the precinct. The search was still going on and their prisoner couldn't be questioned for another five hours at least. It probably wouldn't be done till morning now.

"Status?" Captain Reynolds asked as he sat down and made a motion for them to do the same.

"The package is still missing but could be found any time," Jasper said. "And we have the maintenance man in custody. He's not maintenance. According to records, he's a subby named Willis Frazier. He's done petty theft before but nothing as bold as this."

"He had a maintenance key," Jasper continued. "We've done a check. Its owner was named Lukas. No word yet on how he lost it but he did report it stolen."

"And you?" the captain asked, looking at Brown.

"We have the professor here in the precinct--he insisted. He's pretty upset because it took him years to locate that book and he wants it back," Brown said.

"What kind of book?"

"It's a children's picture book, paper--and, no, he doesn't have any kids." Brown looked a little puzzled by that. "But he's insistent that's what was in the package and he's really upset it got swiped."

"Book lovers." Jasper grinned in spite of himself. He never understood them. He wondered if the professor's precious book had been fed to an incinerator.

"Let's hope his book turns up and the drugs too," his captain briskly said, "but there are changes. Brown, you stay on this case. Jasper, I need you to get over to Section Three, 2

Lily Street, right away. There's been a high-profile murder and I need you there."

Stunned, Jasper opened his mouth to protest then thought better of it. "Victim?"

"Elizabeth West. She owned an entry house."

"The recipe lady?" Jasper abruptly remembered a gray-haired woman who had pressed old-fashioned recipes and baked goods on him and his partner back when he patrolled that section. Part of their weekly inspections had been to check the upper door logs of the West house.

"What?"

"Old woman, maybe ninety now, with a three-story mansion. The top level had an outside entry with logging lock. I used to patrol there."

"Must be the same one. She's dead. I want you over there and I want you to tie up that house," his captain said. "We don't need an entry house being sold right now. You got that? Even if it turns out to be suicide, I want that house tied up."

"Could it be suicide?" Brown asked.

"Not likely. Elizabeth West took the walk two months ago and rejected it. Someone who turns down legal suicide at the last minute isn't likely to kill herself a few weeks later."

Took the walk. Those words made Jasper inwardly flinch. They brought back painful memories of Carol--of kissing her goodbye then holding her hand and waiting for her to die.

His captain hesitated. "Jasper, I know this will be hard on you but, dammit, we need our best people on this. It's a high-profile case and Elizabeth West was a founder of Plains. She deserves the best."

"Understood," Jasper managed to say and then "I agree. Mrs. West was a good woman and not the kind to choose a painful death."

"What was that about recipes?" Reynolds asked.

"She believed in real cooking and always had a treat or two for us when we came to check the door. She'd give us the recipe too and told us to marry women who could cook."

"Tasty bribes huh?" The captain smiled to show he didn't disapprove. "Did you meet any of the family?"

"There was a gawky teenage girl with something weird in her hair," Jasper said. "Big blue eyes. The one time I saw her she disappeared fast."

Brown laughed.

"That might be the granddaughter who found her," his captain said. "The report came in about thirty minutes ago so you'll probably find them at the house."

"Yes sir. Am I completely off this case?" He was reluctant to lose any break they had in the illegal blissex trade.

"No. Brown, schedule the interview of that suspect for tomorrow at seven thirty. Jasper can spend an hour here before going there. Find that package before then too."

"Yes sir." She didn't show any reaction even though that might mean working all night.

"All your other assignments are relieved, Jasper. Just the murder case and this one drug case."

"Yes sir." Jasper accepted the assignment without surprise. He'd spent most of his career working in Section 5 but he'd been loaned out numerous times to other sections of the city. Since not every section had a dedicated homicide unit, it was necessary. Even he pulled double duty between homicide and vice.

"Get moving."

* * *

Jasper took the elevator up to the maintenance level then walked out the precinct's doors. Since they had to maintain order on all levels of the city, the precinct buildings stretched from the sixth level all the way to ground level although the ground level access was just a watch tower and elevator. It wasn't needed often.

The maintenance level held the car park. Jasper selected one of the squad cars, inserted his ident key, and turned it on.

"Computer, plot best course to Section 3, 2 Lily Street."

"Yes sir. Take maintenance corridor to exit 4-C then throughway to exit 3-AB. Enter maintenance corridor at exit 3-B and park at 3-D parking lot. Elevator 3-D up one floor and turn left thirty meters." The best route lit up on the car's screen and he studied it a moment. "Save this screen and highlight progress."

"Confirmed."

The route was fairly simple but he'd learned a long time ago to keep it on screen since too many numbers could get scrambled in his brain. At least he wasn't traveling to the other side of the city. Sections one through five were the oldest parts of Plains and comprised one administrative sector. The city stretched on north along the old interstate corridor for nearly twenty miles to Section 23. There it stopped, construction halted before the planned twenty-five sections when it became obvious there simply wasn't enough water to support additional people.

It never looked like the sections held thousands. Good city planning had provided light rail for inter-sector travel and trams for inside sectors. Bicycles were allowed on both the tram routes and on the pedestrian levels. Since every neighborhood had food markets and clubs and cafes, people mostly traveled to and from jobs and when they had a major shopping day.

Traffic was light right now so Jasper's squad car had no problem maintaining speed as he took to the express lane. A few trams were in the middle lane with their human cargos and bicycle riders clogged the slow lane. No freights. It would be almost five hours before the freights would start rolling through the city. To ease congestion, they didn't run until after midnight and they stopped before five in the morning.

The drive would be fairly short. He should review the West case but wasn't willing to trust the squad car's autopilot. Instead of calling up facts on the computer, he reviewed what he remembered.

Elizabeth West he remembered well even though it was a good thirteen years since he'd patrolled Lily Street. He'd kept the recipes she gave him and a few were family favorites. Why would anyone want to kill her?

It had to be the house or her money. Entry houses were rare. Legal for the first five years of the city, there hadn't been any built since. As the existing ones came up for sale, the city had bought them up and sealed the upper floor entry permanently or tore them down. Very few were still in private hands.

They weren't needed. Plains was ninety-two percent underground and the people liked it that way. The climate-controlled environment was pleasant and they never had to deal with the freezing winds of winter or the endless heat waves that made above ground living so miserable. Above ground was reserved for the orchards. The trees were essential to provide good air, fruit, and insulation from the temperature extremes.

The West house was as hard to forget as Elizabeth West. He remembered it best for its beautiful view of Laramie Peak. A private low-walled garden had lain outside the glass door he checked and beyond that were trees and that glorious mountain rising twenty miles away. He only had to check the logging entry lock on that door but he'd always managed to spend a couple of minutes enjoying that view. Mrs. West hadn't minded. She'd encouraged him and his partner to linger over brownies, cookies, and other treats. After they'd checked that lock and the lock on the house's main door, they'd had coffee--real coffee--and her baked goods and talked about life in the city.

How many people in that family? When he'd been patrolling, her husband was already dead. She had at least one son still living. Yes, there was a Michael West high up in the city engineering staff and there was that girl. She'd been maybe thirteen or fourteen by the looks of her. She'd be grown up now and have a career of her own.

He knew the West family had been one of the founders of Plains. They'd either owned some of the land or had helped finance the city. Either way, they deserved justice. He'd make sure they got it.

Reaching the 3-D parking lot, he scrutinized the vehicles already there--two other police cars, a lab vehicle, and three civilian cars. He eased his squad car into the slot furthest from the elevator. It was unlikely he'd be transporting anyone.

Thumbing on his com unit, he typed in "Bio search Elizabeth West, 2 Lily Street." The com unit responded quickly, giving him her address and picture then her family members. He tapped on Michael West and opened his bio, frowning when he saw that the man was currently on sick leave following a work-related accident. No children.

Going back to Elizabeth's screen, he saw two of her sons were deceased. It was a very large family for Plains. He tapped on the other son who was still living and found he lived in Denver. David West was listed as a lunatech so he wasn't lacking for money. The people who operated the remote-controlled mining equipment on the moon were paid outrageous salaries and they got to live on Earth. The only ones paid more were the mechanics who lived on the moon.

David had one son living. Odd. His other son died the same year as his uncles. Curious, he hit the boy's name. Benjamin West, aged 11, died New Wave Colony collapse, August 23, 2158.

Going back to Elizabeth's screen, he tapped the other sons' names. Rory died New Wave Colony collapse. He noted his wife had also died. No children. He found what he wanted under John. There she was--Jewel West. So she was a grandchild and the sole survivor of her own family--father, mother, sister, uncle and aunt, and a cousin all dead in that disaster.

He felt quick sympathy for her and for the gracious Elizabeth. He remembered seeing the footage of the New Wave collapse when he was in college and how stunned he'd been as the lop-sided dome crumpled like an eggshell, killing more than a thousand people. One of the four survivors had been the reporter that shot that graphic footage. The disaster had mostly stopped undersea colonization. As it was, no large colonies had been built so deep since then.

He pulled his thoughts back to the case. Two sons, two grandchildren, and two of them had wives. Those were his primary suspects unless he found signs of forced entry. Those he had to question and find out where they were today.

He was ready.

Chapter 3 – Crime Scene

Harkening back to a much older day, the exterior of the West house was ornate with a real wood door set into a brick wall. He smiled, remembering the first time he'd seen such opulence on his patrol. The brass doorknocker was still there and he would have put money on it being stolen by now. There was a curtained window to one side of the entry-- another affectation of the rich since it only looked out on the city street.

He used the knocker and almost immediately a uniformed officer opened the door. Showing his badge, he walked past him and down the short hall to the central core of the house. Another man moved to intercept him there and he waved his badge.

"Detective Sanders," the new man said. "You're Lieutenant Stone?"

"Yes. Vice and Homicide, Section 5."

"Vice here," the red-haired detective said. "Trained in homicide though. You're lead."

"Yes." Jasper didn't bother to ask more about his experience. The man knew it and knew he couldn't lead. "She died in here?"

"Yes. She hit the floor over there but there's a second blood spot that doesn't fit the pattern. We were just looking at it."

"Show me. Are any of the relatives here?"

"Yes, in the front room." Sanders led him over the carpeted floor to the impact site. It was by the previously spotless white furniture with scattered throw pillows in flowered pink. Last time he'd been here the furniture was black leather with red and white pillows.

The solid wooden end table had one corner soaked in blood and there was a spray pattern that suggested impact.

The table was still intact but he was sure the head of Elizabeth West wasn't.

"She was lying there," Sanders told him, "But there's more blood on the chair and a blood spot on the carpet beside it. Unless she bounced twice, she couldn't have hit here and there."

"Bounced?"

"Yeah." Sanders led him to the winged chair nearest the wall-mounted vid screen. As usual in this house, the screen was set to show a fireplace fire, a look enhanced by the mantle over it and a tasteful display of figurines. The chair had traces of blood but there was more in a wide spot on the cream carpet. "The girl said she didn't move her. She was dead when she got here."

"Then let's look at the top," Jasper said and motioned to the open ceiling stretching up three floors. Stairs climbed up in stages to the third floor, their wooden banisters the only thing bordering them and empty space.

He kept his hand off the dark wood as they climbed and his eye on the stairs. The white newels were dusty at the base, something he was surprised to see in such a house. It wasn't until they were ready to climb to the third floor that he saw what he wanted.

"Hold it," he said as Sanders started by. "Mind your step." He knelt at the base of the stair and touched a light finger to a drop of blood. It was dry but it hadn't been there long.

Standing up, he carefully examined the banister. The wood looked darker. He touched a single fingertip to the dark area and drew his hand away from the stickiness.

"Blood," he said to Sanders. Leaning over, he looked on the outside of the banister and saw more. He motioned to Sanders to look. "Murder."

Sanders swallowed hard then looked at him like he'd just pronounced a truth. Gee, this guy was green. Jasper knew it before he even set foot on the stairs but that bloodstain cinched it. He didn't have to create any line to keep this house tied up. Someone had killed Elizabeth West. Now he just had to prove who did.

They didn't go back down. Leaving an evidence marker by the blood spot on the carpet and another flagging the banister, Jasper continued up to the third floor. A technician was already there and at work.

This floor was mostly like he remembered it. It was remarkably open with a chandelier hanging over the stair well. The wood floor was immaculate and the wide dance floor that filled three sides of the floor was empty of all save some scattered furniture. The doors to bedroom and bath stood open but the glass windowed door that opened to the outside was closed. He didn't touch the handle but peered into the display on the lock.

"Once this is dusted," he said to the technician, "I need the log from this lock. Go back a week."

"Yes sir."

"It's a Yale Model 53V if they haven't changed it," Jasper said. "That should save you some time."

"Yes sir." The technician betrayed no surprise that he knew.

Sanders did. Looking puzzled, he waved at the door. "How?"

"I was a beat cop in this section thirteen years ago. We checked the logs." He glanced at that glorious view of the Peak but today it didn't hold his attention.

"Then you knew her?"

"Yes, did you?"

"I saw her a few times," Sanders said. "Not recently."

"Good. Let's remember she was a good lady." Jasper remembered her smile and her gracious manner and knew he was going to take this case personally. Elizabeth West wasn't just a face to him.

"Yes sir."

"Now you said the family was in the den? How many?" He headed down the stairs ahead of Sanders.

"Just two. The son is pretty much out of it but the girl is the one who found her and called it in. She's taking care of the other one."

"Any sign of forced entry?"

"The main door wasn't locked when we got here," Sanders said. "The girl said she came in through the upper door."

"Upper door?" Jasper paused on the stairs. "Why?"

"She teaches at the closest school. After classes she came through the gardens to get here. Apparently she does it a lot." Sanders glanced at his com unit and the notes there. "It's shorter."

"Ok, I can see that." Jasper eyed the two blood spots again, one with the white taped figure of a woman. Who could be cold enough to throw a dying old woman over a railing? "What we have is a murder done by someone the victim knew. Agreed?"

"Possible," Sanders said. "Probable?"

"Yes." Jasper pointed to the chair. "She was sitting in that chair and struck with something, probably from behind. She fell on to the floor and bled." He paused. "There's a murder weapon somewhere that was used to club her."

"Right." Sanders studied the chair and made notes. "We'll turn this house inside out."

"Do that." Jasper's cool brown eyes surveyed the scene. He couldn't see anything out of place or anything likely to be used as a club. There were some oriental statues on the mantle but none looked to be missing.

He slowly descended the stairs, looking at the scene from various angles as he went. He realized he'd seen that white furniture before in this house but it was on the third floor not here. Not new after all.

"Why did he haul her upstairs then?" Sanders asked. "If he'd already killed her?"

"To make it look like an accident or...." Jasper hesitated. "She wasn't dead. No, she probably wasn't dead. She bled a lot there," he motioned to the bloodspot "and more on the stairs.

Dead people don't bleed. There might be a drop here and there but no large amounts. She might have survived the blow on the head and kept breathing so he finished the job by throwing her off up above."

"Cold."

"Yes, cold. There was no passion in this. He wanted her dead."

"Why?"

"That's what we need to find out," Jasper brusquely said. "And we aren't even sure it was a man. I remember Elizabeth West as being 5 foot 6 and looking to be about a hundred pounds. Was she still slight?"

"Yes sir."

"So a woman could have done it."

"Possibly." Sanders looked doubtful. "If she lifted. I don't think the girl does."

"What about the son? You said he's here? Which one?"

"I'm not sure. He was asleep on the third floor and didn't seem to hear anything," Sanders said. "He was still asleep when we got here. The girl woke him and told him what happened. He's been out of it since."

"Blissed out?"

"No sir," Sanders said. "A pain killer."

"Prescription?"

"Could be. He's on sick leave because of an injury."

"On the follow-up list." Jasper left the stairs then hesitated. He'd never been in the private rooms of the house--just the central core and the kitchen. No, he'd been in the master suite upstairs too. He'd checked those windows to be sure they couldn't be opened.

"This way." Sanders motioned towards the front of the house. They entered the room with the curtained window.

Jasper got a quick impression of a loveseat with a rocking chair facing it. A desk stood in one corner and the other held a curio cabinet. The colors in here were very neutral and only the green couch cushions showed a woman's touch. Three people were there but Jasper noted the uniform of the policewoman and dismissed her. The two sitting on the loveseat were his only concern.

Michael West was a balding man in his late fifties. Right now his shoulders were hunched over and head down but he was maybe six foot standing. His slacks were good quality cloth and his shirt even finer but he looked rumpled as if he'd slept in both. The face he turned to him showed a moustache and was etched with grief. The man had clearly been crying and even now still looked out of focus.

The girl, on the other hand, was in sharp contrast. Her long chestnut hair was caught back in a look that was half ponytail and half chignon. The big blue eyes she turned to him were sapphire jewels and her lashes were thick when they brushed her cheek. Her full ruby lips parted and she spoke. "Detective?"

"Lieutenant Stone," Jasper said as he thought how beautiful she was. Clearly the gawky teenager he'd glimpsed though. No one else could have such deep blue eyes. He looked from her to the man. "Michael West?"

"Yes," the man managed to respond.

"What did you take and when?"

"Valium," he hesitated, blinking hard to focus. "I don't know. It was after noon. We ate lunch together, Mother and....
" His face crumpled. "Mother." He shuddered and a sob escaped him.

The girl clasped his hand tightly. "It's the valium," she told them with a touch of defiance. "He's not normally like this."

"I understand," Jasper said. She seemed cool and collected but he doubted that calm was more than a touch of bravado. He would have to find out though. "Your name?"

"Jewel West."

"And where were you this afternoon?"

"I was teaching school, West Elementary, fourth grade," she coolly replied. "The school number is 555-8321. You can confirm that."

He made a note of it. "What time did you leave?"

"Three-forty."

"You know the precise time?"

"I saw my last students down the stairs at three-twenty then returned to my room to tidy up. After telling the computer I was walking home topside, I left. It was precisely 3:40 when I clocked out. It takes me between ten and twelve minutes to reach the door of this house. I've timed it before."

"So you came in about three-fifty?"

"Yes."

"Let yourself in?"

"Of course. I have a code and Grandma doesn't climb the stairs anymore."

"She doesn't...didn't?" Jasper corrected.

"No." She glanced at her uncle then back at him. "She broke her hip six months ago. She got depressed because she couldn't climb the stairs then she.... she adjusted. Her bedroom is on this floor now and she just doesn't do stairs. I mean she didn't. There is no way she walked upstairs and fell!"

"Mr. West, where were you?" Jasper turned his attention back to the man.

"Asleep," he muttered then cleared his throat. "Asleep."

"Which room?"

"The third floor. Mother had me take it so it wouldn't be empty."

"Could she have come up there to wake you up?" Jasper asked simply to eliminate that.

West shook his head. "No, no, she would never do that."

"There's an intercom," Jewel put in. "If she wanted him, she would have used that. I can hear it in my room too."

"So you have a room here too?"

"Yes, I've lived here since I was six."

Jasper restrained a smile. Yes, she was the one he glimpsed. Satisfied he had her pegged now, he continued. "So you came in the upper door, saw your grandmother and did what?"

"I came downstairs first, tried to wake her then called for help. She was... She was already cold when I touched her. It was ... horrible." Her voice broke and the reserve she held on to shattered. A ragged sob escaped her and she pressed her palms tightly against her eyes, her fingers clenching and unclenching as she fought for control.

Her uncle gave her knee an awkward pat of reassurance.

Jasper turned to Sanders and held up his com unit to show him the note on the school. Sanders nodded and left. When the girl had regained some control, he spoke again.

"For now I just need to know who woke you up, Mr. West, and when."

"Jewel did but I think the policemen were already here. I didn't know anything, didn't hear anything."

"That I can believe," Jasper said with only a slight hesitation. "About the valium--is it prescription?"

He hesitated. "Not exactly."

"Black market?" Jasper asked.

"Not exactly."

"Explain."

"My prescription for narcoset had run out but I still have a lot of pain. I can't sleep without it," he slowly explained. "My sister-in-law has a prescription. I got valium from her."

"Her name?"

"Jessica West."

Jasper hesitated, instantly recognizing the name of the star. This family was truly connected. "The actress?" He hadn't caught that when he looked at the bios. She must be married to David.

"Yes."

"I'll have to confirm she gave you the valium."

"She'll confirm it."

"Her number?"

"222-777-8342," Jewel said, holding up her com unit to show him. "That's her private line--the one she answers."

"Thank you," Jasper said. "You both look beat and I think I'd better continue this tomorrow when you're both clear-headed. Have you got some other place you can stay tonight? This house will have to be sealed."

Jewel looked taken back then a flash of defiance crossed her face. Her uncle's hand tightened on her knee and he spoke. "I still have my house at Gracee Place. It's number twelve. We'll stay there. Jewel will need her things."

"Of course," Jasper quickly agreed. "Just nothing from this floor. Can I ask why you still have a place?"

"I moved in here after my accident," Michael West explained. "Mother insisted. I could manage the stairs but couldn't cook for myself. She could. It was temporary. Jewel is the only one who really lives here with Mother."

"Thank you." Jasper glanced at the silent policewoman. "This officer will help you pack, Miss West. I'll see you both tomorrow afternoon for further questions. Mr. West, will two p.m. do for you?"

The man nodded.

"I work until three thirty," Jewel quickly volunteered.

"How about four then?" Jasper asked.

"I'll get my things too," Michael West said.

"I'll give you a hand," Jasper said. It wasn't standard procedure to help but both these people were suspects. He wanted to make sure nothing was removed that was essential to the case. He also wanted to look at any valium. If he remembered right, Jessica West had been in rehab before so any pills she provided could be either legal or not. If not, they'd have to be tested for purity. He'd decide whether to bring charges for their possession later.

The policewoman caught his silent command and followed the girl out. She'd keep an eye on her. Michael West was his man--and possibly a murderer.

Chapter 4 - Home

Four hours later he was home. It had taken time to really examine the scene and get the preliminary autopsy report. As he'd expected, Elizabeth West had two head injuries, not one. The other had been from behind.

He'd noted a tea service on the little table in front of the chair and that also fit into his theory that someone she knew was there. There was one cup and saucer, the usual teapot and creamer and sugar bowl and a plate of her homemade brownies. The only anomaly had been two spoons, not one. They'd found the second cup and saucer in the sink drainer with the lunch dishes. Apparently the killer had been canny enough to get rid of his fingerprints but had missed the spoon. There was a chance they'd find fingerprints on it.

It bothered him that the front door had been left unlatched but not much. If you wanted to persuade police it was a stranger who did the crime, leaving a door unlocked helped. It was the move of an amateur though. A professional killer wouldn't leave an unlocked door.

Stretching out his long legs, he sipped his coffee and sighed. The whole crime smacked of an amateur. The bloody banister was a dead giveaway, a clue no one could miss. If he hadn't found it, one of the technicians would have. How long had the killer rested there before taking her the rest of the way upstairs?

He wasn't going to solve it tonight. Resolutely putting it aside, he tried to turn to his other case but he knew better than to call in and find out the status. If they'd found the package, it would be there in the morning. If they hadn't, he'd probably end up going out and looking for it himself. He couldn't afford that. No, he'd better get some sleep.

Rising to his feet, he glanced around his home. Everything was in its normal place. His vid screen was on standby, showing its usual blank face to the apartment, beyond that was his music system and recording equipment. He needed to get that packed but couldn't bring himself to do it tonight. He couldn't sit down and play though or he'd lose hours of needed sleep. He knew what he was like when he played. So did his daughter.

He gazed at it dispassionately, remembering the last fight he'd had with his daughter. She'd kept her threat and gone to live at the college. Mel simply hadn't understood how much he needed to play after her mother died.

His need had faded in the year since but now he played for another reason. He'd kept his promise to Carol to keep it going, keep composing the music she loved so much. In a couple of days the fruits of his labor would finally hit the market. For the first time in nearly twenty years he had a new album coming out.

He knew it would be the end of his law enforcement career. If it got half as big as those albums he'd made in college, there would be reporters trying to find him and they were nothing if not persistent. When they learned who he was and where he worked, the city would come under fire. A sensa artist working in law enforcement? Even though sensa was totally legal, some of the uses it was put to were not. It was one half of the blissex problem.

Sensa combined synthesized music with inaudible undertones to create a heightened musical experience. The right sensa could lift you out of despair, arouse you, or prod you into a frenzy. Combined with blissex, it gave an incredible high.

He'd stumbled on to the secret of great sensa when he was still in college and through his sophomore and junior years he'd composed and released album after album. He'd nearly quit college entirely when he decided to quit sensa instead.

That had been a spur of the moment decision prompted by his brother's death from blissex. He'd switched to law enforcement, hoping to stop the blissex trade but it was like trying to put a bandage on a cracked dam. You could stop the water from leaking in one place but it continued to flow around the blockage. That's all they had succeeded in doing. They got the pushers fairly often and their part of the supply but never the mother lode or anyone above them. The pushers themselves just picked up their packages and made their rounds. The money they collected--never credit--got deposited where they picked the package up. Sometimes the money was picked up in a couple of hours; sometimes it sat for weeks before being collected. Twice the stash the police had under surveillance was never collected.

Possibly a leak in the department was to blame but they hadn't found it yet. In the five years he'd been assigned to the case, they hadn't nabbed more than one man above the pushers and he hadn't known much more than the pushers did. His only job had been to collect money and place supplies. When they traced where he mailed the money to, it had been a dead end.

Jasper sighed. Well this package might mean a break in the case but something told him he wouldn't be that lucky. No, they were going to have to get someone on the inside of the organization before it was done--someone like him.

It wasn't going to happen tonight. Putting that problem on hold, he dimmed the lights and headed for bed.

Chapter 5 ~ Tuesday, 13 July 2179, 7am

Jasper stared at Detective Brown. "What do you mean that package didn't have blissex in it?" He nursed the weak cup of coffee the precinct served and waited, hoping he'd heard wrong.

"It was a book," Lori said, "just like the professor said. He was here most of the night waiting for it to be found--and he wouldn't go home even after we found it until I promised it would be handled with care. He even insisted we wear gloves to turn the pages. The man is nuts."

"Just a book? Nothing else?" Jasper held out the hope there was something in the box, anything, to justify the massive hunt they'd had.

"Nothing," Lori said. "The lab still has it and the book but it looks like we were played."

She sipped her weak coffee and nibbled on a nutrient bar. Jasper guessed she'd been at it most of the night while he'd been sleeping. He felt guilty but that was the breaks. After the wrap up, she could clock out but he'd have a full day.

"Where did you find it?" he asked. "And what time?"

"About ten in a maintenance closet by the elevator," she reported with a grimace. "We started looking a lot closer to where he picked up the car. I couldn't believe he ditched it that fast."

"That is odd," Jasper said. "Did he realize we were on to him?"

"Don't know." Lori gulped down another swig of coffee. "I waited for you to interview him. The snatcher is toast as far as I'm concerned."

Jasper restrained a grin. "Toast might taste good right now." He motioned toward the nutrient bar. "Let's take a bite out of this guy so you can go home. When will they be done with that book?" He still couldn't believe it was just a book.

"They should be done now," Lori said. "Professor Nugent has a free hour at nine and he plans to pick it up then."

"And if it isn't ready?"

"We might not get rid of him," Lori said. "Like I said, the guy is nuts. Teaches history, you know."

"Not all history professors are nuts," Jasper said.

"But this one is," Lori said. "You'll see."

Together they walked down to the interrogation rooms. Outside the block, they spoke briefly to a technician then Brown went to fetch their suspect.

Jasper glanced around the room. It was clean with no visible clue the room was wired. The suspect's seat was the most wired. It could read his heartbeat and blood pressure accurately. Fitting the earpiece into his ear, he spoke quietly, "checking."

"I hear you. Checking," said the technician in his ear.

Jasper sat in the chair and waited.

"It's green. Resetting now." The voice of the technician came through.

Getting up, Jasper moved to the water cooler and drew a cup of water. He was just filling a second when the suspect was escorted in, Lori Brown behind him.

The sandy-haired guy didn't look like a subby. He wasn't broad-shouldered but he didn't have the build of someone who grew up in sub quarters either. His height was good and the slight swagger in his step made Jasper wary. Did he know they'd found the package?

Going straight to the suspect's chair, the man sat down, hands resting on the table. His whole attitude suggested he knew he was going to get off. Well, maybe they could surprise him.

Jasper handed Lori the extra cup. "Name and number?" he asked without preamble.

"Willis Frazier, 101382," the prisoner promptly replied. "How do you do, Lieutenant?"

Jasper ignored the question. "How did you get a maintenance key?"

"Found it," the man replied. "I was going to turn it in but..." he shrugged.

"It was reported stolen."

"Happens. The poor slob had to cover his butt for losing it," he said. "Did he say how he lost it?"

Jasper glanced at his partner and caught the slight shake of her head. "Not yet. Why did you take that package?"

"What package?"

"This one," Jasper looked at the vid screen behind him. On cue the technician threw up the surveillance footage. They watched the crime in progress. "Isn't that you?"

The suspect considered then nodded. "Yup, that's me. Good shooting too. Where was that camera?"

"How about this one?"

The technician threw up another angle of the sales desk and they could see him full face as he slid the package off into his hand and turned to walk out the door.

"Better yet," the man said, looking unruffled. "Looks like you got me."

"Not worried?" Jasper's eyebrow shot up.

"Hey, it was a snatch," the guy said. "Thirty days in the sewage ponds. Done it before."

"There were drugs in that package," Jasper said.

The man's smile disappeared. "You're kidding." He shook off his surprise quickly. "No, you got to be wrong. There was art in that package--old art. Some collector wanted it--no questions asked."

"Who?"

"How the hell would I know?" The guy looked insulted. "I just got the job. I wasn't going to lose it by asking questions."

"How'd you get it?"

"The usual way," he said. "A note on a wall."

"Truth?" Jasper asked.

"Truth," the technician said in his ear. "Only thing that got him excited was you mentioning drugs. He knows what that means."

Jasper knew too. Petty theft was punished in the city. Unless you had three strikes or more in a year's time, you didn't get deported. Drug pushers were different. Even low-level pushers got sent off to Newton. There they did the hard labor of building the newest city in the Rocky Mountain region.

"Why did you ditch the package so fast?" Detective Brown asked.

Frazier shrugged then grinned. "If I'm not caught with it in hand..."

"Lame excuse," Jasper muttered. "Your fingerprints were on it."

"Ok, got me there. I heard someone yell and figured I was busted," Frazier said. "I ditched it and ran. Figured I could go back if you didn't find it. Would have made it too except those bloody doors were locked."

"So you took blissex. Where'd you get it?"

"Not blissex," he denied. "Just plain old bliss. Subbies can get it, you know. It's legal."

"You were out of it," Jasper said. "Totally stoned."

"I was faking." Frazier smirked at him. "I took bliss then faked it. I'm not dumb enough to take the strong stuff."

Glancing at his partner, Jasper saw her shake her head. Blood tests either weren't done or hadn't come back yet. If they weren't done, he wouldn't know. Blissex and bliss both took about three hours to wear off.

"You were a pretty good faker then," Jasper said. "I jabbed the needle in hard and you never flinched."

The guy glanced at his arm then grinned. "Naw, it wasn't you. It was a pretty black thing with big knockers. I remember that."

So he was faking. If he'd been really under, he might have had some hallucinations but no one could mistake him for the buxom lab technician they normally used. At least he hoped not.

As if he read his mind, the snatcher grinned. "You'd look pretty good with knockers, lieutenant."

Lori snorted, hiding her laughter behind her hand. The technician wasn't so smart. The laugh in his ear was abruptly cut off as the technician hit the off switch.

"No tan," Jasper said. "Okay, you were faking. You always carry bliss?"

"Just when I think I might need it," Frazier said. "Don't want to get roughed up. Could lead to unpleasant things."

Jasper knew what he was referring to. A criminal still able to resist could be handled with unnecessary force. If a suspect was blissed out, there was absolutely no need to do that and cops that did lost their badges in a hurry.

"It's close to nine," Lori said. "The other..."

"Yeah, I know." Jasper looked at Frazier and an idea struck him. "We got the package and the book is being returned to its owner. It wasn't any damned artwork."

"A book?" Frazier didn't disappoint him. The smug smile dropped off his face. "A paper book?"

"Yup, we got played and you got played. No big payday for either of us," Jasper said. "But you'll get your thirty days for stealing a kid's picture book."

He waited, hoping the technician would get sufficient readings before he nodded to his partner to take him out. Before the man was out the door, he let loose with a stream of very satisfactory curses. He wasn't smug now.

"What'd you get?" he asked the tech.

"Total surprise on what was in the package," the technician said. "A lot of anger. He's not happy."

"I figured that."

"The rest, well, he told the truth through most of it. He's a pro."

"We'll dig into his records. Maybe we've got enough to move him out."

It wasn't likely, he knew. The real pros kept within the limits. If he'd been busted twice in the past twelve months, he wouldn't have taken this job. He knew it had once been different with petty criminals being locked up for every offense and feeding off the state. Now that was reserved for the real dangers to society. No, this man would be working the sewage farms as he said. He'd even make money at it. For thirty days he'd be monitored and paid for his labor. Some punishment. Since the item was recovered undamaged, he wouldn't even have to pay restitution.

"Do you want to see that book?" Detective Brown asked as she caught up with him outside the interrogation rooms. "I think we have time before the professor gets here."

"Yes." Jasper hesitated. "In fact, I'd like to get him in an interrogation room. Let's bring the book in here."

"That's not legal," Lori said.

"I didn't say I was going to interrogate him. Just maybe a couple of questions." Jasper looked steadily at her. "Not admissible but it might give us a lead."

She hesitated then shrugged. "I don't know anything."

"Right. It's just a room."

She left and Jasper knocked on the technician's door. How much would it cost him to get the tech to leave the equipment on? He'd pay it if he had to.

In the end it was easier than he thought. Word had already spread how fanatic this suspect was about paper books. The technician readily agreed to do the readings because he was curious how deep the man's fixation went. It was such an odd quirk. Officially though the tech was on break and had left his equipment on by accident. Such accidents happened often.

His partner came back with the package and a set of gloves. "He'll be escorted here when he gets here," she explained. "I'd like to see what this is all about too."

She opened the plastic box to reveal the colorful hard cover of the book. It had the figure of a monkey and a man in a yellow suit. The title read "Curious George."

"Curious George is the monkey?" Jasper leaned closer. "Or the man?"

"The monkey I think." Putting on her gloves, she lifted the book out of the package and carefully opened it.

Jasper kept his hands to himself as his partner turned the pages. They were in almost prime condition but he could see a little repair here and there. The copyright date placed the story as being over two hundred years old. He doubted this particular copy was that old. It was in too good a shape.

"It's a good story," Lori said, "but I can't see getting excited over it--or paying two thousand dollars."

"Neither can I," Jasper replied. "The story is probably in the library. Why pay for paper?"

"Because it's rare and you can hold it."

They looked up to see the professor and his escort standing in the door. Lori quickly closed the book but the professor didn't look irritated to see they'd read it. His spectacles were in place and today he wore another old-fashioned suit complete with bow tie. Jasper had never seen one of those outside the theater.

"What did you think of the story?" the professor asked his partner. "And the condition?"

"It's in pretty good condition," she said, "with two or three mended pages. The story, well, I'd never read a picture book this old. Animals from Africa? Did they really capture them there?"

"Yes. Virtual zoos made that unnecessary except for breeding and protection," the professor answered. "It was common when that book was written."

"Why would you pay two thousand dollars for this?" Jasper lightly tapped the book and saw the professor's answering frown. "Why a picture book?"

"Because picture books are the rarest of books," the professor said. "People who owned them used them. Generations of children often read the same books their parents and grandparents enjoyed as children. When the books wore out or got ripped up by a thoughtless child, they got rid of them."

"And this one?"

"A collector who didn't have children herself passed it on to another collector. It's been passed down from one collector to the next for well over a hundred years. I got it with the same stipulations the others agreed to. It must be displayed in public for one month of the year."

"And it will be?"

"Of course. The university will display it in its cultural hall. It's already been arranged."

The professor hesitated. "It'll be sealed in a climate-controlled case. Those who want to read it will have the electronic copy at the same display."

"There's not likely to be many children in the cultural hall," Jasper said.

"No but those who read it will note the title and pull up the electronic copies at home. Those can't be ... destroyed... by careless hands." His voice shook slightly on the word. "Babies chew on books. They rip them. They shouldn't even have paper books!"

"Yet they were written for babies," Jasper said.

"Exactly. When books were common and could be replaced at any store. Did you know some drug stores had a whole aisle dedicated to paper books?" Professor Nugent asked. "I've seen pictures of their displays."

"It was a different world," Jasper said. "I'm Lieutenant Stone. You've met my partner?"

The professor blinked then recovered. "Professor Andrew Nugent. I'm the senior professor of history at Plains University."

"It's good to meet you," Jasper said then offered him the chair. "Do you want to press charges against the snatcher?"

The professor looked uncertain then his thin lips pursed. "Must I leave the book in evidence if I do?"

"Yes."

"Then no," the professor firmly said as he sat down. "I can't allow that. The University is waiting for it."

"Does it belong to you or the university?"

"Me."

"And you can afford it?" Jasper raised an eyebrow. "How much was it again?"

"Two thousand twenty-eight dollars and seventy-five cents," the professor quoted. "Yes, I can afford it. I have my own salary plus money left to me by my grandparents and a substantial stocks portfolio. The University also provides my housing. Books are my one vice and I indulge as often as I can."

"Always picture books?"

"Of course not," the professor snapped then stopped himself. "You know nothing of bibliophiles. Picture books are an investment and a treasure. There are other books out there one reads for the sheer pleasure of reading. The works of the masters are available in many editions even today and one can truly appreciate the feel of paper beneath the hand and the smell of good leather. One cannot appreciate sonnets on a computer screen."

"Sonnets?" Detective Brown asked.

"A form of poetry," Jasper said. "I'll show you some sometime."

"You know sonnets?" the professor asked, surprised. "Which ones?"

"Browning, Shakespeare," Jasper said, unwilling to be bogged down in a literary discussion here. "Do you have any idea why someone would think there was art in that package?"

The professor blinked. "Art?"

"The snatcher was told there was highly collectible art in that package and someone was willing to pay for it." Jasper hesitated then continued, "the man was put out it was only a book so I'm willing to believe he told us the truth."

"You were watching because of that?" The professor took off his glasses and absently cleaned them with another archaic item--a handkerchief. "I was surprised to find police right there in the store--and relieved."

"No, we were told there were drugs in the box. Blissex to be precise."

The professor looked stunned. "Blissex? You were told I was importing blissex? Surely that was a joke!"

"A joke on us," Jasper said. "How do you feel about blissex?"

The professor sputtered incoherently then said in a tight angry voice. "Blissex is the biggest curse of our society. The rich idiots who use it are wastrels not worth the trouble of educating--not one brain between them."

Jasper waited for him to finish then mildly asked. "You are against it then?"

The professor glared at him then spoke. "It should be outlawed. Bliss too. If a student comes to my classes blissed out, he gets shown the door. I will not waste my time teaching them."

"Understood." Jasper consulted his notes. "So did anyone know you were picking up that book yesterday?" He nodded toward the copy of Curious George. "Anyone else who might have wanted it?"

"A few people knew," the professor said. "My secretary, the museum staff, and a few personal friends. I was really quite pleased to be getting it. No, wait, not that many knew when it was coming. I didn't know myself till two days ago."

"Saturday?"

"Yes. I got the call just before going out." The professor's brow furrowed. "A private party of Reach Out. It's my favorite charity. Are you familiar with it?"

"I've heard of it." He knew it gave more opportunities to promising students regardless of financial situation.

"Yes, well, I'm afraid I did mention when it was coming to friends there," the professor said. "Some of them are amateur collectors."

"So people knew when it was coming and what it was."

"Yes, I'm afraid so."

"Anyone in particular you think might have called in a tip?"

"No."

"That's a lie," the technician said in his ear. "He suspects someone."

"Well, no harm was done to the book and you've declined to press charges," Jasper said. "Is there anywhere we can get a membership list of Reach Out? Just to tie up loose ends."

"Of course," the professor said, blinking his eyes in confusion. "But I'll be quite happy if this doesn't go any further. I don't want my friends embarrassed by it. In fact, I'd just as soon they not know about this sad affair."

"I doubt it will go much further," Jasper said. "The membership list is available where?"

"On the website," the professor said. "If you type /memberslist, it will come up. It only includes those who have contributed more than a thousand dollars yearly. Small donors are not actually members, you see."

"Interesting," Jasper said. "And exclusive?"

The professor brushed that aside. "We must have some people with money to get the job done. Scholarships don't grow on trees."

"True," Jasper said. "And I've benefited from a program like Reach Out. It's a good charity."

"Oh," the professor looked suddenly warmer, "could you come to one of our benefits? We like hearing the success stories even if the program wasn't our own."

"Possibly," Jasper left it open, "but for now we must give you your book," he motioned to his partner, "and not take more of your time."

The professor rose on cue, taking the book and returning it to the package with care. Jasper saw him to the door then waited for him to get out of sight before knocking on the door of the technician's booth. His partner was right behind him.

"Well?" Jasper asked. "Was it interesting?"

"Yup," the technician said. "You didn't get many yes or no answers which are the easiest to read but he definitely loves his books and hates blissers. The only outright lie was there at the end. That was quick thinking to get invited to one of their functions, Lieutenant. Very smooth."

"It never hurts--and it wasn't a lie. My last year of high school and first years of college came through a government program," he explained. "It wasn't a charity but it could have been."

"Got it," the technician said. "Still good thinking." He hesitated. "I'm not sure I can get this analyzed since it was unofficial. Can't even officially store it but if you've got a flasher, I'll move it over there. Just don't get forget it's unauthorized."

"Agreed." Jasper reached for his flasher but his partner was quicker.

"This one's fresh," she said. "Label it sonnet."

"Cute," Jasper said. "Let me see..." He changed his com unit to personal mode, looked into his library and pulled out one of his wife's favorites. Touching the unit to his partner's he gave her the file. "That's a sonnet--words and voice."

"How do I love thee?" she asked in an incredulous voice.

"Don't take it personal," he warned as the technician looked up. "The poet and the man she loved have both been dead for centuries. It was my wife's favorite." He hesitated. "Carol's voice. Forgot about that."

His partner looked both embarrassed and touched that he'd given it to her. Damn, he had forgotten Carol recorded it.

Well, no point in getting emotional. It was far too early in the day.

"I'm due over at Section Three. Are we done here?"

"I think so," Brown said. "Turn Frazier loose?"

"Yeah," he said. "No charges. Can you slip a tracker on him without him knowing it?"

"I doubt it," she said. "The guy's a pro. I bet the first thing he'll do is change and shower in case we did."

"And without a warrant, we can't do internal," Jasper said. "Tell communications we're interested in his com traffic and let it go at that."

"Will do."

Chapter 6 - Evidence

Jasper eyed the object in the evidence bag with a puzzled frown. It was very small, less than a half inch in length, and seemed to be wood but not one he'd commonly seen. It was very black and it didn't look to be a stain. The broken edge showed the same wood. "You found this in her skull? What is it?"

The medical examiner hesitated. "It's a piece of carved wood broken off from a larger piece of the same wood. That's all I can tell you."

"Any clues on the type of wood?"

"It's not pine or oak or maple or mahogany," the examiner said. "Those we know. This is a harder wood. We've got a query in about a dark hardwood now."

"But it still broke?" Jasper thought that odd.

"Anything can break if the blow is hard enough," the examiner said. "And this was obviously a protrusion of some sort. Maybe it's a finger. It's definitely not a hand."

"So it could have come off some sort of exotic figure?" Jasper thought back, remembering the statuettes on the mantle at the West house. Those were dark. They'd looked untouched so he hadn't given them much notice. The lab guys might have swabbed them as a precaution. Would they have noticed a missing finger? "I think I know where it came from," Jasper said. "I'll let you know if I'm right."

Slipping the evidence bag into his pocket, he signed the release form. Just then his new partner entered the room, two cups of coffee in hand. Jasper took his and sipped, recognizing the weak brew as standard issue. Well, tomorrow he might have time for a real cup at home. The precincts couldn't afford the good stuff.

"We've got an object to match up," Jasper told him, "and a clue to the murder weapon."

"Good," the detective said. "I don't know how we could have missed it if it was in the house." He carefully didn't look at the body the coroner was putting back into the freeze drawer. "I still can't get over someone killing an old lady."

"It happens," Jasper said. "And it's usually family. Mrs. West was worth a lot of money so we need to know what's in her will and who benefits the most. The granddaughter is working as a schoolteacher so that's one clue and her son recently had an accident and is off work. We have to look at those."

"And the others?"

Jasper motioned him out the door with a nod to the pathologist. "Who all have we got?" He waited for his junior partner to report, curious whether he'd missed any.

"In order of age, there's Michael West then David West--he's the lunatech--David's wife Jessica West, his son Jake, and the granddaughter, Jewel. Jake is also married to a Sasha Kowalski. I don't have anything on his wife."

"What did you find out from the door logs?" Jasper asked.

"The door lock show two uses yesterday," Sanders said. "One was Michael West and the other Jewel West but there's a problem."

"Problem?"

"Yes. Michael West opened the door at 1:03 p.m. and the door registered a continuous error message after that until 2:15 p.m. It cleared up then and worked normally when Jewel entered."

"Door propped open?"

"We tried that," Sanders said. "It doesn't have an error message then. It registers as open if the door is open even three inches. There's a thirty-second delay to allow time for entry then it goes to the open message. I've got a call into the company to see what would cause the particular error message we got. They should get back to us today."

"Good enough," Jasper said. "Are there any cameras we can go to?"

"The one closest to the house was pointed another direction," Sanders said. "There was another at position 3C-- the one by the parking lot. It's a dual view and would have shown us the parking lot and the path but it was out of order. It's been that way for at least three days but didn't get reported until yesterday afternoon."

"Odd coincidence." Jasper frowned. He didn't like odd coincidences. There was usually something behind them. He was all too aware that there were too many coincidences in the book theft. When the snatch happened, they should have been tipped off but they were too focused. "No camera in the house itself?"

"It wasn't required by code," Sanders said. "According to the maid, old Mr. West--that's the grandfather--refused to let the city spy on him in his own house."

"Maid?"

"Yes. She showed up this morning for her regular day. After she got over her shock, she was pretty talkative. Elizabeth West had no enemies and the only family arguments she knew of were about Jake. He's a Mars colonist and due to report to quarantine next week before shipping out. The family was pretty split about him going."

"Why?"

"He's the only surviving grandson," Sanders said. "He had to carry on the family name and they didn't mean on Mars. You know those people never come back."

"How did he come up with the money to go? Did someone in the family cough up?" It was well known that colonists had to provide a million dollars for transport cost and their essential supplies. Most people had to have a corporate sponsorship to do it.

"He got a sponsorship from Centrax. He's a hydro farmer with a geology degree too. Centrax kind of surprised me so I made a note of it. I thought they were just light rail."

"Light rail might be useful on Mars," Jasper said then shook his head. "Surprising though. I doubt they have enough refined steel to even consider it."

Like many people, he made a hobby of following the Mars colony's progress. He'd never go out there but it was good to see the colony was a reality. For fifteen years now they'd been building bases and expanding mining and farming. The population was still small--less than five hundred--but there were children there who had never set foot on Earth. "Can we talk to this maid again?"

"Her next regular day at the house is day after tomorrow," Sanders said. "She's willing to give us her time so long as she gets paid by someone."

"I'm sure the Wests will agree to that. If not, we'll put in a voucher."

Sanders grinned. "I can just see the reaction to that. Maid service--is that supplies or personnel?"

"Informant compensation in this case," Jasper said. "She's not a material witness so she's an informant. It might be more than her usual wage but I doubt it."

Good maids were rare in Plains. Even though there were subbies who could do the work, most were too proud or too lazy for it. A lot of the rest couldn't be trusted in the homes of the rich. He'd had to engage one of the cleaning services for his place. They came in once a week to do the cleaning he had no time for.

"I want to meet her," Jasper said. "Day after tomorrow? What time?"

"Nine a.m."

"Thanks." Jasper made a note of it. He wondered how long she'd worked for the Wests and how helpful she'd be to the investigation. "Have you talked to the other relatives yet?"

"Yes. The grandson, that's Jake, was in Denver when I caught him. He'd been in Chicago visiting his mother then Denver to see his dad. It's his last home leave before shipping out. His wife is visiting her parents."

"And David West?"

"He's coming to town later today. His shift ends at four so he'll take the late train."

"Was he working yesterday?"

"Yes sir. His work week started yesterday so he was in Denver from noon to four."

"That pretty much rules him out."

"Yes sir."

He didn't believe a lunatech would commit this kind of murder. It was well known they earned some of the highest wages in the construction and mining industry. No doubt, David West could buy the house from his mother. He didn't need to murder for it. His wife was known to be even richer-- or she used to be, he thought. He hadn't noticed Jessica West in any recent film. No, he couldn't rule her out.

"Did we get any fingerprints?" Jasper asked.

"Plenty," Sanders responded. "I got the maid's prints this morning so I could rule her out. Michael West is on file as a city employee and so is Miss West. They're sifting through for them now. Since they both lived in the house, their fingerprints are probably everywhere."

"Right." Jasper frowned. "We might not be able to use fingerprints unless we get very lucky and find a stranger in the bunch. That upper door — any fingerprints there?"

"Only one," Sanders said. "Those are probably the girl's since she was the last to use it."

"And the front door--was that clean?" Jasper asked. "You said it was left open."

Sanders looked caught out. "I didn't ask. Let me call them." He walked away a few steps to speak into his com unit while Jasper sipped his weak coffee.

Jasper didn't expect anything on the front door. If the upper door was that clean, the front door probably was too. There could be traces of DNA somewhere but with the killer probably a family member, that was next to worthless. They couldn't date DNA effectively. Even fingerprints were pretty iffy unless they could show them clearly overlapping earlier prints. His best clue so far was in the evidence bag. If they could match that little piece of wood to something in the house, they'd have the murder weapon. It would probably be wiped clean though.

"The front door was wiped clean," Sanders said. "But they've isolated seven sets of fingerprints."

"Seven?" Jasper asked. "How many are in the family?"

"Five plus the two wives," Sanders said. "But there's also the maid. That would make eight. No help huh?"

"Depends," Jasper said. "If they're like most families, not everyone visits. I doubt the actress has been here in quite a while. I think she lives in Chicago, not Denver."

"And the grandson's wife may never have come," Sanders said. "She's a Mars colonist. If they didn't like the grandson going, she might not have been welcomed."

"True. Let's ask about that before involving her," Jasper suggested. "We want to tread carefully with the Colonial Administration." He knew even a hint of scandal could ground a colonist. "Let's not even involve Jake until we have reason," he said. "I want to interview the other three first."

"Yes sir."

"When is Michael West due to be in?"

Sanders consulted his notes. "He should be here at two and the girl at four. Since he's still on medical leave, that's no inconvenience for him."

"True. What do we know about that leave?" Jasper asked. "An accident?"

"That's what the report said," Sanders frowned, "but it was pretty strange. A piece of equipment fell on him. It broke his arm, ribs, and injured his spine."

"What was strange about it?" Jasper eyed him.

Sanders didn't answer right away then shrugged. "It was an air cleaning unit. Those are designed to be hung from catwalks to free up floor space. They also have at least three tie-downs to keep them from falling. This one had just one and that's not standard operating procedure. They disciplined two of the maintenance men for not performing regular inspections and safety checks."

"All that is in the report?" Jasper asked.

"Not all," Sanders said. "I knew about the redundant systems so I called to find out why the unit didn't have them. The investigator told me one had been stolen and one was broken. The last one could have failed at any time and it did when West was in the wrong spot." Sanders frowned. "It's odd that it happened just now, isn't it?"

"When?"

"Almost three months ago," he said. "No, I guess that's not too odd."

Jasper studied him. "Did anyone ever tell you about listening to your gut?"

Sanders grinned. "You think I have a gut feeling?"

Jasper understood his reaction. He'd had almost the same one the first time he'd been questioned about a feeling during a case.

"It looks like you do," Jasper said, "and now I'm getting it. It is odd. We'll check into that a bit more. One question we need answered is how badly was his back injured and could he have carried his mother upstairs?"

Sanders nodded.

"Trust those gut feelings," Jasper said. "Sometimes they pan out. Sometimes they don't. What's really going on is you know something at the back of your mind that doesn't agree with what you consciously know. It'll come out eventually but until then it'll just be an itch you can't scratch."

"You've had them?" Sanders asked.

"All good cops get them," Jasper said. "How did you know about the redundant tie-downs?"

Sanders blinked. "My dad is in maintenance. He took me on tours sometime and I even helped occasionally when no one was looking. Last night I gave him a call and he confirmed how those were secured."

"Good job," Jasper said. "How'd you end up in law enforcement?"

"Mom was a cop," Sanders said with a grin. "I liked hearing about her job too. When the time came that I had to choose, we found out there were more vacancies for cops than for maintenance so I chose that path. I can always retrain for maintenance later if I need to."

"That makes sense," Jasper said. "And it's good to have a backup plan. Everyone should have one." Even him. He knew where he was going though. It would unfold soon, maybe right after this case was done. "Let's see if we can get the medical on Michael West," Jasper said. "Did he sign the consent?"

"Yes sir."

"Then let's do it."

It wasn't easy getting medical files even with a patient consent so the next hour and a half went by quickly. They were shuffled from one level of hospital administration to another before finally locating the doctor treating Michael West. It took even more time to convince him the patient consent form was real and was his patient's before the man would open up his files and explain the findings.

"In light of the damage he suffered, doctor, could Michael West have lifted a hundred pounds?" Jasper asked. "Make it one hundred twenty to be safe."

The doctor looked thoughtful. "It would cause him considerable pain if he did. His spine is no longer perfectly aligned and two of the disks had to be replaced. The muscles around the injury still haven't healed well enough."

"But could he have lifted that weight?"

"For a short time, possibly," the doctor said. "With considerable pain."

Jasper glanced at Sanders then back to the doctor. "Could he have climbed stairs with that weight?"

The doctor looked taken back. "Stairs? With a hundred pounds dead weight? In that much pain? How many stairs?"

"There were four flights of stairs," Jasper said. "About eight steps in each flight."

The doctor shook his head. "No, I don't think he could do it. Mr. West was on almost complete bed rest for a month following his accident. He could climb stairs but not with that kind of weight."

"You're certain?"

"I will be certain after his next visit," the doctor said. "That's scheduled for tomorrow. If you contact me after that, I can give you a definitive answer."

The doctor paused. "I can tell you gentlemen that it's doubtful I'll return him to work status. He's likely to have pain the rest of his life unless he consents to a nerve bridge. Right now our treatment is mostly to control that pain."

"Thank you, doctor. You've been most helpful," Jasper said. He motioned for Sanders to close the connection.

"He has a motive," Sanders said, "but not the ability?"

"A possible motive," Jasper said, "but probably not the ability." He frowned. "The Wests are so rich that not working might not be a hardship to him. He had no problem keeping his house while staying with his mother--and Gracee Place is not cheap living. I've looked at those houses and I know your annual income must be above a hundred thousand to qualify."

"Wow." His partner looked stunned. "That much?"

"Yeah. No one who was just a city engineer could afford them," Jasper said. "They don't have surface access but they're well located and have every gadget you can imagine--and a walking track and citrus garden. Maid service is even included."

His partner looked suitably impressed. Jasper stopped there, not bothering to say he'd been looking for a house for himself. Carol had refused to seriously consider Gracee Place and she'd been right. They wouldn't have fit in with the folks who lived there. They'd settled into a more modest apartment only slightly better than what a cop could usually afford.

Since it had two bathrooms--his most stringent requirement--he'd been satisfied.

Growing up, he and his brother had had their own bathroom. It had been theirs and they'd taken care of it. When his parents had to go on the subby list, they'd been crammed into a small two-bedroom apartment with just one bath. There were no separate bedrooms for him and his brother but the worst thing had been sharing a bathroom with his mother. There were things as a teenager he simply didn't want to know about his mom.

When they moved to Plains and his daughter had started walking, he'd remembered that and had insisted on two bathrooms. Their daughter hadn't thought it was such a big deal having two bathrooms but her friends had been impressed. Now that she was in college and having to share a bathroom with a roommate, her attitude had probably changed.

The Gracee Place houses had more bathrooms than anyone could possibly need. He remembered there was one for guests and one off each of the three bedrooms. There were some units that had four bedrooms but those were rare. Since most families had only two children these days, a fourth bedroom was considered a waste. Those who lived on Gracee Place though could afford the tax burden of having an additional child.

"Does Michael West have any children?" Jasper abruptly asked. "I know he's not married now but did he have any contract marriages and issue?"

"None." Sanders shook his head. "That I checked. If there'd been a child who wasn't legally a West..."

"Right." Jasper gave an approving nod. "Unlikely to be in the grandmother's will but might be in the father's. He didn't have any though?"

"No, he's listed as a celibate under sexual preference. I guess with three brothers he didn't feel the need to have kids."

"That could be." Jasper looked at the clock and saw it was after 3:00. "You did say his appointment was at two?"

"Yes." Sanders followed his gaze and frowned. "They were supposed to notify me when he got here." He picked up his com unit and spoke into it then listened. When he set it down, he looked baffled. "He hasn't arrived or even called. I've got his number..." He touched it into his com unit. "I didn't peg him for an evader."

"Neither did I," Jasper said. "Reschedule him for 4:30. He's probably got reason."

"Yes sir." Sanders put his attention on his com unit.

Jasper considered the doctor's report. If Michael West couldn't lift a hundred pounds without great pain, he was probably out of it. However, the man had taken valium shortly before or after the murder took place. It may be that he needed it after carrying her upstairs. And there was that upper door log. Why did he open that door? He needed to ask that. The fact that the error message had cleared itself suggested someone had reset the door. If the girl's fingerprints were on the door and his weren't, that suggested he'd clean the door. No, someone had cleaned the door. It might not have been him.

He needed to know more about valium too. He knew valium was a sleep aid but wasn't sure it could be that useful on nerve pain. He made a note to do that then turned to his partner as he set down his com unit again.

"He's not answering but I left a message," Sanders said. "Do you think he got more valium?"

"Could be," Jasper said. "He didn't have any more last night but he might have gotten more from another source." He'd been a little surprised Michael hadn't had more but it was difficult getting illegal drugs past inspection sensors. One or two pills were usually let through but never more than that. The city wasn't concerned with stopping small personal amounts but they cracked down on any that might be headed for resale. If Michael West had brought in a couple of valium tablets, they would have let them go through. More than that and they would have been confiscated.

It was odd though that West wasn't using a legal prescription. His doctor would probably have been cooperative. For that matter, there were more powerful painkillers available. His wife had quit responding to narcoset and valium shortly after she got them and they'd given her penatel and narcopen. Both were more effective but even they failed to control her pain in her last year.

Chapter 7 - Jewel

Jewel West arrived slightly breathless but right on time for her appointment. Jasper silently applauded that, still somewhat surprised at the rudeness of Michael West. There'd been no phone call from him and he still hadn't arrived or even acknowledged the new appointment time. He worried he might have to bring him in.

"Ms West," Jasper greeted her with old-fashioned politeness. "Good day at school?"

Jewel's eyes darkened and she brushed a chestnut curl away from her face. "I try to leave my problems at home. If I didn't have the children to teach, I'd be in a bad case."

"Understandable," Jasper said. "Maybe you should have one of your own."

Jewel stared at him in shock and Jasper reddened. Why the hell had he said that? It was far too personal. Well, he'd better muddle through. "I have a daughter and she helped see me through some rough times. It helps."

"I suppose it would," Jewel said. "A reason to get moving in the morning."

"Yes." Jasper thought about the fights he'd had with Mel since her mother died and inwardly shuddered. She hadn't let him sink into his grief. She'd flung it at him, blamed him for letting her mother go, and demanded he take the guilt. He had fought back but realized the only thing he could do was let Mel go too. His music had been his salvation--and his job.

"Uncle Mike was there for me," she said. "We talked a little last night. He was really upset he took that pill."

"Where is he today?" Jasper asked. "He missed his appointment."

Jewel looked puzzled. "That's not like him," she said. "He was very insistent I make mine and not be late. I had to rush. The upper door of the precinct isn't open, you know."

"No, I didn't," Jasper said, "but I'm not surprised. You often use the ground level entrances?"

"It's quicker," she said. "If you know where the paths run, you can get places in a fraction of the time. When the weather's good, why not use them?"

"True." Jasper studied her, noting she was more tanned than most girls and had a nice healthy glow to her skin. Her chestnut hair was either natural or one of the most expensive dye jobs he'd ever seen. He reined in his thoughts with difficulty.

"Where was your uncle planning on being today?" he asked. "Did he discuss it with you?"

"He needed to meet with the mortician about funeral arrangements and tell some of Grandma's closest friends that she was gone. Last night he only told family and he was so upset after talking to Jake that he went to bed."

"Why was he upset?" Jasper asked as they entered the interrogation room. He motioned Jewel to the proper chair and took one across from her. His partner stepped back and let him handle it.

"Jake was probably after his money again," Jewel said. "He desperately wants to go to Mars as a free man with no contract to tie him down. He's got a contract now but he can't do what he wants to do. He'll have to fill the contract first."

"And he would push that even after your grandmother's sudden death?" Jasper asked, surprised. "Does he want it that badly?"

A tiny frown line appeared at the top of her pretty Grecian nose. "I know he wants it. I know he feels it's totally unfair that he can't touch West money till he's thirty and ineligible for Mars. I agree with him that it is lousy that he can't get any of it sooner but Jake could have saved up and made it to Mars on his own if he wanted it that badly. He didn't need to live as well as he has or stay in college so long-- and I would have helped him if he'd had even half of what he needed."

"Do you think Jake could have killed your grandmother?" He put it baldly.

Her face registered her shock but she didn't stay shocked long. "No, I don't think so."

"Why not?" Jasper asked.

"Well, Jake doesn't get things done. Like I said, he could have had money for Mars but he didn't save any. He's got three degrees to make him eligible for the colony but he didn't put any of them to use outside his internships. He stayed in college and did his best to make the right connections to get on the colony list. The only thing he's actually done was gotten married to another colonist. Grandma was really upset about that because she felt she'd married Jake for his money."

"And her name is?"

"Sasha Kowalski," Jewel answered. "I don't like her."

True, his partner signaled. Jasper realized he hadn't put in his earpiece and palmed it. "That's candid," he said as he deftly inserted his earpiece. His partner handed a cup of water to the girl to cover his movement. "Was she ever in the house?"

"Only once," Jewel said. "They visited right after Jake got married. Grandma was polite but suggested Sasha had made a mistake. Sasha asked me later if the family was really so petty to deny Jake his dream. I tried to explain about New Wave but she didn't want to hear about it." Jewel was thoughtful. "She only came to the house that one time but I think she could have done it. She was a lot stronger than Jake."

"Did she have a key code?"

"No but she could have gotten Jake's," Jewel said. "He couldn't say no to her. He needed her to get to Mars. Single men don't get to go unless they're desperately needed."

"And he wasn't desperately needed?"

Jewel shook her head. "He had degrees but not enough experience to back them up."

"What degrees?"

"Hydroponics, mine engineering, and geology," she said. "All bachelors but that was enough."

"But no experience?"

"Well, he had some in hydroponics," she said. "He worked in a Denver hydroponics farm one summer then he interned in a prep facility getting plants and plant seeds ready to go."

"And his wife?"

"She's in livestock," Jewel said. "Animal husbandry. She can tell you anything you want to know about the nutritional value of rabbits versus chickens." She gave him a sour look. "Meat is meat. I don't want to know how long to raise them before killing them."

Killing them? He caught that reference and glanced at his partner. Yes, livestock managers did kill livestock and butcher livestock for processing. It was a very specialized field because of that. And how hard would it be for someone trained in killing animals to kill an old woman?

"I think we'll arrange to question her," Jasper said. "And Jake. We'll have to be careful to make sure neither one is pulled from the colony without cause."

"Now can you think of any reason either of your uncles would want your grandmother dead?" Jasper asked. "Anything?"

Jewel shook her head. "Nothing."

"But someone tried to persuade her to take the walk," Jasper said. "That was family. Who?"

"Uncle David," she said in a low voice. "And Aunt Jessica. And Jake. And me." She looked up, her sapphire eyes shiny with unshed tears. "Uncle Mike said it was wrong because she was just depressed. I knew she was depressed and I didn't really want her to do it but she seemed to want to. It was only when she stopped wanting it that she started fighting back. She got help then and I got my Grandma back."

"So no one in particular pushed her toward it?" Jasper asked, ignoring his own memories. "No one who wanted to gain?"

"No," she said. "None of us needed the money except Jake and he already knew it would make no difference."

"What about you?" his partner abruptly asked. "You could quit working."

"Me?" Jewel looked astonished then laughed. "You think I need the money?" Before the detective could answer she continued, "I'm just teaching this summer because I like teaching and I'd go insane if I didn't have something to do."

Seeing he wasn't convinced, she said. "Detective, I give more than my teacher's salary to charity every year. I don't work because I have to."

"Thank you for clarifying that," Jasper said with a warning look at his partner. "Is there anyone in the West clan that needed money?"

"Only Jake and his wife," Jewel quickly responded, "but now they have sponsors. Jake doesn't need money now."

"What about Jessica? How is her career going?" Jasper asked.

"Her?" Jewel hesitated then smiled. "She's got a clothing line and other things going. She even has real estate. Not many acting roles lately but she's got money. That's not why she wants a divorce."

"Divorce?" Jasper caught that. "There's a divorce pending?"

Jewel's look of dismay was almost comical. "That won't get into the news, will it? It's family business."

"If it shows up in the media, it won't be because we leaked it," Jasper assured her. "But don't be surprised if it does get leaked by someone closer to Jessica West. Actors tend to use such things to get their name back out in front of the public."

"I know." Jewel didn't look at him. "And she's done it before. Yeah, I should expect her to use family business for publicity."

"So you don't like her?"

"I know her," Jewel said. "And I'm glad she doesn't come here. She always tried to lord it over Grandma and Grandma wouldn't stand for it. David got tired of it years ago but he refused to give her a divorce before. Now he's willing."

"Why?"

She set her lips firmly and looked at him. "Ask him. I shouldn't have said anything about the divorce."

"Fair enough," Jasper said. "So you just make a habit of going from the school to your grandmother's house every day?"

"I live there."

"Did you notice anything odd yesterday before you saw your grandmother? Anything out of place?"

She thought about it. "No, nothing odd. The upper door was locked. I did notice the city door was ajar after I saw her. That scared me."

"Why?"

"I thought someone might still be in the house. I ran back upstairs to call."

"You knew your uncle was up there?"

"I knew he should be," she said. "He naps in the afternoon. Grandma does too." She hesitated. "No, I ran back upstairs because I wanted to be able to leave. I know the outside and I have the right code to get in and out. I thought it was safer than the city streets."

"Maybe," Jasper said. "But he could have been hiding on that third floor. Next time just get out the closest door."

"Yes sir." She smiled and even gave him a little salute.

Where had she picked that up? Jasper frowned at her, refusing to find it cute.

She saw his look and sobered again. "I'm sorry. I didn't think about someone hiding upstairs. All I knew was I could leave and no one could catch me on the paths. I know them too well."

"Understood." Jasper looked at the clock and frowned. It was nearly five and still no sign of Michael West.

Opening his com unit, he punched the combo for the main desk. "Has Mr. West checked in yet? " Irritated, he added, "has he even called?"

Getting a negative, he turned back to Jewel. "Still no word from your uncle. I'm going to escort you back to Gracee Place. We'll see if he's there."

"It's not like him to ignore any appointment," Jewel said. "But he did have a lot to do today."

"That's why I won't make this official," Jasper responded. "I'd rather give him a chance to explain."

"Thank you," Jewel said so quietly he nearly missed it. "Can I--can we go now?"

Chapter 8 – Gracee Place

Gracee Place was as he remembered it. The perfume of orange blossoms wafted through the air long before he passed through the security gates into the cul-de-sac and sunlight poured down from the overhead skylight. Orange trees lined the center of the walking track. Benches and a couple of outdoor tables invited residents to sit and talk a while in their own private corner of the city. No one who lacked the proper codes could enter this area--no one except cops and fire control that is.

Jewel entered her code and it passed her through then Jasper entered his own. He might have slipped through with her but many such systems could detect extra bodies and would send out an automatic alert. Gracee Place was rich enough they probably updated their system regularly.

He took in a lungful of the sweet air, appreciating the rich smell of growing things, as he walked the length of the street with her. The afternoon sunlight had brought out a couple of walkers but they were far enough away to not concern him. Maybe he should have tried harder to get a place here. The walking track and garden alone would have been a benefit.

"Here it is," Jewel said. "Number twelve." She punched in her code and the door unlocked automatically.

"Welcome, Miss Jewel," an automated butler said. "You have a guest?"

"Yes. Where is Uncle Mike?" Jewel led the way into the entry foyer. Jasper followed, only half listening to her conversation.

"In his bedroom," the butler said. "He has ignored his wake-up calls."

Jewel hesitated. "Has he eaten?"

"No."

Jasper scanned the large living room and glanced at the open-ended kitchen before frowning. There was something.

He took a deep breath and caught it, his eyes opening wider and hand reaching for his com unit. His other hand snaked out and caught Jewel as she started past him.

"Don't," he warned. Hitting the emergency call button on his com unit, he spoke rapidly. "This is Lieutenant Jasper Stone, Section 5. I have a 10-39 at 12 Gracee Place. Probable homicide. I need a lab crew and a policewoman."

The dispatcher squawked at him.

"I am detached to Section 3, case 10833. This is connected. Notify Detective Sanders to meet me at 12 Gracee Place."

Jewel stared at him with wide shiny eyes. She'd caught his alarm but not what it meant.

"Smell the air," he said. "You smell that sickly sweet odor?"

"Yes." She sounded puzzled.

"That's death. Stay here." He looked about every sense alert even though he knew that smell was old. It was too strong to be recent. Had he been dead all day?

The living room was impeccably clean and showed little evidence of use. Seeing four doors, he headed for the one that was open.

"That's my room," Jewel said. "His door is closed."

"Which one?"

"The furthest one." She started to join him.

"Stay there," he barked. "Don't touch anything," he said in a quieter tone. "Just stay there."

She obeyed, her face pale.

Using the lightest of contacts, Jasper opened the door to the room. It was dark with only the dim glow of a night-light to show any detail.

"Butler," he said. "Police override. Turn on all lights in this house. Authorization code ten eighteen alpha tango, Lieutenant Jasper Stone."

"Complying." The automated butler flooded the apartment with light. The dimness of the living room behind him was gone but so was the darkness of the bedroom.

Blinking fast, he forced his eyes to adjust to the increased light.

The man on the bed was Michael West and he was very dead. The air was foul with death and the smell of human excrement so he'd been dead for hours. There was no sense in looking for an intruder. Forcing himself to take in the scene, he studied the still figure. It looked like he'd just gone to bed. There was no sign of struggle and no pillow out of place. On the nightstand there were two glasses, one full and one almost drained, and a bottle of very expensive scotch. He guessed the empty glass had held some. The bedside lamp was still off so it wasn't connected to the butler.

Unwilling to step further into the room, he returned to Jewel. Tears streamed down her cheeks and her body shook with sobs. He held her, pillowing her head against his shoulder to give her some support. Damn, two deaths in little more than 24 hours. He couldn't blame her for falling apart. Most women would have at the first. He let her cry, his mind racing through the implications. This was more than murder of an old woman who had lived too long to suit someone in the family. Now they were going after other family members. No, they'd gone after Michael before. He suddenly remembered that accident and Sanders' feeling it wasn't and knew he was right. This was the second attempt on Michael. Why?

And how had it been done? He had no doubt Jewel was being set up. It was too pat. In fact, it had looked to him that Michael was being set up before. No, Michael was innocent. He had to be. He was dead.

It seemed a long time before the butler announced, "I am being overridden. Police entry."

Jewel managed to croak out "it's okay" before the lab people entered. Seeing them, she pulled away from his shoulder and tried to look composed but ended up looking like a little girl lost.

Jasper wanted to stay with her but waved to the policewoman. "Take care of her. Victim assistance?"

"Yes sir. Was she here?"

"No, she hasn't seen him."

Jasper left Jewel to her and joined the lab people as they started their procedures. Explaining what he had touched and how far he'd gone into the room, he was then regulated to watching and waiting.

As soon as Sanders arrived, he returned to Jewel. She was composed now but his shoulder was still damp from her tears. He knew now she was hard hit by all this and her calm at her grandmother's death had been misleading.

"Jewel, I have to ask," he said. "When did you last see Michael?"

"Last night," she replied with a ragged breath. "He didn't eat much. We both went to bed around nine--nine thirty for me. He was still upset about Grandma and blamed himself for sleeping yesterday."

"Did he talk to you about it?" Jasper asked.

Jewel shook her head. "A little but then he called Uncle David and Jake. He didn't want to talk after that and went to bed."

"Did he have a heart condition?"

"No." She seemed surprised by that question. "No, he didn't. You think he died from a heart attack?"

"It's possible," Jasper said, "but not probable. Did you talk to him at all after nine last night or look into his room?"

"No." Jewel looked puzzled, her eyes no longer brimming with tears. "I never intrude."

Intrude. No one intruded. Private space was considered private and no one crossed the line into it without invitation. Bedrooms were considered the most private of all.

"Did he die because I didn't look?" Jewel demanded, tears threatening again. "Could I have helped him?"

The policewoman held her hand, talking to her in soothing tones while Jasper waved Sanders out of earshot.

"He's been dead since last night," Jasper said, "and I don't think she did it."

"She was the only one with opportunity," Sanders said. "No one else was here."

"And Michael was the only one with opportunity for his mother's death. Now he's dead. She might be next--and maybe her other uncle will get implicated in that. Someone has a sick sense of humor."

"Unless the uncle turns up dead too," Sanders said. "Last one standing?" He referred to their basic homicide training and how it was always the last relative living that should be looked at hardest.

"Maybe. All right, we take her into protective custody while we look for more facts."

"What facts?"

Jasper thought. "How Michael died then I want to know more about the will--and," he said with mixed dread "what happened when Elizabeth West took the walk."

"What about the uncle? He's supposed to come in on the night train."

"You meet him," Jasper said. "Get him into a safe house."

"He might not like it," Sanders said. "Not with this happening."

"Just do it."

Chapter 9 – Police Custody

Two hours later he had Jewel settled into an apartment within the police precinct itself. Reserved for valuable witnesses and those who needed protection, it was a simple one-bedroom apartment with living room and kitchenette. A police psychiatrist, also female, had replaced the policewoman. She was older, maybe close to sixty, and exuded a steadying influence Jewel might find comforting. She certainly needed her company tonight.

"I need to call Uncle David," Jewel said. She was calm now but it was a fragile calm. Her slender hands twisted and untwisted a cloth napkin she'd picked up at the house. "I have to tell him."

"I Ie's probably on the train," Jasper said. "Do you want to do it now?"

"He's not in a public car," she said. "He always gets a stateroom."

Stateroom? Jasper was reminded once again how rich the West family was. No, David West was. He was a lunatech.

"Always?" Jasper couldn't stop himself from asking.

She nodded, her fingers already at work on her com unit.

It wasn't every citizen who could afford a personal com unit of such quality either. Jasper knew there had been a time when every child and adult had had a cell phone and they had thought nothing of calling anyone around the world but that was long past. Now com units had replaced them and they were expensive. Since public com panels offered free calling and vid panels could also place calls, com units weren't in high demand anyway. It was mostly employees and the wealthy that had them. Well, he knew Jewel wasn't an average citizen. She didn't flaunt her wealth but she had it.

"Uncle David?" Jewel said and her voice quavered. "No, I'm not fine. Uncle Mike... " Her voice broke. "Uncle Mike is dead. I..." She sobbed then handed the com unit to Jasper.

The video was on. Jasper thought David West looked like a younger copy of his brother. He was tanned where his brother hadn't been but he had the same blue eyes and thinning hair. Right now his face expressed his shock.

"Lieutenant Jasper Stone," Jasper identified himself. "Sir, are you alone?"

"No, my son is with me," David said. "What is this? Did she just say Mike is dead? Where is he?"

"We found Michael West a couple of hours ago," Jasper said. "Apparently he died last night at his home on Gracee Place. Jewel didn't know and went to work today."

"I thought she was staying with him," David responded. "How could she?"

"He died in his sleep." Jasper was blunt.

"God." David turned and said "Mike is dead."

Jasper heard his son's exclamation before the com unit was muted. He waited, wishing he could hear. It wasn't long before David returned to their conversation.

"How is Jewel? Where is she staying?" David asked. "We'll be there."

"We have her in protective custody at the precinct in section three. A Detective Sanders will meet you at the station and he'll escort you here. We can extend protection to you too."

"No, no, that won't be necessary," David said. "We have a place to stay."

"Gracee Place and Lily Street are both sealed," Jasper said. "Under investigation."

"Yes, that I understand," David said. "Poor Mike--and Mother too. I..." He rubbed his eyes, bending his head to hide his reaction. "Let me speak to Jewel."

Jasper handed the com unit back, listening intently to what he could hear but there was little of use. His shock and that of his son seemed to be genuine. Well, there was little doubt where they were yesterday. Who did that leave? The actress and Jake's wife. He wondered if they would come.

The doctor had not mentioned a heart condition and Jewel hadn't known of one. He would have to ask the doctor again about that. He also needed to know the specifics of the wills. Elizabeth's will was already in the archives since she took the walk. He didn't know yet whether Michael had one. Given their wealth, he probably did.

Could he have overdosed? Well, the lab was looking at that. They'd analyze any pills and the alcohol too. They'd even taken the remains of last night's dinner for analysis although he doubted anything would be found in that. They'd ordered in from a high-class restaurant and both had eaten the same meal. A quick check of the kitchen had shown him nothing else was there--not even a bottle of ketchup. He wondered briefly if Michael West had even planned on moving back to Gracee Place.

The police psychiatrist caught his attention. "Lieutenant, there are few groceries here. Under the circumstances, do you think we should order in?"

Jasper considered it. "There's a market close by. I'll go get some items. Let me know what. No expense limit."

The psychiatrist nodded and rummaged through the cupboards. "She'll want comfort food if anything. We have ketchup, mustard, and a box of macaroni.... Well, that's comfort food for most people."

Jasper smiled. It certainly was. He remembered his mother saying how she had loved it as a child. He had too. His daughter never turned her nose up at it either. He wondered if Elizabeth West had used the boxed variety though and thought probably not.

Jewel finished her call and sat there with a forlorn expression.

Handing her a tissue, he took the matter in hand. "I'm going shopping for supper and breakfast. What kind of cereal do you like?"

She blinked. "Cereal?"

"For breakfast. We can't have you going hungry."

"I can't eat," Jewel said with a sniff. "I'm not hungry."

"You will be. We've got macaroni. What kind of cheese did your grandmother use on it?"

"Cheddar," she said without thinking. "Sharp."

"Sharp it is," Jasper said. "And real milk. How about a hamburger patty and green beans with it?"

"I'm not hungry," she repeated.

"Ok, hamburger and green beans. I liked the frozen green beans myself," Jasper said.

"Yeah, they're better," she said. "With bacon."

"With bacon," he said. "Now what kind of cereal and what kind of fruit?"

"Frosted wheat cakes," she said. "With strawberries or bananas."

"And whole milk? Coffee?" he prompted.

"I'm not hungry!" She finally glared at him. "Get what you want."

"Ok, chocolate chip ice cream with the works," Jasper said and he had her full attention now. "And donuts. And peppermint sticks."

"You're an idiot." She bit out.

"And you're hungry." He winked at the psychiatrist and went out, confident he'd gotten her out of her grief for a few minutes.

His grin faded as he headed for the market. The next few days were going to be rough on her. Maybe he should spoil her a bit while he could. He knew departmental policy had a limit on what they would supply to inmates and those in protective custody but she was a West. He would buy the extras himself and not submit them to the department. It would be his gift to her.

Chapter 10 – David West

The closest market was small but open. Choosing a quart bottle for the milk, Jasper filled it at the dispenser. Wending his way through the aisles, he picked up a pint of strawberries then hesitated at the bananas. One, he decided. Bananas were imported and always expensive while strawberries were grown by the city. They were much cheaper even if they were seasonal.

At the meat counter he picked up three hamburger patties and four strips of bacon. That should be enough for the beans. He hadn't heard of putting bacon in green beans but he was willing to try it.

Cheese. He backtracked to pick up a small block of sharp cheddar then stopped at the ice cream counter to pick up three servings of ice cream. Those he would pay for. He piled on the toppings, sealed them, and added them to his cart.

Coffee. He wanted real coffee. He grabbed a small bag of the only tolerable kind this market sold. He would have to go to a luxury store to get his favorite brand.

He remembered the beans and cereal on his way out then picked up three peppermint sticks at the checkout. No doubt Jewel would prefer chocolate but the peppermint sticks were a comfort food for some people. They were cheap and a common treat.

One of these days he'd have time for his personal shopping but not tonight. Although it wasn't usual for a police investigator to share a meal with someone connected to a case, tonight he would. Not only did the girl need the distraction but he might glean more information by being informal. Besides, he liked her.

Since the psychiatrist would also be there, it was within regulations. The other two Wests would also be arriving in the next hour or so and he wanted to meet them and see what he could learn.

* * *

His instincts had been good about the food. Jewel, in spite of her grief, took over the cooking in the little apartment. He was able to watch, along with the psychiatrist, as she whipped up a cheesy sauce for the macaroni and turned the green beans into a more interesting dish. She left the hamburgers to him but that was fine. By the time they sat down, even Jewel had an appetite.

"That was delicious," the psychiatrist said as she finished her meal. "And very filling. Did your grandmother teach you to cook?"

"Yes," Jewel said with a tight smile. "She always cooked and I couldn't wait to learn. It's so much better than city food."

"It's incredibly better," she said. "I wish I'd learned. I will remember that about the green beans though. Such a simple trick."

"Most cooking is simple," Jewel said. "Grandma wasn't a chef. She was a cook. We had the best plain food you'll ever get." Her blue eyes got blurry. "Grandma said it was always good to cook when you're down."

"Good therapy," the psychiatrist said. "And I think our lieutenant also cooks."

Jasper set down his coffee. "I learned some. My wife was better."

"You're married?" Jewel looked disappointed.

"Not anymore," Jasper said, reluctant to say more. That was personal.

The psychiatrist rose, gathering up plates. "I can do dishes. It's a good thing they had enough in this apartment."

"Yes." Jasper rose too. "I didn't think to pick up extras."

"I'll dry," Jewel got up quickly. "I don't want to be sitting alone."

"Of course not," the psychiatrist said. "By the way, call me Em. It's short for Emma."

"Nice," Jewel said. "I'm just Jewel. It can't be shortened."

"Didn't you have a sister?" the psychiatrist asked. "Once?"

Jasper waited to see if she would freeze up.

"Once. Amber has been dead most of my life--my parents too. I was only six when they died."

"Terrible," Em said. "Then your grandmother took you in?"

"I was already there," Jewel explained. "I couldn't go with my parents so I was going to stay with my Uncle Rory and his wife. He died too." Her lip finally quivered and she took a deep breath. "Then it was decided I would stay with my grandparents. Uncle David was working and raising Jake and Aunt Jessica was no good with children. I had my grandparents and Uncle Mike."

She stopped, setting down the dishtowel. "I'm sorry. I just can't..." she disappeared into the bathroom.

Jasper thought it was better to leave her be and picked up the dishtowel. "Mind if I call you Em too?"

"It's better than Dr. Rodriguez-Gomez," she said. "Yes, call me Em. If you are concerned she did it, I think you can rest easy on that, Lieutenant."

"Jasper," he corrected automatically. "No, I think she was set up. Possibly she was meant to take the blame for both murders but I don't think so. It's more likely someone knew her schedule well enough to avoid being caught by her."

"I thought she was the last to see her uncle," Em said.

"As far as we know at this point," Jasper said. "But there's still some doubt that was murder."

"Hopefully it wasn't," Em said as she handed him the last dish and reached for a pan. "Thank you, by the way, for such a good meal. How much do I owe you?"

"Not a thing," Jasper said. "The department will pay for the cereal and strawberries and milk and the can of beans and I picked up the rest. I would have had to pick up a meal on the way home anyway. This was cheaper and better."

She studied him, her lips pursed, before saying "You do know I make more than you do?"

His lips parted in a big smile and he resisted the urge to laugh. "No, you don't."

She looked puzzled but just then the door chime sounded and Jasper headed for it. As he expected, it was Sanders with the two West men.

"David West," the older man said. "You're Lieutenant Stone?"

David looked very fit for his fifty-odd years with good muscles under his dark green shirt and a trim waist. His blond hair was thinning and gray at the temples. There were laugh lines around his mouth and eyes but that wasn't what Jasper was seeing now. The man looked grim.

"Yes," Jasper said, shaking the offered hand. His grip was firm. "This is Dr. Emma Rodriguez-Gomez. She's keeping Jewel company tonight."

"Call me Em or Doctor Em," she said as she lightly shook his hand. "Jewel needed some time alone just now."

"I see," David said. "Yes, she would but," he motioned to his son. "Tell her we're here."

Jake West looked a lot like him. His hair was cut short in a spacer's cut but it was only a shade lighter than his father's. Underneath the black jacket he wore, his shoulders looked broad and he looked even more trim than his dad. Of course, Mars colonists had to be physically fit and as close to underweight as possible. Weight took money to move and often it was the colonist with the lowest weight that got selected from those equally qualified.

Jake's face bore more obvious signs of grief as he moved to the bathroom door. He'd barely knocked on it before Jewel flung it open and was in his arms. Jake held her and patted her awkwardly before she latched on to her uncle.

Jasper looked away, aware this was private, and spotted Sanders hanging back in the hall. He stepped out to join him, closing the door as he went.

"Anything?"

"The usual," Sanders said. "Jake hasn't said much but his father's first question was how did he die."

"And?"

"I told him he was in bed. We're still running tests on cause of death."

"Good answer."

Sanders looked uncomfortable. "Lieutenant, I got a call on the way to the station," he said. "The lab found poison in the scotch."

"Already?" Jasper was surprised. "What kind?"

"They don't know that yet but it was the first thing they tested. By morning they should know what killed the rat," Sanders said then hastily added. "The lab rat, not the victim."

"I got that." Jasper smiled at him for his slip. "So they'll be dusting the bottle then tracing it back to where he got it. We'll have to talk to that butler again and check the door more thoroughly. Wasn't that bottle half empty?"

"Yes sir. It wasn't new unless he drank an awful lot last night," Sanders said. "Do we tell them?" He nodded toward the door.

"Not tonight," Jasper said. "Officially, we don't know whether his was natural or murder. Once we say Michael's is murder, they'll want lawyers."

"We should have a fair witness," Sanders said.

"Department regulations allow us to use personnel not directly assigned to police work," Jasper replied. "The psychiatrist will work. That room is also bugged. That's why we're talking out here."

Sanders glanced up and down the corridor before replying. "So we have to talk out here?" he asked.

"Yes." Jasper felt his com unit's silent alarm and picked it up. "Yes?"

No answer. He looked at it, saw the call was from the psychiatrist and realized he was needed. With no explanation, he went back in.

"Jewel, don't be stubborn," David West was saying. "As soon as the services are over, you're going back with me. They'll know where to find us."

"I'm not," Jewel retorted. "It's the middle of term and I can't leave my students. I'll be safe. They'll get this solved." She was actually angry and Jasper realized he'd gotten the alert just in time. What if one of these two was the killer?

"Jewel is right," Jasper said, cutting into the argument. "And until this case is solved, I would prefer she not leave the city. She's a material witness."

"Not a suspect?" David demanded, turning on him. "She was there both times."

Jasper met his gaze. "No sir. The time of death for your mother was between noon and two p.m. Jewel was with her students then and has a solid alibi. Michael didn't but now he's dead."

"You think he killed our mother?" David said, incredulity on his face. "Our mother? He didn't have the guts."

"I didn't say that," Jasper said. "But you say that like you could."

"I was working," David said. "And I wouldn't kill my mother. There's no way in hell I'd be guilty of that."

"But you could?" Jasper pressed.

"I'm a licensed hunter," David ground out, his jaw tight. "So is Jake although he hasn't done it in years. I've killed animals, not people."

Jasper studied him, surprised. He knew some people hunted but they were extremely rare and it was mostly people from farms and ranches. He didn't expect someone worth so much money to do it. Certainly he didn't need to.

"Hunting is a family thing," David said in a calmer voice. "My father took us. After my two brothers died, I was his hunting partner. Mike didn't like it and Jewel and Jake were too young."

"You said Mike had no guts?" Jasper went back to that statement. "Really?"

"Oh, he could pull a trigger," David said. "He couldn't handle the blood. Puked every time. Dad decided he was hopeless."

Interesting, Jasper thought as he recalled how much blood there was at the scene. Could he have forced himself to do it anyway? Possibly but there was that medical report too. It was almost certain that Michael West didn't do it. He might have known who did though. He'd been murdered too.

"We'd already reached the conclusion Michael was unlikely," Jasper said, "based on his doctor's report." He kept an eye on David and hoped someone else was watching Jake. The younger man had turned toward Jewel so he couldn't see his face. "He was there with no alibi but probably not able."

David visibly relaxed. "Thank God for that," he said. "So a stranger?"

"It's not been ruled out," Jasper said. "The front door was open when police got there. What we haven't figured out is why the upper door was open for over an hour--and Michael apparently opened it. I was hoping to ask him about that today."

"I wouldn't know," David said. "That's not like him."

"I thought those doors were designed so no one could leave them open," Jake suddenly said. "Don't they have an audible alarm?"

Jasper eyed him. He looked pale but composed. "Yes, they do--if the door registers as open. This one had an error message so it was not open but not completely closed either. The company said someone must have jammed the lock."

"Interesting," Jake said. "Dad, did you know you could do that?"

"No, I thought that door was fool proof," David said.

"Jewel, did you know?" Jake asked.

"I never tried it," Jewel said. "It never occurred to me to try it," she continued with a tiny shrug. "Grandma wouldn't have liked it."

"True," David said then ran his hand over his hair. "Look, lieutenant, we haven't eaten and we've got rooms at the Grand Hotel. Can we take Jewel with us or not?"

"I'm staying here," Jewel quickly said. "And I've eaten."

"That settles that," David said after a brief hesitation. "I've got two days free for the services and such. Can we talk this over tomorrow?"

"Yes. Will eleven o'clock do?"

"I'm meeting with my lawyer at ten thirty. Can we make it earlier?"

Jasper thought about his dead-ended drug case and nodded. "What time?"

"Nine?"

"Fine. It will be in this building. I'll need to meet with Jake separately," Jasper said. "Matter of form."

"Of course." David glanced at his son. "He'll want to visit with Jewel anyway so he'll come with me. You are taking the day off from school, aren't you?" he shot at Jewel.

"I have the next two days off," Jewel primly replied. "Friday I'll work."

"We'll see," David said. "This city isn't healthy for you right now. Denver or Houston would be better."

Jewel folded her arms across her chest and shook her head, her mouth resolutely set.

Jasper realized that this young woman had a lot more of her grandmother in her than people saw. Elizabeth West had been totally cooperative with police regulations but had refused to bow to pressure to have that upper door permanently sealed. Now her granddaughter was standing firm for what she wanted. He had to admire her for that--and disagree with David. Not only did he need to keep the Wests separated until they solved the case but Denver was split into the old crime-ridden town and the more secure underground. It was far easier to obtain weapons and smuggle drugs in Denver than it was in Plains. He didn't know about Houston but suspected it was the same.

"Until tomorrow," David abruptly said. "See you then." He gave Jewel a hug, nodded to the psychiatrist and Jasper then left with his son and Detective Sanders following behind.

Jewel visibly relaxed, her shoulders sagging and head bowed for just an instant then she smiled resolutely at him and Em. "I'm ready for ice cream."

Chapter 11 - Wednesday

The persistent buzzing of his alarm intruded on his consciousness but it sounded odd today. Off key. He fuzzily tried to figure out why as he dragged himself out of deep sleep--like two different tones fighting. His eyes popped open and he reached for his com unit then reached for his alarm. His hand slipped and the silenced alarm fell to the floor.

"Damn," he muttered and heard his partner's startled laugh.

"Well, you've never answered that way before," Lori Brown said. "Did I wake you?"

"Right on time," Jasper muttered, scrubbing his face. "What's up?" Taking a deep breath to forestall a yawn, he tried hard not to let his partner hear.

"Are you still working the West case?" she asked.

"Yes. There are two murders now, same family."

"Two?" she squeaked.

"Yeah. Ok, I'm awake now."

"I think we have a connection," she said. "I've gone over the membership lists of Reach Out and Elizabeth West, Michael West, and Jewel West were all high level donors. There's also a couple of people I know are executives for Viking Pharmaceuticals and two from Wilson Chemicals."

"You're kidding."

"Nope. That charity has connections both with the company that makes Bliss and their chief competitor but I thought you should know about the Wests right away."

"Thanks." Jasper's mind raced. "Are any other Wests listed?"

"No, just those three. Have you checked into this Michael West? He's a city engineer."

"He's dead," Jasper said. "Jewel could be next but we have her in protective custody."

"God." She paused. "You have been busy. Fill me in sometime?"

"I'll do better than that. If there's a proven connection between our cases, I'll bring you in and buy you dinner too."

"That's a deal," she said. "It might be a good idea to follow up with the professor when you have time."

"I'll make time," he said. "Thanks for the heads up."

"Any time I can."

He could almost hear her smile as she broke the connection. What was she doing working this early? He picked up his clock and checked the time. Ten after seven. That's right. He'd given himself an extra hour because of the late night. Well, he hadn't expected to do more than a quick check-in at his home precinct before heading over to Section Three. Maybe he'd better re-think that. No, Lori had briefed him and Captain Reynolds wouldn't expect more than an update. He'd sent one of those last night with a copy to the captains at sections two and three.

Setting his vid screen to give him his morning update, he started getting ready for the day. There was no international news of worth so he didn't get that. The computerized vid screen did present a report on another death cloud in Mexico, this time in Mexico City itself, and mentioned thirty-two dead. Not that high. Well, they'd take more steps and plant more trees.

Death clouds were nothing new. The biggest were in China more than a century ago. Pollution and stagnant air were the cause. Governments didn't get serious about pollution until the death clouds. Now there weren't any gas cars or coal plants and chemical plants had a lot of safeguards. Reforestation had become a priority too

By then everyone had gotten fed up with the Congressional deadlock and the states had effectively fired most of Congress and put the rest on notice. That had started the Reformation.

The reforms were working. The global temperatures were getting lower and the climate more predictable. More importantly, they had cities like Plains where people could live in comfort and safety. There were still old cities but their surface structures were getting fewer as they expanded their undergrounds and demolished old buildings to add trees and ventilation towers. People didn't like having to deal with snow and heat when they didn't have to.

Jasper didn't either. He'd been raised in new Chicago and moved to Plains when he started his police career. He could handle himself in the old towns but he much preferred the secure undergrounds. Murders were rare, except from domestic spats, and usually easy to solve. The West case was easily the most complicated one he'd dealt with--and he'd never had one that involved a lunatech or a Mars colonist.

Both programs were pretty Victorian in what they required of their employees. Legal marriages, no scandals, and there was a long list of what employees couldn't do if they wanted the privilege of working for Lunarex, the biggest mining firm on the moon, or immigrate to Mars.

He wondered how Jake West would fit in. As he finished his morning routine, he thought about him. The younger West was very reserved and he hadn't said much during that short meeting last night. No doubt he was competent but he thought Jake West would be hard for anyone to get to know. He wondered what his wife was like.

David West was more secure and open. The man had nearly taken charge of Jewel last night and seemed dead certain that Jewel would be safer with him. Was he that set on protecting her or did he want her out of police protection? Jasper wasn't sure. The man was also getting a divorce. He needed to remember that.

"In entertainment news, the new album by Sensor Man has the music world buzzing." Jasper heard Sensor Man and stepped out of his bedroom to watch the report.

"Back Again is the first album Sensor Man has released in nineteen years and it's not in his old style at all. Some have declared it a fake but others are raving at the newness of the music and how it answers a need for a quieter, more thoughtful sensa."

Jasper studied the screen, seeing they had only his album cover. Some of his previous albums flashed in a corner of the screen.

"I like this album," the entertainment editor was saying to the news anchor. "It's almost classic in feel. My favorite number seems to include a traditional hymn I heard as a child."

Jasper grinned. Morning Grace did. He'd tried to create the feeling of the dawn then the sunrise and start of day with that one. An old hymn had laid the theme for it and its melody appeared a couple of times in the number. With luck, that one would make the charts. It probably wouldn't be played in many sensa dens though. It was way too peaceful.

The report ended without speculation on his identity. Good. He had other things to worry about.

Pouring himself a cup of real coffee, he paused to take in the aroma. Nice and strong with plenty of Aruba beans in the mix. At least he had time for this. It was too bad he didn't have a real breakfast to go along with it.

Checking his refrigerator one more time, he grimaced. He had cheese and condiments. He already knew his bread was gone. It was going to have to be a protein bar or buy out. Opting for the protein bar, he went back to dressing.

Shopping had to be on his list today. He could skip reporting in at his home section and head straight for his appointments in Section Three. He hoped David West would be on time but wasn't seriously worried anything had happened to him. The Grand Hotel had good security.

Lab reports. They should know what poison it was and maybe have fingerprints on the bottle by now. He hadn't handled the bottle but he had looked at it and it wasn't new.

More than half the scotch was gone and he doubted Michael West could have drunk it all last night. How much did he usually drink? Another question but would David know it or should he ask Jewel? Not one for Jake. The younger West probably hadn't seen much of his uncle.

He'd find out.

Chapter 12 – Autopsy Report

Death by poison. Jasper read those words and frowned. The poison wasn't named. He looked at the lab technician. "It's not been identified?"

"Not yet," the technician admitted. "It's exotic. We have to isolate it from the scotch to get a clear picture of the molecular makeup. Only one lab in Denver can do that and a sample is going to them today."

"What do you know about it?" Jasper asked.

"Well, the bottle had only the fingerprints of Mr. West. Whoever put the poison in wiped it clean afterward. The bottle was less than half full when we got it so we have to assume it was not a new bottle when the poison was added. The deceased apparently didn't taste the poison because he drained the glass and went on to bed. That eliminates a lot of known poisons. No contortions. That eliminates a few more. He died in his sleep and it looked peaceful."

"How did the rat react?" Jasper asked.

"The rat got tipsy from the Scotch and stumbled about then curled up and went to sleep. Death was not immediate. If it hadn't been for the circumstances surrounding his death, this case might not even have been suspected as poison. Too peaceful."

Jasper realized that was true. A middle-aged man recovering from an accident could easily have died in his sleep. "So a routine autopsy might not have caught this poison?"

"It could have but there's precious few clues. I did the toxicology myself and it barely registers. It could easily be put down to the scotch. This was a very exotic poison." The technician looked like he admired it. "I want to know what it is and how to detect it."

"Is it one of the euthanasia drugs?" Sanders asked. "Those are supposed to be painless."

"Not curare or hemlock," the technician said. "Curare doesn't do much if it's ingested. Hemlock leaves signs on the body. Like I said, this poison is very exotic."

"Ok, so the poison is unidentified." Jasper turned to Sanders. "Anything from the door lock? It was a logger, right?"

"Yeah," Sanders looked unhappy, "but on a week cycle. The only entries were Michael West, Jewel West, and us. Before two days ago, there's nothing. I called management for Gracee Place and found out Mr. West had stopped maid service except for a once monthly vacuuming and dusting. He hadn't listed his home for sale though and the manager wondered if it would be."

"That's not something we'd know," Jasper said. "Good thinking on calling them."

Sanders flashed a smile then turned back to his notes. "On Lily Street, most of the fingerprints have been identified now. We have one set that hasn't. Those were found on both the first floor and the third floor. Besides the maid, we have Elizabeth West, Michael West, Jewel West, David West, and Jake West."

"One of the wives?" Jasper asked, unsurprised.

"The techs say it's a man. We're requesting a check anyway." Sanders frowned. "They aren't the most recent prints. They were overlaid by others."

"What about David and Jake?"

"Those were recent," Sanders said. "Can't place the day but within a few days."

"So the mystery man might not be relevant," Jasper said. "Our suspects remain in the family."

"Can we eliminate Michael West?" Sanders asked. "Or is there still a question?"

"He's doubtful given the doctor's report and since someone removed him." Jasper stopped, thinking hard. "Wait, there's another possibility here."

The technician had risen to go but stopped at the tone in his voice.

"I think we agreed the accident might have been another attempt on Michael West--the first attempt. If that's so and now a second attempt succeeded, he might have been the target all along rather than Elizabeth West."

Sanders stared at him and even the technician looked interested.

"Kill her to get him back to his own place?" the technician asked.

Jasper's mind raced. "What was Michael West working on?" he asked. "Could he have stumbled on something? He obviously didn't know it was important or he would have reported it."

"Maybe," Sanders said, "unless he was involved."

"Even if he was involved, he would have reported it right after the accident," Jasper said. "As you pointed out those air cleaners don't just fall. He would have known that too. Hell, if I'd been dirty, I would have been screaming loud and long or left the city."

"And he didn't do either one," Sanders said. "Yeah, it must have been something he saw but didn't know he saw."

"Unless someone is just out to get the house," Jasper said. "In which case we'll know if another West dies." He hoped it wouldn't happen. He liked Jewel and wanted to protect her.

Hold on, his inner voice said. Like her? She still could be the one. He firmly told it to shut up but he'd heard. He had no business liking a suspect or even a potential victim. It would make him sloppy.

"I think we need to split this case as to possibilities," Jasper said. "Check into what Michael West was assigned to and where he went. At the same time, I'll continue investigating the family angle."

"We don't have enough people," Sanders said.

"We will," Jasper said. "There's another angle we have to consider." Quickly he told him about the Reach Out connection. "At this point, I think I can get Brown reassigned to this case. It's getting bigger."

"Yeah." Sanders grinned.

Jasper knew why. This kind of case didn't come around often and when it did it could make or break careers. He'd never had sequential murders in his entire career, although he'd had a couple where whole families died--murder suicides usually. The worst ones were families about to go on the subby list.

"Lieutenant," the technician said. "I would prefer to continue working on this case with you. It might help if you don't have multiple forensic techs working different aspects. Unless you specify, that can happen."

"True," Jasper said but he knew the tech also smelled opportunity in this case. It was likely to get big and dirty. "Your name?"

"Pedro Kruger."

Jasper raised an eyebrow at that strange combination. The man looked to have Hispanic roots but it was hard to tell what Americans had in them. The technician was short and lightly built and looked almost like a subby boy. He didn't have the attitude though and he must have had a good deal of training to be a toxicologist and forensic technician.

"German father," the technician said. "Named after my mother's dad."

"That happens," Jasper said with a grin. "How are you at civil bureaucracy?"

"Lower levels, pretty good," the technician said. "No actual badge so the upper levels are closed. I can point out a few areas if the detective wants."

Quick, Jasper decided. He even figured out who he'd be working with. "Sanders?"

"Sounds good to me." Sanders took it in stride. "And you worked on Elizabeth West too, right?"

"I was brought in but not lead. It's easy enough to find out anything though. I'm a certified pathologist as well as toxicology."

So he wasn't as senior as he appeared but would like to be, Jasper thought. Was he jumping the chain of command? He'd have to find out. He was senior enough to do the reporting on Michael West. Close then.

"I'll see what I can set up," Jasper said. "Right now we need that last set of fingerprints identified and we have an interview with David West. Let's get that done before we start our secondary investigation."

The other two nodded, Kruger understanding that he wasn't yet on the team. He left first.

Jasper turned to his partner. "Be a little careful with him. He might be a climber."

Sanders looked surprised then thoughtful. "I could find out where he stands."

"Do that. Before I ask, I want to know whose toes I'll be stepping on." Jasper rose to go. He knew it wouldn't matter to him but this was Sanders' home section. He needed cooperation and offending someone in the labs was not the way to get it.

Chapter 13 - Interviews

David West didn't arrive alone. A petite brunette some years younger than him walked in followed by Jewel. The two women looked well acquainted, he thought, before he focused on David.

"My fiancé," David West said. "This is Elinor Ramsey. Jewel told you I was getting a divorce?"

"Yes, she did let that slip. Ms. Ramsey, you're being careful of your safety?" He hated to put it that way but she needed to be aware.

"Yes, she is," David quickly said. "I called her from the train. She's coming back to Denver with me. Jewel says she's not." He didn't look like he'd accepted that yet.

"Good idea. Where's Jake?"

"He'll be along," David said. "Our escort is with him."

"Good." Jasper glanced around the interrogation room. There weren't enough seats. "Let's move the ladies to a neighboring room where they'll be comfortable. There's not enough room in here."

"Fine," David said. "Elinor, Jewel, I'll see you in a few." He gave them a reassuring smile and watched them go out with Sanders then turned to him. "Before we get started, I have a question for you. How did you know my mother?"

Jasper's brown eyes met his. "I didn't really know her," he said. "I met her several times when I was a very young cop. One of my duties was checking the door logger in her house."

"That's all?" David West asked.

"That's all," Jasper said. "Did you expect more?" He wasn't surprised this Mr. West had checked up on him. Did he talk to his captain?

"No, not really," West said and moved to the proper seat. "It's this one, right?"

"Yes. How did you know?" Jasper studied him with his keen brown eyes.

"I got questioned once when I was a brat," David said. "I was twelve and terrified. Dad arranged it to scare me straight. It did."

"Pretty good dad." Jasper's lips twitched but he was still thinking about that question. David West seemed to expect more but that was his only contact with Elizabeth West until her murder. Shortly after he'd caught that glimpse of Jewel, he'd been reassigned to a new section.

"The best," David said with an answering smile. "I haven't been in one since." He settled himself down and folded his hands on the table. "But I know why you do it here."

"Good," Jasper said. "It saves time since we don't have to sort out lies on our own."

"Right." David's blue eyes met his. "I will not lie."

"Truth." The voice in Jasper's earpiece murmured.

"I also waive my right to a lawyer for this interview," David said. "Just for the record. I have nothing to hide."

"Then let's get to it," Jasper said as Sanders re-entered the room. "I already understand the reason for your divorce. Does your wife know about her?"

"Yes. Jessica has her own interests and we've agreed not to bring our partners into the reasons," he said. "I could have gotten her on that any time the last ten years."

"Reasonable," Jasper said. "Very reasonable." He didn't know many women who would decline to use such ammunition. "So a simple divorce?"

"Yes." David West looked uncomfortable then said. "It's all done except for a little disagreement over her share of my wealth. Her lawyer is holding out for more in hopes of getting a bigger fee."

"That happens," Jasper said then voiced a sudden thought. "Will your mother's death affect that?"

David looked surprised. "No, it won't. Jessica's lawyer might think it will change things. I hadn't..." He stopped to think about it then came to a decision. "I don't think Jessica had anything to do with this but you'd better question her too."

"We'll arrange it," Jasper said. "Is she coming here?"

"No," David said, shaking his head. "She hasn't been in Plains for years. It's too remote and she didn't get along with Mother."

"So she wasn't in the house recently?"

"Not that I know of," David said. "Why? Did you find her fingerprints?"

"Not yet. We just have one unidentified set and we're trying to cut down the possibilities."

David rubbed his ear thoughtfully. "As far as I know Jessica hasn't been to Plains in over ten years. She was here after my father died and maybe twice more after that. When we officially separated, she quit coming."

"And when did you last see your mother?" Jasper asked.

"Sunday."

"Last Sunday?"

"That's right," David said. "I was staying with Elinor but I couldn't come to Plains and not see Mother. She wouldn't have stood for it. We had dinner as a family Sunday night then I took the morning train back to Denver for my shift. I didn't see her on Monday."

"Truth," the technician muttered.

Jasper fished out the evidence bag and laid it on the table. "Do you have any idea what this is?"

David picked it up and looked at the little fragment in the bag. "It looks like ceramic or wood. Pretty small." He glanced up at him. "What is it?"

"Part of the murder weapon. We haven't identified it yet."

"Murder weapon? I thought Mother had fallen from the stairs. Where does this fit in?" He handed the evidence bag back.

"She was clubbed first then thrown from the stairs. This was a deliberate homicide."

David looked shaken. He bowed his head and his hands latched together in a tight grip. "God," he muttered then said something under his breath Jasper couldn't hear. "Mother..." he struggled to compose himself. "Does Jewel know?"

"Not about the club," Jasper said. "As I said last night, she has a very firm alibi and I am fairly sure she is not a suspect."

"No, she wouldn't hurt family," David said. "Am I?"

"Probably not," Jasper replied. "If Elinor backs your story and the train records show you left, you're in the clear."

David nodded then wiped his eyes. He took a deep breath. "God, who could have done this? Mother didn't have enemies. She made a point of not having them. And Mike..." He shot him a look. "Mike was in the house--what about him? Do you think he did it? My brother would never hurt anyone--especially Mother."

"According to the doctor's report, it was unlikely he could have," Jasper said. "We did get that far. He had the opportunity but often that's misleading. At this point we are still assuming his innocence."

"Good." David was recovering his composure now. "I don't want his name dragged into it. It was all he had."

"I thought he was rich too."

David managed a crooked smile. "We're all rich, lieutenant. We have more money than anyone could ever spend. What matters are our names. Michael was a fine man who loved his family and did his work well. I don't want him remembered as Mother's murderer."

"Did he ever have children or a girlfriend?" Jasper asked.

"No, no," David said. "He was a celibate. When he went out to a social function, Mother or Jewel was his partner. He never formed any attachments."

"Why was he celibate?" Jasper asked, wondering what his motivations could have been. Same sex marriages were actively encouraged in this day and age but he knew that hadn't always been the case. Could the Wests have been old fashioned in that regard?

"Mike just never got interested," David said. "He was asexual or something of that nature. Later he found out that a lot of great minds were also celibates and he saw no reason to change. The only time Dad put pressure on him was after we lost family. He wanted more grandchildren and my marriage was already in trouble. Jessica was focused on her career and I was raising the boys. I had Jake but I couldn't legally have another child for several years."

"You can now?" Jasper asked.

"Yes, the government restored our rights for every child lost in New Wave. I could replace Benjie--as if that was possible." He looked bitter. Taking a deep breath, he continued, "Dad tried to persuade Mike but that was the one time both Mike and Mother stood up to him. When he couldn't get Mike to marry, he changed the contracts set up for both Jake and Jewel. They won't get their money till they turn thirty instead of twenty-five so neither one could go to Mars."

"I heard," Jasper said.

"You have to understand we were real supporters of both Mars and undersea development. We poured money into both. Hell, it was one of my ancestors who helped develop the lunar mining equipment I work on. When New Wave collapsed, it not only killed more than half our family but it hit us financially too. More than that, it caused Dad to rethink our dreams. We still invest in cutting edge technology but we didn't volunteer to live in it until it's proven beyond a doubt."

"Like Plains?"

"Like Plains. My parents were proud to be supporters and happy to live here. They were newlyweds when the groundbreaking happened and had lived here ever since."

Jasper nodded, getting a more complete picture of the West clan. "So now that Michael is dead and Jake is going to Mars, what will happen?"

David thought for a moment. "Mike's money will go back into the Foundation except for some bequests. Jake has a lawyer to handle his. No doubt, that guy will buy out his contract so he has no obligations and Jake will start looking at what Mars needs that he can make a profit on. That's how we've always made our money--we look to the future and invest in it and help make it happen."

"And you and Jewel?"

David shook his head. "I have my money. Jewel will get hers. Once she finds the right man and settles down she'll be set but it's hard to find a mate that doesn't love your money more than you," he said. "I know. Elinor loves me."

"Congratulations on that."

"Thanks. Elinor and I will have to have at least one child to carry on the name," David said. "We're planning on it. I still have my right and Elinor never exercised hers. She's as picky as the rest of us."

"How old is she?" Jasper asked then mentally kicked himself for being irrelevant.

"Thirty-six," David said. "But she thought ahead. She's had ova in cryogenic storage since she was twenty-five."

"Good for her." Jasper paused. "I know you said Mike was celibate--did he have sperm in storage in case he changed his mind?"

"Nope." David's full lips twitched into a smile. "He was religious about it. He wouldn't donate or in any other way contribute to the genetic future of the human race. That ticked Dad off no end but he had to respect him for it."

"True." Jasper was thoughtful. He knew such sperm donations were never supposed to be released without the donor's consent but old Mr. West might have gotten it done if he wanted grandchildren that badly. It looked like Michael West had won that war though.

Asexual recognition and celibacy had been around since the mid twenty-first century. They'd never been as vocal or as visible as the gay rights community before it but they had gotten recognition. Some still married and had children but the majority didn't. After the monster flu of the 2050s had decimated the world population there had been an attempt to discourage the movement but it had gained in strength instead. Now it was accepted that people had a right not to procreate.

"I wish I had time to know your brother better. He sounds like he was quite a guy," Jasper said. "Do you know if he had any enemies?"

"No, he never mentioned any. He didn't like working on security and inspection systems much but he never complained about the people he was working with."

"Security and inspection?" Jasper asked.

"Yeah," David said. "He said it was hopeless because any system could be and would be beaten but he had hopes for the new prototypes. They still wouldn't stop illegal substances though. You needed people to do that and people could be bought."

"That doesn't sound like he should have been around air cleaners. Wouldn't he have been on level one for that?" Jasper wondered why he'd never met West in his legal capacity if that was his field.

"It was just outside the train station," David said. "A lot of freight came down that street to the warehouses and one of the new Seekers was there, almost directly beneath the air cleaner. If a worker hadn't shouted at him, the cleaner would have got him straight on."

"Sounds like he was on a track that annoyed people," Jasper said. "What do you think of the possibility he was the primary target?"

"He was murdered?" David looked at him in shock then bit off a curse. His hands clenched and unclenched before he spoke. "How? I thought his heart or those pain killers did it."

"We've found a poison in his scotch," Jasper said. "It's still unidentified. Did he drink often?"

"Poison?" David took a deep breath but his hands were clenched tight. "How the hell did he get poison? No, he wasn't a boozer." His eyes shot to Jasper's. "He did drink a shot of scotch before bed. Mother did too. Someone knew?"

"Yes," Jasper said. "We don't know when they got into Gracee Place but the bottle wasn't new and probably wasn't purchased with poison in it. It was what killed him."

"God." David just sat there, his head bowed.

Jasper had no doubt this was new to him. Just when he thought he'd have to terminate the interview, David raised his head to look at him, the lines deeper in his face.

"Jewel was there," he said. "Did she?"

"According to our lab people, Michael died quietly in his sleep. No convulsions and no crying out," Jasper said. "She didn't hear anything. She didn't question his not getting up in the morning but went off to school. She really didn't know until I escorted her back to the house last night and we found him."

"She didn't know," David repeated. "Then she's not a suspect in this one either?"

"Not right now she isn't," Jasper said. "But this looks like someone is targeting your family and we're trying to figure out why--and who. Can you think of anything?"

"Our family?" David repeated. "You don't think it was someone in the family?"

"I'm not ruling that out yet," Jasper said. "But if it's someone else, there may be attempts on you, Jake, and Jewel. What happens to your money and that house if you all die?"

"Our money is protected," David said. "It goes back to the Foundation when we die. The house--I suppose it will go to charity," he said. "In Mother's will we're given joint ownership of it. Jewel is unlikely to approve a sale and Mike was definitely against it."

"You and Jake?" Jasper prompted.

"I can't live in Plains," David said. "At the same time, I don't want to sell it outside of family. I talked it over with Mike and Mother once and told them I'd give my share to Jewel when she got married."

"And Jake would opt to sell it?"

"Yes. Once he ships out, he'll never see it again but he doesn't have a stake in it so long as I'm alive. Jewel does because she receives her father's share." David looked sharply at him, his composure back. "This is because of the surface access?"

"Yes," Jasper said. "Smugglers would pay almost any price to have an unmonitored entrance."

"But it is monitored," David insisted. "Logging lock and all."

"The lock logs and even states time the door was open but authorized users can open it, receive a package, and close it without tripping any alarms. We weren't concerned so long as your family owned it but anyone else we might be."

"I see." David considered it. "Then we need to get that tied up so it can't go into private hands or have that upper entrance sealed."

"Sealing the upper entrance might protect your family more," Jasper said. "The house would no longer be an asset."

"True. Jewel will have a fit though." David finally shook his head. "No, I think I'll set it up so it will go to a nonprofit. They can seal the upper entrance when they get it. I'll let Jewel pick which one to keep her happy."

"You're certain Mike was murdered?" he asked again. "No mistake?"

"No mistake," Jasper said.

"This is one hell of a shitty mess," David said and scrubbed his face. "And Jewel won't leave Plains." His eyes blurred. "I have to meet with my people. I'll make damned sure they know what's going on."

"Are they all here in Plains?" Jasper asked.

David didn't answer right away. "Mike's lawyer is--and Jewel's. Mine is in Denver and so is Jake's. Hell, he's going to have to meet with his too." He looked even more unhappy. "And he doesn't have much time before quarantine."

"A lot to manage?" Jasper asked.

"Mostly oversight," David said. "Something has to be done about..." His voice trailed off.

"I sympathize," Jasper said.

"Even the best people need oversight," David said. "When you have investments, you'll know that."

"I've already had some experience with that," Jasper said.

"Good." David West didn't look surprised to find out a cop could have some investments. "Glad to hear it. Money does better when it's invested."

"Yes sir." Jasper glanced at his notes. "I think we've covered almost everything."

David took a deep breath and let it out. "Poor Mike. I want you to find out who did it," he said, his tone suddenly fierce. "If there are expenses your department won't pay, let me know. I'll see that they are--through official channels too."

"Thanks," Jasper said. "So far the city is still very interested in this case. I'll let you know if that changes."

"I wish Jewel would go with me but she insists on staying," David said. "You'll keep her in protective custody till she sees sense?"

"We'll keep her safe," Jasper said as he rose to his feet. "Do you know when Jake will be back?"

"He should be here any time," David said. "He needed to call his wife and convince her to come. She's only been in Plains once and found it claustrophobic. I don't know how she expects to handle Mars."

Jasper gave him a polite smile but wondered if Sasha Kowalski found her new relatives claustrophobic. Certainly she couldn't have a real problem and still qualify for the colony. Well, she'd only been in Plains once. If her location could be proved for Sunday, Monday, and Tuesday, he'd have no problem ruling her out.

Chapter 14 - Elinor

Elinor Ramsey sat calmly in the chair, her gloved hands on the table. Jasper noted the pretty white gloves and wondered why. They covered her hands entirely, preventing any fingerprints. Did she always wear those?

"Why the gloves?" he asked. The rest of her outfit was pretty normal. She wore a blue dress and white slippers with trim that matched the gloves. Her brunette hair was very short beneath a stylish cap.

"Medical," she said as she pulled her left glove off to reveal a medical compression glove beneath. The transparent glove allowed him to see burst blood vessels in the skin and the fingers seemed oddly fat. "My other hand is ok but it looks odd wearing just one glove so I wear both."

"What happened?" Jasper eyed the hand, thinking it was like no injury he'd ever seen before.

"I'm a lunar mechanic," she said as she pulled her glove back on. "David's counterpart. My space suit had a compression leak in the glove. The damage was localized and not really life threatening but I was out on the surface for almost an hour before I could get back to base. I'm on medical leave."

Jasper stared for a little longer than necessary then recovered. "A lunar mechanic?" He had a hard time picturing this pretty petite woman in a space suit. His image of lunar mechanics was quite different.

She smiled, her brown eyes crinkling at the corners. "Not all lunamechs are men, lieutenant, and I haven't met any--men or women--who look like the vids. No one is taller than five foot six and no one drinks booze on the moon." She gave him a wicked smile. "Not that we wouldn't like to sometime but getting it up there without the company knowing is pretty much impossible."

"I always thought that bit was odd," Jasper managed to say then glanced at Sanders. "That's how you met David?"

"Yes sir," she said with a lingering smile. "He runs them and I fix them."

She didn't look like she could fix a bike. Jasper knew he was being prejudiced and it bothered him but she just didn't seem the type.

"How long have you been down?" Jasper asked.

"Three weeks now," she said. "I can quit with the glove in another ten days."

"Were you over at Lily Place at any time during that period?" Jasper asked.

"Several times," she said. "Elizabeth made it clear I was welcome and was more than willing to cook for me. The last time though was Sunday. David and I went together."

"I see." Jasper hesitated. "How many pairs of gloves do you own?"

She laughed, surprised by the question. Jasper found himself grinning too. Under any other circumstances, that would be an extremely cheeky question.

"Sorry, that was the last thing I expected you to ask," she said. "Six pairs of fashion gloves, three medical ones. I have shoes and hats and purses to match," she added with a wicked grin. "Elizabeth suggested that and I admit it's a lot more fun. Since I can't be normal right now, I'm going for eccentric."

"And David?"

"He puts up with it," Elinor said. "Did you need to know anything more? When David left, for instance?"

Jasper saw her eyeing the clock and it steadied him. "Yes, when did he arrive in Plains and when did he leave?"

"He arrived Thursday on the late train," Elinor said. "I didn't meet him. I did see him off Monday morning at five a.m. He took the early train back to Denver because his shift started at noon."

"That confirms what he said," Jasper remarked. "Company records will back that up?"

"Of course," she said, her smile gone. "So will his pay statement. I suggest you get that instead of bothering the company. They don't like it when cops get interested in employees. He could get suspended."

"Noted. I don't think I need to follow up with them. I might ask for his pay stub later."

"He'll provide it," she said. "David wants this over."

"You seem to know him extremely well," Jasper said.

"I've had five tours moon side," she said. "The last two David has been one of my operators. He's good and doesn't break the equipment. I like that. He also stuck with me when the glove blew."

She studied her hands, her face growing solemn. "It was a hell of a ride back to base," she said. "My hand was freezing and ballooning up and I just wanted to cut it off. David told me I couldn't because it was my left hand and he was going to put a ring on it."

"The doctors were more than willing to amputate it," she said, her brown eyes shadowed by the memory. "And I was in so much pain I almost said yes but David kept telling me it would be ok and he'd see me through it and the ring would look better on a real hand."

"And you got the ring?" Jasper asked.

"You bet!" She smiled and gestured toward her necklace. A diamond ring flashed there in the center of a cleverly crafted pearl setting. "And I'll be able to get it on my finger in another ten days. The skin won't look that good with all the burst blood vessels but there's treatment for that."

"You're lucky to still have your hand," Jasper said. "And David sounds like a very decent man." Could he consider him a murderer? He wasn't sure. With luck, his alibis would hold up and he wouldn't have to. David West seemed sincerely decent and his reaction to Mike's murder seemed real. He'd have to go over the readings with the technician though. .

"He's a romantic," she said, "and no one turns down a romantic."

"I'll remember that," Jasper said. "But we're running out of time and I'm nearly out of questions. I just need to know where you were on Monday between noon and three p.m."

"Day before yesterday?"

"That's right." Jasper wondered at her hesitation. The technician was quiet, had been quiet, for most of this interview.

"I have an elderly aunt in senior care," Elinor said. "A great-aunt. She's my last relative and I try to spend time with her when I'm Earth-side. I was there all Monday afternoon."

"Has she met David?" Jasper asked.

"Yes and he totally flattered her. She didn't buy it but said he'd do." She hesitated. "Auntie is excited about the wedding and we plan to hold it here in Plains for her. Do you think we should change that?"

Jasper thought about that. "How big and where?"

"Only locals," she said. "We'd planned to have it in the chapel at the Senior Care Facility. They invited us to use it so my aunt's friends could attend."

"When?"

"The twenty-fifth. It's still a long way off."

"No, it's not. Let me know when and I'll make time to be there," Jasper said. "If there's some treats, I'm sure Detective Sanders will enjoy providing a little more security." He glanced at his partner and saw him grin.

"Thank you," Elinor said with an answering smile. "I'm glad I don't have to change it."

"This should be solved by then," Jasper said. "And I'd like to see you married." He meant it. She wasn't a beauty like Jewel but she was genuinely nice. He didn't want to suspect any of the family members he'd met so far. Who did that leave? Just Jake and his wife. No, there was Jessica West too.

Chapter 15 - Jake

"Interesting family," Sanders said after Elinor Ramsey left. "Lunar techs, lunar mechs, Mars colonists, engineers, and one schoolteacher."

Jasper looked sharply at him, keenly aware he meant Jewel. "Don't discount the schoolteacher."

"No sir," Sanders quickly replied. "It's just odd they have one in the mix."

"No rebels in your family?" Jasper asked.

"Well, no," Sanders looked sheepish, "but I'm an only kid."

"Married yet?" Jasper asked. His partner looked to be close to thirty.

"Yes," Sanders said. "And two kids--both boys."

"Good. I have a daughter myself," Jasper said. "What have you found out about our schoolteacher?"

Sanders waved his com unit. "A lot of charities and a lot of money," he said. "I got her tax return with no problem and it's all there. She receives a hundred thousand per year from a trust and another forty thousand from a family business. This is her first year teaching so that wasn't reflected there. She donated fifty thousand to various charities, including Reach Out, Forestry Protection, and United Way."

"What about investments?" Jasper asked, his attention fully on his partner. How well did Jewel West do?

"She's got holdings in the Sahara Project, In-Sol, Orbital Air, the Ventura Corporation and various food companies. Isn't Ventura the company that's working on the FTL drive?"

"Yes." Jasper didn't even have to wonder on that. "It's a good long term investment but not likely to pay off in the next twenty years." The shares weren't cheap, either. He'd bought just two at a thousand dollars a share. If they succeeded in developing the drive, they would pay off. If not, he was willing to spend that much on Earth's future.

"Okay, Elinor definitely has her own money and she's marrying money," Jasper said. "Unless she's got some expensive habits beyond hats and gloves, we can probably rule her out. If Jewel needed money, she'd probably just quit donating to so many charities. David has all he needs--unless he has some habits that haven't come out. I think we can almost rule out money as a motive."

"There's still Jake," Sanders said.

"He's already got a sponsorship," Jasper responded. "So has his wife. Sure he'd like to go as a private citizen but..." Jasper hesitated and drew his lips in thoughtfully. "We need to know when he got his sponsorship. That could be a factor. It sounds like it's old news but maybe not."

"Where is he anyway?" Jasper asked, looking at the time. Remembering Michael West's failure to show, he wondered if something had happened to this West too.

"I'll find out," Sanders said.

While he waited, Jasper called his home precinct and arranged for Brown to join him. Their original drug case had either hit a dead end or was getting bigger. He wasn't sure which. Was there a connection to Reach Out? Probably. Did it involve the Wests? Probably not. He wasn't sure if it even involved the professor. It looked like he'd been set up as an unwitting diversion by the tip. He was going to have to follow through on that and, much as he hated to do it, he was going to have to go to the sleep shop.

Soma, Incorporated. Word had gotten around not long after the corporation got its charter that Soma meant sleep in some language and people usually just said the sleep shop. There were hundreds of such companies nation-wide whose business was easing people out of life. Most, like Soma, were also full service mortuaries. Their main business though was euthanasia.

Did he really want to go? No. His memories would never fade of Carol and her decision. She'd been driven by the unrelenting pain of Hades Syndrome to end her life there and he'd been there until the end, supporting her and letting her know she was loved. His jaw tightened and he swallowed hard, his eyes haunted by the memory.

It had to be him. Sanders was too green to know what might be important. Brown was good but she hadn't been through it. She might not notice anything out of the ordinary. He would. No, it had to be him. He wouldn't take either partner though. He didn't know how well he'd keep his composure and he didn't want either Brown's sympathy or Sanders' ignorance. Before he could change his mind, he punched in the number for Soma, Inc. and requested an appointment.

"Jake is on his way," Sanders said as he came back into the room. "He was in a com booth all this time talking to his wife and mother. They've been fully briefed, I think."

"Not surprising," Jasper said. "I won't be surprised if one or both refuse interrogation."

"Can they do that in a murder case?" Sanders asked.

"If we can't prove either one was at the scene, yes," Jasper said. "We have Jake's fingerprints so he can't refuse. Unless that last set of fingerprints belongs to one of them, we can't force either one. Technically, Elinor didn't have to accept but her testimony was necessary to protect David. She placed herself at the house but we couldn't do it."

"Is she a suspect?" Sanders asked.

"Yes but she's an unlikely one. We need to confirm with the staff at the senior care facility she was there. If they can do that, she's off the list. Follow up?"

"Yes sir." Sanders made a note in his com unit. "And Jake?"

"Yes." Jasper glanced around the room, noting nothing was out of place then spoke to the technician in his booth. "Need a check?"

No answer. He frowned and spoke again. "Are you there?" Damn it. The man must have left his booth. Did he think they were done?

"We've lost our tech," he said to Sanders. "See if you can find him."

"Right." Sanders quickly left.

This could be the most important interview and no tech, Jasper fumed. He couldn't even get in there and set the controls because those doors were always locked. He pulled at it to make sure and it was. How the hell had the tech got the impression they were done? They had two interviews--Jasper stopped. He'd done two interviews. The man had good reason to think they were done. Damn.

"Problem?" A uniformed officer said.

Jasper saw Jake just beyond him and inwardly groaned. How long would it take to get the technician back? Hopefully, Sanders would grab any available. "We lost our tech," Jasper said. "He'll be back any time though."

"Do you need to wait?"

"No," Jasper said. "Can you stay?"

"Yes sir," the officer said. "I'm Officer Jim Brody. This is Jake West."

"We met briefly last night," Jasper said. "Lieutenant Jasper Stone."

He turned his attention to Jake. "Did you get your calls done?"

"Yes," Jake said. "Mother won't come even for the funerals. Sasha is willing to be questioned where she is but her schedule is too tight for her to come here."

"We can arrange that," Jasper said. "When do you have to report?" Motioning Jake toward the correct chair, he was also aware of Officer Brody as he took the observer's post. It was out of the way of the cameras and sensors.

"Next Tuesday morning," Jake said. "Then I enter quarantine."

"Final step huh?" Jasper studied him carefully. He looked more relaxed than last night but he also bore signs of grief.

"Yes sir," Jake said. "Do you just need me to account for my whereabouts on Monday?"

"That's the gist of it," Jasper said.

"Here's my cash card and code," Jake said, handing over one of the standardized cash cards and a scrap of paper. "I arrived in Denver about 8 am but Dad wasn't back yet from Plains so I went shopping and watched a movie I wouldn't get the chance to see later. I was at Dad's apartment when he got off shift at six."

"A temporary cash card?" Jake took a look at it. "Why not your regular one?"

"I didn't want to worry about settling up debts before departure," Jake said. "And I can't buy much at this point--just some heavy wool socks for planet side and some light ones for on ship. I'd been warned there's a shortage of good socks on Mars so I bought quite a few. They might be good trade items too," he said with a crooked smile.

"Thinking ahead huh?"

"Got to. It's a long step. Do you know there won't be another ship sent out for ten months?"

"At the next window?" Jasper studied him. "Yeah, I know the schedule."

"That one isn't a passenger ship," Jake said. "If I don't make this one, I'm not going." He looked bleak. "Unless you have a hell of a good reason, you'd better not get me bounced."

"I'm aware how much you want it and how close you are to aging out," Jasper said. "That's why we won't contact the colony authorities or try to put a hold on you without excellent reason. We're doing the same thing with your wife. How close is she to aging out?"

"Sasha is twenty-six. She'll still have a chance but not much of one," Jake said. "Her sponsorship requires her to be on board this ship with her livestock."

"Livestock?" Jasper asked.

"She's in animal husbandry," Jake said. "She's escorting three new strains of rabbits. There's also some pigs but those aren't her responsibility."

"Is she trained in butchering them too?" Jasper asked. "Just curious."

"Of course," Jake said, "but she's never killed larger animals. That's not her field."

"Right," Jasper said. "So where were you at exactly one p.m. Monday?"

Jake hesitated but his hands remained folded on the table. "Either at dinner or watching a movie called First Flight. That one was terrible. They got the details on the reactors wrong."

"I'll remember that," Jasper said.

"My family helped develop the first really commercial reactors. We learned about those over the dinner table," Jake said. "When they get it wrong, we know."

The West-Colman reactor? Jasper put it together and took a deep breath. He'd heard that name in school and even recalled some of the fight to suppress it. The Wests got their money from that? That was very old money and a lot of it. There had been a few improvements on the reactor since but the basic technology was still West-Colman.

"Is Jewel as up on the technology as you are?" Jasper asked.

"The basic stuff, yeah," Jake said. "Her major field is programming. The men in the family all take engineering. It's expected." He said that last with a bit of sarcasm.

"Not what you wanted?"

"It seems every other applicant for Mars is an engineer," Jake said. "I had to get other degrees to get on the colony list."

"How long have you been on it?"

"Two years," Jake said. "I was pre-selected when I was sixteen but only confirmed then. I couldn't get a ship date till I had my sponsorship though."

"And when did that happen?" Jasper prompted.

"Two months ago," Jake replied. "Centrax bought it. We were in talks for a month before that."

"That was cutting it close," Jasper said. He tried to fit that into place with the murder but couldn't. It looked like Jake had nothing to gain either.

"I kept hoping family would come through," Jake said with an edge of bitterness. "But not even Mom and Dad helped. I'm tied down with a bloody contract for three years then I can buy it out for twice as much as they paid for it. It will cost me two million to get free."

"You can do it?" Jasper raised an eyebrow.

Jake met his eyes. "When I turn thirty--not a day before-- I'll be worth sixty million dollars. I have to wait though. Grandpa made sure of that."

Sixty million? That meant every West had to be worth at least that much. Suddenly he understood why Jewel could afford to give more than her salary away. It also made his income look small.

"So what will you do when you get it?" Jasper asked.

"Buy out my contract and look around to see what Mars really needs that no one is offering," Jake said. "I won't be coming back to Earth so what I have will eventually end up on Mars. Maybe we'll be able to get the system ferries going." Jake studied his well-groomed hands before continuing. "And lots of kids. They'll be tied to Mars but the West name will go on. If Jewel and Dad don't have kids, mine will be the only Wests."

"Are you planning on that?" Jasper asked.

Jake shook his head. "No, not really. I want Jewel to get married. She just hasn't liked her choices so far and I don't blame her. That friend of Uncle Mike's is a real stuffed shirt."

Who? Jasper almost asked but was stopped by the reappearance of his partner. Sanders nodded to him then motioned Brody out before taking his place.

"Equipment is on," a voice said in his ear. "He's coming in clear. Sorry, lieutenant, for the delay."

"Almost done," Jasper said for the benefit of the tech as much as Jake's. He'd covered all the essentials. "So who is this friend of your Uncle Mike's who's interested in Jewel?"

Jake hesitated. "I only met him when Grandma took the walk. Jewel called him Drew and she was giving him the cold shoulder then. Uncle Mike," his breath caught on his name, "Uncle Mike thought he was a good choice. He was a teacher, had money, and all that. You'll have to ask her."

"Was he at your grandmother's house a lot?"

"Yes." Jake's reply was short.

"His pulse just jumped," the technician said. "Either he didn't like the man or he didn't like him being there."

"Jewel said she didn't want to marry him," Jake quickly said. "And I didn't like the idea of them pushing it. I had to get married. She doesn't."

"Do you like your wife?" Jasper quickly asked.

"Yes." Jake's answer was firm. "Sasha understands me. We'll do just fine."

"Truth," the technician murmured.

"She's better than I deserve," Jake said. "I wish I could be better."

"Mixed emotions on that one but probably truth."

"We all wish that," Jasper said. "When you think you deserve your wife, you'd better look to what you aren't seeing."

Jake smiled. "Voice of experience huh?"

"That's right." Jasper mentally went down his list and couldn't think of anything else to ask. "I think we're done for now," he said. "We'll verify where you were, of course."

He picked up the cash card and saw it was for five hundred dollars. "Do you have credit still left on this?"

"About thirty dollars," Jake said. "There's not enough to worry about. I already have another one for four hundred. That should get me through till I check into quarantine. Staying with family is cheap."

"We'll get you a voucher for what's left. If it doesn't come through by Tuesday, where do we send it?"

"My attorney," Jake said. "Let me..." Standing up, he pulled out a slim wallet and handed over a business card. "He handles all my financial affairs. He'll probably charge me more than the voucher is worth to process it."

"Probably," Jasper said. He noted the Kucera name and wondered why it sounded familiar.

"On second thought, make the voucher out to Jewel. It's so low I don't want to bother him. Can I do that?" Jake asked.

"It's recorded. No problem."

"He's my own attorney," Jake said. "He'll look after my interests here."

And the family won't be involved, Jasper thought. In spite of the civilized appearance of things, Jake was still at odds with his family. He was leaving though. He had his sponsorship. He had nothing to gain from murder and everything to lose.

Chapter 16 - Analysis

After a brief lunch Jasper assembled his team in a conference room. Detective Brown was still viewing Jewel's interview and would have to go over the others but they were together. He'd even got Officer Brody to sit on this meeting since Jake's interview had mostly not been recorded and he needed a second set of eyes and ears for that one.

"Done," Brody said. "My initial report on the West--Jake West--interview." He looked at Jasper. "I think I got it all. Let me know if I didn't."

"There's always something missed," Jasper said as they touched com units and the file transferred. "I did set my com unit on record at the beginning. Poor substitute but better than nothing." He looked at the technician who had the sense to be nervous.

"I'm sorry, Lieutenant. I thought we were done after the second interview and I got an urgent message I was needed. I went to the lab--only when I got there the gal who I thought messaged me wasn't there and no one knew what it was about."

"Lured away?"

"I'm not sure," the technician said. "When I retrieved the message I found it was from an outside number. I'll see what I can find out."

"It was too convenient you were called away." Jasper scowled and held out a hand for the com unit. He scanned the message and its tag. It came from someone he didn't know. "Who is this Garcia?"

"Juanita?" Their forensic technician perked up.

"It says J. Garcia," Jasper said.

"I thought it was from Juanita," the tech mumbled.

"Juanita is on vacation. She went to Denver a few days ago. I doubt she would have sent a message," Pedro said.

Jasper handed the com unit back, wondering briefly if this Juanita kept men on a line. The tech had certainly jumped at the bait.

"Let's consider Jake first," Jasper said. "Since we don't have his interview all taped, I want to get it out while it's fresh."

"He told me he was in Denver from eight a.m. until six and backed that up with a temporary cash card he was using." He handed the card over to Sanders along with the slip of paper giving his access code. "He did some shopping, had dinner, and went to see that movie First Flight," he added. "Has anyone seen that yet?"

Pedro raised his hand. "Yes sir. Good movie. They killed Tommy Beacon in it."

"Did they have the West-Colman reactors?" Jasper asked.

"Yeah, they went into a spiel on those. I don't think it was right though." Pedro frowned. "They got the dates right but some of the physics were funky."

"Other than that?" Brown asked.

"Other than that, it was a pretty good movie. I doubt many would have caught the bad physics."

"Jake did," Jasper said. "I think we can assume he was there. Do we have a time for him at the movie?"

"One thirty," Sanders said. "He paid for two lunches before that at the Brown Palace."

"Ritzy," Brown said in surprise. "Two? His wife was there?"

"I don't think so," Jasper said. "Someone he neglected to mention." He added it to his notes. "She could have given him an ironclad alibi."

"Or he," Brown added with a smile. "An old friend," she said before anyone could question it. "Some people have them."

"True." Jasper dismissed it. "Let's move on to David West."

"The train station here was cooperative," Sanders said. "They also know him quite well. I have confirmation of his ticket for the morning train and a ticket agent who saw him get on the VIP car. He always gets a stateroom."

"Do we know he stayed on the train?" Brown asked.

"If he didn't, he had no other way to get back to Denver in time for his shift," Sanders said. "He could have gotten off in Cheyenne and taken a later train to Denver since they run hourly but not from here. The next train would have left here before the murder and arrived in Denver after his scheduled shift had started."

"So if he was on shift, he's clear," Brown said.

"He's unlikely. Even if he had a car here, the murder happened after his shift began." Jasper knew he was running out of suspects and didn't like it.

"That leaves the granddaughter," Sanders said. "And Michael West."

"The other victim?" Brown looked interested. "Could it have been murder suicide?"

"According to the doctor's report, he wasn't capable of lifting a hundred pounds and carrying it up that many stairs," Jasper said. "Unless the autopsy showed something different?" He looked at Pedro.

"I saw trauma to his spine," Pedro said. "I can't tell you how much pain he was in but the level of drugs and alcohol in his blood indicated he'd been trying to damp down a lot of pain." He hesitated. "He probably would have taken the walk in time. People aren't willing to live with pain anymore."

"True," Jasper said, hiding his own reaction. Brown shot him a look but said nothing.

"We also have what might be a prior attempt on Michael West," he said. "His field was inspection sensors so he might have gotten too close to a smuggling operation. If that's the case, he was the primary victim and his mother was secondary--not the other way around."

"So it might stop with him?" Brown asked.

"Might," Jasper said. "I'm not counting on it right now. There's also that house. If it goes on the market, the new buyer would have to be considered a suspect." He should have asked Jake about the house--Elinor too. "David West plans to designate a non-profit to receive it but prior to this it was agreed that Jewel would get it as a wedding present. David and Michael had agreed to that. Jewel doesn't know, I think."

"So she could be the next victim or the killer," Brown said and got shocked looks from the others. "Hey, women have killed for less. That house might mean more to her than money or family."

"If that's the case, she won't be selling it," Jasper said. "And she practically has it anyway. She's lived there since she was six and, if her grandmother hadn't died, she'd be there now."

"Money?" Brown asked. "A better bedroom?"

"She could have wanted the master suite," Sanders reluctantly said.

Jasper snorted. "Reaching, people."

"What room does she have?" Brown asked. "There has to be more than three bedrooms."

"The master suite on the top floor was being used by Michael West. His mother was using a bedroom on the first floor. Someone called it the maid's bedroom. Unless there's another bedroom on one of those floors, that leaves Jewel on the second floor somewhere--and she's probably the only one using the second floor."

"Nice," Brown said then added. "Ok, I can't see her killing her grandmother when she already had the run of the house. At least, not for the house."

"She also has an alibi," Jasper said, "Nineteen students and the school's logger. She couldn't have slipped away from her class for any length of time--certainly not long enough to club her grandmother and haul her up the stairs."

"She would have had blood on her too unless she changed," Brown said. "Was any bloody clothing found?"

"I don't think so," Jasper said. Going down his list, he recalled it. "There was an empty pill bottle in Michael's room. What was in that?"

"Narcoset," the technician said. "Filled on the first and already empty."

"Doubling up?"

"Doubling or even tripling," the technician said. "He was in pretty serious pain."

"So could he have suicided?" Brown asked. "Was he that depressed?"

"He didn't act like a suicide," Jasper said. "He had appointments with me, the funeral home, and expected his brother. No farewells either. Jewel said he was upset and went to bed early but that was normal. Has the poison been identified yet?"

"Not yet," Pedro said. "They aren't familiar with the molecular structure. I think they're putting in queries on similar deaths now."

"No time table on when it was put in the bottle?" Jasper asked Sanders.

"The door logger at Gracee Place didn't register any entries in the week prior. Unless Michael or Jewel put it in the bottle, it had been there at least that long."

"So someone guessed he'd move back home eventually and they planted it," Jasper said. "That sounds like a contract hit."

"Really?" Sanders looked surprised. "For him?"

"It fits," Brown agreed. "Amateurs get rushed and sloppy. A lot of professionals set it up and walk away, knowing that their mark will eventually trip the trap. They don't like to be anywhere near when it happens."

"But Elizabeth's murder was sloppy," Jasper said with a sudden flash of insight. "Except for the lack of fingerprints, it smacks of an amateur. He had to kill her twice. Do we have two separate cases here? Two different killers?"

That brought silence as they each thought about it. He let them think. The murder at Lily Street had been anything but clean and professional. It looked more like she was meeting with her killer and he decided to club her from behind. When that didn't kill her, he had to throw her down the stairs. A pro would have succeeded with the club and left. He wouldn't have left dishes or any other sign he'd been there.

Brown then Sanders and the rest slowly came around.

"So we rename the cases 10833A and B?" Brown asked. "So we keep the connection but treat them separately?"

"That sounds good to me," Jasper said. "And we've covered the major suspects who have alibis. Now we have the wives and fiancés--Elinor, Jessica, and Sasha."

"And the unnamed suitor," Officer Brody volunteered. "Just a possibility."

"You're right," Jasper acknowledged. "Maybe he'll fit that last set of fingerprints." He paused. "Elinor was in Plains. The other two apparently weren't. We'll need to confirm exactly where she was from noon to four on Monday. Sanders, have you checked at the senior care facility?"

"In progress."

"Brown, I want to be updated on that other case. Let's see what we can dig out," Jasper said.

"And the other two women?" Sanders asked.

Jasper hesitated. "I think I'd better make a very diplomatic inquiry on Jessica West. See if she'll grant me an interview. The other one.... No, I'd better handle that one too. Let's see if we can get her to cooperate without making it official. That's it for now."

Chapter 17 – Sensor Man

Jasper sighed and sat back in his chair. It was a borrowed chair in a borrowed office in a borrowed precinct. God, he wished he could get this case done. There were too many delays. He was waiting for callbacks from Jessica West, Sasha Kowalski, and Reach Out.

Jewel was in the company of both her uncle and cousin and he figured having the three Wests together was less dangerous than having them apart. Ms. Ramsey was also with them. He should have put tracer tags on them but couldn't do it without their consent since no one had been charged.

His com unit buzzed and he picked it up without thinking. "Lieutenant Stone."

"Jazz?"

Jasper straightened up, surprised. "Milt? What's up?"

"Video please."

He complied, throwing the call onto the vid screen of the office. His publisher looked harried and a bit guilty. "Ok, what's up?"

"We had a leak," Milt said. "I know you intend to go public soon but, well, it might be sooner." Milt Anderson was only a year older than Jasper but had stayed in the music industry after their college days. Jasper had helped him make the leap from agent to publisher years ago in return for guarding his identity.

"It's been a madhouse here," he said. "Reporters have been calling and fans too. They all want to talk to you, of course. I hired some temps who don't know anything to field the calls with Mary supervising. When someone said he was Sensor Man and wanted to talk to me, they gave her the call. She took it and said "Mr. Stone?" and a man replied, "Yeah, that's me." Since he didn't sound like you, she asked for video and he hung up." Milt took a deep breath. "They got your last name. Sorry, Jazz."

Jasper frowned then thought about it. They could use this. It was too damned bad it was this week and not next though. "You aren't going to fire her, are you?"

"Not unless you want," Milt said. "Under the circumstances..."

"No, I don't want." Jasper made a quick decision. "Bring her in to the call." He waited while Milt asked her into her office. Mary was a middle-aged woman who usually wore a professional don't mess-with-me attitude. Now her composure was shattered and she looked on the verge of tears. Of course, she knew how he guarded his privacy.

"Mary, how would you like to go to dinner at the Lantern tonight?" He saw her eyes widen in shock and Milt showed his own amazement. "You and one of your friends? Or--are you married?"

"Twenty years," she managed to gasp. "I'm sorry, Mr. Stone."

"Don't worry about it," he said. "It was bound to get out sometime. The press is nothing if not persistent." A thought struck him. "You did say Mister Stone and not Lieutenant Stone?"

She looked confused.

"I never mentioned your rank in the office," Milt said. "The staff knows you only as Jazz Stone. Most of them aren't even sure my college buddy Jazz is Sensor Man."

"Good." Jasper turned back to Mary. "Ok, Mary, Milt is going to give you three hundred dollars and charge it against my account. I want you and your husband to go to the Lantern tonight. Make sure you're there around eight. Milt, you might have to pull some strings to get them a reservation."

"I'll do it." Milt looked puzzled. "Why?"

"Now, Mary, I want you to talk about it with your husband at the Lantern. Make sure you mention Mr. Stone and Sensor Man several times. Tell him you aren't getting fired but you were afraid it would happen. It won't, by the way. I know Milt trusts you and likes your work and if he weren't married..."

"Cut that out," Milt hastily said. "Now you're just trying to cause trouble."

"Ok. How is Brad, by the way?" He knew Milt had been firmly married to Brad for nearly fifteen years.

"Same as always," Milt said. "He doesn't like the fuss and he said to tell you that you owe him one."

"When it's all out, I'll come visit with a case of premium Aruba," Jasper said.

"Just send the coffee. He'll be happy."

"Ok. Mary, do you understand what I want?" Jasper turned back to the secretary and saw she had recovered her composure.

"Yes sir. Go to the Lantern for dinner tonight with my Jack and tell him I goofed up." She still looked confused but her voice was steadier. "But, Mr. Stone, the Lantern is crawling with reporters at that hour. I know some of them."

"That's right. Right now we have one clever reporter out there who knows that Sensor Man is a Mister Stone. What you're going to do is make sure the whole town knows that much. Try to avoid saying Jazz but if you slip up on that, it's not going to give them much. You know that's not my legal name."

"Yes sir," she answered. "Mr. Stone, I really am sorry I was so.... unprofessional. It won't happen again."

"I know it won't and you saved it for the best time. Just do that little job for me and all is well. Can you get your husband to go to the Lantern on such short notice?"

"Yes." Her voice was so firm that he knew there would be no argument. "We'll be there."

"Good. Milt, get her those reservations and make it four hundred dollars. They might need to grease a palm or two to get a good table."

"Right." Milt looked relieved. "Thanks, Jazz."

He broke the connection and sat back thinking. He'd be lucky to get a week's grace now. Once they found him, he'd have to move too. His name was all over the property records for his house on C Street. There was no time to get it listed for sale but he could start the process of moving.

Deliberately he speed-dialed his daughter's number. As he expected, he got her voice mail. His messages always went to voice mail. He tapped the urgent code so she'd look at it then started speaking. "Mel, this is Dad. It's starting to break. If you need any more of your stuff from the house, you'd better get it in the next couple of days. I don't want reporters getting in your face. Love you, girl."

He really didn't want reporters finding out he had a daughter. Mel had taken her mother's last name so that would help and Carol had done the necessary paperwork to claim Mel exclusively as her child, leaving him free to have another. He wasn't forty yet so there was time.

Well, Mel would probably go to the house while he was working since she'd been avoiding him for over a year. He was sure things would change as she got older and wiser but for now all he could do was let her have her space.

Captain Reynolds. He tapped in his number then cancelled it. No doubt he'd be busy. After some thought, he typed up a status update. On a second page he inserted an urgent flag and typed in a warning that his past was likely to come to light in three or four days. Reynolds knew what that meant. They'd discussed it often. Certain things would have to be set in motion and he wasn't even at his home precinct. Events would have to unfold without him.

His com unit buzzed. Without thinking, he picked it up then wondered briefly who the person was when he threw the call on to the vid screen.

"Lieutenant Stone? This is Sasha Kowalski West. They said you had questions for me."

"Sasha? Yes, that's right. I understand you can't come to Plains?"

"No, my schedule is pretty full. My parents are insistent I have to stay for the party." Her pale blonde hair flashed in the light as she tossed her head. She was nice-looking but her nose was a shade too large and her cheekbones a bit too sharp for beauty.

"I need to know where you were on Sunday, Monday, and Tuesday," Jasper said. "With receipts if you have them."

"That will take me a while," she said. "I'll get it ready. I can tell you I wasn't anywhere near Plains. I've been in the Saint Paul area for over a week. Before that, Jake and I were both in Florida."

"Do you have lots of family in Saint Paul?" Jasper asked.

"More than you can shake a stick at," she said.

Jasper grinned, catching the aggravation in her voice. "So you're going to Mars to get some peace?"

"You got it." She smiled back then sobered. "Seriously, I wish I could be there for Jake. He was pretty torn up about his uncle. Mike was the only one who thought the family should support him in getting to Mars."

"But he didn't give him the money?"

"No." Sasha frowned. "He could have but he wouldn't. His father could have but didn't. They made him get it on his own."

"You got yours on your own?" he asked.

"Yeah but I didn't expect to do anything else," she said. "My family isn't made of money like them. After I got to college I worked for the rest."

"There's a lot to be said for that," Jasper said. "If you'll send your itinerary to this number with your receipts, I should be able to work from that. You said Jake was upset about his uncle?"

"Yes, he was pretty shook."

"What about his grandmother?" Jasper asked.

"He didn't say much about her," Sasha said. "He talked mostly about Mike and he was worried Jewel might be in danger." She hesitated. "He's really worried about Jewel. Is she going to be ok?"

"Right now we're keeping her in protective custody when she's not with her family," Jasper answered. "Until this is solved, we'll try it keep that way."

"Good." She glanced off screen. "I've got to go. You'll have everything by morning."

Morning? It would have to do. "Good enough," Jasper said.

So why was Jake focused so much on Mike's death and so little on his grandmother's? He mulled that over as the call ended. Mike's death had hit Jewel harder too. And David had been more shook by his brother's untimely death. Could they have already braced themselves to lose Elizabeth?

She'd taken the walk. He knew family members got counseling both before and after. He'd been through it. Well, they probably had too. He'd have to ask Jewel.

His com unit beeped again and he saw he'd received an email. It wasn't from Jessica West but her secretary. It contained a list of the star's activities over the previous three days. The attachment no doubt contained receipts, pictures, and blurbs about the actress. He sent the message on to Sanders to decipher. There were other things he needed to get done.

Deciding he could follow up on Reach Out from his home, he headed out.

Chapter 18 - Mel

Jasper ran his hand through his hair as he looked at everything that still had to be packed. His wife's few treasures he'd packed up months ago but there were still a few things he'd left out for Mel and simply because he liked seeing them.

Damn, he still needed to get over to Lily Place and match up that piece of wood. Where had he put it? Checking his pockets, he found the evidence bag and laid it on his dresser. Tomorrow. He'd do it tomorrow.

Digging cases out of the largest storage closet, he started disassembling his equipment. Speakers, modulators, and the keyboards were easy. Stopping to check on his dinner cooking in the kitchen, he flipped the vid screen to a local channel while he tackled the computerized heart of his system and the more delicate sensa equipment.

The door rang briefly and he glanced up just in time to see Mel enter. Surprised, he waited to see if she'd brought one of her friends. She usually did to keep things from getting too ugly but this time she was alone.

Mel looked good, almost like her mother, with her auburn hair caught up in a twisted braid that made her look far too old and professional. It wasn't perfect though. One rogue strand had escaped to curl on her cheek.

"Hi, Dad," she said.

He smiled. "Hello. You got the message?"

"Yeah. I thought I'd come tonight and get it over with."

"Help yourself. I've got baked chicken and noodles parmesan for dinner."

She sniffed and gave him a tremulous smile. "Luxury."

"Yes," he said, "and enough for two--if you want to stay."

"Please," she said then continued in a rush. "I'm sorry, Dad. I've been a jerk."

He waited, restraining the urge to agree with her. When she didn't continue, he cautiously asked "what brought this on?"

"My friends," she said. "They keep playing your music and pointing out how good it is. It is. Even I like that morning one and you know how much I hate sensa."

"The old sensa," he said. "I'm glad you like mine."

"And it's all because of Mother?" she asked. "Really?"

"Really," he said. "If it weren't for your mother, I never would have started up again and I wouldn't have been looking for peace. It's all for her."

The next instant she was in his arms, apologizing in a babble of confusion. He patted her back and let her run out, not surprised to find for the second day in a row he was getting soaked by tears. He blinked back a few of his own, glad to have his daughter home.

"It's okay, Mel, it's okay," he crooned till she was calmer. "Dinner is going to burn if you keep it up."

She pulled away from his shoulder and looked up at him with a teary smile. "Can't have that."

"Not at the price of real parmesan," he said. "Why don't you go check it?"

She obeyed and he sat down next to his system.

"What next?" he wondered. Did this mean Mel would want to live with him? His eyes darkened. No, he couldn't allow that. The next weeks were going to be hectic. He would have to head that off.

"So how's college?" he asked as his daughter busied herself in the kitchen. By the sounds of it, she was setting the table for both of them.

"Pretty good," she said. "I like history."

"I thought you were still in that math and software program," he said.

"Dad, you have to have some history credits to graduate," she said, coming back into the room. "And music. I didn't take music this semester though."

"I'm glad," he responded. "I think you'll enjoy it more if you aren't still reminded of me."

"But I always will be," she said. This time she actually smiled. "Mother too. I won't mess with instruments though. Just vocals."

"Good idea. That won't remind you of me," he said with a laugh.

Her smile widened. They both knew he couldn't sing worth a damn. Mel had inherited her mother's singing voice and didn't croak like him.

"So what's this about reporters?" she asked. "Are they really going to find you?"

He sobered. "Yes. It's almost certain they'll find me in the next week. I don't want them finding you too. They're a nasty breed."

He saw her shudder. "I'll get my things out tonight and tomorrow. How are you going to avoid them?"

"Rent a room somewhere so my name's not on the property lists," he said. "Then put my equipment in storage till I find a new place." He gestured toward the half-packed equipment. "It'll die down in a month or so when I start slapping injunctions on them. I won't be able to work though. The city will either put me on a leave of absence or suggest I leave permanently."

"Oh, no," she said. "You loved police work."

"It's not the end of the world," he said. "Things change. The new career might be challenging for a while."

"For a while," she said. "But... Dad, I don't want to see you all over the news with girls hanging off everywhere. It's not you."

"No, it's not me," Jasper said. "And I plan to be as private as I can. Besides, when I want girls hanging all over me, I can always call you and your friends."

"You!" She glared at him, half laughing. "Darn it, they'd love to. Sensor Man is my dad. They always thought you were rad anyway."

"I thought I was grup?" He raised an eyebrow. "The old generation?"

She shook her head. "Not that grup. Sara wanted a dad like you and Misty thought you were a lot cooler than her dad. Rad."

"And what do you think I am now?" Jasper asked and waited for her judgment.

"Just dad," she finally said. "My own dad. I don't want to trade you off anymore."

"I'm glad to hear it," he said, hiding his disappointment. It was almost as good as being rad, he decided. Hearing the timer chime, he brushed past her to the kitchen.

She was there almost as quick, pulling out a small bottle of wine and splitting it between two glasses. He divided the chicken and noodles into two portions then added a roll to each plate. In moments, they were seated and enjoying the first meal they'd had together in more than a year.

"Heavenly," she said as she savored her first bite. "Real food. No one cooks as well as you do, Dad."

"I learned. Are you going to hold out for a boy who can cook?"

"You bet."

They didn't say much more until the last bite was eaten and the dishes clear. It wasn't a large meal because he hadn't planned on her being here but it was sufficient. The rolls made up for the shortcomings of the portion sizes.

"I bought some fudge bars for dessert," he said and saw her eyes light up. He wished he had bought them for her. "Now what do you like about history?"

"It's the way it's taught," she said as she cleared the table and ran the dishwater. "You know I didn't get much history in high school--and I wasn't interested. Now I'm enjoying it," she said. "We're learning why the Reformation happened and the professor is really good at showing us why Congress had to be decentralized. Did you know corporations were actually running the country by then?"

"Yes, it was bad." Jasper took over washing their few dishes. He had retained that much from the endless hours of history he'd sat through in his own school days. It had taken term limits, a line-item veto, and decentralizing Congress to limit the power of lobbyists and the career politicians. Once that had been done, the actual Reformation had begun. The Constitution still stood intact but the federal government was smaller and more efficient now--and a lot less intrusive. "So who is this great teacher that has you thinking about governments?"

"Professor Nugent," she said.

"Professor Andrew Nugent?" he demanded, remembering the eccentric book collector. "Collects books?"

She giggled. "You heard about that. Oh, he was so mad. He told us in the old days they would have strung up the guy from the nearest tree and he wanted to do it!"

Jasper grinned. "Maybe," he said, "but he wasn't that mad when I met him. He refused to press charges."

"Really?" She cocked her head. "I thought he'd demand a firing squad."

"What's that?" Jasper asked.

"Something with bullets," she said. "Dad, you know that!"

"Yup, I wasn't born yesterday."

She splashed water at him like she did when she was little. He grinned and pulled the plug. "Get the fudge bars, brat."

She did, joining him in the living room where the forgotten vid screen was going through local news.

"In this week's obituaries, we have a mother and son. Elizabeth Sullivan West, age 86, was a founder of Plains and granddaughter of President Gene R. Sullivan. She passed away at her home on Monday and is survived by her son David and two grandchildren, Jewel and Jake. Michael West, her oldest surviving son, passed away at his home on Tuesday. He had no children."

"That's sad. Mother and son one day apart," the commentator said.

"Really sad. The Wests were major contributors to charities in the city and will be missed. Her grandson, Jake West, is a Mars colonist and due to ship out next month. Funeral services will be tomorrow at one pm at the city cathedral. At the request of the West family, attendees are to wear bright colors to celebrate their lives."

"You knew them?" Mel must have seen his expression.

"Yes." He looked at the fudge bar absently then sighed. "I'll tell you about it when it's over."

"Oh," Mel said. She was sharp enough to catch what he hadn't said and smart enough not to ask about his cases. "Odd news is next, I think."

"Yes," he said, "let's see if the book gets mentioned."

Every day the oddest crimes in the city were aired for the public to wonder at. Most of the time they were nothing special but occasionally one really tickled the public's fancy. The department had a special website where people could take a crack at solving--or humorously unsolving--a case. When he was younger and lower in seniority he'd often been assigned to read the stupid suggestions and an occasional intelligent insight into the crimes. He still went there occasionally for a good laugh. Some of the crimes were so stupid there were periodic accusations the police or news service had made them up but they were all real. Most were unsolved and only of note because the person had got away.

"And now for odd crimes," the commentator said. "These are the crimes that leave us wondering why. This week Section Five wins with two of the top three. First off we have a stolen book."

The screen cut to show a display case with the book in it. "This copy of Curious George was stolen from the import store right after the owner received it. The thief was caught and the book returned but we have to wonder why someone would steal it in the first place. Got a reason? Be sure and send a comment to the website."

Mel grinned at him but didn't leave off nibbling at her fudge bar.

The screen changed to an indoor fountain and some ducks swimming there. "Over in Section Eight, the Grand Hotel is searching for two of its prized ducks. The birdbrains were apparently lured away from the fountain and out of camera range on Saturday. There are no clues to the fowl crime but police are not holding out hope for the ducks' survival. If you see the ducks or their feathers, please contact police."

"Someone had roast duck, I bet," her fellow reporter said.

"That's the theory but we want to know what other uses two ducks could be put to. Be creative, folks. The winner will get copies of the hottest new album on the market: Back Again by Sensor Man."

Mel rolled her eyes at him but declined to comment. Her mouth was too busy.

"And what is our winner this week?" the reporter asked.

"The top head scratcher this week is also from Section Five," the commentator said. "Why, oh, why would anyone steal," her voice dropped suggestively, "tablecloths? Yes, you heard me right. Tablecloths! Red tablecloths and from a subby cafeteria no less. These were real cloth and at least five are missing. We have to wonder why."

Jasper snorted. That he'd never heard of. The only reason he could think of is some subbies wanted red clothes. Stupid though. Police would notice if they turned up on any subby's back. He'd hate to be the cop investigating that one.

"Are they going to stop every subby wearing red?" Mel asked. "Oh, I think I want to hand out red scarves...."

"You would." Jasper glared at her. "Don't. They don't need to be hassled like that."

She subsided and he was sure she'd think twice before she did it but her school friends might think it a huge joke on the police.

"You know, a lot of people might have that idea," he said. "I got a better one. I want to see leaf green scarves on subbies. If I count thirty between now and next Wednesday, I'll give you signed copies of Back Again to hand out to your friends."

"You'd do that?" She was stunned. "Dad, you never sign them."

"I'll be public by then," he said. "I told you the press is hot on my trail. Your friends can have the first if they come through."

"Oh, they will!" She looked delighted. "Dated too?"

"Dated too."

"I'll let them know."

His evening was far more pleasant and productive than he thought it would be. After Mel left, he checked his messages and found one from his captain that brought a thoughtful frown to his face. The West Foundation was checking him out? David and Jewel West were from that family? He thought back and realized David had casually mentioned money going back to the Foundation so it must be true but why were the Wests living here instead of at some fancy estate? Why was Jewel teaching school? It wasn't anything new if Elizabeth West had lived here half a century.

He turned it over in his mind and tried to fit that new piece in to the puzzle of his case. Jake West seriously wanted Mars but the Foundation wasn't helping him any more than his family so maybe the link between the West family and the West Foundation wasn't that tight. After all Jewel was teaching school and David had his own job. They had money but probably no control over the Foundation. That was too bad. He liked what he'd heard of the Foundation and their projects. He especially liked their motto of "Building a Better Future Today."

Maybe it had no bearing on the case. Maybe it did. The Foundation had apparently been interested enough to contact his captain about him. He'd keep it in mind.

Chapter 19 – Thursday

Soma Incorporated was just as he remembered it. Jasper studied the wide front entrance and inviting lobby for a long time before he crossed the street and opened the glass door. Instantly the sounds of the Pastoral Symphony and the calming smell of lavender assailed him.

Recoiling, he had a wild thought of retreat. It was too familiar and brought back too many memories. He just didn't want-- Carol? Carol was gone. He forced himself to take a deep breath and step through the door. This was just a business. This had nothing to do with Carol. He forced himself to walk across the lobby to the first free receptionist.

"Good morning, sir. Can I help you?" The receptionist was good, her eyes just widening when he produced his badge.

"I have an appointment with your manager. Jasper Stone." He kept his voice low to avoid disturbing an elderly man a few feet away.

"Yes sir." She beckoned him to follow her, leading him away from the usual reception rooms and down a small hall.

Mercifully, he couldn't hear the music here. Normally he liked Beethoven but not that tune here. He didn't think he'd ever like the smell of lavender again.

The manager's office was more Spartan than any of the other rooms he'd seen. Here there was no fake grass carpet and the walls were a warm tan instead of the blues and greens used to comfort people. A vid screen dominated one wall and photos he assumed were family decorated another.

The middle-aged woman behind the desk looked like she belonged here. Her conservative brown suit was business-like and clearly set her status. Her employees, all of the ones he'd ever seen, wore pseudo-medical garb. A stylish close-fitting cap covered her hair.

"Detective Stone," the receptionist said, getting his rank wrong but his name correct. Jasper didn't bother to correct her.

"Thank you, Maggie. Ask Rachel to join us when she's free," the manager said then smiled mechanically at him. "Ruth Cordova, Manager of Soma 23."

"Lieutenant Jasper Stone." He showed her his badge. "I'm investigating the Elizabeth West murder."

"Murder?" The manager blinked then recovered. "Of course. It couldn't be suicide." That last was a flat statement, not a question.

"You know that?"

"Please have a seat." She motioned him toward a chair. "I'm a psychiatrist, lieutenant. Moreover, I specialize in the psychology of death. Those who come here occasionally suicide before our process is complete but we have never had someone who has chosen life commit suicide at home. They come back here six months to several years later but they don't suicide. There's no need for it once they've been evaluated and approved for euthanasia."

"How did she die?" she abruptly asked. "Was it messy?"

Jasper hesitated, remembering the blood. "Yes."

"Again murder," she said. "Women don't like leaving messes when they go. Men sometimes do but women like to leave a clean house and they usually don't want to mess up their bodies. It's vanity, I know but it's also a very female thing. That's why most female suicides are by use of drugs or, if they want to bleed out, they do it in a bathtub."

That much he knew. He'd never seen a messy female body where it wasn't murder or, in a few rare cases, accidental death. Suicides were always a lot cleaner.

"I regret seeing Elizabeth West go," the manager said. "She was exceptional."

"You knew her?" Jasper asked.

"Not through here," the manager replied. "Socially. We were both patrons of the theater. Since I knew her, I couldn't wait on her. It's not something the company encourages."

"I suppose not." Jasper knew it must be doubly hard to

help a friend or relative to rest. It was bad enough being the friend or relative.

"You remember those you help," the manager said. "We don't want to remember anything more than necessary. It makes the job too hard. As it is, most of our employees leave after four years."

He hadn't realized the career life of people in this industry was so short. It must be far harder than he thought. He imagined having to help someone like Carol and his jaw set. That couldn't have been easy.

"My employees will help as much as possible," the manager said. "But I want you to understand that not remembering is part of the job description. If they've forgotten something, it's not intentional."

"I understand."

"Since Elizabeth chose to leave, it will be different with her, of course. She chose life. The parting was joyful, not sad. Rachel was assigned to her case from the beginning," the manager said. "Until Elizabeth chose life, she was under her care. After that it was Mary who assisted her. She'll be available when Rachel is done."

"Thank you." Jasper rose and turned toward the door when another person entered then his eyes widened in recognition. She went pale at the same time, her eyes shooting from him to the manager and back to him.

"Lieutenant Stone!"

"You know each other?" the manager demanded, surprised.

"I'm sorry, I... Lieutenant Stone's wife was one of my clients a year or so ago. I didn't know."

Rachel wore a pretty blue uniform now but she was the same blonde Jasper remembered. When he dreamed of this place, she'd always been there and he hated her for it. He fought back the memory, trying hard to get his objectivity back. This had nothing to do with Carol.

"This is highly irregular," the manager said with a stern

look at him. "Lieutenant, I think it would be better if you sent another officer to do the interview."

"I don't think so," Jasper managed to say. "I'm the most experienced. Rachel, I know it's unusual but I assure you I'm only interested in what happened with Elizabeth West."

She looked doubtful but turned to her manager. "I can do it," she said. "And it might be good for both of us to have some other memory than what happened."

"True," the manager finally said. "However, you are to keep out of the public places with this. I won't have other clients disturbed. And you'll keep this with you." She handed a call button to her. "If there's a problem, I expect you to call me."

"Yes ma'am." Rachel clipped the button to her belt. "If you'll follow me, lieutenant."

He did, noting she used his rank although she knew his name well enough. Good. That would put a barrier between that time and this. He followed her back to the lobby and across it and through a wooden door.

This office held no desk but a comfortable set of chairs and a couch. Two vid screens were hung on opposite walls and an office chair waited with a discreet keyboard mounted on a swing arm. Both vid screens showed a mountain vista.

"How do you want to do this?" Rachel asked. "Is she really dead? There's some information I can't give you if she's still alive."

"She died on Monday," Jasper said. "We're looking for the reasons someone would want to kill her."

"I don't think I'll be much use but we'll go through it. I find it easier to remember in linear time."

"Then we'll use that," Jasper said. "How long ago did she come in?"

"I first saw her in February, I think," she said. "Let me verify that." She motioned him to a seat and sat down herself in the computing chair. Swinging the keyboard into place, she began typing. The vid screen in back of Jasper changed to her desktop. The other screen remained a mountain scene. He had to crane his neck to see the one behind him.

"No, it was January--the fifteenth."

"And her next visit was?"

"The last day of March," Rachel answered. "It's typically six weeks from first visit to second. They have to get the psych evaluation done before we go any further. I really didn't expect to see Elizabeth back. On her initial visit she was still recovering from a broken hip and was really depressed about not being able to get to her own bedroom. I thought her spirits would lift as she got her mobility back."

"Did anyone come with her?"

"In here? No. She was in a wheelchair the first visit so someone did bring her but I never saw them." She studied him. "Lieutenant, it's really not usual for anyone to come to Soma and be interviewed with a relative watching. We allow it but it sends up a flag. Do they want to go or does the relative want them to go? We're very careful about that."

Jasper nodded. He hadn't come with his wife for her interview either. In fact, he hadn't known she had it. A friend had helped her get here then helped her home again while he'd been at work.

"What did you find out at the first interview?" Jasper asked.

"Not much," she said, "the usual. I explained the procedure and gave her the forms to fill out. She didn't have a regular psychiatrist so I gave her a list of those we recognized. She also paid the retainer as required."

"How much is that?" he asked.

"Five hundred dollars," she said. "It's kept steep enough so only those who are serious will pursue it further. The psychiatrist charges them more, of course, and must see them a minimum of three times over the course of the six weeks."

"And you can trust the psychiatrists to do that?" Jasper asked. He knew that was required by law but that didn't mean it was always followed.

"Those on our list, yes." She looked at her notes again then at him. "She asked for a recommendation and I suggested Doctor Madden. She's in her seventies and understands the aged better than some of the others."

"Was that who evaluated her?"

"No, she went to Dr. Riley," she said. "No reason given. He's good too."

"Did she discuss family at all during the first meeting?" Jasper asked. "Anyone in particular?"

"Oh, she mentioned several of them in passing but her main concern was she was tired, she was in pain, and she couldn't get to her room without help. She didn't want to go on."

"I really didn't think I'd see her again," Rachel said. "Her hip was still healing and she hadn't finished therapy. I figured her attitude would get better when she was mobile again. "

"But she came back."

"Yes," Rachel said. "Still in a wheelchair too. She was very insistent she wanted to go so I scheduled the follow-up appointments. Those happened in early April. You want impressions of all of them?"

"Yes, let's start with Michael West," he said.

"Ok," she said then threw the records up on the second screen. She must have seen him craning to see. "Michael West." She frowned. "He missed his initial appointment and we had to reschedule him for one three weeks later. An accident?"

"Yes, he had an accident," Jasper confirmed.

"He wasn't happy his mother wanted to go," Rachel said, "but he fought it less than the others. I... He asked me what he would need to do it in that interview. That wasn't usual. Sometimes a spouse will ask but I've never had a son ask before. He didn't suggest a double ceremony but he was interested."

"Double ceremony?" Jasper asked.

"Yes, that's where a married couple decides to leave

together," she said. "We actually get that a lot in the elderly group. They just don't want to live without the other. It's allowed under the law."

"There's never been a mother and son arrangement though," she said. "I checked after the interview with Michael West and it just hasn't happened. A few times a child has opted to leave for medical reasons and the mother has followed but I've never even heard of both being in the works at the same time. I don't think a psychiatrist could sign off on something like that."

"So the only unusual thing about Michael West is he inquired on his own behalf? No opposition to his mother going? No pushing her?"

"No, no pushing," she said. "It was her decision and he supported her in that. He didn't actively support it but he didn't oppose it either. He was more interested in what he needed to do. I know he was in a lot of pain too."

"Did he come to subsequent meetings?"

"There was only one after that for him and family. That was the reading of the will. He was there."

"Good." Jasper thought of Jewel but kept to his order. "Now David West."

"The other son? He didn't like it."

"Why?"

"Selfish reasons," she said. "He was going to get married again and wanted her there for that. He was fairly certain his son would go to Mars and he was concerned his mother might make it possible. Michael was injured. Jewel was engaged. Just bad timing."

"Jewel was engaged?" Jasper caught that and sat straight up. Engaged? To who? That stuffed shirt?

Rachel looked at him in surprise.

"What do you know about that?" Jasper asked in a more professional tone. He had no business caring about that but it was damned odd no one but Jake had mentioned him.

"I know she had a boyfriend," Rachel said. "He wasn't

included in the evaluations but he did make it to the will reading. I doubt they're still together though. He was far too old and looked rather reserved. Jewel didn't even mention him in her interview."

He was going to have to find out who this man was. "Do you have a name?"

Rachel checked her files and was busy for several minutes before she gave him an apologetic look. "I don't have a full name. The family called him Drew. Since he wasn't part of the family, there was no need to interview him."

"Not even if he was engaged to the only granddaughter?" Jasper asked.

"Like I said, she didn't even mention him in her interview and I did her before David because she lived here. Michael didn't mention him either. David was the only one who did so I thought maybe it wasn't a formal arrangement. Even at the will reading, he didn't arrive with Jewel. He came with Michael."

"There was no mention of him in the will," she said. "Not one word."

"Can I have a copy of the will?" Jasper asked.

"Of course," she said. "You'll have to sign for it. The will probably hasn't been probated yet so no public release is allowed."

"Got it." Jasper handed her his com unit and pressed his thumb to the signature pad she handed him. For good measure, he wrote in his authorization and the case number. "What was your overall feeling about this family?"

"They were close and they weren't likely to fight over stuff," she said. "I was concerned about that when I checked into Elizabeth West's financial worth but both sons had more money and Jewel wasn't poor by any means. It was only Jake who seemed interested in money. He was still trying to get on the Mars colony list and upset that the will didn't give him the money to do it."

"Was he in favor of Elizabeth taking the walk?"

"He was very in favor of it," she said. "At the will reading, he changed. He told his father that all she had was depression and she shouldn't kill herself over that. He also said she could just put in an elevator if she wanted her room so damned much. The others weren't happy with him but I think it goaded Elizabeth. She told him no one was going to put an elevator in her house as long as she was alive."

Jasper grinned. "Sounds like she found some fire. What a time to do it."

"I know," Rachel said. "I thought she was going to call it quits then but she actually took the walk before she changed her mind."

Jasper kept himself from thinking too hard about that. Not yet. He thought about their conversation and realized he was still missing people. "Did either of the wives come to anything?"

Rachel shook her head. "No, I knew there were two wives but David had filed for divorce and didn't want his wife involved. Jake's wife had only met the family once and wasn't interested. Since she wasn't named in the will, there was no reason to ask for her to come." She thought a moment. "David West mentioned a fiancé but she wasn't available. On the moon?"

"Probably," Jasper said. "She's a lunar mechanic. She's on Earth now and I've met her." He thought. "That leaves Jewel. You said she never mentioned being engaged but this Drew fellow came to the will reading anyway as a friend of Mike's. What was Jewel's attitude toward the whole thing?"

"Her grandmother or her so-called fiancé?" she asked.

"Both." Jasper knew the boyfriend was unlikely to be a lead but it bugged him he still hadn't been positively identified. If they didn't get an ID on him today, he was going to have to come right out and ask Jewel who he was and how serious she was about him.

"About her grandmother, she didn't like it," Rachel said. "She wasn't opposing it because she wanted her to be happy but she clearly didn't like it." She paused and looked at him with a bit of a smile. "Not one word about the fiancé."

"How about at the will reading?"

"She sat with her grandmother on a loveseat and left no room for him. I am fairly sure she didn't want him and was letting him know it."

"Did they leave together?" Jasper asked.

"No. He left right after the walk--alone." She closed her files. "Lieutenant, you've made this part fairly easy on me. Do you want to see the walk?"

"Yes." Jasper braced himself. "I need to know anything I can--and what Elizabeth might have been thinking."

"The only place we can get that is the walk. I'm sorry," Rachel said. "Really I am."

"Let's keep to the business at hand," Jasper said, knowing this was the same walk that Carol had taken.

She led him through a comfortable sitting room adorned with more furniture and he spied what must have been the loveseat Jewel had preferred. His lips twitched. Yeah, he'd experienced that tactic before. Carol had never done it to him but there were a couple of girls in college who had made it clear he wasn't welcome.

Off the sitting room there were two doors. One was clearly labeled "Family" and he knew what lay beyond that door. He'd walked through it before and he'd been alone. Mel hadn't been there. She'd been too angry to come even for her mother's sake.

The other wasn't labeled. It didn't need to be. He followed Rachel through to find what must be a changing room. Right now it was bare and sterile but there were hooks on the walls and other things. He caught sight of a box of adult diapers on a counter and frowned.

"They get prepared here," Rachel said. "There's not much to do. The women like to do their makeup so they look good. Then they put on their nightgowns or pajamas and the rest." She didn't mention the diapers.

Jasper realized he hadn't even thought about what must be under the clothes. "Heart sensors?"

"No," Rachel said. "The bed has those. In the old days the patients had to wear them but we did away with that a long time ago."

"What's next?" Jasper asked, wanting to be out of this room.

"The walk itself," she said. "Let me show you." She opened up one more door to show a long hallway. They walked down it in silence to where it took a corner. At a second corner, there was a small sitting area with one chair, a prayer bench, and two doors. One opened to the left and was labeled "Death." The other opened to the right and simply said "Life."

"What's this?" Jasper asked.

"The final moment of decision," Rachel said. "The moment everyone must look into their own soul and decide which door to open. Once I escort the client here, I have to leave them. I can't stay and comfort them. No one can. They have to be here until the timer runs down."

"What timer?" Jasper looked for it.

"No, they can't watch a clock either," Rachel said. "This is the moment of decision. No plants, no music, no sound, and no company. For ten long minutes, they have to be alone with themselves and make their choice. Sit down and try it," she said. "I'm going to see if Mary is ready." She slipped through the door marked life and disappeared.

Left with no company, Jasper sat down and tried to imagine Carol sitting here all alone with her thoughts and her pain. This was why it had taken so long for her to appear in the last room. He had imagined a long painful walk that carried her from floor to floor in his dreams. Was this any more comforting?

Sitting there, his hands on his thighs, his brown eyes moving from one door to the other, he thought. Carol had chosen death but Elizabeth West had chosen life. Why had an old woman gone so far along the path then turned aside? He knew why Carol hadn't. He remembered the long nights when he had held her, massaged her, and played music for her until she could sleep again. Elizabeth had been old but not in severe pain. Should she have been here in the first place?

His lips twitched ever so slightly. Apparently not. He needed to know more though. Wondering where his guide had gotten to, he started to rise.

"Five minutes," Rachel said as she came back in. "That's about as long as the lifers wait. The others might get up and walk around but they sit back down and wait. The other door will not unlock until they've been here ten minutes."

"You call them lifers?" Jasper asked. "Do you get many?"

"A little less than a third," Rachel said. "Most of them back out before this point and don't make it through the whole process. A few get this far. We've never had one back out on the bed but it's happened before in other cities."

"And how does your company feel about lifers?" Jasper asked and his eyes widened at her smile.

"The company loves them," she said. "More than those we help. I love them too. The ones who choose life give me hope."

"How could your company possibly love them?" Jasper asked, mystified.

"It's easy," she replied. "We get paid no matter their choice. Paid in advance for the private customers and paid by the city for subbies. That takes the legal conflict out of our contracts. We don't get paid if they die. We get paid for offering them the chance to die."

Jasper thought about it. "So it doesn't matter to you one way or another."

"Oh, it matters." She was openly smiling now as she leaned close to his ear. "The dead are never repeat customers."

He stared at her in shock. "Did you just say...?"

She nodded, her face solemn again but her eyes were merry.

He had to force down a laugh. It was so preposterous. Here they were standing before two doors marked life and....

death, talking about business. It got him back to reality. This woman was not the angel of death he saw in his dreams leading Carol away but simply a woman paid to do a job. Carol had chosen death but this woman would have cheered if she had chosen life in the end. She wasn't to blame.

He took a deep breath and felt his tension ease. "Thank you," he said, letting his face relax into a smile. "Let's get on with this."

He turned toward the door marked life.

Chapter 20 - Life

Jasper stepped into a room filled with sunlight and plants and heard the trickle of running water before he saw a fountain against one wall. Stunned, he stopped to take it all in. This was what Elizabeth was greeted with?

This was what was missing from the hall, from the waiting area. There had been no plants at all, no hint of sunshine. It had been dead quiet. To go from the sterile quietness of that to this garden must really feel like being reborn.

He turned to his guide, only then noticing a second woman sitting quietly by the fountain. Unlike the others, she didn't wear the pseudo hospital garb but street clothes. Her hair was uncovered and she looked so normal. "Mary?" He recalled her name with an effort.

"That's right," Rachel said. "Come on." She led him to the fountain.

"How do people in the other room know someone has chosen life?" Jasper asked. "Buzzers?"

"Nothing so startling," Rachel said. "No, the music changes to Handel's Hallelujah Chorus. That's how I knew Elizabeth had changed her mind."

"It did startle them," Rachel said. "I had to explain Elizabeth wasn't going through with it and then there was the reaction: A lot of hugging, some crying, and demands to see her. We couldn't allow that and David was unhappy he couldn't take his mother home."

"What about Jewel and Mike?"

Rachel stopped and thought back. "Jewel was clinging to Mike and crying, I think. He was too busy comforting her to...." she shrugged. "Jake looked both relieved and unhappy but he'd been unhappy most of the day. David was the most vocal about wanting to see her."

"And Elizabeth was here," Jasper turned to Mary. "You

waited for her?"

"There's always someone waiting for the choice," she said. "I'm Mary. I used to do Rachel's job but now I'm an advocate. I help the reborn get to the core of their real problem and help them deal with it."

"And Elizabeth's was?"

"Simply put, it was her bedroom." She smiled at his shock. "Yes, that was the core. She couldn't live like she had. She was frustrated. I let her cry herself out and we talked. I kept her overnight then we went into her house with movers and rearranged things to her satisfaction. Her furniture came downstairs with all her belongings and everything she'd left in place because of her husband went upstairs. She told Michael he could have the master suite and declared the first floor to be her house and she was going to rule it."

"It was entertaining," Mary added. "Once she decided to live, she got her spirit back."

"And the family stayed out of her way?" Jasper asked.

"They were told to get out of the house while the movers were there since it was necessary that Elizabeth be the only voice in where things went. The movers were good. Everything she wanted was put in precisely the same places on the first floor. The only real adjustment was the big dining room table got banished to the third floor and she got a small one that would sit four instead of eight. I helped her pick that out. We also got rid of a couch no one used so she could put her desk in the front room. We bought new curtains too. Except for the lower amount of sunlight, she was happy."

"Sun globes?" Jasper asked.

"Yes, we put some of those in too." Mary nodded. "And I took her to therapy. The therapist said she was uncooperative before and was pleased by the change. She thought she could have her walking with no more than a cane in a couple of months."

"And what did you think?" Jasper asked.

"Since she got up from her wheelchair and walked into

this room unaided, I thought it possible," Mary said. "She wasn't very steady but she did it. I found out she walked around her kitchen without help. The wheelchair was in the way, you see."

"Yes, I can see that," Jasper said. "And Elizabeth West did love cooking."

"She did," Mary said. "I had several follow-up appointments and she was baking by the second one. Both Michael and Jewel seemed relieved by that."

"She also got active again socially, I understand," Mary said. "Our last appointment got cancelled because she had another obligation and it was never rescheduled. I got another client about that time and she was too busy. I had to actually warn her not to overdo and clutter her life with trivial things."

"Is it normal for people to do that?"

"To a degree, yes," Mary answered. "Elizabeth was more extreme. David's fiancé had an accident and came back early from the moon. They set the date for the wedding and Elizabeth insisted on doing some of the planning. She wanted it big and formal but they put their foot down. They were still talking about it the last time I met with her."

"How long ago was that?" Jasper asked. "And was it at her house?" He remembered that last set of fingerprints.

"At her house, yes. It was about two weeks ago. We had tea and some delicious double chocolate brownies." Mary smiled and looked at Rachel. "You remember those? I brought you a couple."

Rachel nodded, a smile on her face. "I'd give anything for that recipe. Lieutenant, they were so wonderful."

Jasper grinned too. "I'll send you the recipe."

They both looked at him.

"She was very generous with her recipes," Jasper said. "And I used to patrol that area. She fed me brownies and handed me a few recipes. That was one of them."

They both looked envious then their faces changed as they realized the bad side of that. He was investigating her death.

"Do your superiors know you knew her?" Mary tentatively asked.

"They know," Jasper said. "They also know I won't let this case go unsolved."

There was no question of that for him. The more he dug, the stronger he felt about the death of Elizabeth West. The few pieces he'd picked up on Michael had gotten him deeply committed to his case too. The shattered, drugged man he'd briefly met was not the true Michael West. No, Michael West was a city engineer trusted with surveillance and inspection systems and a good son and great uncle. Someone had killed him when he was down and he wanted to get that man.

"Someone murdered Elizabeth West and Michael West," he said. "I'll find out why and bring them to justice. That's my job." He took a deep breath and continued. "Thank you, Rachel. Mary too. Going through this has been instructive and good for my soul too. It's brought home to me how much you really care about what you do."

"Thank you," Rachel said and he saw her wipe away a tear. "Mary, his wife took the walk a year or so ago. I.... I'm going to say something now he needs to hear."

Jasper waited. Mary turned away; ready to go but he stopped her. He didn't want to be alone.

"It's not much," Rachel said, "and I never thought I'd see you again but Carol.... She was really concerned you wouldn't go on with your life. She said you were a musician, a brilliant one but you'd set it aside for your career. She didn't want you to do that again. She was also afraid you'd never marry again--and your daughter...."

"Our daughter is talking to me again," Jasper said. "And I kept my promise to Carol to keep on with the music. I had to. It was the best therapy I could get." He thought about telling them who he was but decided against it.

"Two out of three isn't bad," Mary said.

Jasper smiled. "I'll try to make it three one of these days," he said. "When I meet the right woman." Unbidden his thoughts turned to Jewel West. Ridiculous, he knew. The woman could buy and sell him several times over. She was just pretty and he wanted to protect her. That boyfriend of hers had better be good or get out of her life.

"That's all she asked for," Rachel said. "She really wanted you to be happy. She just couldn't be."

"I know. Hades syndrome is murder," Jasper said it and this time he didn't bother to correct himself. It was. It hadn't existed before euthanasia but the nerve killing disease eventually forced every sufferer to this end. He knew that. Carol had lasted longer than most out of sheer determination to see her daughter graduate. Now she was at peace.

"I think I've let her go finally," Jasper said. "Really let her go. Thank you."

Chapter 21 - Funeral

Jasper stopped long enough at his apartment to change. Mindful of the admonition to wear bright colors, he'd chosen the most whimsical tie he owned--a black silk one with splashes of red, yellow, green and blue. The black suit and white shirt he wore as a uniform he changed for an expensive tailor-made dark blue suit which he paired with a light blue cotton shirt. Carol had loved that suit and he knew he looked good in it. He'd had it made for their seventeenth wedding anniversary--the last real celebration they'd had.

The tie was much older. Mel had picked it out for him when she was three. She had given him two more over the years but this one was the one he liked. It was different and something no one really expected him to wear. Well, he was different too. Soon he'd be able to set aside black suits and white shirts and wear what he wanted. There wouldn't be many ties but if he needed one, this one would stay in his closet.

Done adjusting his tie, he studied his reflection. His hair was fine, still neatly trimmed over his ears, the dark brown color showing not a trace of gray. His chin was smooth and slightly rounded on either side of the small cleft. Running his hand over his mustache line, he felt some stubble but not much. He could go a couple more days before using the hair removal crème again. He only needed it there, having had the rest of his beard permanently removed. Beards just didn't suit him and he'd taken the treatment while he was still in college. Since it was irreversible, he'd left his upper lip alone. He could tolerate a mustache and might grow one again someday.

His blue suit was cut to conceal the slight bulge of his trank gun and com unit. Idly, he pulled his snub-nosed trank gun and checked the level of its charge. He knew there were enough darts to take a half dozen people out. They were effective, better than bullets, and could be used on anyone older than four years old. Since it was sometimes necessary to trank innocents to get at fugitives, they were the preferred police weapon. He still had a Henry automatic and wore it when it was needed but he'd never had to fire one except on the practice range.

He was lucky, he knew, to be serving in Plains. In the cities that were still divided between underground and a topside, cops carried their police-issued guns. In Plains, it was rarely necessary--one of the reasons he'd spent his career here. A trank gun was enough. There was a stun grenade too in its own compartment at the bottom of his holster but it didn't need to be checked. Only the charge in the trank gun required monitoring and it was good.

His vid screen showed messages waiting but none were from the moving company he'd called that morning or his daughter. They could be dealt with later. Checking the time, he headed out for the cathedral.

* * *

The six-floor cathedral was the main attraction of Section 2. Located close to the original city center, it was the tallest building in Plains, rising over forty feet above ground to allow natural light to flood through the stained glass windows. Like most major churches, it was non-denominational Christian, although there were scheduled services for other faiths as well.

As he expected, the cathedral was crowded and almost full to capacity on the ground floor. Seeing the Wests were occupied with mourners, he just waited till he caught David's eye then did a quick survey of the cathedral. Nothing unusual.

Showing his badge to an usher, he took the stairs to the upper floor. Halfway up, he saw Sanders was following. Between the two of them, they did a quick walk-through.

"All clear?" Jasper asked as they met back at the stairs.

"All clear," Sanders said as the first strains of the organ

music came to them.

"Join them down below. Brown is on the left side of the aisle toward the door. Try to sit halfway up on the far right."

"Do you expect trouble?" Sanders asked.

"Probably not. Just do it," Jasper said. "I'll take a post up here."

"Yes sir." Sanders left him on the stairs.

Looking around, Jasper decided the choir loft was the most likely hiding place for a villain and took a spot there. It allowed him to see the entire room and hear the important things. At the same time he was invisible and he liked that.

The crowd was what he expected. He recognized some of the worthies of Plains and some he was sure came from elsewhere. The mayor, the city attorney, two of the deputy mayors, and even the director of Soma were here. On the altar table large portraits of Elizabeth and Michael sat beside the empty crematory urns. Later, after the bodies were released, those urns would be full and the family would do whatever they planned in their private memorial.

Listening to the eulogies, he wasn't surprised to learn Elizabeth had taught cooking and was an accomplished equestrian and photographer. Ranch girl, they said, and granddaughter of a U. S. president. Her son's eulogy focused on his philanthropy and service to the city. Reach-Out was mentioned but not the West Foundation.

The slide show wasn't as boring as most. Elizabeth West had been a beautiful woman when she was young and the show included pictures of her as a newlywed and at the groundbreaking of Plains then shots of their house from the outside and inside. Little boys then bigger boys were always somewhere in the pictures. He studied a family shot with more interest, picking out Michael and David with ease and guessing the smaller of the two girls was Jewel. Her husband and other men were in the shot and he knew without asking that this was the last shot they'd taken as a family. One of the two smiling men was Jewel's father and the other was the uncle who died with him at New Wave. Now only David, Jewel and Jake remained.

He'd lost relatives too but he'd never had the closeness of the West family. Josh had been three years younger than him and had died at eighteen. His father had passed away shortly after that. His mother had gone into a mental hospital for a while then moved to Louisville. He occasionally heard from her but hadn't seen her in years. Once she'd remarried, there didn't seem to be a point.

No, there was just him and Mel. He supposed Mel would find a husband in the next few years and then there would just be him. He hoped he'd like the man. He hoped he got grandchildren.

God, funerals made him morose. He was too young to be a grandfather. Giving himself a mental shake, he studied the crowd below. In the family pew there were David, Elinor, Jewel and Jake. No boyfriend. Elinor's great-aunt wasn't even there but she was in senior care and those elders didn't get out much. A lot of times they weren't even told of deaths unless they had to be told. At least, that's what he understood. He hadn't known anyone in senior care and had never had a case there. You had to be more mobile to commit crimes.

Rising to his feet when the others did, he went downstairs. It was only then that he noticed a medium-sized man sitting close to the doors in a nearly empty pew. Jasper didn't have time to catch his picture but there was something about him. More importantly, the man was definitely moved-- enough so that he left before anyone saw it.

In the next minute, Jasper put him in the back of his mind. Lori joined him and gave him a quick hug.

"You look great. Are you okay?" she quietly asked.

"Fine," he said and meant it. Going to Soma had been a trial but it was well worth it. "Let's see your colors," he said, pulling back from her.

She hadn't disappointed. A canary yellow blouse and a skirt of forest green showed off her coffee-colored skin to advantage. A wide flowered sash around her hips concealed her badge, com unit, and trank gun. Definitely not police issue.

"Nice," he said. "Carol would have liked it."

"She would have borrowed it, you mean," Lori said with a quick smile. "I seem to remember that tie. Didn't you wear it to a Christmas party?"

"Yes," Jasper said. "Mel."

"Of course." She looked away as Sanders joined them. He was the only one who looked like he might be a police officer in his white shirt and duty suit. Well, Jasper knew he was green. Hopefully, he'd learn when not to stick out.

"All quiet," Sanders said. "What's next?"

"You can stick around for food or go off duty," Jasper said. "Your choice."

"You're staying?" he asked.

"Yes, for a few discreet questions."

"Then I'll go," he said. "I really wasn't prepared for this."

Jasper thought he meant wardrobe wise but quickly noted his somberness. "Best to go then," he said. "Remember she had a full life."

"Yes sir." Sanders nodded to Brown and left.

"I have to feel for him," Brown said. "First messy murder, I take it?"

"Definitely the most involved one," Jasper said. "Section 3 has no permanent homicide squad. They pull them in when needed so he's normally vice."

With few complicated murders and twenty-three sections in the city, there was no need for a lot of homicide units. The top three homicide detectives in each district were routinely loaned to other sections as needed. For the past four years, he and Lori had been ranked in the top three in their district and both had been loaned out although not together.

"Well, two of the most popular sensa dens are located in Section 3," Brown said. "I checked last night and they started getting busy around ten o'clock. The new blissex is here."

"And today's the fifteenth. Right on schedule," Jasper replied. "Missed again. Now we just have to figure out how."

"Right." She smiled as a group of people passed her and muttered condolences. "Food?"

"There's a reception hall and its open. See whose here." He idly watched as she made her way through the crowd, stopping to talk to a couple of people along the way. Lori was good at her job. When he'd first met her ten years ago, he'd had doubts that a woman so beautiful could make a good cop but she was talented at dressing down and blending in. More than once she'd been borrowed for an undercover operation. He really should introduce her to the Wests but he wasn't too worried about her being spotted as a crasher. No, they'd just assume she was with someone they knew.

Making his way back to the doors, he spent some time thumbing through the guest book. There were over two hundred signatures, many of them with their company names and messages of condolence. He wasn't surprised to find not one but three major caterers had representatives here. By the comments, he gathered Elizabeth had been a valued patron.

There were two Wilson Chemical executives. He noted their names out of habit--Mark Baxter and Rosalyn McCormick. He didn't know either of the names and wondered if they were the two in Reach Out. He'd have to check.

He almost laughed when he saw the remembrance card. On the front were pictures of Elizabeth and Michael and a short poem. The backside though contained two of her most prized recipes. Brilliant. No one would discard these laminated cards. Remembering his promise to those at Soma, he tucked three into his jacket pocket.

"Glad you came," David West said almost in his ear.

Jasper turned, surprised and a little guilty but David must not have seen. He looked tired and very much his fifty some years.

"I would not have missed it," Jasper said. "Your mother

was quite a woman."

"Yes," David absently said, "and she'll be remembered most for her brownies and lemon bars," he gestured toward the stack of remembrance cards, "long after everyone here is gone. Not a bad legacy, I guess."

"Not at all," Jasper said. "Real food and a real pleasure."

"Well, Mike won't be entirely forgot," he said. "I wish he could have been remembered for something else besides being my mother's son. Except for some patents and a lot of giving, he didn't do much."

"He'll be remembered by the people he helped," Jasper said. "I know I remember the people who helped me."

"True," David said. "Well, come join us. We need some color today. Nice suit."

Jasper saw him eyeing his tie. "I have a daughter," he said and saw a quick smile flash across David's face. "She's in college now but..." he tweaked his tie. "It's the most colorful thing I own."

"Mother would have liked it," David said. "Mike would have burned it."

Jasper grinned. "Not a father."

"No. I'm really thankful I have Jake," David said. "He's given me some bad moments but some good ones too. I just wish he would reconsider going to Mars."

"You still don't want him to go?" Jasper asked.

"It doesn't matter if I do or not," David said, raising a hand to pinch the bridge of his nose. "Sorry, the service got to me." He took a deep breath then continued. "Jake's a man and he's made his choice. It's going to be hell having him on Mars and knowing I've got grandkids there but that's life. You can't stop it."

"But you weren't willing to help him?"

"Hell, no. If he wanted it that badly, he needed to do it on his own." David looked around. "We'd better get over to the reception. I came to get these," he said as he gathered up the remembrance cards.

"I'll carry the book," Jasper quickly said and gathered it up along with the pen and a small basket of cards. "Lead on."

"Thanks."

Jasper followed his lead; glad he had something to do in this. Just inside the door of the reception room he spied the yellow shirt of Detective Brown and saw an urgent expression on her face. Before he could figure out why, he heard Jewel's voice above the crowd.

"Let me go."

His head turned that direction just as David quickened his pace. Clutching the book, he followed, getting halfway to Jewel before the man she was pulling away from turned and Jasper came to a dead stop.

Drew! Professor Andrew Nugent. The history professor had let her go but he looked embarrassed by her rejection. Before he could move away, David was there.

"I've told you I'm not interested," Jewel said in a quieter tone. "This doesn't change that. I can survive without you."

"I didn't mean to upset her," Professor Nugent said to David. "She misunderstood."

"I'm family," David quietly said and there was an edge to his voice. "You aren't. Leave it, Drew."

"As you wish." The history professor turned away and found himself face to face with Jasper. "Lieutenant Stone," he said in surprise.

Shifting the book in his arms, Jasper could only nod to him, his face expressionless as he put it all together. He should have known. How many teachers were there with enough money to satisfy the Wests?

"You know each other?" David asked.

"Acquaintances," Jasper said then quickly recovered. "Professor Nugent suggested Reach Out would be interested in hearing about how I was helped off the subby list. It's not set up yet."

"That's right," Professor Nugent quickly said. "The lieutenant is a success story. We'd like to hear about it."

Jewel eyed him, her expression changing from surprise to confusion. "You were a subby?"

David's face had lost its warmth.

"My parents were for two years," Jasper said. "They got off the list as fast as they could. I was in high school at the time and got help with college. I started out in mathematics, moved into music, and finally ended up in law enforcement."

"Quite a combination," David said. "At least you've done well in the last one."

"Yes," Jasper said. "Honest work. There was a time when I thought music wasn't." He wanted to say more but not in front of the professor. What the hell was he doing chasing after Jewel? He had a good twenty years on her.

He must be the friend of Mike's that Jake objected to. He certainly was a stuffed shirt. Even with the admonition to wear bright colors, the professor hadn't unbent. He was still in a tweed suit and the only color visible was wide red stripes in his bow tie.

"Where do you want these?" Jasper asked, lifting the book higher.

"Right," David said, recalled to what they were doing. He led the way to a side table, Jewel tagging along until someone stopped her with a question.

"You said you had investments?" David asked in a quiet tone. "Or was that meant to impress me?"

"I'm with Kleinman & Jones," Jasper said and heard his sharp intake of breath as he named one of the biggest stockbrokers in Chicago. "Jazz Stone, 3738."

"Sorry," David said. "I had my doubts back there."

"You're protecting family," Jasper said. "Go ahead and make inquiries. They'll assure you it's honest money."

"Good." David finished arranging things and stepped back. "I don't want Drew around Jewel. I used to think he was a good choice but now that I know where Jewel stands on it, no."

"I can keep her in protective custody maybe three more

days before we'll need other arrangements," Jasper said. "Maybe move her back to Lily Place and get her a couple of house mates."

"We might have to do that," David said. "God, I hope you can get these murders untangled. Right now I'm even suspecting Drew."

"So am I," Jasper said, his eyes on the history professor. "We had an unidentified set of fingerprints in the house. Can I assume they're his?"

"Probably," David said. "He was a friend of Mike's and knew the entire family. They shouldn't be recent though. Jewel told him off pretty spectacularly a week or so ago. Even Mike told him to stay away till it blew over."

"I'll find out where he was Monday," Jasper said.

"I'd appreciate it." David rubbed his eyes. "But it would really help if you could convince Jewel to come to Denver with me. Right now she's being stubborn and citing damage to the kids and how she needs to work."

"I'll try," Jasper said. "Where's Jake at?"

"Mingling," David dismissed. "He's going to take the late train tonight. There's still friends he wants to see before checking into quarantine."

"And you?"

"I'll take the early train tomorrow," David said. "It looks like I'm needed. Excuse me." He headed off in the direction of Elinor and Jewel.

Before Jasper could move, Brown was there. "Of all the people to run into," she said. "You think he's involved?"

"Maybe. Did we get prints on him over the book case?"

"Yup."

"Run them against the prints at the West house. I want to know if he was there," Jasper said.

She nodded and left.

Jasper looked for Jake but didn't see him. Failing that, he found the professor and attached himself loosely to his group. Waiting until the others had drifted off, he motioned the professor to a quiet corner.

"You are a surprise," the professor said. "I never dreamed you knew the Wests."

"It's official," Jasper said. "Can I ask where you were on Monday before the import store?"

"Teaching class," he said. "Where I am most Mondays. You can verify that with the college but I wish you wouldn't. The scandal..."

"I have other sources," Jasper said. "Was it American History?"

The professor looked at him, his spectacled eyes widening. "No, no, that's on Tuesday and Thursday afternoons. You know someone in my classes?"

"Yes," Jasper said. "But she's in American History. What were you teaching on Monday between one and two?"

The professor looked torn then shook his head. "I wasn't. I have classes in the morning on Monday. In the afternoon, I grade papers and do other things."

"Where at?"

"My home," he said, looking more nervous. "I'm sorry. I guess I don't have any proof. That's what you need, right?"

"Yes." Jasper studied him. He looked uncomfortable as hell but he wasn't making stuff up. That suggested innocence and he hated that. "Look, I'm going to have to ask you back into a chamber. Not tonight though. What's your schedule tomorrow?"

"I'm free tomorrow afternoon between 1 and 5. Where do I go?"

"Precinct in Section 3. They've got jurisdiction," Jasper said then added. "I'm on detached duty."

"Right." The professor stood a little taller. "Thank you for keeping this quiet. It's bad enough about the book. I really don't want to give people anything else to talk about. And now Jewel is..." He nodded toward where she was chatting with well-wishers. "I promised Mike I would look out for her. With him gone, it's essential she have someone she can trust."

"No, it's not. If she doesn't join her uncle in Denver, I'll help them make other arrangements for her safety. She doesn't want you involved."

"No, she doesn't," the professor said, his hand clenching on his glass. "Very well, lieutenant, I will keep my distance."

Jasper watched him leave then casually walked through the crowd. Pausing at the refreshment table, he looked around, hoping to see Jake. Instead Jewel came over to help herself to pate and crackers. A waiter poured her a drink and she tasted it before she spoke.

"Are you scaring Drew off for me?" she asked. "You don't have to but I appreciate it."

Jasper smiled at her. "I'll scare off anyone you don't like," he said. "Got any more disappointed suitors I should know about?"

She blushed, the color creeping up her neck and into her cheeks. "That is an awfully personal question, lieutenant."

The beginnings of a smile tipped the corners of his mouth as he studied her, fascinated by the rise of color. "Not really, Miss Jewel," he said with deliberate politeness. "I'm still working on the murders. Any one of them could be of interest."

The color left her face as quickly as it came. He leaned closer and spoke quietly. "I don't know if any are guilty but I don't want you alone with anyone till this is done--not even your uncle or your cousin."

"They wouldn't," she whispered back.

"They probably wouldn't," he said. "I like your uncle and his alibi is pretty airtight. So is Jake's. But we still have two of your relatives dead and the motive is still unknown. Promise me you'll be careful."

She nodded and he straightened then sipped his own drink.

"Uncle David still wants me to go to Denver," she said in a low voice. "What do you think?"

Jasper debated then spoke his mind. "I'm not comfortable

with it. I'd rather keep you in protective custody a few more days. When does term end?"

"Three more weeks," she said. "I can't miss it."

Jasper nodded. "We'll find a way to make it work."

"Thank you," she said.

"If you see a woman in canary yellow with a green skirt, she's my other partner," Jasper said. "You can trust her."

"No Sanders?" she asked then was hailed by another mourner. She walked away.

Still no Jake. Jasper started to wonder if he'd left already. It was David who joined him, his expression more cheerful.

"I owe you an apology," David said. "I called them and they assured me you are solvent and it is legit. I would like to know how a police detective with a subby background could be worth more than a million dollars though."

"Long story," Jasper said.

David looked ready to wait for it.

Jasper was wondering how much to say when his com unit went off. "Excuse me," he said and checked the unit. "I have to take this. Police business."

He stepped back and thumbed his unit, seeing it was a message from his captain and marked quiet delivery. Obediently, he put the com unit up to his ear and listened.

"Damn it, Stone, I thought you said we'd have three more days." His captain sounded irritated. "We've got reporters all over the place. Don't come back here. You're on detached duty."

Damn. The message ended and he quickly typed in a special code. Half a minute later, he was looking at the street outside his house. He counted six people who had no business there and two--yes, two--he recognized from the network news. Rex Allen was there too. He knew that reporter and had used him as a source.

Typing in another code, he switched to his internal security camera. As he feared, the boxes were still in the living room. The moving company hadn't made it there before the reporters. He couldn't go home and he couldn't get his stuff. Damn.

"Problem?" David asked as he put the com unit away.

"Yeah," Jasper said. "It's nothing to do with the case. My house got infested."

"Better call an exterminator," he suggested. "Unless you prefer a cat?"

Jasper smiled. "I would love to call an exterminator but it might be worse than the infestation." He had never liked reporters getting in his personal life.

He was about ready to make his excuses when he caught sight of Jake headed their way and he didn't look happy. Before he could ask why, the younger West stopped in front of his dad.

"Dad, you were right about Kucera," he said. "I'm going back to Denver and revoke the assignment. Do you mind if I ask your lawyer to represent me?"

"Not at all," David said. "Is he stealing from you?"

"No, not that," Jake replied. "I just can't..." He stopped abruptly and walked away.

"Kucera? Wilson Kucera?" Jasper suddenly placed where he'd heard the name before. He was CEO of Wilson Chems.

"No, his brother," David said. "He's a lawyer but he's in family law, not estate law. He's better known for being a professional lobbyist."

"It's better for him to find out now," Jasper said.

"Yes." David looked concerned. "Now maybe Jake will give me his power of attorney. I've got no objection to him having his money on Mars. He can do a lot of good with it."

"No objection now?" Jasper asked.

"No objection now," David confirmed. "It'll be his money on his thirtieth birthday. He can use it however he wants. He's going anyway. I can't stop him."

This was new, Jasper thought then went over David's previous statements. No, it fit. David didn't approve of his son's decision and had refused to help him get there but with his money he could have kept his son from getting this far. Instead he had stood back and let his son succeed or fail on his own. Now that his son had succeeded, he was accepting the inevitable.

David sipped his drink then looked at him. "How about joining us tonight?"

Jasper opened his mouth to say no but David was quicker.

"Not exactly social. Jewel has this idea I will cart her off to Denver in a sack if she eats with us tonight. I might be able to convince her it's safe if you're there to escort her back to her quarters."

"I could assign an escort," Jasper said.

"No, I want you. You're more dependable and better company than some poor guy in a uniform. Besides, you owe me a story."

Jasper nodded and gave in. "When you're ready."

Chapter 22 – The Grand Hotel

The Grand Hotel--Jasper knew that was the only way to describe it. The duck-filled fountain, the sumptuous lobby and the sheer elegance of the restaurant added to the charm of the best hotel in Plains. Cloth covered tables, the trickle of water from the fountain and ornamental screens, all of them sound deadening, gave a welcome ambiance to the restaurant. Overhead a domed skylight filtered the afternoon sun, softening the light. Jasper had been here before at night and knew that dome had stars embedded in it to give the impression of a night sky rising above the diners. Classical music masked the conversations and the clink of silver ware. Jasper didn't recognize the piece this time but thought it sounded like Chopin. It didn't matter.

Their party was shown to a table set in an alcove with solid walls, not screens, on two sides. A third side was screened but the last side was open to allow a good view of a small empty stage ringed with flowering bushes.

Jasper's hand casually brushed the fine cloth napkin before resting on the equally fine white tablecloth. An arrangement of glow flowers lit up the center of the table. Beautiful, Jasper thought. There were few places in Plains he could appreciate for sheer beauty but the Grand's restaurant was one. The setting was perfect, the food excellent, and he never felt rushed when eating here. Not that he came often. The last time had been with Carol. Since their final parting, he'd not felt like coming here.

A waitress came around in a nice black frock with white apron and handed them real menus. Here there were no vid screens to order from but real people. Few places had such old-fashioned service.

"Have you been here before?" Jewel asked from her place on his right. "They have some incredible dishes."

"I know. Their Baked Alaska is great," he replied.

"Yes, it is. So what are you going to order?" Her eyes didn't leave her own menu.

"Macaroni and Cheese ala Jewel," he said and her startled eyes met his before she gave him a shy smile. "It's even better."

"You wouldn't dare," she said. "You're just kidding."

"I am," he admitted. "It will have to be Beef Wellington. What do you want?"

She didn't answer right away. When she did, it was with an eye on her uncle. "Freefall Salad."

"I knew it," David said as he laid his menu down. "Brat."

She smiled at Jasper. "If the waiter falls…"

"The salad is free," Jasper finished with her, his lips turning up at her embarrassed smile. Why did they always think that was a new joke? "I have a daughter."

"Right," Jewel said, her eyes falling to her menu. "Ok, I'll have the Beef Wellington too. And what would you really like, Uncle?"

Jasper wondered if he should have played along with her joke but it was older than the oldest space station. He'd annoyed his father with it and he was pretty sure his dad had pulled it on his parents. Old.

David eyed her but didn't answer. It was Elinor that spoke up.

"A small steak medium well with a baked potato and green beans," she said. "It'll be heavenly after months without."

"Hardly a challenge, my dear," David said. "The chefs will be insulted."

"Let them be," she said. "That's what I want."

He smiled at her. "Then we'll make it two."

Jewel caught Jasper's gaze and rolled her eyes. On impulse, he caught her hand, leaned forward so the other couple couldn't see their faces and winked. Jewel giggled like a schoolgirl.

"Hey, you two," David suddenly said and Jasper retreated, worried he'd gone too far but David's eyes were on Jewel, not him. "You'll remember the lieutenant's reputation, Jewel. He can't go home with lipstick on him."

Jewel's smile faded but her eyes shifted to Jasper's left hand. He wasn't wearing a ring. After a year of mourning Carol, he'd taken it off and put it away in a keepsake box. Interesting that she looked though.

The waiter came round and took their orders before they spoke again.

"There's been something I've been meaning to ask a cop for years," David said, a frown on his face. "You said you were vice and homicide, right?"

"Yes sir."

"What is going on with blissex?" David asked. "I know it's a serious problem but no one has really made it clear to me why blissex is a problem and bliss is legal. I thought they were the same drug but others have said they're not."

Jasper wondered if he was serious but the two women also looked politely interested. Didn't they know? Well, he couldn't see them as users and David, at least, was too old to have run into blissex in his college years.

"They are the same drug," Jasper explained, "but different doses. The legal form is low dose and safe--just enough to give someone a nice high and relax them. There's no hangover and no worries that they can't operate equipment after a good night's sleep. It's a nice, safe relaxant."

He hesitated. "But Blissex is anywhere from five to seven times stronger. It still wears off in the same time and is undetectable from legal bliss after a good night's sleep but it pushes the mind to an incredible high. Those who use it say it's better than sex."

David looked skeptical. "I thought it inhibited that."

"Oh, it does," Jasper said, "at least in men. All the blood rushes to the brain and the pleasure centers there. With women, it's different." He glanced at Jewel and quickly dropped that part. "Blissex is such a high dose, it's pushing the limits of what the brain can handle. If someone has a weak heart or another health problem, it can kill. It's also addictive. The kids love it and the kids who can afford it come from wealthy families."

"So they put pressure on police to get it stopped?" David asked.

"It needs to be stopped," Jasper said. "But as long as bliss is legal and we can't confiscate it, I'm not sure it can be. Even with changing the color of bliss every six months and the packaging every two months, the counterfeiters manage to keep up with the changes. That's the real reason we can't stop blissex."

"Why don't they use the old system?" Jewel asked. "Legalize--oh, bliss is legal. Never mind."

"Legalization works on the natural drugs," Jasper said with a smile. "Marijuana, cocaine, heroin, and others. Once they were legalized and available in legal doses, they weren't profitable enough. That's why the criminal syndicates fought them being legalized. They knew that would happen. It doesn't work with Bliss because only one company makes it and has the legal license to make it. The counterfeiters got hold of the formula and went into business for themselves."

"So if more companies made it, there would be less of a problem?" Jewel asked.

"No, because the counterfeiters would still be out there," Jasper said. "We think it's from one source. A couple of the chemists who developed the Bliss formula disappeared about the time Blissex was first noticed. That was about twenty-two years ago."

"Interesting," David said. "So we might have to get Bliss outlawed to stop the whole thing?"

"Either that or make it illegal to carry even one bliss tab into a public place," Jasper said. "Like the sensa dens. If the dens themselves could provide legal bliss and keep the blissex tabs out, we might see a difference."

"I can't see that happening," David said. "Too complicated."

"Right," Jasper said. "And they'd probably find a way around it."

"Well, that tells me more than I knew. As you can guess, our family hasn't had much to do with Bliss. I think the wildest thing I've ever done--other than good scotch-is adding marijuana to Mother's brownies."

Jasper nearly choked on his coffee.

David laughed and Jewel struggled to hold back her own. "Ah, c'mon, lieutenant, surely you've heard of that."

Jasper cleared his throat to where he could talk again. "I didn't expect you to do..."

"Neither did Mother but the brownies were especially good that night," David said. "When Dad found out, he just laughed and told me not to do it again. The brownies were good enough without it."

"That wasn't what landed you in the chair?" Jasper asked, remembering David's confession.

"No, that was something truly stupid," David answered, his smile fading. "And not something I talk about."

He looked at Jewel and Jasper got the unspoken warning. There were some things Jewel was not to know--that he understood. He might never know what David did but neither would she.

Jewel looked puzzled and curious so she hadn't missed his oblique warning either. Elinor tried not to look interested.

"So, lieutenant, you promised me a long and interesting story," David quickly said. "About college, I think, and money."

"Yes." Jasper shook out his napkin and thought how to begin. "I told you my parents were on the subby list. I was sixteen then and graduated early with top scores in mathematics then went straight on to college. Once I got there, I started learning about the relationship between math and music. The next thing I knew I was composing little tunes. After that, a few albums." He made light of it. "My junior year I got serious and switched to law enforcement but the albums have continued to make money."

"Over a million dollars' worth?" David asked, one eyebrow rising.

"Yes sir," Jasper answered. "Of course, I learned enough about math and investments to make it grow more--and I've never been given to spending. Subby living taught me the folly of that."

"Carol had her own career," he added. "And she worked for most of her life. It was only when her condition got too painful for her to concentrate that she stayed home. She died about eighteen months ago."

Jewel looked shocked but David just nodded. Of course, he probably checked into him as soon as he had his name.

"What was it?" David asked.

"Hades," he said, "the most virulent form. Carol stayed till our daughter graduated high school but then she took the walk."

"You can't blame her for that," David said. "I knew someone who had Hades. He didn't last a year."

"Carol had it for six years," Jasper said. "It was very hard on her." His eyes darkened and he stared into the glow flowers. "It's not genetic," he finally said. "We did the research and there's never been a repeat case in the same family."

"Thank God for that," David said. "Someday they'll find out why it happens and we'll be rid of the damned disease."

"Yes," Jasper said. He didn't want to talk about it.

"Here's our meal," David said.

Jasper appreciated the timing. Except for a few words of sympathy, the women let the subject drop. The conversation revolved around the food until they were nearly done then Jewel looked at her uncle and laid down her fork. "Uncle, I want to set up scholarships for Uncle Mike and Grandma and I don't want to wait until I'm thirty to do it."

David nodded. "Shouldn't wait," he said when his mouth was free. "How many and what qualifications and how much?"

"I don't know," Jewel said. "I haven't thought that far. No sports though."

"I agree," David said. "There are enough sports scholarships. Academic based?"

Elinor laid down her own fork and dabbed her lips with her napkin. "Can I suggest academic and need? That way you can limit it to children who really need it to finish college."

"There's a problem with that," Jasper said. "Sometimes a middle-class family has other necessary expenses sucking up their income. Even though it looks on paper like they can afford to pay for a child's college, doesn't mean it's so in real life."

"True." David nodded. "Although with our birth rates, it's not likely to be extra children these days."

"No, I was thinking on-going medical costs. Universal health care doesn't cover everything," Jasper said, "and old debts. Those belong to the parents but can keep a child from getting a good education."

"I hadn't thought of that," Elinor said then looked at David. "I think Lieutenant Stone is right. If you use a need criteria, you should set it very high. Keep the children of millionaires out but let practically everyone else in if their academic performance is good enough."

"Jewel, are you okay with that?" David asked. "Oh, and how many--one each or three each?"

"Three please." Jewel looked thoughtful. "I'm not sure if I want them restricted to Plains or not."

"We'll work it out," he said. "Michael was a first-rate engineer and programmer so I want his limited to engineering students. We'll have to get Jake's thoughts on all this but I like the scholarships." He folded his hands in front of him. "Now I need to know if you'll come to Denver with me. Final decision."

Jewel's chin came up and she looked him in the eye. "I have obligations."

"The school might think you being a target is a hazard to

the kids," David said. "You might damage them for life."

"I'm staying," Jewel said. "I can't live cooped up in a tower."

"Elinor?" David turned to his fiancé. "Can you help her cope?"

Slowly she shook her head. "David, I'm used to being cooped up. She's not. Within a week she'd be clawing her way out or killing us. Don't push it."

"Ok, I give," he said. "Lieutenant, can you keep her safe?"

Jasper eyed her, uncertain he could but knowing he would try. "If she uses some common sense, probably," he finally said. "If she doesn't duck out."

Jewel looked surprised he even asked. "I won't. I've got more sense than that."

"Then we'll see how it goes," David said. "I assume she'll have to move out of protective custody soon. Which house would you prefer?"

"Lily," Jewel quickly said.

Jasper frowned. "Gracee Place is more secure."

"But Lily is home," Jewel said, insistent. "I have my own rooms."

"I think Lily would be a better choice," David said. "There's room for her and any security. If the city doesn't see fit to provide them, let me know and I'll get people here. Is Lily Place still considered a crime scene? Can she go back there any time soon?"

"It's still a crime scene. We're still missing the murder weapon so I want to go through the house again before it's released." Jasper frowned. "It's probably not in the house. The lab people are pretty thorough."

"Still that little piece you showed me?" David asked.

"Yes." Jasper nearly cursed, remembering he had left the evidence bag on his dresser. He had to get back into his house.

"Piece?" Jewel asked.

"A bitty piece about so long." Jasper motioned with his fingers. "Pretty black and pointy like a fang."

"A fang?" Jewel looked confused. "Snake fang?"

"I don't know," he said. "It could be a hand too. There's not enough to tell except it was carved and it's wood. I don't have it with me tonight. I'll show it to you tomorrow."

"There are some figurines in the house but no animals or snakes. Mostly they are mythological gods. Grandma liked those," Jewel said. "Especially the Oriental ones."

"Didn't we have one of Daniel in the Lion's Den once?" David asked.

"Busted it," Jewel said. "Anyway, the lion had his mouth shut."

"And what were you doing to bust it?" David asked, his lips twitching.

Jewel glared at him. "Okay, I was little and I wanted the lion and I didn't know it would break. You've heard about it before."

David grinned. "She needs real toys," he said to Jasper. "Otherwise she'll break museum pieces."

"I think I'm ready to leave," Jewel announced.

"Just a minute," David said, his smile disappearing. "Wait here." He rose from his chair and headed toward the bar.

"I take it the lion is a sore point," Jasper said.

"Very sore," Jewel said. "No one told me it was worth a fortune and they've never let me live it down."

"Well, I'd never force a kid to go without a toy zoo," Jasper said. "Or a farm."

She gave him a grateful look.

Jasper met her sapphire blue eyes and thought again how lovely they were. His slender fingers found hers and she didn't draw back.

Elinor coughed.

"Problem?" Jasper asked as he quickly shifted his hand.

Elinor reached for her water glass and took a long drink before responding. "No, I just swallowed wrong. I wonder what's keeping David?"

They waited in awkward silence until David returned

with three little liquor bottles. He set them down in front of Jewel.

"I bought them at the bar. They're still sealed. If you feel a need, use them. I don't want you getting into an old bottle like Mike did." His voice was gruff.

Jewel quickly stuffed them into her handbag.

Jasper's eyes met David's, expecting to see them somber but he looked amused.

"I saw something interesting on the vid in there," David said with a nod toward the bar. "You watch yourself, Lieutenant Stone."

"Damn." Jasper let the word out, knowing exactly what he must have seen.

David's smile broadened. "I thought so. Jewel, keep our lieutenant safe. He's the man of the hour."

"David, what are you talking about?" Elinor demanded.

"I'm Sensor Man," Jasper said in a low voice. "Word just got out it's me and it's going to be a hell of a mess the next few days."

"Sensor Man?" Jewel looked confused.

Elinor's sharp intake of breath told him she knew what he meant.

David chuckled. "Musician indeed. I think he needs the ivory tower more than you do, Jewel. You have a standing invite, lieutenant. Just bring Jewel so you can get in."

"Can we go?" Jewel abruptly asked. "I really want to get home."

"Home where?" Jasper asked.

"I've got to go to Lily Place and get more clothes," she said. "Can we go there first?"

"Infestation," David said, chuckling again. "And exterminators."

Reminded of the reporters, Jasper thought quickly. He couldn't go home. Maybe if he went by Lily Place first then escorted Jewel back to the precinct, those reporters would be bored enough to go home. He just needed in to retrieve the evidence bag and some clothes. After that he could book a room at a modest hotel.

"Lily Place, first," he agreed. "You can help look for the tooth or fang or whatever."

They left David still smiling and Elinor looking distracted. No doubt, she would pump David for all he knew as soon as they were alone.

Chapter 23 - Lily

They caught a tram back to Section 3, Jasper using the short ride to pull up the video of his apartment. Three reporters were still there including Rex. More than half of them were gone.

Jewel studied the little screen then asked, "Are they waiting for you?"

"Yes," Jasper said and turned off the screen. "Bunch of sharks. I've never liked them."

Jewel sat in silence until the other riders got off then she fitted her hand into his and leaned closer. "You can use Lily Place."

Surprised, he looked at her. She was serious. Jasper considered it then shook his head. "I'd have to get authorization. I'm also assigned this case. Too many conflicts."

"But it would solve my problem and yours," Jewel said. "You can even convince Drew there's no need for him to protect me."

But who's going to protect you from me? Jasper nearly groaned. This woman didn't seem to know how damned beautiful she was or how inviting and here she was making it so easy for him. No, he had to keep his distance. When this case was over, he'd be on to a far different one--and caught in the fishbowl of the press. She'd be better off without him.

"Your uncle would have a fit," Jasper said.

"Uncle David likes you," Jewel said. "He doesn't invite just anyone to dinner at the Grand. And he's been after your life history all night. He's probably got hold of your banker too."

"Maybe," Jasper said. He had gotten hold of his stockbroker. Had he played into that? He wanted David to know he wasn't a liar or a social climber because he wanted the man's respect. That left him wondering why that was important to him. David West was still a suspect but he couldn't help liking him. He felt the same way about Jewel.

His instincts told him they were both innocent. He wasn't sure about Elinor yet but she probably couldn't lift a hundred pounds in Earth gravity.

Jake could. He frowned. Jake was the only one who hadn't talked to him a lot. He made a mental note to check over Jake's alibi more carefully.

Jewel pulled away from him, sitting straight in her seat. "Silly idea, I guess," she said. "Our stop is next."

Jasper reached out to touch her hand. She pulled it away. Wondering what he'd done wrong, he let her get off the tram by herself.

"Wait a minute," Jasper said. "I'm fairly sure no one is watching Lily Place but I want you to stick close and if I say run, run. You got that?"

"Which direction?" she asked. "There are no public buildings..."

"To the house. You can key in fast?" he asked. "No, wait. It's got a police seal. Hold on." He called up the information he needed. "Access code is 911834. Can you remember that?"

"911834," she said. "Won't it know I'm not a cop?"

"Not that lock," Jasper said. "It will take that code from anyone. Don't forget it."

"Yes sir." Jewel looked happy.

He was going to have to reset the code before they left. If she thought he'd just given her carte blanche to come home, she'd learn different. It was far too dangerous for her.

The precautions were unnecessary. The few houses on Lily Street were prosperous ones but there was no traffic at this hour and few places anyone could hide. The bushes dotted along the street were kept short and bushy, their grow lights on even at this hour. The overhead lights were on night cycle so they turned on only when they detected movement. They seemed to be alone.

He didn't relax even when the door of Lily Place was closed behind them. First he checked the lock for the last entry then nodded to Jewel. She turned on the master light switch and light flooded down from the chandelier on the top floor.

"Wait here," he whispered then spoke louder. "Brown, check the first floor. I'll take the upstairs. Watch your step."

He headed for the stairs, doing a thorough sweep of the third floor first then a quick check of the second. Nothing looked like it had been disturbed. Rejoining Jewel on the first, he saw she'd already been through those rooms.

"Anything?" she asked, her voice only slightly shaky. "There's a dumbwaiter from the kitchen to the third floor. I've already looked there."

"Good." Jasper refrained from telling her how risky that had been. "Any hidey holes?"

She thought about it. "Not in the walls," she said, "but Grandma kept a flat box up there when it was upstairs." She pointed to a curio cabinet in the parlor. "There's a shelf on top."

Jasper reached up and felt around, bringing down the box she'd mentioned. Jumping up, he eyed the rest of it but the rest was empty. No club.

Jewel took the box and unlatched it, showing him a small selection of rings, one jeweled bracelet, and a couple of flashers. "This one is insurance records," she said and touched the red one. "The other is financial plus some family history."

"And the rings?"

"They all have a bit of family history to them," Jewel said. "Nothing all that valuable. Grandma kept the pricey ones in a bank vault."

"Did you keep any pricey ones here?" Jasper asked.

Jewel shook her head. "I don't wear a lot of rings. I have some pearls and a couple of necklaces I really like. Scarves are more in fashion so I rarely wear even those."

"Any other hidey holes or safes?"

"There's a storage room down here," she said. "And a safe in the master bedroom--a wall safe. It has maybe two thousand dollars in it and a couple of cash cards. Grandma always kept some money on hand and I preferred cash cards."

"I noticed Jake used prepaid cash cards too," Jasper said. "That's a family thing?"

"Yes. Grandpa drummed it into us at an early age not to expose our bank accounts. The only thing I've ever used my debit card for is to buy a cash card out of a machine. I usually buy them at the bank though. It's safer."

"Right," Jasper said. "Well, I'll want to look in the safe. You have the combination?"

"Handprints," she said. "Combinations are amateur."

Jasper resisted the urge to tell her handprints weren't much safer. If someone were really determined, they'd still get in. Depending on the safe model, they also have overrides. "So your family doesn't keep other important papers here that a burglar could use?"

"Not in hidey holes," she said. "Grandma's will, her own copy, is in her desk. Financial stuff is mostly on flashers. Everything legal is at the law firm or the Foundation or our broker's."

"Sensible," he said. "Did Jake or David know about this?" He put the jewelry box back into its hiding place.

"Uncle David might remember it," Jewel said. "Jake never lived here so he probably doesn't know. I grew up here."

"So the only fingerprints likely to be on that are yours, mine, and your grandmother's?" Jasper asked. "How about Mike's?"

"He couldn't raise his arms that high," Jewel said. "If his are on it, they'd be old. The last time I took it down was before Grandma took the walk. Oh, wait, this cabinet was upstairs. The movers brought it down here. They might know."

"Great." Jasper thought about the movers-and Mary. They must know every secret the house had but none had left fingerprints. Well, it was almost two months ago. The house had probably been cleaned thoroughly after they left. "Do you know what moving company it was?"

"No," Jewel said. "Soma hired them. Grandma did have me tip each of them for doing a good job but I don't know...

Oh, it was Crosstown. I remember the coveralls."

"Good company," Jasper said. And they keep good records. He hadn't called them for his move but maybe he should have. They probably wouldn't have delayed coming. With an effort he controlled his irritation. He really couldn't expect a moving company to show up within six hours.

"Ok, let's go check that safe," he said. "Then you're packing."

He followed her up the stairs. The house was quiet--too quiet for his tastes. They hadn't turned on any vid screens yet but there were plenty here. Besides the silent one in the living room, he'd seen a small one in the kitchen and other big ones in every bedroom. The largest was on the third floor in what he'd learned was the solar. It was part dance floor and part family room but its main feature was the windows, the door, and that incredible view of the peak. It must have hurt Elizabeth a lot to lose access to that floor.

Jewel touched a wall plate and discreet floodlights came on around the big room, lighting up the recesses not lit by the central chandelier. Her hand wasn't quite steady when she did the same in the master suite.

It still showed signs of disorder. The covers were in place but wrinkled since Mike hadn't taken the time to make the bed in his packing. A water glass still stood on the nightstand with a little bit of water in the bottom. The pills, he'd forgotten about the pills.

Jewel stared at the bed a long moment, her eyes brimming with tears then she wiped them away. "Uncle Mike was always a bit of a slob," she said. "I...."

"Go sit down a minute," Jasper said. "I'll look around here. When you're ready, you can do the safe."

"Right." Her answer was strangled as she disappeared out the door.

Jasper picked up a discarded pair of pants and checked the pockets before tossing them in a hamper then flicked the covers back and made the bed properly. No pills. He checked the nightstand then the dresser top but there was no sign of valium. Forensics had taken the garbage sack so he couldn't look for discarded wrappers. Mike had said Jessica provided the valium but if she hadn't been here in months, how had she? And how much had she given him? There was no pill bottle and Jasper hadn't seen Mike pocket a blister pack. He was going to have to ask.

Pulling out his com unit, he tapped into the medical database and made a query. No, Michael West hadn't filled a new painkiller prescription. He hadn't resorted to a legal dose of Bliss either. He must have had some valium left but how had he slipped it past him? The only pills he'd seen him pack had been a bottle of low dose aspirin.

Leaving the bedroom, he saw Jewel curled up in a corner of the black leather couch, her face turned away from him. "Jewel," he spoke softly, carefully keeping his distance. "Another question. Did Mike have some valium at Gracee Place?"

She sniffed, not looking at him. "Yes, he took some out of a blister pack and put the pack into the incinerator. Gracee Place has one."

Jasper froze. Of course Gracee Place would have one. It had every gadget. "Did he tell you why he was doing that?"

"No," Jewel said. "I didn't ask. I guessed that was the valium Jessica sent but...." she sniffed again then turned her face toward him. "It wasn't his prescription."

"Ok, another question. If Jessica sent the valium, how did she get it here?" Jasper asked. "And when did he get it?"

Jewel shifted, changing position so she could look at him. "Mailed it?"

"Can't," Jasper stated. "The inspection sensors would have caught it. If it had been brought in through the city, it would also have been noticed. We don't worry about legal prescriptions or single pills but a blister pack with no id would have been confiscated. Procedure."

Her eyes widened.

"That leaves the upper door," Jasper said. "And Mike opened it. He took delivery."

"But he wouldn't," Jewel's voice quavered. "He wouldn't let anyone in."

"Somehow he did," Jasper stated. "And he probably destroyed the blister pack because he thought there might be prints. Jessica's?"

"Oh, no," Jewel said, her face pale. "Not her too."

"Let me check," Jasper said. He turned on his com unit and searched out the file Jessica's secretary had sent to him. Scanning it quickly, he looked at Monday. It noted she was traveling to Las Vegas that day for a meeting. At 12:30, she should have been sitting on a plane. There were frequent flights out of Denver though to LA and she might have left her scheduled flight. No, no time. She was at the meeting that evening. He still needed to know.

"Got your com unit?" he asked Jewel. "Call Jessica. She won't answer mine."

Jewel fumbled in her bag and found the com unit. Dialing it, she handed it to him. As he expected, Jessica West answered promptly.

"Jewel, darling, what is it?" She stopped on seeing him, her voice going icy. "Who are you and what are you doing with this com unit?"

"Lieutenant Jasper Stone," he said. "A couple of quick questions, Mrs. West. Did you send some valium to Michael West? If you did, who carried it?"

"Valium?" Her confusion looked sincere. "No, I didn't send him any. What is this?"

"You're sure?" Jasper said.

"Of course, I'm sure," she said. "It's illegal. If Mike had wanted some, he could have gotten it legally. I don't have a problem getting it."

"That's what I heard," Jasper said. "But Mike said he'd gotten some from you, just not how it was delivered."

"That's ridiculous," she said. "I haven't been near Plains in years--and my secretary sent you my itinerary."

"Yes, ma'am," Jasper said. "I just couldn't ask Mike about it again. Here's Jewel."

Her face changed to an almost maternal look as he handed the com unit to Jewel. The next minute Jewel was telling her about that awful day and what Mike had said. To Jessica's credit, she patiently put up with a long, distressing call. He hadn't thought she would. When Jewel was finally done, she handed the com unit back to him.

"I can see why you thought," Jessica said. "And I'm really sorry about the family. Lieutenant, I did not supply any drugs to anyone. I haven't used valium myself for six years. It nearly destroyed me."

"Thank you."

"I'll verify that with your department," Jessica said. "I just can't come to Plains right now."

"If there's a need, I'll ask," Jasper said. "Will you take my call in the future?"

"Yes," Jessica said, "now that I know who you are."

Damn, had she seen the news too?

"You're protecting Jewel, I gather," she continued. "And she needs that. I'll accept calls from you and no other."

Maybe she hadn't seen the news. He hoped he was being judged for who he was and not whom the press said he was.

"Thank you," he managed to say. "And thank you for your time."

She gave him a gracious nod and disconnected.

So if Jessica West didn't provide the valium, who did? Someone Mike knew and would have opened the door for. That suggested family--or a good friend.

Chapter 24 – Murder Weapon

"So what now?" Jewel said. Her face was tear streaked but she had regained a fragile calm. "I wish Uncle Mike had told me..."

"He could have made this simpler but-- You said he only talked to David and Jake that night?"

"I don't know," she said with a sniff. "I know he talked to them. I don't know if... Excuse me." She abruptly left, ducking into the master suite. When he followed, he realized she'd gone into the bathroom.

He waited for a minute then began another search of the room. It was unlikely he'd find anything now but you never knew. A lot of Mike's things were here, a testament to his long residence but no computer. Of course, he'd taken that with him to Gracee Place. He'd even carried it downstairs for him. He wondered if the lab had confiscated it.

"I'm ready now," Jewel came out of the bathroom, her face freshly washed and composure restored. "The safe?"

"Yes." Jasper had already located it on the wall the closet shared. He'd peered in to see how the back was secured but there was no obvious back. Someone had done a good job and incorporated the safe into an organizer. Unless he missed his guess, the back was behind a tie rack.

Jewel swung a small painting out to expose the blank face of the safe. Placing her right hand in the middle, she let it register her prints then did a quick finger tap in a sequence too rapid for him to follow. The safe screen went green and she opened it.

Impressive, he decided. He couldn't even be sure of the safe model and he hadn't seen one that used both fingerprints and a sequential combination. And they just kept money in it? He flipped through the bills, eyed the cash cards, and checked for anything else. Nothing.

"Can I take one of those?" Jewel asked. "Mine is getting

low. I could buy a new one but I'd rather use these up."

"Not a problem," Jasper said and handed her one. They were standard issue and each had a value of five hundred dollars. "I'm putting the rest back. Please close the safe."

"Yes sir." She managed a smile.

"Let me note it's been opened and checked," Jasper said.

He recorded a note on his com unit then hesitated. "I think we're done up here. Let's go down to your room. I can record my notes while you're packing."

"Rooms," Jewel absently said then explained when he looked at her. "The second floor has four bedrooms, a playroom, and a sitting area. Oh, and one huge bathroom my father and his brothers all shared. I've had a bedroom and the playroom for my own since I was six and I sort of took over the sitting area. Before Uncle Mike moved up here, another bedroom was his when he stayed over. Uncle David had permanent dibs on another one."

"But he didn't stay here?"

"Not since he and Elinor got engaged," she said. "Jake occasionally used it but he was rarely in Plains. Anyway, I have two rooms, the playroom, and the sitting area."

"Nice. It must have been hard sharing the bathroom with your uncle though."

That got him a quick smile. "The best thing about him moving upstairs."

They were on the second floor now and she let him peek into her tidy room then showed him to the sitting area. He tactfully didn't mention he'd seen all the rooms on his walk-through. He knew the other room she claimed made the mess her Uncle Mike left look immaculate. It still wasn't too bad, just windblown. His daughter's had been on the tornado scale.

He busied himself recording notes until she came out with a small suitcase. Sending off his notes to Brown, Sanders, and Kruger, he turned back to her. "And you have?"

"Clothes, my toothbrush since I forgot it before, makeup and the usual things men don't want to know about. No valium and no murder weapons."

"I'll take your word for it," Jasper said and picked the suitcase up for the trip downstairs. "Kind of light. Don't you want more?"

"No, I plan to be back here as soon as possible," she said. "Then I'll sleep in my own bed and stretch out in my own tub." She stopped, a flush creeping up her neck for the third time that night.

Jasper laughed. "Hey, I like my own place too. I'll do what I can to get you back here soon."

He led the way downstairs and sat the suitcase down near the door. "Look around and tell me if you see anything missing, I'll be right back." He headed back up the stairs.

"What are you doing?" she asked.

"Checking something. I'm going to stand over by the outer door and talk," he called down. "I want you to listen really hard and tell me what I say."

He stood over by the outer door and, not sure if she could actually hear, decided to recite a harmless nursery rhyme. Going back to the staircase, he peered over. "Hear anything?"

"Not a word," Jewel said. "But I could have told you that. The house doesn't echo."

"Really?" Jasper clapped his hands sharply.

"Ok, it does on the stairs," Jewel amended. "If you step back about four feet, it doesn't."

Jasper put it to the test, walking around the third floor clapping his hands then giving a high-pitched whistle. The acoustics were impressive. There were some pretty good speakers built into the walls too. He just hadn't spotted the sound system. There was no time now. Regretfully, he headed down the stairs.

"Did you hear any of that?" Jasper asked as he got down to the first floor.

"I think I heard a whistle but it was pretty faint," Jewel said. "What were you doing?"

"Testing. I wondered if your grandmother would have

heard someone come in or any conversation Mike had up there. Apparently not."

"No, she wouldn't. One of the reasons we have intercoms to each floor," Jewel said. "Saves hollering and climbing steps. It's on the kitchen wall."

"Yes, I saw that," Jasper said. "Well, did you notice anything missing?"

"An end table, an area rug, one chair, and some pretty large sections of carpet." She motioned toward what was left of the living room. "I'm going to have to get new carpet." She shuddered. "And I'm going to get rid of that furniture. I can't stand looking at it now."

"Take a deep breath," Jasper advised. "Sit down and close your eyes for a minute and try to see the room as it was."

She obeyed.

He waited till she was calm then spoke again. "Can you see the room as it was?"

"Yes."

"Then I want you to look at it again now. Compare the two rooms. Look for something missing that shouldn't be-- besides the carpet and stuff."

Jewel opened her eyes and looked around, a tiny frown appearing between her eyes. She finally sighed and threw her hands up. "I can't see anything. What do you want me to see?"

"That I can't tell you." Jasper gave up. "Look, I'm going to reset the lock with a new code. We'll be ready to go after that."

She stayed in the chair, closing her eyes and opening them again, while he reprogrammed the lock. She didn't seem to be getting any results though. He frowned, seeing the figurines on the mantle again. They were dark, almost black.

"Can I get some food?" she asked. "There's plenty here." Before he could answer, she was out of her chair and headed to the kitchen.

He followed her. "Nothing that's been opened," he said, "and no bags or boxes. Or produce," he added.

She glared at him. "That doesn't leave a lot."

"Better safe," he said and moved a fruit bowl out of her reach. "It would be better to throw all this stuff away."

"Scandalous!" She grinned at his reaction. "Sorry, I couldn't help it."

"I don't like it either but I won't have others getting poisoned. Here, you can take this." He handed her a can of beets and another of corned beef hash.

She made a face at him. "Terrible combination," she said but took them anyway. "There's a can of pork and beans. I'll take that."

"You have the oddest tastes," he remarked and grinned when she stuck her tongue out. "Going to have it with scotch?"

"Men." She glared at him, unexpectedly playful. "You always have beer with pork and beans. I thought every macho man knew that."

"Interesting diet that. Do you have enough for tonight?"

"Yes. I just need a sack." She opened the pantry door and grabbed an empty cloth sack. "That should do it." She started putting her booty in the sack, her face turned toward the living room. When she paused, he followed her gaze.

"What is it?"

"Something odd," she said. Closing her eyes, she took a deep breath then opened them again. Giving a little cry, she abandoned her booty and went straight to the mantle. "There's one missing. It's Fukurokuju. He's gone."

"Pardon?"

She gestured at the wood figures. "There are seven in this set. It's the Seven Lucky Gods from Japan. Here's Hotei, Jurojin, Bishamantu, Benzaiten, Daikokuten, and Ebisu." She touched each as she named them, picking up one and moving it to the end of the line. That left a vacant space. "Fukurokuju went here. He was the god of happiness, wealth, and longevity. Did someone take him?"

Jasper looked blank. "Describe him."

"Well, he was ebony like the others but it was mostly head. He was supposed to be very wise. Stood about so tall."

She measured him off with her hands. "Why would anyone take him?"

"The murder weapon," Jasper said and saw her go pale. "Is there a picture of him in those insurance photos?"

She nodded and he went to retrieve the box.

She followed him, sitting down at her grandmother's computer. Within moments he was looking at the complete set of figures. There was the club.

Pointing to the tall-headed god, he said, "I need a copy of this. Transfer it to my com unit?"

While she was doing that, he studied the picture a bit longer. Could there have been a more perfect club? The head was about eight inches long and the body another eight. The hands were folded inside the Japanese robes but he could see where the piece must have come from. The shoes were long and pointy.

Ebony, she said. That's why the lab hadn't been able to identify it. Ebony was exceptionally rare, yet here was an entire set of figures carved out of it.

"How much is that set worth?" he finally asked.

"Intact, about twenty-five thousand dollars," Jewel said. "More museum pieces. They're over three hundred years old."

"So you never played with them?" Jasper asked, remembering the lion.

"I didn't break them," she said with a trace of a smile, which quickly faded. "Here you go," she said, handing his com unit back. "I'll be a minute."

She disappeared into her grandmother's room, shutting the door a little too hard.

Jasper knew without asking it would be more than a minute. He found a plastic bag and went back to the mantle to eye each figure carefully. There was no dust, nothing to betray that the set wasn't complete. Carefully, he lifted the last figure, the one she'd moved into the bag, and put it back on the mantle. It would have to be checked for prints. The murderer had moved it too.

Chapter 25 - Friday

Jasper rubbed his eyes and waited patiently as a string of freight cars went by. He'd taken too long to get Jewel back to the precinct and settled. Now it was after midnight and the freights were out and would be till around five in the morning. More delays and he was so tired.

Dr. Em had answered his call and returned to the police apartment, ready to take over with Jewel but the girl had been reluctant to let him leave. Em had finally given her a little sedation to calm her down.

Then he'd had to brief Em as much as he could as to what set her off. That had taken almost an hour. The only good thing about the delay was he knew most of the reporters had gone home. Unless one returned, he'd only have to deal with Rex.

He tucked his squad car in behind a string of freights and followed. He'd better not use autopilot with freights ahead since they were notorious for peeling off down sub routes without warning. They could maneuver through any city highway or maintenance level but weren't allowed on the pedestrian levels. Their jointed bodies were simply too hard to stop in an emergency.

He could get within a block of his apartment using the squad car but then he'd have to walk upstairs or go an extra block to find an elevator. He'd take the stairs this time. How the hell was he going to get the rest of his stuff out? Had Mel gotten hers? He had no idea.

Everything would have to go to storage or the reporters would find him. The movers should be willing to run the gauntlet but he wasn't sure how confidential the moving company might be. It didn't matter right now because he had no place to move to. When he pulled the stuff out of storage, it would matter.

Leaving his squad car in a parking spot, he checked his

com unit again. Still only Rex and he looked sound asleep. Well, he owed him for some of the leads Rex had given him over the years. If he could just convince him to keep quiet tonight, he'd make it worth his while.

Alarm clock. He'd need that after tonight. And that evidence bag. Scrubbing his face, he tried to get his edge back. Damn, he'd have to return the squad car to Section 3. It would be missed in the morning.

Slowly he walked down his own block, wondering if Rex would wake. The reporter didn't look comfortable in the portable chair he'd brought but that didn't concern him. What did was what was on his apartment door.

He studied the device, seeing it was a two-in-one police bar designed to give off an audible alarm loud enough to annoy the neighbors and send a signal back to its owner. It was also illegal. He took a picture of it for future use, identified the model number, and called up the police override codes the manufacturer had built in. He doubted Rex had set it so he fully intended to find out who did and they would be the first to get an injunction. Magnetically attached to the door and door jam, the bar came loose when he used the override and fell with a clatter.

Rex woke up with a startled jump then sagged back into the chair. "Did you have to?" He eyed Jasper through bleary eyes. "Jasper," he identified him with some difficulty, "leading us a chase."

"Get up and I'll make you some coffee," Jasper said.

"Would rather be in bed," Rex replied.

"Me too," Jasper said. "Don't hang around out here."

"Ok." The sleepy reporter was still only half awake. "You got the bar off? I knew you would. Worthless things."

"Yup," Jasper said as he started the coffee. He needed it bad. How long had it been since that dinner? The aroma of the prime Aruba did them both good as it filled the kitchen. Not waiting for it to get done, Jasper went into his bedroom and started packing. The evidence bag went into his jacket pocket.

His hand encountered the remembrance cards and he grimaced then tossed them into his suitcase. He'd worry about those later.

He could hear Rex in the other room messing around with dishes. A minute later he joined him in the bedroom and pressed a cup of fresh brew in his hand. Neither one spoke till the cups were drained.

"You're in a mess," Rex finally said. "How are you going to stay on the force, Sensor Man?"

"I'm not," Jasper said. "You're the first to know outside of the force. Papers will probably be through next week."

"Involuntary?" Rex asked, his eyes sharper. "Jasper, you were a hell of a cop--one of the few I respected."

"And you are one of the few reporters I'll talk to," Jasper said as he added more to his bag. "You didn't send out an alert, did you?"

"Hell, no. Those network vultures went to bed."

"Who owned the bar?" Jasper asked.

"Alyssa Sanders, Entertainment TV3."

"That figures. She's not getting it back." Jasper tucked some socks in and grabbed more clothes. "Ok, I expect to be free by next Friday," Jasper said. "You get first interview. Give me your number and I'll contact you as to when and where."

"Straight up?" Rex sat upright. "Jasper, I didn't expect..." He stopped. "What do I give you?"

"Tell them I'm staying with friends in Denver."

"That won't work," Rex said. "First time you're spotted in the city, I'll be toast."

Jasper thought about it and knew he was right. "Ok, I have to stay." He dug around in his closet and came out with a kit he hadn't used since his college days. He hoped the makeup hadn't dried up. If it had, he'd have to get more.

"So where are you going to go?" Rex asked.

"Staying with friends inside the city," Jasper said. "I'm wrapping up a case. I'd appreciate it if you could get them to cut me some slack."

"Give it in writing that I have first interview," he said. "I'll wave that in their faces and they'll back off. They won't like it or me but if they want to use it in the rebroadcast, they'll have to."

"Done."

Jasper hesitated as he wrote the note. "One more thing. I have a daughter. She's off limits. Anyone bothers her and Plains will lose their newest celebrity. Let them know that."

"If anyone uncovers that, I'll tell them," Rex said. "It might not stop the national guys but Article 8 will."

"That's only good after the fact," Jasper said. "Protection of minors."

"Yeah but the big networks fire people for violating it. She is still a minor?"

"She's seventeen."

"Not a problem," Rex said. "This might blow over before she's legal."

"I'm hoping," Jasper said. "I will be visible this time and you'll get your interview."

"Thanks," Rex said. "I know how it got out. Do you need details?"

"Yeah, I'd like to hear."

"Some secretary talked about it at the Lantern in Chicago. Thought she was going to get fired for letting it leak."

Jasper stopped, remembering. "Ok, that one I know about. I knew it would work."

"You planned it?" Rex looked surprised. "You wanted this to happen?"

"I didn't expect it this soon but I knew it would happen. The secretary let it slip to one reporter and I told her to really let it slip and give you a level playing field."

"Son of a bitch."

"I'm not." Jasper grinned. "Hey, we wouldn't be having this conversation otherwise. Be glad I controlled it."

"Right," Rex said. "Ok, I'll quit feeling guilty for being in this."

"No need to. I appreciate being able to get clean clothes tonight." Jasper zipped up his suitcase and set the makeup case with it. "Your number?"

"Right," Rex said and fumbled for his card. "Can I get one for you?"

"Bad idea," Jasper said. "They'll weasel it out of you. I'm sure they've got this home number already. If you send a message marked archive, I'll read it. No urgent flags."

"Got it." Rex checked his watch. "It's nearly two. You'd better get before those turkeys show up."

"You'd better take your post outside," Jasper said. "Grab another cup of coffee to keep you company. When the movers come, give them the cup."

"Deal."

Jasper watched him leave then checked his lights and the coffee pot. Grabbing the last of his Aruba, he stuck the package in his suitcase. He wouldn't have to do without. Finally he added the police bar to his stack.

Setting a silent alarm that would just alert him if someone entered, he left.

Now he'd have to find a hotel for the rest of the night over in Section 3.

Chapter 26 – Murder Scene

Jasper sat quietly, his eyes narrowed as he tried to imagine the murder scene that had played out here in Lily Place. It was quiet on this first floor and he had no problem ignoring Brown and two other technicians searching the upstairs for the murder weapon.

Clearing his mind of other distractions, he tried to piece together exactly what had happened here. Elizabeth knew her killer. That much was clear since she had made tea for him and turned her back on him. He'd also left at 2:15 pm through the upper door--or did he? It was true that the upper door was jammed between 1:03 and 2:15 but the downstairs door had been left open too. He could have left that way.

No, that didn't work. Michael had opened the upper door then it had been jammed. That couldn't have been accidental and whoever did it had planned on leaving that way and didn't have the necessary code to open the door--or didn't want to use it. He wondered if the professor had a code for the door.

The lower door was a standard coded entry but not a coded exit. The upper door, for security reasons, required codes for both.

Michael had known or expected the person he'd let in. He'd been confident enough of him that he hadn't checked the door but had gone ahead and taken some valium and gone to bed. Did he think the person had left? Or did he know the person would leave later after visiting with his mother?

No, he couldn't have left the person in the house, Jasper decided. No matter how much pain he was in, he couldn't imagine Michael West abandoning a guest to go nap. The person must have jammed the door and left then returned a bit later.

The acoustics in the house were too good. Elizabeth wouldn't have been able to hear an upstairs conversation and once the intruder was on the first floor, Michael couldn't have heard his mother. He might have heard the man come back in but maybe not. The master suite was twenty feet away from the entry door. If he had the bedroom door closed, he might not have heard him even if he was still awake.

So the person had probably walked downstairs, surprised Elizabeth and been invited to tea. Could it have been Drew? Unlikely. He was Michael's friend. If he had come down the stairs without Michael, Elizabeth would have been suspicious.

He couldn't trust the lack of fingerprints though. Remembering the cotton gloves Drew had provided for their examination of the book, he was sure the man had a good supply of them. Gloves were normally quite rare in the city but now he had two suspects with a supply. He couldn't afford to forget Elinor either.

Could Elinor have come through the upper door? Her alibi was nearly nonexistent for the time in question. She'd been visiting her aunt but her aunt had gone down for a nap shortly before one. She'd stayed at the senior care center reading a book.

Well, Elizabeth would have welcomed her and Michael wouldn't have been expected to be with her. Her presence was more likely that way. He still had doubts about her physical ability to lift Elizabeth West. There was also the issue of blood.

Hell, he could rule her out anyway. Traffic to the outside was monitored. If Elinor Ramsey hadn't gone outside, she couldn't have come in here. He tapped in a query for information on exits under the name of Elinor Ramsey.

Thinking about it, he also typed in queries on Jake, Jewel, and Michael West. He was fairly certain Michael would not be found but he was curious on the other two. As an afterthought, he added Professor Andrew Nugent.

"Lieutenant, we found something," Kruger came down the stairs, an evidence bag in hand. "A maintenance coverall with blood on it."

Jasper rose to his feet. "You're kidding."

"Nope. It was tucked into a music cabinet. Sloppy work missing that." He looked disgusted.

"Murder weapon?" Jasper asked.

"No, just this and a towel we found with it," Pedro said, turning the bag so he could see the towel too. It was soft tan and Jasper recognized it as belonging to the house.

"One of their towels. The coverall is more interesting. What's the size?"

"Medium."

"Hmmm." He thought about it. A medium wouldn't fit Drew Nugent or Jake but it would fit the women if they rolled up the legs and arms. "I might need a clean one same size. Get that blood matched?"

"Yes sir."

Jasper sat down again, pondering this new piece. A maintenance coverall? Could the killer have brought one with him? Just when he thought it had to be one of the men, something like this turned up. He didn't want to suspect Elinor and he was fairly certain Jewel didn't do it. It would be easy to suspect Drew Nugent--he didn't like him--but his instincts kept leading him back to Jake.

He rubbed his eyes. Why the hell would Jake do it? He was going to Mars. His family money was secure and could not be circumvented. He had nothing to gain from killing his grandmother or his uncle and far too much to lose. What he had worked for his entire life would be gone. Even if he were accused then cleared, he'd never get to Mars.

His wife? Maybe another colonist was an alternate if he couldn't go? He would have to check. If this were a frame-up though, it was too good. Nothing pointed directly at Jake--and it still had to be someone Elizabeth knew.

He opened his eyes, trying to see the sequence of events. After the killer had come downstairs, she'd made him tea. He had walked around her to pick up the club from the mantle then hit her with it. He'd even moved the pieces just enough to cover up he'd taken one.

Not right, Jasper thought but had trouble picking up on his thought. He walked over to where the chair had been, envisioning Elizabeth West sitting there and her killer grabbing the piece and hitting her with it. He'd done it with force, enough to embed the wood into her skull and break the figure. Why did it feel wrong?

"Brown, I need you," Jasper said into his com unit. She was upstairs with the others.

She came down the steps with a quick, bouncy gait. "What is it?"

Jasper explained what he thought had happened. "There's something wrong with it," he said. "I can't get it."

Brown stared thoughtfully at the scene then pulled the remaining wing chair into position by the fireplace mantle. "Act it?"

"Tried that," Jasper said. "Still not clear."

"We're missing pieces," Brown said with a nod to the mantle. "Let me find subbies." She disappeared into the dining room and came back with two other Oriental figures, these carved in ivory. "Stand-ins. This can be the one with the big head." She arranged them on the mantle.

Jasper pantomimed getting up, walking around the armchair and grabbing the piece off the mantle. Mindful of the value, he stopped short of hitting the chair. He stood there for a minute then tried to rearrange the figures on the mantle as Jewel had shown him.

"Cold," Brown said. "Damned cold. Are we sure this wasn't premeditated?"

"You're right. Rearranging the figures doesn't fit with the rest of the crime." Jasper folded his arms and stared at the figures. "And we have that coverall," he said. "Clubbing Elizabeth looks almost like an act of desperation but the rest looks premeditated. Rearranging the figures, putting the teacup in the sink, bringing a coverall...." he ticked them off on his fingers. "And leaving the door open."

"Why leaving the door open?" Brown asked. "A pro

wouldn't do that."

"I don't think an amateur would either," Jasper said. "He had his escape planned upstairs. Why would he leave a door open? Who would need it?"

"A second man," they said almost in unison.

"It fits." Jasper gave her a grim smile as the pieces fell together. "Michael was killed by a pro. This job is half amateur and half pro. The clubbing was spur of the moment but Elizabeth's death was planned." He stopped and yelled up the stairs "Kruger" before remembering to use his com.

"What?" Kruger came barreling down the stairs.

"The tea cups," Jasper said. "Did anyone do a toxicology on them?" At the man's mystified look, he changed tactics. "Did you check Elizabeth West for drugs?"

"No, I didn't do the autopsy..." Kruger stopped, a look of horror on his face. "Poison too?"

"Possibly," Jasper said. "But I bet she didn't get much. That's why she was clubbed. Go check it out. Now."

"Yes sir." He bolted out the door.

"Why a pro?" Brown asked. "No, why trust an amateur if you've got a pro?"

"Good question," Jasper said. "I can see why an amateur would want a pro but not why a pro would want an amateur. Unless he couldn't get in."

"In which case the amateur should be dead," Brown said. "None of our suspects are."

"Except Mike." Jasper didn't like where his thoughts were going. "Hell, he could be the one. He might have needed the pro to carry his mother upstairs."

"Client, not victim?" Brown asked.

"The guy came prepared," Jasper said. "He provided the poison, wore a maintenance coverall, and knew how to clean the scene. I bet the only unscripted part was the club." He felt sick. "Mike was an engineer who worked on inspection systems. He would have known how to jam the lock. The upstairs door was the red herring, not the lower one."

"And the valium?"

"The pro could have provided it," Jasper said. "The only thing unexplained is why the pro took Michael out. It would have been more to his advantage to keep him alive and blackmail him."

"Maybe he was being blackmailed," Brown suggested. "And this was an attempt to get more to pay off the blackmailer."

"Possible. We're going to have to look a whole lot harder at Michael West." His com unit buzzed and he saw there was a vid message from David West. God, he was going to hate telling him.

He thumbed it on and threw the image on the big vid screen for Brown to watch too.

"It's David," he said with a worried expression on his face. "Jake didn't stay at my apartment last night. He also hasn't been to see Kucera. It's got me bugged. There was one other thing. I got a text message from him simply saying 'Don't see Kucera.' I've tried calling him about it but it goes to voice mail."

He looked off camera. "I have to go on shift. This may be nothing but it's not like him to do this. If it helps, his personal number is 308-555-8762."

Jasper replayed the message. On the third time through, he finally looked at his partner and saw she was thinking the same thing.

"Good theory, wrong person."

"Maybe," Jasper said. "Still no motive. Let's check them both out."

"Drop the professor?" Brown asked.

"Hell, no. I want to know where he was Monday before the import store. He's got a motive and a good one."

"He does?" Brown asked.

"Yeah, he wants to marry Jewel," Jasper said. That had occurred to him last night and he didn't like it. Jewel had told him no but now the two relatives she counted on were both dead. Under those conditions, could she be persuaded to say yes? He wasn't going to give him a chance to find out.

Jewel was worth a ton of money and could only get richer. She was also the prettiest girl he'd seen in a long time--and nice. She felt good too. She deserved better than a stuffed shirt professor of history.

"Then we'd better get going," Brown said. "I'll tell those upstairs. You'd better do something about that face of yours."

Jasper nodded and headed for the bathroom. He'd already got ribbed by Brown, questioned by Sanders, and seen some incredulous envy from the other people he worked with. Brown, of course, had known for years. Every time internal investigations had looked at him, they'd brought it up.

Them he could work with. It was the people on the street who might recognize him. He set about changing his look.

Chapter 27 - Professor

The trip back to the precinct was uneventful. Having changed the shape of his face with some cheek pads, Jasper walked along with his usual confidence. He'd learned exactly how to go unnoticed in college and, even though he hadn't used it much outside the line of duty, he could use it now. Only Brown's occasional evil grin drew attention to them. He was still relieved to get off the street.

"There's something I have to do first," he said. Heading for his temporary office, he took the police bar with him. Setting it on his desk, he did a quick search for the legal department of the network he wanted. The first secretary put him through when he mentioned his rank.

"Who is this?" The lawyer behind the desk looked mildly irritated. "Police?"

"This is Lieutenant Jasper Stone, Plains Police Department, Plains, Wyoming. I am also known as Jazz Stone and as Sensor Man." He'd removed his disguise for this call. "I want to show you what I found on my apartment door last night. It was left by Alyssa Sanders, Entertainment TV3. Her fingerprints are all over it."

He shifted so the lawyer could take a long look. "This a police bar, model XG5. Use of one requires a court order and it must be done by a duly appointed law enforcement officer. Any other use constitutes a violation of Civil Code 383 and Federal Law 1062. I have the means here to arrest Alyssa Sanders."

The lawyer went pale.

"Now you will keep Ms. Sanders and every other reporter from TV3 off my back or I will use this. Got it?"

"Yes sir," the lawyer stammered.

"For your information, my first interview is scheduled and will be with Rex Allen, Plains TV2. Thank Ms. Sanders for helping me decide that."

He cut the connection. He'd have to get the police bar to the lab for fingerprinting then he'd add the damned thing into police inventory. He was fairly sure the network would never call him on what he'd just said. The law was on his side.

Ms. Sanders would get a reprimand he was sure but he doubted it would go beyond that. Reporters tended to get rewarded for skirting the law and fired when they got too blatant about it. Unless he actually filed a suit, she'd stay.

One down. That left five more networks to go. He hoped word would get around fast that illegal tactics would result in legal action.

Being a cop had its advantages. He wasn't a lawyer but he'd been well versed in what cops or reporters could legally do and what the consequences could be. There were times when it was necessary to skirt the law to nail someone but they'd learned to be very careful doing it.

Dropping off the bar at forensics, he filled out the necessary paperwork then went to join his team.

"What have we got at Gracee Place?" He looked at Sanders.

"It's clean. I think we can release it."

"Not quite yet," Jasper said and briefly told Sanders of their new suspicions. Kruger wasn't there so he must be working on the toxicology.

"This just gets bigger," Sanders said. "So who are we investigating for what now?"

"Good question," Brown said. "Is there anyone we can quit working on while we concentrate on others?"

Jasper thought about it. "We need to concentrate on Michael West and Jake West--and the professor if this interview doesn't come out right. Let's drop Jewel and David West."

"And Elinor?"

That reminded him. He checked his com unit. "I have it verified that Elinor Ramsey didn't exit Plains on Monday. Jake West, no records. Jewel West left the city and didn't report entering--shocking. Michael West, no records. Andrew Nugent, no records."

"So none of our suspects used the upper door except Jewel," Brown said. "I can see why she failed to log that with the city."

"So can I." Jasper waved it off. "Wait a minute." He looked at hers again. "She left the city at 2pm and returned at 2:40. Then she left the city again at 3:40."

"The door malfunction happened at 1:03," Sanders said. "And it cleared at 2:15. Doesn't fit."

"No, it doesn't. Did she go back to school?"

"Yes, I escorted her," Sanders said. "She promised no outside duty so it should be pretty safe."

"That's right," Jasper said. "Maybe she had outside duty on Monday. That would account for the two o'clock thing."

Both Brown and Sanders looked relieved. Had they fallen for her too or were they just relieved they wouldn't have to follow up on her?

"Now for Jake. Sanders, find out if he took the afternoon train to Denver yesterday," Jasper said. "And call his number. If it's still on voice mail, it won't help. We need to get him to talk to us. If he took the train and didn't get to Denver, could he be in Cheyenne or Fort Collins or beyond Denver?"

"The train line stops at Boulder," Sanders said. "If he wanted to go beyond that, he would have to change in Denver."

"APB?" Brown asked.

"Not yet," Jasper said. "We do that and they'll ground him. Let's do our checking first."

They looked doubtful so he went on. "Jake has no motive for doing this. He also did a good interview and his alibi is pretty solid. Until something cracks, we can't justify holding him on suspicion."

"I'd like to go over his alibi," Brown said. "Dig into it. There also might be something about that Kucera guy. I assume it's not Wilson Kucera?"

"No, it's Edward." Jasper dug into his wallet and pulled out the card Jake had given him. "Use that."

"Will do." She glanced at the clock. "I'd like to watch from the tech booth and let Sanders have the watch position this time. Let's keep the professor off balance."

Reminded of the interview, Jasper wrapped up the briefing quickly. He wanted to get this done.

* * *

"Testing," Jasper said after putting his earpiece in. It was the same room, would it be the same technician?

"Confirmed," a female voice answered. "The chair please."

Jasper sat down in the chair and the female voice asked, "Are you Jasper Stone?"

"Yes," Jasper answered.

"Were you here this morning at eight o'clock?" The technician asked.

"Yes," Jasper said in a deliberate lie.

"Calibrated. You're good to go, lieutenant. I'm Technician Bradley."

"Nice to meet you. We will be interviewing Professor Andrew Nugent to establish his alibi for past Monday. Suspect in case 10833A and possibly case 10833B."

"Noted. Thank you, sir."

Jasper rose and was drawing his usual cup of water when the Professor was ushered in.

This time the man didn't look so calm. He had dressed with his usual care, bowtie and all but he lacked the confidence he'd had about the book. Jasper eyed his hands on the table and saw they were restless. Finishing his water, he set the cup aside.

"It's good to see you again, Professor," Jasper said. "This is a formal interview to establish where you were for this past Monday between the hours of noon and three pm. There are two or three other specific questions I will ask pertaining to the West cases. Do you want a lawyer?"

"No," Professor Nugent responded.

"Good, this shouldn't take long. First, where were you at one pm on Monday?"

"In my office at home," Nugent said. "Grading papers."

"Truth," the technician said. "He's nervous but it's truth."

"Good. Where were you at 2 pm, same day?"

"In my office at home," Professor Nugent said. "Still grading papers."

"Did you leave your home at any time between 1 and 2?"

"No." His voice was firmer now. "I have regular hours."

"But no one saw you there."

"No," he said, "it would be unusual if someone did."

Jasper studied him. "Why did you wait until 2:40 pm to go to the import store?" Remembering the man's desire to have his precious book, it didn't fit.

"I have regular office hours even when I work from home," Professor Nugent said. "I did leave before my usual time because I wanted..." he reddened slightly. "Normally I don't leave my work until three but my book was waiting. I left as soon as I had finished grading papers."

Jasper studied him with cool brown eyes, reminded again how precise this man was. "So you left around 2:15?"

"No, it was 2:20." The quiet statement was firm.

"Truth," the technician said. "Not a waver."

"Then we'll accept you were home," Jasper said. "Did you supply any valium to Michael West?"

"Excuse me?" The professor looked startled. "Valium?"

"Bear with me, professor, and just answer yes or no to the question. Did you ever supply valium to Michael West?"

"No." He looked puzzled. "For his pain?"

"Yes, for his pain," Jasper answered. He turned to the room's vid screen and pointed his com unit at it. "Have you ever seen this object?"

The long-headed god of whatever showed up on the screen. The professor squinted at it then answered. "Yes, I've seen it. Elizabeth collected such figures. This one is Japanese, I think. Yes, it is. She had another set in ivory of Chinese gods."

"Did you see this figure at any time last Monday?"

"No, no, of course not," the professor said. "I haven't been to their house in almost two weeks. Why are you asking me about this?"

Jasper considered then decided to see what he would get with the truth. "This particular figure was used to club Elizabeth West. The murderer knows that already."

The professor looked at him in disbelief. "Clubbed her? I thought she'd fallen."

"Clubbed first."

"I didn't know." He pulled a handkerchief from his pocket and mopped his face. "Poor Elizabeth to die that way."

"He's genuinely surprised, lieutenant, and upset. You've caught him out," the technician muttered in his ear.

"What was your relationship with Michael West?" Jasper idly asked, not expecting much.

The professor didn't answer right away and the technician hissed. "That's got him. There's something there."

Jasper eyed the man but the professor wasn't looking at him but his own hands. Idly Jasper noticed a couple of rings. The professor refolded his hands and finally looked up.

"Mike West was a very good friend and a very intelligent man. I will miss his company. His death leaves a vacuum in my life."

Jasper hesitated, unsure how to take that. Michael was a celibate but that sounded like they had been lovers. Before he could ask the obvious, the professor went on.

"We weren't involved," he denied, "except on an intellectual level. Mike liked history and we were both interested in helping young people get an education. That's why we both belonged to Reach Out."

"Thank you for clarifying that," Jasper said. He wasn't absolutely sure that was the truth but the technician didn't tell him it was a lie.

Jasper glanced at Sanders then steeled himself for the question he most wanted the answer to. "One more question, professor. If you could get the West house without marrying Jewel West, would you do it?"

The effect was immediate. Professor Nugent sprang up, his face going pale and his voice shaking with anger. "That is crossing the line, lieutenant. You have no business suggesting I would do something so despicable."

"Answer the question, please."

"I will not. If you mean to accuse me of murder, I want a lawyer. If not, I am done." He waited for Jasper to say something then abruptly turned and left.

"Book him?" Sanders said as the door shut behind him.

"No," Jasper said. "Did we get anything on that last question?"

"Before he jumped up, yes. His blood pressure elevated. It wasn't enough of a reading to say whether he was alarmed or angry," the technician said. "Hell of a motive though. Killing for a house?"

"You haven't seen the house," Jasper replied. "Huge. He could put a lot of books in it."

"That might be what he planned," Brown said as she rejoined them. "That house would make a great library. You really think he wants it enough to kill?"

"Unknown at this point," Jasper said. "But it would explain why a man his age has taken so long to court Jewel-- and why she doesn't respond to him. I doubt he can love a woman as much as he loves his books."

"She's lucky to be rid of him," Brown said. "But she'd better find a man who can protect her." She looked at Jasper. "An ex-cop would do."

Jasper set his jaw but didn't meet her eyes. Had he been that obvious?

"Ex-cop?' Sanders repeated in confusion.

"You don't really think they'd let me stay once the press tracks me down?" Jasper asked of Sanders. "Not unless it's a desk job."

"I hadn't thought about that," Sanders said. "But I did think about something else. There's a problem with the Michael West theory."

"Let's hear it."

"He was killed by poisoned scotch placed in his house at least a week prior to him being there. Granted, it was a pro that did it. It couldn't be the same pro."

"How do you get that?" Jasper asked.

"If it had been the same pro, he would have killed Michael at the house. Even if he left, that front door was open. He could have returned at any time and killed Michael in his sleep. Murder suicide or two murders but no waiting and taking a chance Michael would talk."

Jasper thought about it then looked at Brown. "You're right. It makes no sense. Let's follow up anyway because this whole damned case hasn't made any sense."

"Right."

Chapter 28 - Outside

Jasper stared up at the thick clouds that obscured the sun and wondered if it would rain. The forecast called for it and, damn, he wished it would. His suit hung off him and he could feel the sweat. "What's the damned temperature out here?" he asked his partner.

Brown managed to look cool even out here, her black hair neatly pinned up and her black suit seemingly impervious to the heat that was making him swelter. "41 Celsius."

"Cute. What's that in the old scale?" Jasper asked.

"One hundred six," she replied. "I prefer Celsius. It sounds cooler."

Jasper had no answer for that. He knew one hundred six was not considered dangerous but it was still far too hot for him. He preferred the seventy-six degrees of the city in July. Well, the sooner he got done with this search, the sooner he could get back below ground.

"These strawberries are pretty good," Brown said as she popped another into her mouth. "They need to be picked too."

"Right." Jasper's hand slowed as he found one too tempting to resist. They were doing a check outside Lily Place for the murder weapon. Technically they weren't breaking any codes picking strawberries inside the low-walled garden of the private residence. He didn't think Jewel would mind. He would tell her they needed picking. He picked another then scanned further along the path and tried to ignore the afternoon heat.

Strawberry plants were the preferred ground cover in the city gardens since they grew in thick and produced fruit too. They also grew just high enough off the ground that they could conceal something the size of that club.

"I think we're going to have to bring in pickers for this job," Jasper finally said. "It would be quicker. If the figure was discarded in one of the beds, they'd find it."

"Agreed," Brown said, straightening with a small handful of berries. "Not that I mind searching right now but it'll take too long. It might not even be close to the house."

She popped another berry into her mouth. "Did you see that snatcher when we left the precinct? I think he saw you."

"Yeah." Jasper remembered the wide-eyed look on Frazier's face. "I think he saw the news too." He was glum. "But that's two arrests in one week. He's going to have to talk fast to get out of it."

"If they don't drop the charges like the professor did," Brown pointed out. "It seems he doesn't have much luck though. He should just go straight."

Jasper grinned. "Yeah, I had him pegged as a pro but now I don't think so."

"I'd better get Jewel's permission to harvest the strawberries in her garden," Jasper said. "The rest isn't a problem."

"It's Friday," Brown said. "And late enough in the afternoon, they might not get to it. Call it in now?"

"Yes." Jasper carefully stepped back to the path, his eyes still scanning the ground cover. He knew the odds of finding the weapon were slim since there was a pro involved. Even if they did find it, the automatic sprinklers might have wiped it clean of fingerprints by now. Still they had to eliminate possibilities. If the killer had come out this door and simply discarded it on his way to a public entrance, it could be recovered. The nearest public entrances were both over a hundred feet away. The parking lot was closer but private cars were rare. Ranchers and farmers drove trucks or sometimes a ranch car but they would park a lot closer to the mall or take their produce to receiving. The only vehicle he saw in this lot now was a city-owned work cart with some gardening equipment sticking out of the back. He looked around for the driver then stiffened as he saw a class of kids in the distance.

Looking up Jewel's number, he activated it. Could she be outside?

"Hello," she answered. "Anything important? I'm with my class."

"Are you outside?" Jasper demanded. The long silence was answer enough. "I'm seeing kids headed west of me. Is that your class?"

"Yes." Her answer was faint. "I had to get out. We're going to the track. It should be safe enough."

"I'll join you." He disconnected and turned to Brown. "She's outside after all. Can you take care of this while I play bodyguard?"

"Yes." Brown looked irritated. "You might have to get her restricted."

"I know." Jasper headed off toward the group, wishing it was cooler. They were easy to follow since they were almost in a direct line with the landscape's most picturesque feature. Laramie Peak seemed to loom over the city and the gray clouds behind it made it look ominous today. He wondered how long it would be before it rained--if it rained.

The long oval of the track wasn't deserted. Seeing that, his frown deepened. Another class was there. He spotted Jewel's class and made for her then stopped. It was no use chewing her out and he shouldn't do it in front of a pack of kids. It would be better to see to her safety instead.

There was a male teacher speaking to his assembled students. "Some of you are getting lazy so I've asked Miss West to bring her fourth graders today. They're going to be the bears and you'd better outrun them."

That brought mock cries of fear from what he guessed were sixth graders.

Jewel's kids were stretching with enthusiasm, some of them growling at the older students as they did so. The older students responded by waggling their butts and laughing.

Jasper had to smile, remembering this game. The fourth graders would be chasing and trying to catch the other runners. It inspired both groups to put more effort into their running since the successful bear could demand his capture to do pushups or sit-ups if caught. Sometimes there were other incentives too.

Jasper eyed the empty bleachers then walked down to the finish line and back. By that time Jewel had gathered her students together into a huddle. He got close enough to hear.

"Chocolate milk for everyone when we get back," Jewel said. "And anyone who catches one of those uppity sixth graders gets a chocolate bar. No tripping but any other catch is good. I don't want you to spend your time roaring if you're up. That's wasted energy. Let's do it."

Her students cheered.

Jasper wondered if it was safe for kids to be running in this heat as she tagged the three students who'd go first. He knew 106 was considered a fairly good temperature in July and they didn't start restricting outside activities until it reached 115. At 125 not even gardeners and maintenance men were allowed out in the heat of the day and special misters would be run to keep plants cool.

Six older students took their places in the lanes, giving the bears a good choice on whom to catch. Most of them made faces at the fourth graders but a couple looked ready to settle down to business. He wondered if those were two of the slower ones or the top runners.

The bears also noticed the quiet ones. They were allowed to pick their own prey and two settled into lanes six feet behind the serious ones. The third chose one who was goofing off more than the others. The bears waiting their turns roared but the three in the lanes had listened and paid attention only to the race.

Another school employee had taken up a post at the finish line and the male teacher was midway down the track. This race was short, about forty meters, so the bears would have to be quick.

Jasper took up a position where he could watch the start and Jewel at the same time. The kids went off, the bears lunging forward in hope of catching the runners at the start then running for all they were worth. A shout went up as one of the sixth graders got caught. It was one of the serious ones.

The goofer had proved more nimble.

Another shout went up at the finish line. This time it was the teacher verifying another catch. Two disgruntled sixth graders went over to sit in the "captured" box. The others took seats on the bleachers to cheer their fellows on.

After that first round, it was harder for the fourth graders. Out of the eighteen, only five managed to capture their prey. The sixth graders didn't goof off much either after the first round. Seeing two fall so fast, they got serious.

Jasper watched the races but he also noticed a maintenance man in the green overalls of a groundskeeper join the students at the bleachers. He had a shovel and some garbage bags so he might have been on legitimate duty but he didn't think so. A shovel would have little use on the track.

By the time the races were done and five sixth graders had done their penalties, the man was gone and a light breeze had sprung up, helping to move the humid air around.

"Jewel said you inspired this," the man she called Mr. Forester said with a broad grin. "Thanks. That's the best times I've had out of my students in a long time."

"You thought of the bear race," Jasper said. "Lieutenant Stone."

"Lieutenant?" He grinned. "Well, I'd expect nothing less out of Jewel. She's a real treasure."

For once Jasper couldn't think of an answer. He mumbled something before the man walked away. A treasure? Wouldn't expect anything less? He thought he was Jewel's boyfriend? He was torn between setting the matter straight and not.

Shortly after excited students surrounded him and, as he sorted through the babble, realized they thought he was too. What had Jewel told them? Well, it explained his presence. He should be thankful they didn't know he was protecting her-- and them--in case of trouble.

As they started the walk back to the school, he managed to fall a little behind with her. "I saw one maintenance man at the bleachers," he said. "No one else."

Her smile slipped but only for a second. "There's always maintenance and subbies around."

"True." He didn't mention the shovel. "So I'm supposed to be a friend," he said.

Her cheeks went pink. "You are. Well, I think you are. And I thought it was the easiest way to explain to...." she motioned to her students.

"I have no problem with it," Jasper said and he didn't. It was unprofessional to think along those lines but he didn't want this girl hurt. And it might be easier to protect her if people did think they were a couple. Thankfully, no one had recognized him from the news.

"So how many chocolate bars do you have stashed?" he asked.

"Just enough," Jewel said. "Everyone gets chocolate milk but the bars are what they all work so hard for. We've got to catch up," she said as the students yelled at them. "They can't get in without me."

"Right," Jasper said. "When school is done, I'd like to take a walk with you. Would that be all right?"

She hesitated then nodded. "I'd like that."

Using his police ID to enter the school, he said later to Jewel and headed for the principal's office. Once he was satisfied Jewel would not be assigned outside duty again till the case was done, he returned to Jewel's classroom. There were mostly girls there now, the boys having been taken off somewhere. Some were busy gathering up milk-stained glasses and washing them in the classroom sink and others were sweeping or tidying up the room. It was the normal end of day routine.

There was just one boy in the classroom. Jasper eyed him, realizing he hadn't been on the track. He also didn't look happy or engrossed in the portable reader he was holding. Clearly a new subby, he thought, looking at his short hair and all gray clothing. The other students, subbies or not, had added flashes of color to their school uniforms. One girl even had pink and green hair. Jasper caught Jewel's eye and motioned toward the boy sitting by himself.

She hesitated then came over to him. "That's Tommy. He's new to being a subby. Can you talk to him?" she asked. "Oh, and he lost his mother about a month ago. He's very angry."

"Got it," Jasper said. He sat down next to the boy, taking a quick look at the reader he held. "That's a girl's book."

"What do you know?" Tommy retorted then looked embarrassed as he realized he wasn't talking to another kid. "Who, I'm sorry, sir."

"Don't be," Jasper said. "Jasper Stone. It sucks being a subby," he said it as a mere statement of fact. "People look down on you."

Conflicting emotions crossed the kid's face before he blurted out. "You know?"

"I was one," Jasper said. "I'm not there now. I think you'll be one that gets out too."

"I want to," Tommy said with a scowl.

"What's your favorite subject?" Jasper asked.

"Science," Tommy said. "I like rocks mostly. They don't change."

"Good reason," Jasper said, having no trouble following the boy's reasoning. "They need good geologists and mining engineers, even miners. If you aim for one of those careers, you'll get college."

"Will I get into space?"

"Maybe." Jasper leaned closer. "I know a lunar mechanic now. She says don't believe the vids. The lunar mechs are never six-foot-tall boozers."

Tommy finally grinned. "No kidding."

"No kidding. By the time you grow up there will thousands of people on Mars and probably some in the asteroid belt. Studying rocks could get you out there. You'll need math too."

"Thanks."

The last bell rang and he waited as excited students

gathered their things together and headed out the door. The rest of the boys appeared from a room down the hall and he tagged along as students one after the other touched an ID panel and started down the stairs into the city proper. Some piled on to the drop slide next to the stairs, sliding down the two floors.

He couldn't blame them for taking the slide. It looked like fun. He knew it was to speed evacuation of the school but it was practical too.

When the last student had gone, Jewel smiled at him. "I'm ready."

Chapter 29 - Revelation

The buzzing of his com unit broke the quiet left after the students' departure. Jasper glanced at the number and answered. "Lieutenant Stone speaking. Yes, this is Jasper Stone." He listened intently as the woman kept on talking. "Yes, I'm interested in talking to Reach Out. It will have to be scheduled in September. No, that's the earliest I'll be available. Thank you for calling."

Jewel smiled as they walked to the outside exit. "Let me guess. That was Rosalyn Krantz."

"Got it in one," Jasper said as they logged out of the city. "Is she the social secretary for the charity?"

"Pretty much. By the way, you held out on me last night. I didn't really hear until breakfast what everyone else in the city knew," Jewel said. "Sensor Man is my protector," she declared in melodramatic tones.

"Don't say that too loud," Jasper warned with a grin for her drama. "You'll have to share." He took off his suit jacket and threw it over his shoulder, deciding he had to have relief from the heat.

Jewel's eyes slid down to his trank gun, now visible on his belt but it didn't hold her back. "Uncle David thought it was hilarious," she said. "How on Earth are you going to keep from being recognized?"

"I have my ways," Jasper said. He hated to disturb this playful mood she was in. Searching for a safe topic, he remembered the boy. "So what is this about Tommy? Why wasn't he with the other boys?"

"Counseling session every Friday," Jewel answered. "He hates them but hasn't learned to lie yet."

"Lie?" Jasper stopped walking to look at her, surprised by the casual statement.

"Oh, come on, everyone learns to lie. Didn't you ever have counseling?"

"Well, yeah," Jasper admitted. "You did?"

"For almost a year before Grandpa said no more. Jake wasn't so lucky. He had years of it--first because of Benjie and then because he was aiming for Mars. He learned to tell them what they wanted to hear."

"Tommy will learn," she said as she started to walk again. "As soon as they think he's adjusted to his mother's death, he'll be out of counseling."

Jasper didn't follow, his thoughts going over what she'd just said. Of course Jake had counseling--they required it when a child lost a family member. He'd been through it when his brother died even though he was legally an adult--and Mel had fought with him because she had to go through it after her mother's death.

He hadn't lied that he remembered but he hadn't been young. They'd mentioned in training though that extended counseling really didn't work on young kids. They didn't want to dwell on what happened so they would get uncooperative, even lie.

Could Jake be that practiced a liar? Could she? He took quick strides to catch up.

Jewel hadn't gone far before stopping again, her hand shading her eyes from the afternoon sun as she peered toward the road that ran around the city.

"What do you see?" Jasper asked, his hand drifting to his trank. His eyes scanned the road and parking lot but there was nothing in sight beyond trees and the usual structures.

"Nothing," Jewel said. "I just look."

"Look for what?"

"A car that looks like a white Sport Javelin," she said. "I saw one on Monday and it just gave me chills. I thought it was Uncle David's car but he was on shift. So now I'm just hoping I'll see it again so I can get it out of my mind."

"David has a car?" Jasper turned that over once in his mind then abruptly changed direction, pulling her along with him. "Come on."

"Where?" She looked confused when he pointed to the gray stone precinct tower marked with a big number three. "But we can't get in that way."

Jasper was already speaking into his com unit, clearing himself for ground level entry. "You need to pack," he said. "We're going to Denver."

"I don't want to," Jewel said.

"You're free until Monday. You need protection and you're going with me."

"One more thing," he said before they entered the precinct. "I need to examine that car first. Don't call anyone."

By the time he'd washed up, put on a fresh shirt, grabbed his own luggage and called to reserve a place on the next train, she was ready. Thankfully, it was the five thirty train and they had staterooms. The last thing he needed was someone recognizing him now.

Jewel looked pale but composed until she saw him. "What did you do to your face?"

He popped out a cheek pad and one half of his face returned to normal, giving him a very off-balance appearance. He leered at her and she lost it, fending him off with a slightly hysterical giggle.

Ignoring the few curious stares, he popped his cheek pad back in and grabbed her slender hand. "Just hold it together, Jewel, till we get on the train. We have to get to Denver tonight."

Her gorgeous blue eyes met his and her smile faded.

"That's better," he said, quickly letting her go. Aware she could have lied to him, certain that Jake had, he vowed to stay professional.

By the time the squad car reached the station, she was collected and just another young woman taking a weekend trip to Denver. Jasper asked one of the station people if Jake West had taken the train the night before and was assured he had. He knew better than to ask if Jake had stayed on the train till Denver. They wouldn't know here.

Placing his suitcase on the rack next to Jewel's, he glanced around the stateroom. Each was furnished with a sink, toilet, drop down table, and two comfortable couches in a deep red brocade. They even had a coffee maker and enough outlets for three personal computers. A large vid screen took up one wall. Luxury.

Latching the door, he turned on the sink. A few minutes later his cheek pads were out and rinsed. Thankfully, the train was kept at a reasonable temperature and didn't run above ground for most of its journey. He settled down to make some necessary calls.

"Can I text David we're coming?" Jewel asked. "Nothing about the car."

Remembering the security of the Lunarex Tower, Jasper nodded. "Just let me see it first. Ask him to meet us."

She worked for a bit then showed him the brief message.

"You have me for the weekend. Arriving 5:30 train. Meet us please," he read. "Good enough. He'll know you aren't traveling alone."

"Wait," he stopped her, "would he use the car to meet us?"

"No, a Javelin is only a two-seater," she said. "Not very practical. That's why he rarely drives it anymore."

"Who can drive it?" Jasper asked. "Besides David?"

"You don't think it was him then?" Her face regained some color.

"Not likely. His alibi is solid. I want to know who else could have."

"Jake and probably his mechanic. I never got a license. Maybe Elinor. She learned to drive on the moon."

He looked at her, struck by the absurdity of that statement. "That doesn't mean she can drive on Earth."

"Why not?"

He shook his head and went back to his calls.

By the time the train stopped in Cheyenne, he'd finished alerting Sanders and Brown about the developments and knew they would step up efforts to find out where Jake was.

He'd also called the Denver police and arranged for a forensic team to go over the car. It would have to be driven to their laboratory but they would have someone available at eight to do just that.

One more call. He wished he didn't have to use Jewel.

"Try calling Jake and text him too. Don't tell him you're coming to Denver but ask where he is. Let me know if you get through."

Thinking that would occupy her for a few minutes, he put in a number he knew by heart. "Sensor here. I need to talk to Carlson."

He was put through quickly.

"Sensor, I thought you'd be calling."

"I'd like to meet. I'll be in Denver all day tomorrow but I'm not sure of schedule yet."

"Stay at the Silverado," Carlson said. "Send a text about 45 minutes before we can meet there."

"Will do." The call ended.

"I didn't get a reply from Jake," Jewel said. "Voice message went to voice mail. I don't know if he saw the text or not."

"He'll respond if he wants to," Jasper said. "He reports for quarantine on Tuesday, right?"

"Right--at Elk Mountain."

"Jake will turn up then," he said. "It'll be okay."

He felt lousy for lying to her but he didn't know yet whether Jake had driven that car. Until he did, there was still some doubt. If he had though, Jake West would never get to Mars.

Chapter 30 – The Javelin

The train glided into the Denver Hub precisely on time, the VIP car sliding smoothly to a stop at the carpeted VIP platform. Jasper looked out, seeing David and Elinor were already there and the other man he expected. It didn't look like Detective Jameson had made himself known to them yet.

Security was notoriously tight in Lunarex Tower and difficult for even the local police to penetrate so they had suggested meeting Jasper at the train. Since he needed an impartial witness to the car inspection, he'd agreed. He just had to smooth it over with David West.

When the doors opened, Jewel went straight into her uncle's arms and gave him a hug like she hadn't seen him for months. If she shed any tears, they were quickly hidden as she hugged Elinor too.

"It's official," David said, his face already settling into lines of grief. "Did you find Jake?"

"No sir." Jasper saw the relief in his face and realized he thought Jake had been found dead. "We're looking for Jake. Any contact?"

"Not here." David frowned at the waiting Jameson and it deepened when Jasper motioned him over.

"Badge, please." Jasper examined the proffered badge and ID then handed it back. "David West, this is Detective Jameson, Denver PD. I've asked for his help in examining your car."

"My car?" David asked. "The Javelin?"

"That's right. I wasn't aware you had a car until this afternoon. We need to confirm it was here on Monday."

"Let's get out of here," David said as another couple glanced their direction. "I have a limo. There's room enough for all." He ushered them toward the exit.

Jasper hid his surprise at seeing a Crown Elizabeth limo at the curb. He'd ridden in one a couple of times when he was still in college and being wooed by publishers so he knew the elegance of their interiors. Jameson was a little less prepared but tried hard not to show it.

"You'd better get used to it, Jasper," David said as the limo pulled away from the curb. "Appearance and security."

"I suppose so," Jasper said. "But not in Plains."

Denver was an old town. Like Chicago, the newer sections had been built underground but there were still plenty of skyscrapers, shopping and even housing developments on the surface. Most were connected to the underground but not all. The Lunarex Tower, sometimes referred to as the Ivory Tower, was not.

Inside the seventy-floor tower were the residences of all their Lunar Techs, plus high-speed communications with the mining equipment they operated via remote control. Basic shopping was also available and a theater, several restaurants, bars, a lounge, gymnasium, and even a school for their children. It was very secure and a very expensive place to live.

"So have you heard from Jake?" Jasper asked. "Jewel hasn't."

David glanced at Jameson then shook his head. "Not directly. Two texts came in while I was on shift. The first warned me again about seeing Kucera. The second said he'd changed lawyers. That was it. I tried calling back this evening but no response."

"He didn't say what lawyer?"

"No, no details at all. I hate those damned text messages. They never give you what you need." David rubbed his eyes. "Now what's this about the car?"

"Uncle, I saw what looked like a white Javelin Monday when I was out with my class. I thought it was your car but I knew you were on shift. When I saw it I just got a shiver. It didn't go away so I hurried home right after work."

David studied her then sighed. "Like Mother, I suppose." He turned to Jasper. "You'd better check it out but I want you to know I haven't driven it since May. My mechanic had it in for a tune-up a couple of weeks ago but it hasn't moved since then."

"What is this about shivers?" Jasper asked.

"Premonitions," David said. "Sometimes they pan out, sometimes they don't. Mother had one when New Wave collapsed. It was pretty intense and she was hysterical long before the phone call came. She knew." He looked at Jewel. "I'm glad only the women in the family get them though."

Jasper glanced at Jameson and saw the skeptical look on his face. Another kind of gut feeling? He wasn't sure but he was here because a car would have made it possible for Jake West to get to Plains and back again regardless of his alibi.

Jasper's eyes went back to David. "Any other calls from anyone?"

"Kucera called wanting to know if I'd seen Jake. I told him no. He called again while I was on shift and tried to get an appointment to see me. Elinor took that call but refused to set it up without talking to me."

"Good. Do you have any idea what set Jake off yesterday?"

"Not a clue," David said. "You were there. He wasn't like that during the service or we would have noticed. Just that one quick line and he was gone."

"Are we talking Edward Kucera or his brother?" Jameson asked.

"Edward," David answered. "You've had run-ins?"

"He's of interest," Jameson said. "He spreads money around in some unusual places and it's suspected he has some sort of tie to Blissex. Never proven but suspected. What we'd really like is to get his brother but Wilson Chemicals is clean."

"I'd like to know more about that," Jasper said, his interest keen. A thought struck him. "Is he a donor to Reach Out?" He looked at Jewel. "A major donor?"

"Well, yes," she said mystified.

"Does he ever come to events at Plains?"

"Sure. Not all of them but we had a party just last week

and he came."

Bingo, Jasper thought. Maybe he'd just found the source of the anonymous tip.

"What's that about?" Jameson asked.

"Different case," Jasper said. "I'll fill you in later." He really shouldn't be concerned with that case right now but he would pass on what he suspected to Brown. She'd be taking it over when he was no longer available.

"I can't see Jake doing anything to Mother," David abruptly said. "There was no reason he should. He had his sponsorship and everything was set. He really had no motive. At least, he doesn't have any more motive than anyone else in the family."

The limo turned into the wide avenue leading to Lunarex Tower. Jasper glanced briefly at the looming whiteness, noticing that the evening lights around its base were already on. It wasn't full dark yet but the lights banished any shadows from the structure.

"No, he doesn't have a motive that we know of," Jasper agreed. "But everyone else has solid alibis. His looks solid but I don't think it is. He could have paid someone to go to the movies for him and have lunch at the Brown Palace. Until we go over surveillance tapes, I can't say for certain he was there. If he didn't drive the car, I'll rethink it. Right now...." he shrugged.

"Fair enough," David said. "Elinor, why don't you take Jewel upstairs? I want to get this over with."

Elinor nodded. Jewel didn't say anything as the limo pulled up to the door of the tower. While the doorman was assisting them with the luggage, the two detectives followed David West into the guarded lobby.

"You'll have to sign in," David said as they stopped at the guard desk. "No badges, just names. They get suspicious of official visits."

"Yes sir," Jameson answered first and signed his name then put his thumbprint next to it.

Jasper thought a moment then signed Jazz Stone and put Sensor Man under it. The guard's eyes widened but he didn't say anything.

David saw his signature and quickly said, "We're going down to see my Javelin. Mr. Stone is interested in buying it. Note that we're in the garage please."

"Yes sir," the guard responded and waved them on.

"Sensor Man?" Jameson asked as the elevator doors closed behind them. "That's you?"

"Unfortunately, yes," Jasper answered as David smiled. "This is my last case for the department."

Jameson looked impressed.

"It's entertaining watching him duck the press," David said. "The only good thing about this week." His jaw tightened and his smile faded.

When they stepped from the elevator, the garage lights came on, showing a number of high value cars, each one assigned to a generous sized parking spot. Jasper was reminded again how much a lunatech got paid. Few others could afford such rich toys they never used.

They walked in silence to where the Javelin stood in isolated glory, its gleaming white body immaculate. Jameson squatted down to peer at the tires. "Do they have a car wash in this garage?"

"Yes," David answered.

"I thought so. Tires are too clean," he muttered. "Maybe driven and maybe not."

"It's a Javelin," David said as he put his thumb to the lock. "It keeps a log of everyone who has driven it clear back to when it was in the factory."

"What's in that log exactly?" Jasper asked.

"Driver, number of miles, and fueling log," Jameson answered for him. "It's also got a GPS built in. Anytime it sits idle for more than hour after changing location, it logs it."

David nodded, unlocking the car so Jameson could take the passenger seat. He sat in the driver's seat and brought up the appropriate logs. Jasper had to content himself with watching their faces. There was simply no room in the speedster for a third body. Would he be wrong?

Jameson's face lost expression, settling into the set face of a cop on the job. It was David who went pale then cursed. He tried to climb out of the car then sat down heavily, his head in his hands.

Jasper froze, unable to believe it was actually true. He was torn between wanting to comfort David and seeing for himself. When Jameson left the car, he leaned in to read the display. Last user: Jake West. Last use: Monday, July 12, 2179. Last fueling, Monday, July 12, 2179. Distance traveled: 410 miles. He didn't need to see the GPS log. He reached for his com unit

"This is Lieutenant Jasper Stone, authorization code ten eighteen alpha tango, " he quietly said. "I want an APB on Jacob West, aka Jake West, civilian ident number in file. Wanted for questioning." He sent the recorded message to both Brown and Sanders then walked around the car to David.

David West looked defeated, his jaw slack and his eyes staring off into the distance. Jasper touched his arm and David shifted his gaze to him but it took him a moment to recognize him.

"Why did he do it?" David asked. "Why the hell would Jake do something so...horrible." a ragged breath tore through him. "He's my son."

"We don't know yet," Jasper gently said. "Now we have to find him. Can you think of anywhere he might go?"

David shook his head then cradled his head in his hands. A tear escaped down his cheek. "Nowhere. There's here. There's Plains. He could have gone to the Sullivans but he'd need a car for that and it's here."

"Sullivans? Could he have taken this car there?" Jasper sharply asked. Could they be wrong?

"No, no," David said. "They're much further west. It

would have taken more than 500 miles to get there and back."

"He's still my son and I'll stick by him. God, I wish he was on Mars!" He rose to his feet with an effort and, taking out a handkerchief, mopped his face. "I have to tell Jewel."

"Sir, I need you to unlock the car," Jameson said. "I'll drive it back to the precinct."

David hesitated then nodded. "Right. Sorry. I wasn't thinking. Come over here."

He sat back down and typed in a code. The computer panel went blank then showed an outline of a hand. "I'll authorize you. I'm not going to unlock it for just anybody. Put your hand on the screen, Detective."

Jameson did. The screen flashed green and the handprint was replaced by a box.

"Thumbprint there," David prompted. The screen flashed green again as it accepted his prints. "You're an authorized user now. Take care of the damned thing."

"Yes sir. "

Jasper watched as Jameson took the controls of the car and carefully backed it out of its space. As the big garage door opened to allow exit, his attention was drawn back to David by a muttered curse.

"I never want to see that car again." He glared at Jasper then shook his head. "Not your fault. Jake did this all by himself." He took another ragged breath. "Damn it, he's lost Mars. Does the little fool even realize that?"

Where the hell was Jake anyway? Did he know he'd lost? Did he intend to hide until he could go in quarantine? It wouldn't work. Until they actually got into space, law enforcement could still remove colonists from the list. Quarantine was twenty days long. Only a fool would think this secret could be kept that long and Jake West wasn't a fool. There had to be something more here but he wasn't seeing it-- not yet.

Chapter 31 - Saturday

"The hottest news item this week is Sensor Man. We have reports that he's actually a police lieutenant in Plains, Wyoming. Plains TV reporter Rex Allen claims to have an interview scheduled with Jasper Stone, the fabled Sensor Man. If so, that's a pretty major scoop for a small town reporter."

Jasper snorted. Yeah, they would make a big deal out of that. Well, he'd chose his own shark. Rex was not as cutthroat as the rest. In the years that he'd known him, the reporter had also kept his word and that was unusual in his career field.

He watched the news report a little longer, making sure they made no mention of his daughter. Under Section 8, the children of celebrities and public figures were guaranteed privacy. Even if they got pictures of him in public with Mel, they were required by law to edit her out. The only exception was if he took her to a public event related to his own career-- and that wasn't going to happen. He would never use Mel to get headlines.

He had to be public this time around. When he'd concocted his plan, he knew it would only work if he were visible and accessible. For the past year he'd been laying the groundwork for the biggest job in his life. Now it was about to begin.

Carlson would get here soon. He needed to get this over with then see if he could trace Jake and he needed to talk to David and Jewel again. If Jake had left the train in Cheyenne or Fort Collins, he would probably stay in a hotel he already knew. The Hitching Post? No, too obvious. If he were hiding, he wouldn't pick the richest hotel in Cheyenne. Little America was out too. It wasn't connected to Cheyenne's underground and security was tight but it was too far away from everything.

In Fort Collins, he might choose the Rings Hotel or Futura House. Both had good security but both would probably require a personal debit card. No, he could probably eliminate those too. If Jake were hiding, he wouldn't use his personal debit card. Transactions were too visible by any law enforcement agency. Now that an APB had been issued, that could be used without his consent. The warrant Sanders was securing this morning would open other doors for the investigation.

Damn, he still couldn't come up with a reason Jake would do this. He'd just thrown away his future in the most useless way possible. There was almost no doubt he'd killed his grandmother or that he'd known the professional that had come in afterward. It made no sense.

Why had Jake used a public com station to call his mother and his wife? Why had he waited until morning to call them? He knew about Mike's death the night before.

Most people who had com units liked the option of being able to throw a vid call on to the nearest vid screen. That was really the major reason anyone with a com unit would use a public com booth--that and privacy since the booths were shielded from sound and sight. The enclosed booths weren't free to use like the basic com panels but they also didn't have a five-minute time limit built in. Jake might have needed that and the privacy.

Did his escort know he had called his mother and his wife? Could he have called others? Who? And did he use the public com booth for the bigger screen or to prevent leaving a record of whom he called on his personal unit?

Damn, how many things had Jake slipped by him? He cradled his coffee mug in his hands and thought.

They hunted. David had said that when they were discussing Mike. He hadn't paid attention because no guns were involved and his focus had still been on Mike.

Jewel had said something too. Jake didn't finish anything. He had to take that with a big grain of salt. Jake had his reasons for getting so many degrees-and he had finished them. He just hadn't got experience.

His com link buzzed and he picked it up, his coffee cup still in his other hand. Without thinking, he transferred the call to the vid screen. It was Brown.

"What's up?" he asked. She looked jubilant.

"We've got something! Those tablecloths..."

"Tablecloths?" Jasper repeated.

"Yes, tablecloths. Didn't you see it on the odd news?" she asked then went on quickly. "Hunter gets the credit for this one. He realized the tablecloths came into the city on Monday in a shipment to a subby cafeteria. They came in sometime between 2 and 6 pm. We'd pulled their inspectors for our stakeout so the boxes weren't checked in until Tuesday."

Jasper's mind worked quickly. "And the tablecloths were gone through during the night? Do you think it was Blissex?"

"We're pretty sure it was," Brown said. "Hunter tucked a legal bliss into the folds of the tablecloths and ran it back through the inspection scanners. It didn't show. The material is thick enough to hide the shape and not even the metallic foil gave off an alarm. It was perfect. He brought it to the captain's attention before saying anything."

"And the captain told him to leave it out of his report?"

"Yes. Jasper, this is the first concrete lead we've had. Five tablecloths were missing. That would have left room for almost a thousand chews. This one is major." Her grin got fiercer. "And there's more. You know who bought those tablecloths for the subbies? Reach Out!"

"You're kidding."

"No, I'm not. One of their people actually insisted we find the missing tablecloths--a Mrs. Krantz."

"Rosalyn Krantz?" Jasper asked, remembering the woman who called him.

"Guess so. Hunter said she was really insistent. They have an event coming up and needed the tablecloths to make it "special." She snorted. "As if tablecloths matter to subbies. They'd rather have jobs."

"Agreed." Jasper thought hard about it. "See if you can get

Hunter to keep quiet about it. We don't want rumors circulating about Blissex and Reach Out until we've investigated."

"Right. He's a good cop and he knows there's something there."

"He's not assigned to Vice. It might be a good move to get him there," Jasper suggested. "Ask the captain."

"Yeah, hey, I heard there's going to be an opening in Vice," she said with a wide smile. "How's that going?"

"I have no idea. It's out that I'm a cop. Now it's up to the city to get me unemployed." Jasper hesitated. "I hope they don't move too fast. I need to wrap up this case."

"Still no Jake?"

"No. Once we have him, we'll get all the answers--I think."

"Is there any question of him going to Mars now?" she asked. "Is it certain he's the one?"

"It's certain. It took his handprint to unlock the car and activate the systems. It's also certain the car went to Plains. Jewel can put it there and the mileage matches. What bugs me is why he did it since he was already set for Mars. He didn't need the money and he wasn't going to get it."

"So we're stuck without a motive?" Brown made a face. "You know I hate cases like this. Nothing is ever tidy."

"Tell me about it. Has Sanders got the warrant?" He sipped some more coffee.

"He's working on it. Are you staying with them?"

"No." Jasper remembered how difficult it had been to leave them last night. Jewel had begged him to stay but it was a family moment and he was already having problems with his objectivity. "I'm at the Silverado. I needed some place more accessible than the Lunarex Tower."

"Well, that's pretty accessible," she said. "Oh, I walked by your house. Five reporters still there but the biggies are gone. I think they've figured out you aren't coming back."

"Good." He sighed. "Damn, I still need a place to call home."

"You'll figure it out. I'm going to head to Cheyenne on the noon train. I don't think Jake is here and that's a good place to start."

"True," Jasper said. "Oh, David said he mentioned switching lawyers. It might be good to query those in Cheyenne."

"This is Saturday," she reminded. "Law offices are closed."

"Damn."

She laughed. "How about you visit some Reach Out members? Denver has five that come to Plains pretty often: Nestor, Kucera, Mushti, Stephens and Davies."

"Give me those names again," he switched his com unit to note mode. "I need an address on Kucera."

She was still rattling them off when the doorbell chimed.

"Got to go," Jasper said and abruptly ended the call. He reached the door just as it chimed again. As he expected, it was his new mentor.

Roy Carlson was in his fifties with thick black hair just starting to gray at his temples. He'd chosen to look casual for this meeting in a hotel known for a touch of elegance at an affordable price. His blue polo shirt and khaki pants were nondescript enough he could blend in to any group.

"Jazz," he said and made his way in, setting a small computer case on the sink counter. "How's your case going? I saw you'd put out an APB."

"I'm pretty sure he's the one," Jasper said. "No motive yet but we've got evidence."

"So how long do you think it'll be?" Carlson asked. "Until you're ours?"

"I'm officially on detached duty but I expect to be off the force entirely by Wednesday," Jasper said. "First interview as Sensor Man on Friday."

"That will work," Carlson said and opened his case. "We can't get everything done today but I can get everything I need to get you certified. Have you thought up a code name? It has to be totally unrelated to you. I'd ask the department but they come up with the worst names."

"Wolfgang von Blitzen." That got him an odd look.

"Can I ask why?" Carlson said as his fingers moved over his keyboard. "German?"

"Well, I'm not German. That's one thing. Wolfgang is for Mozart. That's the only music connection. Blitzen, well, I've been told I was born during a snowstorm. It wasn't much of one but still snow fell. I also liked the connection to Blitzkrieg and just plain old Blitz."

"Not the reindeer huh? Ok, Blitzen it is. Wolfgang von Blitzen," he corrected. "Now I'm going to enter it in official files the short form is Wolfgang. If anyone calls you that, know it's a leak. Those authorized to meet you will call you Blitz."

"Suits me. We might have just got a break, by the way." He told him about the connections between Reach Out, the missing tablecloths, and the Wests. "I've already started making overtures to Reach Out. They're interested in Sensor Man. I think I can use that and a hefty donation to get inside."

"Good." Carlson hesitated. "Reach Out? That's on our radar."

"It is?" Jasper's pulse jumped. "Why?"

"It's a national organization," Carlson said. "And it's got way too many members connected to pharmaceuticals--and a lot of millionaires. It's a very rich group. I know they're dedicated to helping children get better education but it's still too interesting not to watch. Keep me posted on anything you find out."

Carlson turned back to his computer and typed something more. "Ok, now I need your hand prints. Left hand first."

Jasper set down his coffee cup and placed his hand on the digital screen then the other hand. "Eye scan too?"

"No. You have that on file in police records. I just want to embed these in your ID." Carlson jabbed a few more keys. "Ready. This is a microchip ID. You were told about that?"

"Yes." Jasper felt for the chain he always wore around his

neck. "I have the right place for it. This locket is shielded on front and sides." He unfastened the silver chain and showed him the piece with its eight-pointed star on a black enameled background. On the back was a picture of Carol. He took out a penknife and pried the cover off then carefully removed the picture. There was a slight cavity beneath it.

"That will work," Carlson said. Taking the locket, he used a pair of tweezers to lift the tiny blue microchip he'd been working on. Less than a sixteenth of an inch wide and only an eighth inch long, it was similar to what they tagged animals with. This one though held his official credentials if he should ever need them. It was readable by a variety of scanners but only from the back of the locket.

"Nice," Carlson said as he put the picture back in place and snapped the cover on. "And something Sensor Man would wear--and Jasper Stone. I assume she was your wife?"

"Yes," Jasper said as he refastened the chain. "I've worn it since before she died. Her last gift." He had found it hard to put on at first because he knew she was saying goodbye but now he wouldn't part with it.

"Sure it won't flip?"

"Not on its own. The design doesn't allow it." That had been one of his concerns too but Carol had shown him the wide oval connector the chain fed through. Unless he turned it deliberately, the star would always be out.

"Interesting," Carlson said. "Well, I'll take your word for it. Here's your contact number in Plains and mine in Denver. I don't recommend staying here when you're Sensor Man," he said with a glance around the common hotel room. "It wouldn't fit your image. We'll have to arrange something else later."

"I have no home just now," Jasper said. "Any preferences on where you want me?"

"Just some place secure," Carlson said. "And suitable for a star musician. Since you're bearing the everyday living expenses, stay within your budget. If you break the case, all expenses will be met. I think we agreed salary would be paid through your publisher?"

"That's the least suspicious way of doing it," Jasper said. "I've set it up with him. If he forwards it to me quarterly, it will look like just another royalty check."

"Noted. Well, you are now a deep cover agent for the DEA. Let's hope you have a hell of a lot more success than the others."

Jasper shook his hand and held the door open for him to leave. That was done.

Chapter 32 – Lunarex Tower

Getting back into Lunarex Tower was as difficult as he expected. Mindful of David's warning not to reveal his police status, he had to wait while they called up David. He or another resident would have to escort him. While he waited, he became all too aware that people now knew who he was.

The security man was apologetic about the wait but it was regulations. Not even someone they knew could get in without the physical presence of a resident or a staff escort.

Jasper was aware of onlookers but that caught his attention. "Not anyone? Not even maintenance?"

"That's right," the guard said. "Mostly they use the people who have been vetted and employed by the tower but if it's someone who hasn't, they have to be escorted. We can't allow operations to stop because someone didn't follow the rules. It could cost millions."

"Right," Jasper said. So no one could get to David without him knowing it. No one could slip into his apartment and poison his scotch. Suddenly he understood why David would want Jewel here. "Is Jake West an official resident?" he casually asked. "That would be David's son."

"I think he is. Usually the children of company personnel are included--after proper vetting of course." The security guard checked his computer. "Yes, he is. There's a flag on him though. We're to notify his father if he arrives."

"Typical?" Jasper smiled.

"Parents," he said. "They lose track of their kids and want to know when they get home and who with."

"So have you ever met Jake West?" Jasper asked, wondering why he would say that of a man in his late twenties.

"Not that I can recall," the guard said. "But we have over a thousand people living here and another four hundred support staff come and go."

"I knew the Tower was large," Jasper said. "But that's pretty impressive for a stand alone structure."

"Well, it's residential, commercial, and industrial," the guard said. "Triple use. Higher population." He shrugged it off. "Excuse me, Mr. Stone. If you'll just have a seat," he said waving a couple of teens forward for security check.

"Are you really Sensor Man?" A teen girl asked and Jasper realized they weren't there to check in. He stepped into the waiting area, the teens following when he beckoned them.

"Yes, I am," he said, admitting it for the first time to fans. "Got something for me to sign?"

"Oh, yes." She whipped out the souvenir cover for his new album and a pen.

"Let me make sure they got it right." He turned the cover over and went briefly down the list of songs. All there. The front didn't have his name, of course. His cover would have been blown weeks ago if they had.

"This one is going to be a collector's item, I think," he said as he signed and dated it with the month and year. "In September there will be a new release with my name actually on it and this cover will get pulled. Keep it safe."

"Oh, I will," the teenager said in a breathless voice. "Thank you, Mr. Stone."

God, had he ever been that young?

The first teen stepped back and let her friend in and he repeated the procedure. It felt funny doing it. He used to have nightmares about being mobbed when he was in college and hadn't liked it so he'd kept his identity secret. Now the reality was far different. Maybe it was because he was a cop. Maybe it was because he was no teenager. He didn't know.

Two more teens had appeared from somewhere, he didn't know where, and Jasper was relieved when he saw Elinor watching him sign the last souvenir. "Let's get out of here before they multiply," Jasper said.

"At least you know you're appealing to kids." She completed his sign-in and led him to the elevator, her smile disappearing as the doors closed. "David isn't taking this well. I had to recommend he take a family bereavement leave. They've taken him off shift for a week." Her lip quivered as she spoke but she didn't dissolve into tears. "I couldn't let him work. Not when I know what it's like up there."

"You did right," Jasper said.

"A distracted operator makes fool mistakes," she went on, "and breaks equipment and sometimes gets mechanics killed. David can't get it together. I couldn't let him work."

He didn't know what to say. Was she going to break down too? He was thankful when the elevator doors opened and another couple stepped in, the woman carrying a toddler.

Elinor was trying to compose herself. Searching for some way to distract her, he made a face at the toddler peering over her mother's shoulder. The brown-eyed girl stared at him with wide-eyed wonder until he crossed his eyes then she giggled. When her mother looked around, he was solemn and just another man. Elinor had seen though and it gave her a smile.

"You're shameless," Elinor whispered as they got off the elevator. "Making eyes at a toddler. I think I should warn Jewel you're a cradle robber."

"Warn Jewel?" Jasper pulled her to a stop. "Warn her against me?"

Elinor smiled. "You're all she talks about. She's upset about Jake, of course but she was really unhappy you left last night. You should have stayed. We had room."

"There were other things I had to do," Jasper said. "Follow-ups."

"I thought so," Elinor said, "but she will try to get you to stay tonight. Be warned."

Damn. So it looked like Elinor was putting them together too. How was he going to continue in this case if Jewel was involved? Could he turn it over to someone else? No, he knew he couldn't leave this case. Not only did he like the West family but there was that Reach Out connection. That was the first important lead they'd had in the Blissex case. He tried not to think how important Jewel might be to that or to him.

Entering the apartment, he got a distracted wave from David and a brief smile from Jewel before she turned away. The vid screen showed details of a bank account.

"Jake's account?" Jasper asked as he took a seat next to David. "You had the codes?"

"I always have," David said. "There were times when he overspent and I bailed him out. In return he had to let me have them so I could see he wasn't doing anything stupid."

"But he uses cash cards," Jasper said.

"For minor things, yes," David agreed. "Not hotel rooms. I was hoping I'd see where he was staying."

Jasper studied the last entries on the card. There were two about a week ago for purchase of cash cards. A third was for his train ticket back to Denver. A fourth was not specified. Fifteen hundred dollars. The vendor name was a number. The rest of the transactions were more than a week old.

"Let me record that last one," Jasper said. "It looks interesting." He took a picture with his com unit.

"It might be the lawyer," David said. "It looks like it could be."

"I'll know when we get the vendor code," Jasper said. "It will just take a minute." He stopped punching keys.

"What's wrong?" David asked.

"It's Saturday. State offices are closed. I can't get the vendor code until Monday."

"Not online?" David asked.

"Not secure enough," Jasper responded. "You know how paranoid government is."

"True," David said. "I never thought I'd wish it were different."

"It used to be," Jasper said. "Too many lives were ruined by easy access."

"They could save one today," David said, his calm exploding with such savagery that it propelled him out of his chair. "Damn it, Jasper, where could he be?" He scrubbed his face.

"We're working on it," Jasper said. "Sanders is getting the warrant. Brown is checking with hotels in Cheyenne. Do you know which one he preferred?"

"I don't think he ever stayed in Cheyenne," David said. "It was too close to home. Maybe the Hitch."

"I thought of that one," Jasper said. "They'd require his personal debit card and we just looked at that. No charges." He hesitated then continued. "You do know he's lost Mars? Maybe a lot more."

Jewel looked pale but David just shook his head. "I don't give a damn about Mars and if he's lost it, he's done it to himself. I just want him safe." He paced the floor. "And I want to know what the hell he was thinking!"

"I agree," Jasper promptly said.

David stopped pacing and turned to look at him.

"We have no motive," Jasper said. "There's nothing Jake stood to gain by doing this and he stood to lose everything he's worked for so why did he do it? And why did he warn you against Kucera?"

"You think he had something to do with this?" David demanded. "That misbegotten son of a--" He stopped, one eye on Elinor.

"I find it interesting that the only messages Jake sent you had to do with not seeing Kucera and changing lawyers," Jasper said. "But I'm not sure whether he was afraid you'd learn something from Kucera or whether he was afraid of him. What do you think?"

David rubbed his head, his anger dissipated. "I don't know. I do know that bastard has called me again. He seems really concerned about Jake and wants to know if I've seen him--and he wants to talk to me in person."

"Don't do that."

"I have no intention of seeing him." David sighed then said, "how about you? Can you see him?"

"Tried," Jasper said. "I've been told I'm out of my

jurisdiction. He'll still see me but I'll have to make an appointment with his secretary on Monday."

"Does he know who he's talking to?" David asked, his smile returning. "You could be a rich client."

"I'll never be his rich client," Jasper said. "And, no, I didn't think to use that."

"Do next time," David said. "It's one thing no other cop has got. Money--and fame--opens doors. Jessica taught me that."

"How is she? Does she know Jake's missing?"

"Not yet," David answered. "She won't accept my calls and I think we'd better wait for all of it before Jewel calls her."

"And Sasha?" He could see by their blank looks no one had thought of her. "She's his wife. He could have called her."

David reached for his com unit but Jasper was quicker. He also had Sasha under important numbers just like he did with all his current cases. He didn't throw the call on the screen immediately though. It wasn't Sasha who answered but a blond-haired boy about seven who handed the call off to a plump middle-aged woman. The room he was seeing looked to be above ground and was littered with toys, mostly colorful blocks, and featured a large comfortable couch.

"Sasha, yes, she's here. Hold on a moment." She walked over to a door and let out a holler that would have deafened him if Jasper had had the com unit to his ear.

Jewel was trying to see over his shoulder so Jasper threw the call on to the vid screen. It wasn't long before Sasha appeared but in the short interval, they'd seen two more children, both girls, one very large dog, and a white cat.

"Madhouse," Jewel said under her breath as the cat got scooped up by one of the girls and disappeared off camera.

Jasper looked sharply at her, surprised by the criticism.

"That's how Jake described it," Jewel said. "A madhouse. They're farmers. Animals everywhere and--" She shut up as Sasha dashed into the room nearly breathless.

"Ok, what?" she said then saw the screen. "Yikes, Mom!"

Jasper grinned. She was dressed but the coveralls were stained so badly he could practically smell the barn. The classy hairstyle she'd worn before was just one long blonde braid now. She dashed off camera and came back ten seconds later in a halter-top and shorts and no shoes. She didn't look old enough to vote, much less go to Mars.

"I think I'm seeing the real Sasha," Jasper said as she stood in front of her camera. "Working hard?"

"Always," she said. "Hi, Jewel. Where's Jake?"

"We were hoping you could answer that one," Jasper said. "Have you heard from him in the last forty-eight?"

Her mood completely changed. The vibrant girl became a totally serious young woman in a flash and Jasper forgot how she was dressed.

"What is this?" she asked. "Where is he?"

"When did you last hear from him?" Jasper asked.

"I got a love note from him on Wednesday. It was just the usual," she said. "Oh, and a text Thursday night. He said he'd meet me in quarantine. He was going to just chill until then."

"Could you send that one to me?" Jasper asked.

"Why? What's going on?"

"Jake is missing," Jasper said. "We're trying to locate him. He's also under suspicion of murder."

Her jaw dropped and they heard her mother's exclamation off camera.

"That can't be," Sasha insisted. "Jake loved his Uncle Mike. He was really torn up about him."

"We weren't talking Mike," Jasper said. "His grandmother. What did he say about her?"

Sasha got quiet. "I don't know what to say," she finally said. "And....damn him!" Her lip quivered then she turned away from the camera.

The room they were looking at had gone quiet except for Sasha. The children were gone and not one animal popped into view. It seemed like everything had stopped. Her mother came back into camera range to hold Sasha but they seemed to be forgotten.

Jasper waited, hoping she'd tell him more but it was a middle-aged man who finally appeared on screen. Like Sasha, he wore coveralls. He blocked their view of her and roughly demanded what had got her into tears.

Jasper explained, seeing the man's eyebrows furl as he took it all in.

"As far as I know, Jake hasn't called here in a while. I'll check into it though and get back to you. Your number?"

Jasper gave it.

"Hell of a mess, lieutenant. If the Colonial Authority gets wind of it..."

"They will get wind of it, sir. We have proof Jake West was there at Plains when the murder took place and he covered it up like a pro. Once he's found, he'll be charged."

The man glanced behind him.

"I'll find out what my daughter knows. And I will swear on a stack of Bibles she was here working with me on Monday." He looked fierce. "She had nothing to do with it."

"Understood," Jasper said. "She's not under suspicion."

"Damn kid just had to ruin his life." He snorted. "Thought he was better than that."

He ended the call.

"She could lose her place too," Jewel said in a low voice. "They could reject her. I didn't think about that."

"None of us thought about that," David said, "and she deserves better."

"I thought you didn't think much of her," Jasper said.

"We didn't. Jake married her because he had to be married to get on the list. Barbaric requirement and always has been," David said. "Seems she cares for him though." His voice was softer. "Damn, I wish this hadn't happened."

Jasper agreed.

It was Elinor who broke the uneasy silence. "We need to eat," she said. "All of us. David, I think Jewel and the lieutenant can pick us up some Italian downstairs. Mario's is open and they've got lasagna. I want some salad too."

"I can go out?" Jewel asked.

"With the lieutenant," Elinor said. "But I want you both back here in an hour."

Jewel rolled her eyes.

"Don't sass me, Jewel. Until you're married, I'm the oldest bitch in this house."

"You'll still be oldest," Jewel said then grinned and ducked behind Jasper as Elinor stalked toward them.

David grabbed his fiancé by one arm and pulled her close, his dark mood lifting. "Go get us some Italian. They only fight when they're hungry. Jewel can pay."

"Like hell she can," Jasper said but he was willing to escape. He could only take so much of the somber mood.

Jewel's mood shifted again as soon as they were out of sight of the apartment. She clung to him in the elevator and his arms encircled her, one hand in the small of her back. He just held her, knowing she just needed comfort but acutely aware of her proximity and a faint smell of flowers. When she finally looked up, her eyes were dry.

"I still don't believe he did it," she said. "Not Jake. He'd never hurt family."

"The car."

"The hell with the car," she said and pulled away. "I should never have said anything about it. Jake couldn't do it. He, he never did anything."

"He got on the Mars colony list," Jasper said.

"Big deal," she responded, her tone angry. "I bet it was his money got him on."

"I hadn't thought of that," Jasper said. "You think they selected him because of his family money? You can't tell me Sasha has money. She wouldn't be mucking around in barns if she did."

Jewel shook her head but her full lips twitched. "I don't think I'll ever forget that."

"You wouldn't."

"Well, I didn't like her when Jake brought her home to meet the family. She was so formal. Now she seems human."

"She was probably scared stiff of meeting a family worth more than the entire population of her town," Jasper said.

Jewel looked thoughtful. "Yeah, I guess we can be frightening. We didn't try to be though. It's just that Jake had to marry someone. He couldn't wait for the right one."

"Like you are?" Jasper asked then mentally kicked himself.

Her reaction was not what he expected. She gave him a sharp look and her cheeks turned pink. When the elevator doors opened and another couple stepped in, she buried her face in his shoulder. Automatically, he held her.

She was just the right height, a little taller than Carol. His arms fit around her slender frame and he liked the feel of her. Her breasts were not too small and not too big but just right for her and they felt firm as they pressed into him. Natural too. When Jewel looked up at him with those big blue eyes, he bent his head.

Her lips molded to his, parting under the pressure of his kiss. It wasn't a deep kiss and he ended it quickly, appalled he'd done it. She hadn't pulled away but still this was not the time and place. She was too vulnerable right now.

She sure as hell didn't look vulnerable when they parted though. Giving him a wicked smile, she murmured. "You take too long. I wanted that days ago."

"Hussy," he said without heat.

She laughed then hastily slipped out of his embrace as the woman looked at them. Her husband just smiled and put his arm around his wife. When the elevator came to a stop, the couple hurried off.

"Go up again?" Jewel suggested and tried to slip into his arms again.

He shook his head and pulled her off the car. "I'm not safe with you," Jasper said. "Let's get that Italian."

Chapter 33 - Jake

Dinner was almost pleasant. They'd brought back lasagna, salad, garlic bread, and a recommended bottle of wine from the upper scale Mario's. Jasper had almost passed on the wine but Jewel persuaded him to take half a glass. The shameless hussy had asked her uncle if there were security cameras in the elevators when he resisted.

He was going to have to watch out with her he decided as he sipped the excellent wine. Now that he'd slipped up, she wasn't going to play fair. Of course, he'd never known a woman who really did. Carol would have liked her and her tactics.

Carol. He realized he was starting to compare Jewel West to her. He drew in his lips thoughtfully, his eyes half closed as he thought about Carol and this sweet young woman--never a girl--and what Carol would have thought of her. The thought made him pensive.

"Stop that," Jewel said and nudged him. "No dark thoughts at the table. I'm not kidding."

"Is she always this bossy?" he asked, fighting the urge to smile. One kiss and this minx was trying to run his life. He was still a cop assigned to their case and he wasn't about to let it happen--not now.

"Only when she's hungry," David said, his attention still on his plate. "Got to keep women from wanting."

"Stop that." Elinor glared at him and Jasper got the inkling David weren't referring to food. What the hell?

"What?" David looked innocent but he winked at Jasper.

Jasper gulped, certain now of what he meant. Of course they had cameras in elevators but did David have access to those? Or had Jewel told him? How deep was he into this? Damn, this could be serious trouble.

Jewel's color was high and she was paying a lot more attention to her meal so she hadn't missed it either. Did she think David wanted them together? Obviously. Hell, he'd been checking into him for days.

His com unit buzzed and he answered it with a sense of relief. He almost threw it on the vid screen before he saw the private flag and recognized Brown.

"I've got a message for you," she said and Jasper hurriedly put the com unit to his ear, his dinner forgotten.

"Repeat please."

"I've got a message for you," Brown said. "Secure?"

"Just a moment." Jasper stood up, walking to the far end of the living room. "Where is he?" That code phrase told him it wasn't good.

"Cheyenne morgue. He came in as a John Doe around midnight. No ID."

"Where was he found?" Jasper asked.

"Inside a com booth at the old post office. He'd been there for hours."

"We'll come to Cheyenne," Jasper said and noticed David had left the table and was standing a few feet away, watching him.

"Not them," Brown quickly said. "Jasper, this was a professional hit. It wasn't suicide. Someone is still out there and the rest of the family could be next."

"Right." Jasper was glum as he looked at David. He was going to have to tell him. "I'll come alone. Keep me posted."

"Will do."

He ended the call and turned to find they were all there. By their expressions, they'd heard enough. "Jake's dead," he said. "I have to go to Cheyenne."

"Suicide?" David asked.

"No." Jasper was blunt. "Brown says it was a professional hit. I'm sorry you can't come. I'll get Jake's body transferred to Denver as soon as I can."

David stopped listening, collapsing into the nearest chair, Elinor beside him. Jewel reappeared with another glass of wine and pressed it into her uncle's hands.

Damn, he had to leave them like this.

* * *

The trip to Cheyenne was uneventful. He'd caught a cab from Lunarex Tower to the station and caught the first train heading to Cheyenne. It had no VIP car so he settled into second class. The seats were roomy enough but there were people all about him and it was a far cry from the luxury of the stateroom. There were no power hookups. Since the train traveled for most of the distance underground, he had nothing to look at except for a couple of stations. He couldn't even call Brown for more up to date information.

God, they'd be calling Jessica now and Sasha would have to be told she was going to Mars as a widow. He wondered if she would go. Probably. He would have to make it clear to the Colonial Authority she wasn't a suspect. Hell, he'd like to get the whole West clan off the planet.

He'd fallen for more than just Jewel, he knew. His objectivity was totally gone. He liked them all--even Jake--and that was dangerous to a cop. He'd gotten far too close to them. When had it happened? They were like family.

He stared out the darkened window and tried to think. Was he going to end up with Jewel? How would that affect his work for DEA? Could he protect her and still do a good job? At the same time he needed her. She had connections to Reach Out and that house--his pulse quickened. That house would lure any drug smugglers close to him. The uncontrolled access was an incredible asset--he'd known that from the beginning but now he looked at the house again as more than just bait. It had perfect acoustics and he could do something with that. It was a house that Sensor Man would have.

"Damn," he said. "Perfect." His seatmate looked at him curiously and he shut up.

Jewel. He could have her, have the house, and have the connections but he doubted he could call it in the line of duty.

If he married her, he'd have to mean it--and he would. How the hell was he going to protect her?

It would definitely put an end to his law enforcement career. The plan had been to use his new album and the notoriety it caused as the reason for him being forced to leave the Plains PD--and they wanted to make it a less than voluntary decision. They'd known all along that was weak but hadn't been able to come up with something better. Now-- well, if he got involved with a suspect or even a woman he was assigned to protect, that would be just cause for termination. Hell, he'd deserve it.

As the train glided into the Cheyenne station, he pulled himself together. There was nothing he could do right now. He had to concentrate on Jake.

"You look like hell," Brown said when she met him at the station.

"I feel like hell," Jasper said. "I think I've lost it."

She didn't answer until they were in the squad car. "You haven't lost it," she said, "but I think this one is under your skin. Jewel, right?"

"No, it's the whole family. I'm getting too close," Jasper said. "And the hell of it is I want to get closer."

"Ok, you've lost it," Brown said. "It's good you'll be off the force."

Jasper shot her a look but she wasn't smiling. "How bad is it?"

"Clean kill," she said. "So clean they almost didn't catch it. He came in as a John Doe and it looked like heart failure. When they ran his prints, they found out who he was and the APB."

She hesitated. "They had just found the puncture wound when I left. It was curare. The assassin must have got him into a com booth first then injected him. Curare kills too fast for it to be any other way. No ID and no com unit. The man was thorough."

"Where was the puncture wound?" Jasper asked.

"Behind the right arm and down a bit," Brown said. "It's not possible to self inject there."

She paused. "The pathologist said it was a pretty odd place to inject. There's no major blood vessels and the curare would have taken longer to work."

"Curare paralyzes," Jasper said. "When it stops the lungs, you suffocate." He wished he'd never learned that. Carol hadn't been conscious when she got it but he had watched her last struggling breath before it killed her. "It must have been hell for Jake to just sit there and wait for it."

"Yeah, don't think about it," Brown said. "If he killed his grandmother, he deserved it."

Brown pulled the car into a curb and Jasper saw they were still above ground. The antiquated state capitol building lay in front of them, its golden dome shining in the afternoon light.

"He was up here?" Jasper asked, trying to ignore the hot humid air that hit him when he left the car.

"Right--in the historical district. It would be pretty odd except there are also a dozen law firms here and a post office. That's where he was found."

Jasper studied the imposing facade of the post office. Like the Capitol, it was stone but it wasn't nearly as old. Set back from the road, it stood about four stories tall.

"Only the first floor is post office," she said as they walked in. "There's a lot of law offices upstairs and a small bank through there. They have everything except a restaurant in here."

The blue and yellow com booths sat near the door, the first one with yellow police tape across it. The building seemed to be deserted and he guessed it didn't get used on Saturdays with the offices being closed.

"So do you think he went to one of the law offices upstairs then down here?" Jasper asked. "Did he mail something?"

"Yes. The reason the police found him so fast is someone tried to break into the mail drop. They didn't succeed. It wouldn't have done them any good anyway since the system is fully automated here. The package was probably in a crate for shipment within minutes."

"Have they looked for it?"

"No, it takes a court order to stop the mail. Since they don't know where it was headed, they haven't tried." Brown looked disgusted. "We can't claim it was a bomb so they won't cooperate."

"But they know when the break-in happened. Any footage?"

"Yes." She pulled out her com unit and punched a few buttons before handing it to him. Jasper saw a small image of a man in a ball cap walk over to the mail drop with a cheap grabber and watched as he fished the grabber down the slot and an alarm went off. The man fled, leaving the grabber behind.

"That's all?" Jasper asked.

"No." She took back her com unit and pushed some more buttons. "When they responded to the theft alarm, one of the cops noticed the com booth was busy. He checked it out and it was sealed so he unsealed it with a police override. They didn't know if the guy had actually left or just ducked into it. They found Jake instead."

"Surprising," Jasper said. He could imagine the shock of the police officers on the scene. People did die and a hefty percentage were found by police but in connection with an attempted robbery?

"They got a figure on how long the booth had been occupied and checked the footage for that too. They wanted to know if he was alone, I guess. They got this."

Jasper studied the footage closely, wishing he had a bigger screen. It showed Jake West exiting the elevator, quickly walking over to the mail slot, and dropping not one but several packages in. Before he stepped away another man walked into the picture and grabbed him by the arm, twisted it behind his back, and started marching him to the com booths.

"I'm going to enjoy putting you out, shit brains," the hit man said. "You made me kill her."

What Jake said was inaudible but clearly scared. The terror on his face changed to something--resignation?--as the man shoved him into the com booth. Jasper hit the pause button as the killer turned, freezing it on his face. He was wearing some sort of stealth mask to fool the camera but he got a clear view of the guy's eyes and the shape of his mouth.

"I've seen him," Jasper said. "At the West funeral. He was by the door."

"You're kidding." Brown studied the image. "I missed him. What was a pro doing there?"

"I don't know," Jasper said, "but he clearly wanted to do Jake." He watched the rest of the vid with a sick feeling. He couldn't see into the com booth but he did see the man back out about three minutes later without Jake. The adhesive stealth mask effectively hid everything about his face except those eyes and his mouth. Highly illegal, the patterning was on every level the camera could see down to frequencies human eyes couldn't. A camera simply couldn't get past that technology. If he hadn't seen the guy at Elizabeth's funeral, he wouldn't have been able to pick him out.

"His MO is poison. Professional hitman. We need an ID," Jasper said.

"They're working on it," Brown said. "Cheyenne has claimed jurisdiction. I'm being informed but they won't let me in."

"We'll fix that," Jasper said.

"Tried," Brown said. "We'll get a decision on Monday."

"Damn, no cooperation at all?" Jasper looked at her.

"They were cooperating till they found out who Jake was. Now it's a high profile murder involving millions and a professional hit man. They want credit."

"Screw them," Jasper muttered. "I want the hit man and who's behind him."

"Me too," Brown said. "Where's the girl now?"

"I left her in Denver. She's locked up in Lunarex Tower with her uncle standing guard," Jasper said. "She's not going anywhere till I collect her."

Brown smiled. "The fair princess? Are you the knight?"

He glared at her. "I told you I'd lost it."

She laughed and his frown got deeper.

"Carol would love it," she said and put a hand on his arm. "Jasper, you've been alone too long. Let it happen."

"When I know she's safe," Jasper said. "Not now."

Brown sobered. "Ok, what do we do next, partner?"

He surveyed the scene then walked over to the building directory. Touching the word Law, he changed it to display the names of legal offices in the building then snapped a couple of shots with his com unit.

"Follow up on those?" Brown said. She copied his actions.

"Yes. It might be Monday before we can start but we have that." Jasper studied the directory again but no name jumped out at him. Who would Jake choose? Did the Wests know any of these guys? He'd have to ask.

"I'd better go back to Denver," he said. "Can you try to match our hit man with transit records? If he was here on Friday, he probably left Plains shortly after Jake did."

Brown nodded. "Sanders can help. There's lots of video."

"No, wait," Jasper said. "I saw him at the funeral and Jake left two hours later. Maybe we can pin it down. There's an early morning train, a ten o'clock, the noon train, one at three o'clock, and the next at five thirty and the last at seven. Jake took the five thirty. Check the one at three and the one at five thirty."

"Will do," Brown said. "Let me give you a lift back to the station. You might make the next train."

"Copy me those files first," Jasper said. He had to go back. He couldn't leave David or Jewel waiting to hear. This was hard enough on them without that.

Chapter 34 – Fish Eggs

Jasper called from the train station and wasn't too surprised to find David himself waiting at the security station of the tower. Check-in was quicker and Jasper was grateful for that. He wanted to get this over with.

"The girls can wait," David said and took the elevator up to a different floor. "We're going to talk." His firm tone brooked no argument.

Jasper wasn't ready to give him one. It was late and he needed a drink. The small bar David took him to had shielded booths and an automated serving system. He preferred the human touch but not tonight. It was better to have no ears for this conversation.

"How are you doing?" Jasper asked. "And can you handle it?"

"Yes," David responded. "I'm over the shock. I can't do a damned thing for Jake but I can help you get his killer." His tone was savage.

He ordered their drinks then sat back and looked at Jasper. "How did he die and were there any witnesses?"

"No witnesses except security cam. I've seen it."

"Show me," David ordered.

"No sir." Jasper was just as firm. "I'll tell you what's on it but it will take a court order for me to show it to you. It's not pretty."

They locked stares but it wasn't long before David's eyes shifted. "You got guts, Sensor Man," he finally said. "Tell me."

Jasper described the scene, only omitting the look of terror on Jake's face and how the curare had been deliberately mis-injected to prolong his death. David was shaking when he was done but he just ordered another drink.

"So who was this hit man? Who does he work for? He sure as hell didn't work for Jake," David said. "I want him and his boss too."

"We're working on it," Jasper said. "But at this point we have to assume your whole family is targeted."

"They can't get me unless I let them," David said. "And Elinor is officially a resident of the tower since yesterday. She's not going back to Plains except for the wedding."

"What about Jewel?" Jasper asked.

"Can't convince her," David said and finished his drink.

"Can't you order her?" Jasper asked then knew how stupid that was. This wasn't the Middle Ages and David wasn't even her father. "Forget that. Stupid idea." He ordered himself another drink.

"Yup, stupid. She needs a tower of her own," David said. "Can't keep her here unless she wants to be kept. Elinor would probably kill her in a week anyway. I can't keep them apart."

"They seem to be getting along for now," Jasper said.

"It won't last," David responded. "I give it about an hour after the funeral. We can have one, can't we?"

"I'd keep it small and have it here but yes," Jasper said. "The body is still evidence but we'll get it released as soon as we can."

"I need to see him before he's cremated," David said in a ragged voice, "just to say goodbye." The hand around the glass was white-knuckled and Jasper knew he was still struggling for control.

Jasper knew seeing him was necessary. God that was going to be hard on more than just David. Such a waste.

"What's going to be said about him?" David asked after finishing another drink. "Is this going to be public?"

Jasper considered it then shook his head. "His death was homicide and he was a victim. That's all the public statement can say."

"But Mother..."

"We can put him at Plains and we know he lied about being there but we can't definitely put him inside the house. Since we can't and he wasn't formally charged..." Jasper knew the department might see it another way but technically he was right. "You can sue anyone who claims he was a murderer--including the department."

David's sigh of relief was palpable. He scrubbed his face and shoved his fourth drink away. "That's what I needed to hear. Worst thing." He rubbed his eyes. "God, I think I had one too many."

Jasper laughed. He hadn't tried to match him but he also hadn't eaten since the Italian food eight hours ago. He was feeling it but it had been good scotch.

"Damn, Elinor is going to like this," David said. "Think we should just stay here till it wears off?"

Jasper tried shaking his head but David was already ordering coffee and some potato skins. Jasper put in a second order for ice water and cheese sticks. They waited in companionable silence till the table opened and the dishes rose to the surface. Their last drinks sat untouched.

"Damn, I like you," Jasper finally said and knew he'd had too much too fast.

David blinked then gave him a sloppy grin. "I like you too," he said, "but we've got to talk about Jewel."

"I like her too," Jasper said then gulped some ice water.

David's eyes crinkled and his grin got wider. "And Elinor?"

"You can have her," Jasper said and David burst out laughing.

Jasper laughed too but his mind had gone fuzzy. Damn, that was good scotch. He forced himself to eat the greasy appetizers. It wasn't until he was on his third potato skin he identified the black stuff on top just under the sour cream. "Caviar? On potato skins?"

"What's the matter? Don't like fish eggs?" David chuckled before taking another for himself.

Jasper shook his head then stopped as things threatened to move. "Just didn't expect them," he said. "Better on skins than crackers." He was reminded again how rich the Wests' were. Could he get used to caviar on potato skins?

"I have to be drunk to order these," David said as he took another one. "Fish eggs. My father would think I was insane. He hated them and their price. This is the only way I like them."

"How about Jewel?" Jasper asked.

"Oh, she'd laugh in your face if you suggested buying them. Don't worry," David said. "Jewel is an excellent cook but she's not fancy. She won't make you eat truffles and fish eggs."

"Good." Jasper grabbed a cheese stick. His head was starting to clear with the help of the ice water and appetizers.

"Skipped supper huh?" David said. "No wonder that scotch hit you so hard."

"Some days are like that," Jasper said, shrugging it off. "Damned good scotch though."

"Only the best," David replied. "Now about Jewel. It would solve my problem and yours if you just said yes."

"Your problem?" Jasper asked, confused.

"I can't keep her here and I sure as hell can't move back to Plains," David carefully said. "And you need her."

"Are you trying to get her married off?" Jasper abruptly asked and got a bark of laughter. "You know she's got to want to." Was he really having this conversation?

"Hell, she's been panting after you like a bitch in heat," David said then scowled at him. "Do you want her?"

"I think you're making a mistake," Jasper said and his voice was almost even. "You've known me less than a week. I'm also going to be an unemployed ex-cop very shortly. You know how many enemies I might have? I've worked vice for twelve years and homicide for eight."

David seemed almost sober now. "Jewel is the one who needs protection. You can have your choice of Lily Street or Gracee Place. No, take them both. I don't want to deal with them."

Jasper frowned, his head suddenly clear and his appetite gone as he realized David was quite serious. "You don't understand. I could have people coming after me."

"So? She's got people after her. You're better equipped to deal with this than any man I've met and I want you beside her." He studied him with pale blue eyes then added, "if you're worried about spending her damned money, don't be. It's impossible. You won't ever have control of it and, even if you did, you'd have to build your own space station to get rid of it. There's just too much of the blasted stuff."

Jasper's lips twitched. "You make it sound like a curse."

"Oh, it is. The best thing you can do with that kind of money is give it away." David picked up his discarded drink then firmly set it down and picked up his coffee instead. He looked and sounded sober now. "I can handle my own salary. Elinor can handle hers. I haven't touched my share of the Foundation money in years except to invest it or give it away." His blue eyes clouded and he cradled the cup in his hand. "Damn, I wish I'd given it to Jake."

"You think this was tied into his sponsorship?" Jasper asked, glad to be off the topic of Jewel.

"I don't know," David said, his eyes on his cup. "I know he didn't get it confirmed until after Mother did the walk. It was Kucera who got it for him." His eyes met Jasper's. "That was when he switched lawyers too."

"Got it," Jasper said, his wits back to normal "I'll get on that. So was he with the family lawyer until then?"

"No, no, he had another one in Chicago--Jessica's lawyer. He switched from him to Kucera. Jewel and Mike have—had the same law firm. Mother's been without for a couple of years. She outlived two and didn't want a third. She claimed she knew more about estate law than the up-and-comers anyway."

"I think I should see Kucera," David said with sudden decision. "He'll have the answers to all this."

"It could also give him an opportunity to kill you," Jasper responded. "That may be what he wants. As you pointed out, you're safe here. If he wants to see you in his office, I wouldn't go."

"Good point," David said. "Both text messages I've gotten have suggested an appointment there. The phone calls we didn't get that far."

"Then hold off on meeting him," Jasper said. "This is the seventeenth. If we haven't got this solved by the thirtieth, maybe a meeting. I want to be with you."

"Right. As Jewel's fiancé, I hope." David's smile was grim and he seemed confident.

"Determined, aren't you?" Jasper said with an answering smile but he was no less determined to put this off.

"You do know she's not as helpless as she's been acting?" David suddenly said. "She's twenty-seven."

"Yes, I know." Jasper didn't know when he'd figured that out but Jewel wasn't a shy young miss. She hadn't even tried that act until… was it the dinner at the Grand? "I've been chased before."

He paused to consider it and knew David was right. Jewel definitely wanted him. "I'm not going to say anything to her until this is over."

"Fair enough," David said then glanced at the remains of their impromptu meal. "We're going to catch hell for making them wait. Want some more anesthesia to dull the pain?"

Jasper just shook his head. "I'd better get used to it." He knew he'd committed himself in spite of his words but it wasn't a firm commitment. Depending on how the investigation ran, David might change his mind--or Jewel would. If not, well, he knew he was attracted to her and David's arguments had made sense.

Chapter 35 - Sunday

Jasper walked off the train in Plains with his cheek pads once again in place and a privacy cloak over one arm. His suitcase and makeup case he'd left with Jewel, knowing he'd have to be back in Denver at the end of the day. First, the precinct.

Wishing he could just report back to Section 5, he knew it would be stupid. The reporters were gone from his house but they might not have given up on the precinct. Besides, headquarters for this case was still Section 3. He found the right tram and boarded it, knowing it would drop him off less than a block from the precinct at the center of Section 3.

He'd warned Brown he was coming and she was busy getting the rest of the team to come in on a Sunday morning. Some would be reluctant, he was sure but this was also their biggest case. They'd be there or face being shut out of other such cases. They'd have down time later.

The shopping area around the precinct was nearly deserted at this early Sunday hour since those businesses that opened on Sundays, with the exception of the restaurants, wouldn't open until noon. He could smell some of the food as he walked from the elevator to the precinct and it smelled good, much better than the egg sandwich he'd had in the Cheyenne station. After this meeting, he'd try to find a decent meal.

Brown met him at the door, looking too rested and cheerful to suit him. "How did you get away?" she asked.

"Took the 4am train to Cheyenne then waited for the 6am to here. Did you know the Plains train doesn't have staterooms then?"

"Staterooms?"

"Yeah, I'm Sensor Man."

She laughed at his sour tone. "He admits it!"

"Not so loud," he said. "Not so early."

"Not so crabby," she jibed. "Ok, you're short on sleep and low on coffee. I can see that. The team is in Conference 3. I got us real coffee because it's Sunday."

"Good. Rolls too?"

"Yes. You're paying."

"Fine, I might order lunch too." Jasper hesitated. "Any unhappy spouses?"

"Sanders' wife. She wants the case done with. This morning I don't think she's your fan."

"Who are you going to poke fun at when I'm gone?" Jasper demanded.

Lori grinned. "Hey, I've been saving it up for years. I get less than a week to use it all." She punched the elevator button for him.

"Torture," Jasper said then got serious. "I want this case done with too. As soon as we get the hit man and his employer, we're done."

"Any theories on who that is?"

"One." He yawned. God, he was tired. He hadn't slept on the Cheyenne train at all. He'd bought a privacy cloak--a blanket and hood combination people wore when they had to sleep on trains but still hadn't managed more than a doze. He was all too aware there was a hit man out there and he might make his list. Even being assigned to the West case could be hazardous to his health. If it got known he might join the family, it definitely would be.

God, he'd be glad when this case was over. He just wanted some time with a keyboard and his music but he wasn't likely to get it any time soon. The movers had finally cleared out his house and everything was in storage but now he'd have to get it delivered to Lily Street.

He smiled ruefully. The only thing that had diverted Jewel's irritation last night was the news he'd agreed to move into Lily Street. She'd been ecstatic, even offering him the master suite. He'd tried to refuse that but David had told him to take it. Jewel was too comfortable on the second floor and that bathroom was hers. Neither one mentioned that Mike was the last to have that room. There had been no hint of romance. He was Jewel's protector--and moving into Lily Street gave Sensor Man a place to hide. Quid pro quo.

"You definitely need coffee," Brown said as they left the elevator. "Inside. It's the good stuff."

Jasper could smell it when he walked in and saw a plate of rolls and, to his delight, sandwiches. He grabbed a beef sandwich and a cup of coffee and took his place. The others hadn't been there long and were willing to give him time to eat while they enjoyed their own coffee and rolls. Sanders and Kruger were watching the video of Jake's murder.

"We've got at least two packages," Sanders said as he paused the tape. "See? Not quite the same size. And I think there's two letters too."

"I think you're right," Kruger said. "Now who do you think he would send mail too. His father, yes. His wife, probably. Maybe his old lawyer?"

"Probably. He was quick to get those in the mail slot and it was good thing too. Our hit man was waiting."

"Did the hit man show up on other surveillance footage?" Jasper asked. "Or had he kept to blind spots?"

"It's hard to say," Brown said. "Cheyenne PD didn't share that with us. Jasper, we may need to bring the FBI in. If this spreads to Colorado, we'll have to."

"I agree. Kucera lives in Denver so we'll need the FBI." He'd already thought of that possibility. "Let's see what we can get done here. As I see it, we need to find Jake's new lawyer to prove Kucera had a motive. That would allow us to bring him in for questioning. He's already refused to see me as a courtesy."

"Why do you think the hit man went back and tried to jimmy the mail slot?" Sanders asked. "I mean, why did he do it later? There's a panic button on most of those where the mailer can get it returned if he dropped it in the last thirty seconds. After that, the machine cycles and the mail gets shunted away."

"There's also an urgent button," Brown said. "See if Jake pushed it. That starts the cycle immediately."

They went over the video again and Jasper finished his sandwich. Lori absently poured him another cup of coffee as she watched the video.

"I can't tell if he did or not," Sanders said. "But the hit man didn't even check. So maybe he didn't know how important that mail was likely to be? His boss told him later?"

"That could be," Jasper agreed. "And he picked up a disguise before he went back. That suggests he'd run out of stealth masks or he didn't want to be tied to Jake on camera."

"I don't blame him. Pros don't like returning to the scene."

"Have we got any idea who he is?" Jasper asked. "Based on his MO? He likes poison."

"The Elizabeth West murder doesn't fit the pattern of the other two," Sanders pointed out.

"Actually, it does," Kruger interrupted. "Lieutenant, I have the toxicology. Elizabeth West did get some poison."

"You're kidding," Brown said. "When? And why wasn't it in the autopsy report?"

"I didn't do that," Kruger said. "And I would have missed it too since it wasn't what killed her. There were traces of cyanide on her gums and tongue--very minute amounts. She didn't ingest any of it. Apparently she tasted it and spat it out--some people can taste it."

"Yet she wasn't suspicious enough to call the cops," Brown said. "Just bad tea?"

"Could be," Kruger said. "If she drank tea regularly, she probably noticed the difference right away. Still, most would have swallowed. She didn't."

"So Jake might have tried to poison her and, when that didn't work, he clubbed her. Not planned. That would explain something else." Jasper looked at the screen. "Let's get that line the killer said to him."

Sanders forwarded the vid frame by frame until the killer

appeared. Running it from there, they watched him twist Jake's arm up behind his back and say again, "I'm going to enjoy putting you out, shit brains. You made me kill her."

"Made him kill her?" Sanders echoed. "Jake botched it and he had to do it?"

"More than that, I think." Jasper felt old. "This guy uses poisons. No blood. He's neat. That suggests he's either a woman or a homosexual. He's also very professional in what he does and Elizabeth West's murder was anything but professional."

"So he enjoys killing the guy that botched it and made him clean up," Brown said. "Yeah, I think I would too. We'd better discount her murder from his MO."

Kruger grinned. "Then I got a possibility."

"You do?" Jasper looked at him. "How?"

"The exotic poison," Kruger said. "They still don't have a name for it but it's like adenia volkensii. That's a passion flower. There's more in it but the passion flower causes drowsiness and weakness, followed by paralysis and death. No convulsions. No vomiting. It's a very neat poison and it's only shown up on the crime scene in the United States during the last four years."

"Who uses it?" Jasper asked.

"The euthanasia industry considered it years ago but passion flowers are hard to get in the right stage and they couldn't get a big enough supply to make it viable. No other commercial use."

"It's been showing up in toxicology labs though," Pedro went on. "A half dozen times. Some other suspicious deaths have been linked but not proven since cremation took place before they thought to look for it."

"Half dozen times huh?" Brown seized on that. "So probably just one hit man uses it. Have they got a name for him?"

"They've dubbed him the Executioner," Kruger said. "Strictly murder for hire. Planting poisons is his specialty. As far as I know, this murder of Jake West is the first time he's actually been there for a kill--oh, and Elizabeth West but we know that was abnormal."

"No fingerprints?" Jasper knew the answer without asking. "Can we isolate a voice print from that video?"

"Yes," Kruger said. "And if you get a warrant to tap Kucera's com lines, we might get a match if they're still in contact."

"We'll try," Jasper said. "If Kucera has any brains, he'll have multiple numbers and the one he uses for illegal activities will be buried under another name."

"If Jake's com unit shows up," Brown suggested but they all knew that was unlikely. The killer had undoubtedly disposed of it.

"What about curare? How hard is it to get that?" Jasper asked. "I know it's used by the euthanasia industry."

"It's not easy," Kruger said. "But there's a lot being transported to euthanasia sites. It's also used in medicine in a weaker form. If a shipment got lost, there'd be an investigation but that's about it."

"And cyanide?" Jasper asked.

"You can make it at home," Kruger answered. "Too common. Lots of industrial uses too. Other hit men have been known to use cyanide but curare and the exotic poison are rare. Deaths using the exotic poison are the only ones linked together and attributed to the Executioner."

"So we have a label for our hit man," Lori said, a pretty frown marking her disapproval. "A very melodramatic one. I'm going to call him Ex."

"Suits me," Jasper said. "And let's make him an ex. I want this guy before he targets any more of the West family."

"Yes sir." They sipped their coffee or nibbled on rolls while Jasper thought. "What else have we got? Is there anyone interested in Lily Street or Gracee Place?"

"Gracee Place, they wanted to send in a cleaning crew to get rid of any smell," Sanders said. "Section 2 allowed it. Since we released it as a crime scene, they didn't see any harm. A realtor is also interested in listing it but wasn't sure it was wise to contact the Wests directly. I told her to lay off for at least a month."

"Good. I want to go over it again after I'm done with the force and make sure nothing else is poisoned. I'll do the same with Lily Street although it looks like no one has gotten in there."

"Wrong," Brown said.

"Wrong?" Jasper asked, looking at her for an explanation.

"We don't know how long our killer took to clean the scene or what he brought with him. There could be a bottle of liquor, a jar of mayonnaise or a bottle of ketchup with poison in it. There might even be a contact poison in some soap. I admit the contact poison is reaching but the next target would have been Jewel. I looked in her bathroom and she's got a wide range of soaps and lotions. Those will have to go."

"You're right. Hell, she even brought some into protective custody." Jasper thought about it then decided not to worry about it. "Well, the ones she has with her seem to be ok. She hasn't turned into a raging lunatic or broken out in rashes. I'll get the others out of there."

"So are you moving into Lily Place?" Sanders asked. "To protect her, I mean." He turned bright red and Jasper had to struggle not to smile. Lori didn't bother to hide hers.

"Yes, it's been agreed that my next job is protecting her," Jasper said. "And hers is protecting me from the press. Until I find a permanent place suitable for a star musician, it will do."

"There couldn't be a better place in Plains," Brown said. "Have you fallen in love with that view of the peak?"

"I may not want to be in the city," Jasper said. "I'll look at ranches."

"Ha," Lori responded.

She knew him too well. He had little experience outside of cities. Having access to all the cities had to offer mattered to him and he really liked the controlled temperatures of the undergrounds. Well, he could change--other artists had. Living away from cities meant privacy. Living on a ranch or farm meant you had privacy when you wanted it and company when you didn't. You just couldn't order out or go to the latest concerts. He'd think on it.

"Oh, unrelated question," Jasper said, changing the subject. "Nothing to do with the case. Have any of you noticed subbies wearing green scarves?" Remembering his deal with Mel, he was curious if anything had happened.

Sanders and Brown looked blank but Kruger smiled. "Yeah, I've seen them. I was over in Section 5 and saw a bunch of school kids wearing them. They looked like a gang."

"Any red ones?" Jasper asked.

"A couple. What's with the green?" Kruger asked.

"A bet I made with my daughter," he said. "If she gets me to notice thirty of those scarves, I owe her signed copies of the new album."

Lori laughed.

"Nice," Kruger said. "You've lost."

"I haven't seem them yet," Jasper said. "But she'll get them anyway. It's easy enough to do."

"And for us?" Kruger asked with uncommon boldness. "Sanders could use one to placate his wife."

"For you too." Jasper easily agreed. "Now that I have an address for them to be shipped to, I'll get it done."

"To Lily?" Lori asked.

"Not directly. I think I'll pick them up at the import store."

"That works," she said then quietly added. "I'm glad Mel wants your album. That's a good sign."

"Me too." He eyed the donut plate but decided he didn't want anything sweet. Water, yes. More coffee and a good hamburger steak then he wanted to get over to Lily Place.

"Good work, Pedro. If you come up with anything else, let me know. Sanders, you can go home and kiss your wife. I think Brown is following up on the lawyers. I will be too as soon as I can."

He waited until the other two had left before turning to Lori. "Can anything be done on the lawyers today?"

"I've already done quite a bit," she responded. "Some are criminal law and they wouldn't be interested in estate work. A couple specialized in land titles. There's only five who might possibly take on an estate case and one of those was out of town on an extended trip. That gives me four to actually follow up with tomorrow. As soon as I run that vendor code you gave me by the state, I should have him."

"Good."

"Oh, before you go, there's another thing. That snatcher has been asking for you."

"What snatcher?"

"Frazier. He's being charged this time. He's been screaming he wants to see you."

"Why me?" Jasper was puzzled.

"I don't know," Brown said. "Maybe he just wants your autograph but I don't think so. He won't talk to me."

"Then let me see him," Jasper said.

* * *

Fifteen minutes later he was sitting across from Willis Frazier in an interrogation room. The snatcher looked the same but his smart attitude was gone. He'd been issued an orange coverall--a clear sign they intended to keep him. It wasn't a simple snatch job this time.

"What did they get you for?" Jasper asked without preamble.

"I got caught with two blissex," Frazier said, rubbing a hand through his sandy hair. "They weren't mine. I was delivering. I was only supposed to take one but the asshole selling them gave me two by mistake."

"Tough luck," Jasper said. "That's deportation. I thought you didn't take blissex?"

"Lieutenant, they weren't mine," Willis said, his tone

insistent. "I was set up."

"Truth," the technician said in his ear. "He believes it."

"And why would anyone set you up? You're just a delivery boy."

"It's what I know," Willis said but there was no smart grin. Whatever he knew, he was serious.

"About blissex?" Jasper felt his pulse quicken. Could this be his break?

"Naw, it's what I heard," Willis waved the blissex matter away, "about murder."

"Murder?" Jasper sat up straighter. "What did you hear?"

"Not so fast," Willis said, his square jaw jutting out. "I want out of these charges. I didn't know I had two chews and I'm not going to take the rap for two chews. I'm not even going to take the rap for one chew if you want to hear what I got to say."

Jasper stared at him, hope giving way to anger. This dirt bag was holding what he knew over him. Sure, he could make such a deal but what if the information was worthless? He'd let this guy loose again in Plains for nothing.

"I've got a wife and a kid, lieutenant. They're here in Plains. I don't want to go to Newton. Have you got a kid? You drop the charges and I'll tell you what I know."

"Is it about a specific murder?" Jasper asked. "Give me a detail. Has it happened or pending?"

"Happened," Willis said. "A woman."

Jasper folded his arms. "Lots of women die. How do I know it was murder?"

"It was messy," Willis said, "and the guy wasn't happy."

Jasper stared at him. It had to be Elizabeth West. Had this snatcher met the killer? Did he know where he was? Could he get the hit man before an attempt was made on Jewel?

"When was this?" he asked.

"Nothing doing. I want the charges dropped. You can do it." Frazier folded his arms and waited. He wasn't smug but desperate to deal.

"Why did you pick me?" Jasper asked, stalling for time while he thought it through. "Why not some other cop?"

"You're a lieutenant," he said. "And I know your rep. Word is you stick by your deals."

"Not because I just hit the news?" Jasper asked, surprised.

Willis barked laughter. "That shit? Whose gonna believe that shit? The real guy is probably laughing his ass off while you get all the guff."

"Yeah, pretty good joke," Jasper said with an answering grin, wondering how long it would be before this snatcher found out he was wrong. "Ok, I'll bite. Tech, I need a record for legal."

"Recording," the technician said over the room speaker.

"In consideration for information given, I ask that charges against Willis Frazier for possession of two chews of blissex be dropped on condition he not get caught with blissex again in any amount in the next two years. If he is charged again with possession of blissex, these charges should be reinstated. Lieutenant Jasper Stone, authorization ten eighteen alpha tango, case 10833A."

"Ask huh? They gonna give it?" Willis cocked his head to one side. "Maybe you don't got the pull I thought you had."

"I can ask," Jasper said. "Recording off in there." He leaned closer to Willis. "No one can say the charges are dropped. It's not up to me and you know it so quit screwing around. If you want to stay in Plains, start talking."

He leaned back. "Recording on."

"Ok, ok. It was an old lady. A kid was supposed to whack her but he botched it. The lady was still breathing. The guy finished her by throwing her down the stairs."

"Go on," Jasper studied him. "What did this guy look like?"

"I didn't see him," Frazier said. "I just heard him. He was real mad about it. Said the kid was so green he had to clean up and he didn't like doing little old ladies."

"How could you hear but not see him?" Jasper demanded.

"Where was this?"

"In church."

"Church?" Jasper stared at him in disbelief. "You heard him in a.... church?"

Willis grinned at him. "Lieutenant, I swear it's true. It happened last Thursday. That's my regular day for picking up a little cash by cleaning the church. I was in the little room behind the confessionals sweeping up. It's not really a room, they just kind of used the confessionals to screen it off so there's no wall there."

"Anyway, these two guys climbed into the confessional. I knew the priest wasn't in there and started to say something before I started hearing this whacked conversation. The first guy says all this about the old lady and the other one tells him not to worry about it like it's no big deal. The first one said it was and he wanted to kill the kid. Loose lips and all that. The other said he still needed him for the job in Denver. After that he could do it. Really cold people talking about murder that way." Frazier stopped, his flippancy gone. "Last thing I heard was the first one saying he was going back to Denver."

"What did the other one say?" Jasper asked, keenly interested now.

"I didn't hear," Frazier said. "The priest came back and I went down to the kitchens. I couldn't stay to see what they looked like."

"Did the priest see them?" Jasper asked.

"He might have but people get in the wrong boxes all the time there. They've even got signs but folks can't read. They do some strange stuff too. You know how to tick off a priest in a confessional?"

"How?" Jasper asked.

"Ask for the toilet paper." Willis guffawed.

"Is that all you have?" Jasper asked.

"Yeah," Willis said with a serious face. "Lieutenant, I got a kid. If they send me to Newton, he'll grow up wild. I got to keep him in school."

"Frazier, you owe me," Jasper said. "I'll let the deal stand but I want you to know you owe me. If you see or hear those guys again, I want you to find me and tell me."

"Yes sir." He was dead serious now. "You think I was set up?"

"No, I don't," Jasper said. "If they never saw you, they'd have no reason to. And that hit man you overheard doesn't mess with blissex. He's called the Executioner. If he saw you, you'd be dead."

Frazier stared at him. "That guy? Shit."

Chapter 36 – Lily Street

Jasper stared out at Laramie Peak but didn't really see it as he sipped his coffee and went over the Frazier interview again in his head. There wasn't a lot there they hadn't already guessed but Ex was not happy with his employer. He'd left for Denver but that was before he turned up in Cheyenne. Had he tracked Jake? Possibly. Jake's killing was more personal than the others. He'd really ticked Ex off.

He'd sent the interview to the rest of his team. Since that had happened on Thursday, it must have been before the funeral. It was interesting they used confessionals that way but not too surprising. The Catholic Church had never allowed recording devices in them and there wasn't a church in Plains that allowed mounted cameras. Under the law, they were considered private, not public, places and no supervision was allowed. There might be street cameras. Brown would probably check that.

He set down his cup when his com link buzzed. Glancing at it, he saw it was his auburn-haired daughter. "Hi, darling. Are you here?"

"Yeah, I think so. You did say Lily Street? This place looks fancy." She swung her com link to show him the doors of Lily Street. "Is this right?"

"Yup, I'm upstairs. I'll be right down to let you in."

Damn, those stairs were going to be a problem if he had to open the door a lot. Maybe they needed a remote entry lock. He didn't want to hop up and down stairs constantly.

Mel wasn't alone. Her boyfriend of the moment stood by her, looking a bit sheepish for the intrusion. His eyes widened at seeing him but he gave no other sign he recognized him from the news.

"Hi, Dad. This is Corey," Mel said. "Corey, my dad." She breezed past him, leaving Corey in the hall.

"Wow." She turned around in the living room, taking it all

in. "Dad, are you really buying this?"

"No." He motioned to Corey. "You'd better come on in."

"Thanks." The teenager grinned.

He wasn't a bad looking kid. Mel never had gone for the ones with spiked hair and flashy body paint. This one looked a bit too normal with his short black hair and tanned skin. His only body jewelry were two earrings, one of them a cuff, on his left ear. His features were fine and waiting to be asked in was a good sign.

Mel was already up the stairs. "Wow and double wow!"

He didn't hear anything else she said so he hurried Corey up the stairs.

Mel was just standing there, staring at the view of the peak. Her auburn hair was loose today and she wore jeans and a clingy red top. Jasper caught his breath. She looked so much like her mom.

"Now this is rad. Dad, you got to buy it."

He laughed then said, "it's not for sale." It was nice to know she approved.

She looked at him and waited for more. Corey though was going over the rest of the room.

"Great room," he said. "Are you going to make a studio out of it? It sounds good." He clapped his hands.

Jasper's eyebrow shot up. "You're a musician?"

He stared at his daughter. She had hated musicians--especially him--just a few weeks ago. Now she was dating one? He could see her embarrassed smile.

Corey stopped. "Sorry, sir. Yeah, I play a bit but only guitar and cello."

"If you can play cello, you're decent," Jasper said, "especially if you have one and not a synthesizer."

"Yeah, I do." Corey waved it away. "It's nothing though."

"That's where you start," Jasper said. "We'll talk later about playing. I'm on a tight schedule today. Mel, downstairs please."

"Dad, what's this?" Mel poked at the bar across the door.

"Don't touch it. Just a police bar." He'd retrieved the one from the evidence room and set it on the door. "It will warn me if anyone tries entering the house that way."

"Oh." She headed down the stairs, frowning a little as she noticed the living room with its torn carpet. "What have you got to eat?"

"Nothing here," Jasper said. "Mel, I'm not buying this place. I'll be staying here for a few weeks. After that, we'll see."

Corey hadn't stopped in the living room. "Hey, there's food in here, Mel."

Jasper moved fast, dashing across the living room and into the dining area. "Don't touch it," he barked just as Corey raised a home-baked brownie to his lips.

He swept it out of the startled boy's hand and pushed him toward the living room. The boy looked scared and even Mel looked shocked.

"Look around you," Jasper said in a gruff voice. "This is a crime scene. None of the food in this house can be trusted. I don't know what's poisoned so I'm getting rid of all of it."

His daughter looked frightened now. Corey took in the missing carpet and an evidence flag still dangling from the banister and his eyes widened.

"Sorry, sir, I didn't think." He opened the hand Jasper hadn't grabbed and revealed another very crushed brownie. "Two. I was greedy. I'll put it back."

"Do that and wash your hands then come back and let me look at them," Jasper said. He wasn't about to let the kid off. It was unlikely any contact poison was on the food but it would have taken just seconds to inject cyanide in something. He had to bag it all up and get it to the public incinerator. There was too much for a small household one to handle--and those weren't designed for liquids. They were meant for sensitive papers.

"Dad, what's the story?" Mel asked. "I mean, why would anyone poison food? Can you tell me?"

He realized she was scared for him. "There's a hit man who uses poisons and this family was targeted. Three are dead. Since I'm leaving the force, I've agreed to protect a fourth. It's her house."

"Her?" Melanie's eyes went to a portrait of Jewel with her grandmother.

"Yeah." It was a good picture of them both taken maybe a few months ago. He hoped Jewel wouldn't shunt it off to a bedroom till her memory was less fresh.

Corey returned and held his hands out for inspection. Jasper checked them front and back. The boy had done a good job of washing them down to his short manicured fingernails. No redness that he could see. Jasper asked him to swallow.

"Any numbness in your mouth?" he asked.

"No sir. I didn't eat anything," Corey answered. "Just handled it. I didn't think."

"Teenagers rarely do. Next time you come I'm sure there will be food. Not this time. Now help me bag the stuff up and you can walk with me to the incinerator."

He drafted both teens. The kids relaxed and started talking as they worked. Not much was of note until Mel poked him. "Have you seen any green scarves yet?" she asked.

"Not a one."

Her eyes fell and he hastily added. "I've been in Denver for two days. One of my team said he saw them though. You've won the bet."

"So when do we get them?" Mel asked.

"I called today. I should have them by Friday and they'll be collector's copies."

"Great!" She and Corey exchanged happy grins and he knew this was the kid who had convinced his daughter to listen, really listen, to his album. He was probably going to like him.

Jasper went through the cupboards one more time. There were a couple of sealed spice jars and several cans of food but no more boxes or open jars. He'd swept everything out of the refrigerator, only saving a couple of containers he thought Jewel would miss. The contents of those went into the bag too and he'd left the containers to soak.

He still needed to do the upstairs but time was getting short if he wanted to make the four p.m. train. He'd have to do that later.

"Let's go. I want to make sure these get incinerated and then I have to catch a train."

Ushering the kids out, he made sure the lights were off and his cheek pads were in his pocket. "Mel, did you get your stuff out of the old place?" he asked. "Or is it in storage?"

"In storage," Mel said. "By the time I got there a whole bunch of reporters were in the street. I just walked on by."

"Good thinking," Jasper said. "When I get the storage emptied, you can come over and help."

"Corey too?"

"Yes, you can drive Jewel crazy and eat her cooking for a change. She'll love it."

"That sounds good to me. Thank you, sir," Corey said.

He'd chosen the four pm train because it had staterooms and it would get him back to Denver by seven. He knew Sasha and her parents were coming for Jake's funeral on Monday and he had done what he could to get Jake's body transferred to the Denver forensics morgue. He didn't know if he'd been successful or whether Sasha would be allowed to see it but he hoped so. It would ease her mind to see it even if it wouldn't lessen her grief. Whether or not that happened, they needed to have the funeral tomorrow since Sasha had to report to quarantine Tuesday afternoon.

David's apartment was too small to hold seven people so he had arranged for a suite at the Brown Palace for all but him and Elinor. Jewel was determined to join them so Jasper had agreed to the change too. He liked the Brown Palace better anyway--and he'd made some arrangements of his own.

* * *

"So the cow dropped her calf on your brother?" Jewel asked then burst into giggles when Sasha nodded.

Jasper chuckled, imagining the scene but more amused by the two young women sitting on the floor talking like kids half their age. After an uncomfortable dinner with David in the elegance of the Lunarex Tower, the Kowalskis had been happy to retreat to the Brown Palace and be more at home in their three bedroom suite.

Sasha's mother had already announced she was ready for bed but Jewel and Sasha were still wide awake. Sasha's father, Ivan, mostly ignored their antics to talk to him but occasionally contributed a story of his own. He was a burly man, muscled from years of handling animals and doing farm work. A little shorter than Jasper, he bore himself with the confidence of a man who could lead and did. Jasper had already noted his Masonic ring and wasn't surprised. Most of the Masons he'd known had been good people.

Ivan caught him eyeing his hand and smiled. "Pretty good craftsmanship, isn't it?"

"Craftsmanship?" Jasper repeated, uncertain what he meant.

"My hand," he said. "Actually, my arm. It goes all the way up."

Jasper watched as Ivan flexed his hand and this time he could see something was not quite right about the movement of his fingers. There was a slight hesitation, almost unnoticeable, when he set down his beer mug and picked it up again.

"Bionic?"

"Yeah, I'm a cyborg," he said and grinned at him. "I've been one since I was twenty two. I lost it on a job."

"Tough luck," Jasper said.

"Not at all. I met Molly at the hospital and carted her off to the farm. Best luck I've ever had." His face softened at the memory.

Jasper smiled too. He'd seen that look before although he doubted he'd ever get it for someone like Molly Kowalski. Her hair was unnaturally red and curly and there was just a bit too much of her for his tastes. Well, she suited Ivan.

"I'm glad you came," Jasper said. "I think you've made a good impression on the Wests."

"I hope so," Ivan said. "They're quite a bit different from what Sasha told us--and I like talking hunting."

Jasper nodded. He didn't but David and Ivan had found that in common. The rest had talked cooking and that he'd enjoyed. Sasha had briefly lamented the absence of ice cream on Mars but swore she'd get by.

Sasha still got teary when Jake was mentioned but she seemed determined to know Jewel and the family better before going into quarantine. Jewel had the same determination. Jasper knew they were trying to build a relationship that hadn't had much importance before. It was strange what grief could do. Without Jake in the way, the girls were free to be friends. It was just too bad it would last less than 48 hours.

Jewel had kicked off her shoes and was sitting on the floor like a teenager with her chestnut hair down around her shoulders. Sasha was just as barefoot and sat cross-legged, her blonde hair spread out as she combed her fingers through it. She was prettier than he first thought, Jasper decided but he liked Jewel's chestnut hair better than her blond. Sasha was leaner and more fit looking but remembering that kiss in the elevator, Jasper knew he wouldn't trade Jewel for her. Was that really just yesterday? Or was it the day before? He couldn't remember. All the days seem to run together now.

"What was that?" Jasper said, realizing he'd missed something.

Ivan Kowalski chuckled. "Sleeping on your feet? I said the missus is going to bed and I'm going to join her soon. You want me to break those two up?"

"No, let them be. I'll be up a while."

"How short are you on sleep?" he asked. "Did you get any last night?"

"A couple of hours," Jasper said. "But I got almost three on the train back. I can navigate."

"Well, you know best. My wife and I are still on farm time. She feels it more than I do but I can only take so many old tales before I want my pillow. Are you going to sit here and listen to them?"

"No, I'm going to take a walk," Jasper said with his eye on the clock. "Would you like to join me?"

"No, I think I'll try to catch the news. It would help if you'd take them."

Jasper wanted to say no but stopped. He'd reserved the salon. Did it matter if those two kept it up down there? He knew once he started playing he'd barely know they were there--and Jewel had to hear him sometime. If they were going to share Lily Street, she wouldn't be able to avoid it. He needed to get it over with.

Tossing a shoe at Jewel, he got her attention. "I've got a surprise for you two. Get your shoes on and come along."

Within minutes the girls were ready, both having kissed Sasha's father good night and given him the remote. With Ivan ensconced in front of the vid panel, they followed Jasper out the door.

"You're shameless, Jewel," he said, "trying to get into Sasha's family that way. Why don't you just admit you need one of your own?"

"Why don't you just help me?" Jewel said then looked shocked it had come out.

Sasha giggled.

Jasper felt his face get hot but shrugged it off. He'd brought that one on. "What have you been drinking?"

"Grasshoppers," Sasha said. "No, wait, it was vodka and cope."

"Coke?" Jasper asked.

"Yeah, coke," Sasha said more carefully. "Wish I had a

grasshopper though. They're yummy."

"I'll see what I can do," Jasper said and steered both girls to the elevator. Down on one of the social floors, he spoke to a hotel employee. The man nodded and bowed him into the small salon.

It was an elegant little room with a good view of Denver from ten floors up. He could see the Lunarex Tower off to the west and the raised track of the monorail that served the city. Off to the north the massive train terminal spread across several city blocks. Beyond it, he could see the lighted domes of the underground.

What he most wanted to see was right here in the room. Leaving the girls to admire the view, he ran his hand so lightly over the keyboard there was no sound. The ebony bench beckoned. The piano itself was a very old, very grand Steinway. It was elegant, almost as elegant as the Brown Palace itself with its fine black finish. If it played as well as it looked, this was going to be fun.

Softly he stroked the keys, getting the feel of it. The notes were clear and perfect. He smiled and stretched his fingers for the first song. Starting simply with Amazing Grace, he built on it, adding chords and soft treble notes to the harmony. The music soared and filled him with joy, pushing the cares of the last days away.

He forgot about the girls as his hands shifted into the main theme of Morning Grace. He could almost feel the quiet dawn building into the sunrise as he played. The piano was too limited for him to hear the multiple parts, the birdsong, the rustle of leaves on the trees, and the true waking of the day but he remembered those and mentally filled them in as he played.

Giving himself up to the music, he was barely aware when someone set a drink down beside him. Remembering the years he'd resisted, he felt foolish. Only now was he free.

He began a third number, a new improvisation, and abruptly stopped, unhappy with the passage of notes.

Tinkering with the keyboard with one hand, he felt a cold drink pressed against the back of the other and looked up to see Jewel smiling. Jewel? For a moment he couldn't remember why she was there then he took the drink and left off stroking the ivories.

"My dirty secret," he said in a voice gone hoarse. "I forgot you were here."

"It was beautiful," Jewel said. Leaning over, she whispered in his ear. "Never stop playing."

Catching her head with his free hand, he brought it closer, his lips brushing hers. She leaned into it, kissing him back with a passion that surprised and pleased him. Tasting her minty lips, he devoured them, hungry for more. Desire quickened his pulse and she, she was trembling under his hand, her body half sitting on the bench.

A chink of glass intruded on his awareness and he reluctantly let her go when she pulled away. A second chink and he remembered Sasha. They weren't alone. He abruptly dropped his hand and looked for the source of the noise.

It was worse. Sometime during his playing, Sasha's parents had joined them. Molly was dressed so it had been some time and Ivan had a pleased grin on his face. Sasha looked like the cat that swallowed the canary. It was clear they'd seen it all.

Lacking words to say anything, he jumped into Beethoven's Fifth Symphony. By the time he finished another set, going from one tune to another, his arms ached and he felt bone tired.

Jewel scooted on to the bench beside him and captured his hands in hers. "It was gorgeous," she said. "And I want you."

"Not here," Jasper said. "Not tonight. It's not right."

"It's never right," she said but moved off the bench. "You've been playing for hours. You need sleep now and so do I."

"But I haven't finished my drink," he said, only then realizing he'd gotten a grasshopper too. The minty flavor was still good and the liquor warmed him but the ice cream had long since melted.

"Bring it upstairs. You start playing again and I'll go to sleep under the piano." She yawned.

He yawned too suddenly aware he couldn't go on. Jewel might want the floor but he wanted a bed.

"When did they go upstairs?" he asked as he picked up his drink.

"A couple of hours ago," she said. "Farmers. They can't stay up past midnight." Slipping under his arm, she led him back to the elevators.

"I'm not much better," Jasper said but he was grateful he wouldn't have to explain that kiss. What had he been thinking? Not about anyone else for sure. He resisted the temptation to kiss her again but didn't pull away from her warm presence at his side.

Chapter 37 - Monday

The morning was well advanced before Jasper opened his bedroom to face the world. He'd gotten ready for the day first, putting off this moment as long as he could but the living room of the suite was empty except for Jewel. Relieved, he eyed her. She beckoned but didn't move from her position on the couch. Seeing the room service tray, he crossed to it first and poured himself a full cup of coffee.

Jewel giggled.

"Okay, what's going on?" he asked, suddenly suspicious but the coffee was good and just the right temperature. Drinking half a cup, he idly watched as Jewel stretched and slowly rose from the couch. God, she was pretty. Her tanned legs were long and sinuous and her slender waist showed beneath a shortie top. Chestnut hair tumbled on her shoulders, framing those beautiful eyes and luscious lips but it was her body that held his attention as she moved with studied grace, every motion sending out sharp warnings of what she was about.

"Why aren't you dressed?" he said then "no, you don't," and he thrust his coffee cup out to ward her off as she tried to wrap herself around him.

She burst out laughing. "I win," she said. "I told Sasha you'd go for the coffee first."

He grinned to hide his embarrassment then tried to look stern. "Hussy, I suppose you've told her of your little plot to get me in your bed." Damn, she looked good in that shortie top. He could just see the bottom curve of her creamy breasts and she was way too enticing. With an effort, he focused on her blue eyes.

"I had no choice! She was lying in wait for me when we got back. She wouldn't let me sleep till I spilled the whole story." She headed for her room. "They're downstairs in the restaurant so you can relax. It's just the two of us."

"I think I need a chaperone," he said and she giggled again.

What the hell was he going to do about her? He took the cover off the tray and decided that problem could wait. Omelets couldn't.

Damn, she was so eager. He had wondered if David had mistook her interest for a need to be protected but it didn't look like it now--and she wasn't a teenager even if she acted like one. She'd be twenty-seven next month. Hell, Sasha wasn't either. She was just past her twenty-fifth birthday. From the looks of it, she not only had her degree in animal husbandry but a lifetime of experience on her parents' farm. She'd be a real asset to the Mars colony.

He was half done with his omelet when Jewel reappeared, this time dressed for the day in a becoming white dress with a red and black sash. Pearls adorned her lovely throat and studded her ear lobes.

"Hungry?" he asked and waved her toward a seat.

"You were," she said, her lips curving into a smile. "Yes, I'll just have to have food though."

"Wicked," he said but kept on eating. "You need to behave yourself. You'll shock them."

She smiled. "They're farmers," she said. "They've seen it all. You know animals still do it when people are watching."

"But we won't." He was firm, wondering if she had those tendencies. "Today is not the day. I expect you to behave."

Her smile slipped. "Yes sir."

"Don't call me sir."

"Well, what should I call you? Jasper is so formal. I can't see using it all the time."

"Jazz," he said. "My daughter is Mel."

"Melanie?" she asked.

"No, just Mel." He frowned at her as he laid his napkin down. "No more hijinxes today. I know you're just having fun but it's not right. We need to think about Jake."

"I don't want to think about Jake," she said. "I don't want

to think about him ever again. He..." Her lip trembled and she bit it.

Surprised, Jasper reached for her hand. It was just the wrong move for she burst into tears and fled to the couch where she curled up into a ball and cried. How the hell was he supposed to handle this? Aware the Kowalskis could be back any time, he scooped her up and carried her into his bedroom. She clung to him like a leech and all he could do was pat her back and let her cry.

Damn it, he was getting soaked again. He shifted her a little. She made little sounds of apology but she was also cursing Jake for being a half-baked idiot and other things. God, she was really letting loose.

He should have let it be. Now he knew she'd used him to avoid doing this. So how did she really feel about him? He knew what he wanted but did she?

Faintly he heard the Kowalskis come in and tried to shush Jewel. She had to stop. All too aware what they might think they were doing in his bedroom, he decided to try another tack as he saw Sasha peer through the open door.

"Jewel, Jewel, we've got company," he repeated. "Come on, do you want them to catch you in my bed?"

She hiccupped then gave a half-hearted giggle.

Sasha didn't retreat. As she came further into the room, Jasper realized she wasn't going to be any help at all. Unless he missed his guess, she was going to fall apart too. He motioned her closer then extracted himself from Jewel. Pushing Sasha into his place, he got himself free before either girl was aware he was leaving. He pulled the door closed behind him but unsure whether they would follow, held on to the doorknob.

Both parents looked at him in surprise.

"I had to," Jasper said. "Need coffee."

Mrs. Kowalski brought him a cup, which he drank while still holding on to the doorknob.

"So what happened?" Ivan asked. "Did she fall apart?"

"Yes," Jasper replied. "I told her to quit fooling around and--" He grimaced. "I think Sasha just lost it too."

"Yes, she's been doing that," Ivan remarked. "Last night was a relief and she needed the distraction. Does West know about you and Jewel?"

"Yes, he approves but she wants to go a hell of a lot faster than me. I should have known it was reaction. She's lost a lot this month."

"True. Well, it was entertaining."

"I loved the music last night," Molly Kowalski said as she refilled his cup. "And Sasha insisted on buying your album. I don't blame her. You're incredible."

"Thank you." He wasn't sure what else to say. "Soon it will be my only career. I'm leaving the force when this case is done."

"You should," she said. "Now are you going to let them out? If not, let me in there and I'll get them settled down again."

Jasper stepped away from the door and let her in then went back to his breakfast. He motioned for Ivan to join him.

"Sasha still wants to see Jake," Ivan told him. "Can you arrange it? She just needs to be sure he's dead. I think you know the problem."

"Yes," Jasper said. "I want Jewel to see him too but I'm not sure she will. She's madder than hell at him right now. I know his father wants to."

"It has to be done today," Ivan said. "We're taking Sasha up to Wyoming this evening and we'll stick with her until she enters quarantine. I'd like to know what Jake was thinking too. This was supposed to be for both of them, now it's just her."

"She might find someone else on Mars," Jasper offered.

Ivan snorted. "Not likely. Do you know they have seventy-three more women than men now? It's stupid. I know that women bear the next generation but you've got to have enough men to keep them happy. They're going to have to change their selection process and do it soon."

"True. Well, Sasha can deal with it when she gets there." Jasper looked for his com unit and realized it was in the bedroom. Were they still crying?

"Sasha needs to talk to you about all this," Ivan said. "But I'd do it some place official to hold her together. This is too comfortable."

"I'll remember that. I need to get my com unit," Jasper said and rose to his feet. Peering into his room, he saw both girls were subdued and sitting with Mrs. Kowalski, heads resting on her shoulders. Deciding it was safe, he snagged his com unit and began calling.

Chapter 38 – Jake's Will

Jasper exited the limousine first, eyeing those on the street before he opened the door for David, Jewel and the rest of their company. He felt he was being paranoid but it just felt wrong bringing the last surviving members of the West family to the city morgue today. He almost wished they hadn't gotten Jake's body transferred.

The city morgue and police headquarters were located in the old town of Denver and only accessible via the surface streets and a subway stop a block away so David had ordered the limousine again. Half of them could have walked the three blocks from the Brown Palace but Jewel was with them and Jasper had agreed it would be better to arrive together and in style.

Showing his badge to the uniformed police officer in front of the Justice Building, Jasper ushered his group in to the security desk. There they were forced to wait a few minutes while Ivan Kowalski produced his medical card and let someone peer into the electronics of his arm. By the time that was done, they'd been joined by three others.

Jasper eyed the one in the lab coat and guessed he was their guide. He turned to the other two. "Lieutenant Stone, Plains PD. You are?"

"Detective Evans, Cheyenne PD and this is Mr. Norton. He's here to see David West," the taller of the two men answered. His shorter counterpart was clearly not police. He was short, not too heavy, and wore a tailored suit.

"Why, Mr. Norton?" Jasper asked.

"I have papers for Mr. West. They are quite crucial to this case. His son Jacob asked me to draw them up Friday."

"You're Jake's new lawyer?" David West nudged Jasper aside. "What's your name? Did he get it done?"

"Richard Norton, sir. I'm an estate specialist although I

also do family law. I'm sorry I couldn't call yesterday but the police advised against it. Given the size of the estate and the circumstances of Mr. West's death, it was also imperative that I register the will with the State of Wyoming. That was done this morning."

"Good," David said. "Is there some place we can talk? Have you got copies for me?"

"Yes sir. I do have copies but..." He looked at a loss for a place to talk.

"Mr. West," their guide said, "there are a couple of waiting rooms and offices this way. Just follow me. They're a lot closer to the viewing room too."

"Could you take charge of both girls," Jasper asked Ivan in a low voice. "I need to hear what this lawyer has to say."

Ivan nodded. When they reached a small meeting room, it was only Jasper, David, the lawyer and the Cheyenne detective who went inside. The others, including Elinor and Jewel, continued on to the morgue's viewing room.

Jasper was torn between being there for Jewel or staying but he had no choice and she had Elinor with her and the levelheaded Kowalskis. She'd be safe enough.

The lawyer laid his briefcase on the table and unlocked it, picking out a set of papers he handed to David West. "They're all in order, Mr. West. Your son was insistent they be done properly and completely before he left. We even called up one of your financial advisers--Mr. Harris, I believe--to get more accurate information."

"But Harris didn't call me," David said as he idly thumbed through the stack.

"He was asked not to until Tuesday," Mr. Norton said, "after Jacob entered quarantine."

"There's probably something in here I won't like then. I need to read. Jasper?" He settled himself at the table and began going over the papers.

"The top one is the reassignment of attorneys," Mr. Norton said. "Then there's a power of attorney for you and his will."

"Thank you." His brow furrowed with concentration as he started reading.

Time to divert this lawyer, Jasper thought. "Mr. Norton, how did Jake come to pick you for his lawyer? Had you met him before?"

"No, never," the lawyer said. "He just walked into my office at ten thirty Friday morning and asked if I could help him. Of course I agreed when I found out who he was. He was quite insistent though that it had to be done on Friday."

"Didn't you find that odd?"

"I did but he explained he was entering Mars quarantine on Tuesday and everything had to be changed. He was unhappy with his current lawyer and there would be no time on Monday to get it done." He sighed. "It was unusual and he was excitable but I saw no reason not to help him."

"Did he say who his current lawyer was and why he was unhappy with him?"

"Edward Kucera," Mr. Norton said. "He said Mr. Kucera was in some sort of legal trouble but he didn't give me any details."

"So what was Jake West doing while you were drawing up the papers? Did he leave?"

"No sir. I allowed him to use a spare office. He was busy writing for much of the day. Oh, and he ordered in lunch for my entire staff as well as himself."

"How many staff?"

"Me, two secretaries and an office clerk," Norton answered. "I have a partner but she's away at the moment. My secretaries are both notaries. I used one of them to witness the will along with my office clerk. My other secretary notarized it."

"Was there a witness who didn't work for you?" Jasper asked.

"Mrs. Feingold from Feingold & Blum," he responded. "She's also a lawyer and their offices are down the hall from me. I'm afraid most people had left the building by the time we got done. I had hoped to get Judge Blum but he had left for the day. Lois was kind and agreed to witness."

"So Jake had you draw up papers appointing you as his new attorney and notifying Kucera he no longer had control? And a new will?"

"Yes, that's correct." He nodded.

"What time did he leave?" Jasper asked.

"It was about five thirty. I left right after with my secretaries but didn't see him. The papers I locked in the building's vault. That's on the first floor just behind the old post office counter. It contains safety deposit boxes for the law offices."

Jasper shifted his gaze to the Cheyenne detective. "When did Jake show up on the surveillance tapes? I thought it was later than that."

"It was. Six ten, I think. It sounds like he waited upstairs for a while hoping Ex wouldn't be there when he came down."

"He would have done better to leave in a crowd," Jasper said. "So your department is calling him Ex too?"

The detective shrugged. "It's a natural way of putting it. We want him exed out."

The lawyer looked uncomfortable.

"So how and when did you find out Mr. West had died?" Jasper asked.

"Sunday morning it was on the news," Mr. Norton said. "As soon as I realized it was our Mr. West, I called Cheyenne PD. They suggested I call my staff and not open on Monday which I thought was reasonable. I retrieved the documents and stayed in protective custody last night. They were concerned this Mr. Ex would somehow locate me."

"That is still a possibility," Jasper answered. "Although he might not be interested now that the will is registered with the state. Very thoughtful move," he added. "That puts it completely out of their reach."

Not every will had to be registered with the State of Wyoming but it was strongly encouraged that wills with sizable estates be protected by that system. Those that were registered could never go missing or be altered. The official legal will was the one the State had scanned into its archives.

David laid the last paper down and rubbed his eyes. It was a moment before he spoke. "You did pretty good, Mr. Norton. I'm familiar with the forms these days and I'm sure this will hold up in court."

"Yes sir, it will," Norton replied with calm certainty.

"At least Kucera won't be into his affairs after this," David said.

"Was there anything you didn't expect?" Jasper asked.

"Not really," David replied. "He gave Sasha a half share in his estate instead of a quarter but that's allowable. Hell, I might do the same with Elinor. I didn't with Jessica. She only gets a tenth part."

"You'll let that stand?" Mr. Norton asked. "He was quite concerned whether you would or not. Since there are no children, he felt you might disregard her."

David snorted then wiped his eyes. "There are some things even a son can't be sure of. I would never cut the woman he married adrift with no money. Even if I wanted to, which I don't, I sure as hell wouldn't try to break this will. There's no point in that."

He looked at Jasper. "He left Jewel their grandfather's pool table. I have it in storage. I'll see that you get it before Jewel gets anxious about it."

Jasper nodded, not bothering to ask what was important about it. Jake had simply left it to her.

"I've got to see him now," David said. "This though is a load off my mind. Mr. Norton, let me give you the card for my attorney at the West Foundation. I would appreciate it if you would send him copies. You can also send your bills to his office for payment until probate is accomplished."

"And after that?"

"If the Kowalskis agree, I'm going to recommend you represent Sasha's interests. I think her father has her power of attorney already so he's the one you'll need to impress. If they decide otherwise though, don't be surprised. They're based in Minnesota. Thank you for coming."

"Thank you for your patience, sir, and I am so sorry for your loss."

Chapter 39 - Sasha

Jasper had taken Ivan's suggestion and picked a regular office to talk to Sasha. To increase the distance between them and make it easier on her, he'd also agreed to include the Cheyenne detective. He was lead. He'd made that clear with the help of the Denver detective whose office he was taking. Since this murder led directly into the two older murders, it couldn't be any other way.

Sasha was alone but looked less like a teenager in the office environment. She'd done her crying, he decided, and was entering that numbness that follows the outpouring of grief.

"You want to know what Jake told me," Sasha said, her fingers shredding a tissue. "Just since we parted in Florida? That was the fifth of July."

"How was he before that?" Jasper asked.

"Pretty normal," she said. "We were all getting edgy, of course. It was only two weeks till quarantine and it was sinking in that we were actually going to leave Earth and not come back. Jake couldn't wait. He wanted to get it over with. If he could have reported for quarantine earlier, he would have."

"And you?" Jasper asked.

"Well, I wasn't that eager. I'm going to miss my family and the farm but Mars is exciting and I thought I was going to have Jake to share it with." She stopped and dabbed her eyes. "Sorry."

"Ok, let's move on," Jasper said. "Your father said you made a list of when Jake called you and his attitude?"

"Yeah, we worked it up with Uncle Uri," she said. "He was on the force in St. Paul."

Jasper wasn't surprised. The Kowalski family seemed to be numerous and diverse. From the stories last night, there seemed to be a ton of kids although not all of them were related.

Sasha pulled the paper out of her purse and handed it to him. "He really didn't call much. Jake was much better at writing letters--mostly love notes," she explained, her cheeks going pink. "Mom's read those and doesn't think there's anything of interest to you."

"I'll bet." Jasper glanced at the Cheyenne detective and saw his slight nod. "I don't think we'll need them but if we do, my most trusted partner is Detective Lori Brown. She'll keep it quiet."

"Thank you," Sasha said. "But I really, really don't want to share those. It was bad enough letting Mom read them."

Jasper could guess their nature. A little surprised Jake was so eloquent on paper when he hadn't been in person, he just nodded. They were unlikely to be useful.

"So other than the love notes, what calls did you get?" Jasper asked.

"He called once to say he was going to Denver early but wouldn't be staying with his father," Sasha said. "I had his com unit number so I didn't think much about it. It sort of surprised me he was leaving his mom's so soon but maybe her schedule was full. Anyway, that was on the eighth. It was just a voice mail. I didn't talk to him."

"Another voice mail on the ninth. He said something about Centrax was thinking of pulling his sponsorship and he had to stop it. That one had me worried so I tried to call him back. He didn't answer." She frowned. "He did send me a text message saying it would be ok but it was really brief."

"How about the twelfth?" Jasper checked the list in his hand. 'The day his grandmother died?"

"Nothing," she said. "But on the thirteenth he called and told me his grandmother and his Uncle Mike were both dead. I was stunned. I wanted to come out but he said no and my family had stuff planned. His dad heard that call. He was there."

"From the train or his hotel room?" Jasper asked.

"From the train," she said. "I didn't know there were staterooms on trains until then."

"Shocking huh?" Jasper said to lighten the mood.

"He called back again late that night," Sasha said, her eyes darkening. "No witnesses. It was just us. He was really upset about Uncle Mike. He barely mentioned his grandmother but it sounded like he was trying to convince himself that Mike died of a heart attack. The shock, you know. He also said something about if it was anything else, Jewel might be next."

"He said that?" Jasper asked. "Might be?"

"Yeah, that scared me. I'd only met her once but I knew Jake thought the world of Mike and loved Jewel like a sister. When he fought with his father, he usually ran to Mike. His uncle sort of mentored him. His grandparents were both against him going to Mars so he tended to avoid them when he could. Anyway, I told you he was scared for Jewel."

"I remember," Jasper said. "Any other messages?"

"A couple of text messages and a voice mail," she said, her lip trembling. "He kept saying he'd meet me in quarantine."

"Anything after noon on Thursday?"

"The two text messages," she said. "I wrote them down. The second one said don't worry. He'd see me in quarantine." She paused and her lower lip trembled. "Damn it, he lied. I thought that was just another bit about Uncle Mike but he lied to me. He wasn't going to make it and he knew it. I...." She sobbed and buried her face in her hands.

Jasper knew the interview was over and she'd probably given him everything she thought might help. Opening the door, he ushered her waiting mother in and he and the detective departed.

"Let me make a copy of that," Evans said with a wave at the list. "Not that it's very useful."

Jasper let him have it then turned to study the hall. He half-expected to see Jessica West somewhere but so far the vid star hadn't made an appearance. Well, maybe at the service. That was set up back at Lunarex Tower. One of the Tower's social directors had promised it would be small and private and she would see the famous Jessica West got admitted.

That sort of relieved him. He'd been recognized again leaving the Brown Palace and had signed some more albums. The Kowalskis had been amused by it all since Sasha had already produced hers up in the suite and got him to sign it. No doubt, her signed copy would be the only one of its kind on Mars.

Well, Jessica West might take the heat off him. She was certainly more famous. He wondered if Jake had called her with anything more significant. Probably not. Jessica had already denied supplying the Valium Jake must have brought with him. Where had he gotten it? For that matter, how did Jake know how to jam the lock on the upper doors? Had Ex taught him? He'd talked to the manufacturer and knew it took a magnetic plate of a specific size and thickness to trick that model door. It wasn't something you could easily buy even in Denver. He also knew there was a fix for it and he'd install it as soon as he could.

Well, unless Jake had called his mother and said something more significant, interviewing her might be a waste of time. He'd do it anyway if he got a chance.

Turning down the hall toward the viewing room, he peered through the window. The girls weren't there but David was. Even as he watched, David let go of his son's cold hand and turned away. Jasper scanned his face as he walked toward him but saw only the usual signs of grief. If he was still angry with his son, it wasn't showing now.

"I'll be ready in a moment," David said and gestured toward the men's room.

"No hurry," Jasper said and entered the room to pay his last respects. He'd no sooner entered than an older man in a blue lab coat came in through a windowed door. Seeing he was a lab technician, Jasper made a guess. "Pathologist?"

"Yes sir, from Cheyenne. I'm Luke Wallace, senior pathologist. They asked me to come down in case you had questions. You are Lieutenant Jasper Stone?"

"Yes sir." Jasper showed him his badge. "I just want to know where he was injected at and how much."

"Let me show you," the pathologist said. "Windows first." He pressed a button that caused the windows to go opaque white.

"This was pretty unique," he said as he lifted Jake's arm and moved it across his lifeless chest. "The injection was clean with nothing to indicate he'd missed but the site he chose in the back of the arm was very strange. There's no major blood vessel there so the curare had to find its way through smaller vessels to the artery. Instead of dying in seconds, it must have taken the victim several minutes to die. Very risky. He could have called out and probably would have if he hadn't been prevented."

"Prevented how?"

"A rough gag. It was removed after and tossed in a wastebasket. Since it's standard procedure to collect the contents of waste baskets it was found."

"Did the killer leave any DNA on it?" Jasper asked.

"No. He didn't leave the syringe either. No fingerprints. He did leave bruising on the victim's wrist but that was insufficient to tell us anything but his size."

Jasper looked at the tiny red dot the doctor indicated and felt sick. It was no bigger than any other injection sites. What must have gone through Jake's mind as he looked up into the face of his killer? Could he feel the curare seeping through his muscles? Did he wonder why it hadn't already killed him? It was a hell of a way to die.

Jake looked peaceful now but he knew that was the usual mortician's illusion. He'd been murdered and Jasper knew he couldn't hate him. There had to be a reason Jake did it and he was going to find it. Was he going to have to talk to Centrax? Or did the line stop at Kucera?

"How much did he get?" Jasper asked.

"That's impossible to say," the pathologist said. "It was

enough but I can't tell you whether he got a minimum dose, the recommended one, or a lot more. For a man his size it should have been seventy ccs but fifty ccs is known to be fatal."

Jasper nodded. That fit with what he remembered of Carol's death. The recommended dose for her had been much smaller but what she'd received was a good ten ccs over that dose. He was suddenly thankful Soma knew their business and had seen to it that Carol had a good death. He was still haunted by images of the hit man shoving Jake into that com booth. He had to find him before he killed again.

"What happens next?" Jasper asked as the pathologist rearranged the body. "Is the body released?"

"Yes, we've done all we can. Mr. West has signed a crematory release so he'll go for cremation tomorrow afternoon. It's department policy to hold a body like this an additional 24 hours in case something should turn up."

"Good policy," Jasper said. "Thank you for your time."

The pathologist just nodded as Jasper turned to go. His com unit buzzed and Jasper glanced at it as he reached the hall. "Jasper here. How's it going in Plains?"

"Pretty good. You're about to get fired. Happy?" Brown answered. "I have the lawyer's name and address. He's not in though."

"Let's see, his name is Norton and he's in Denver today," Jasper said with a grin and watched his partner's expression change.

"He showed up there?" Brown asked. "You got him already?"

"Yes, I'll send you a report when I get a chance to sit down. He's registered Jake's new will and lawyer assignment with the state and came here to hand deliver copies to David. Jake was with him from ten thirty a.m. on Friday until five thirty."

"Any word on where he stayed?" Brown asked.

"Not yet. I'm sure Cheyenne P.D. is checking that out."

"Good. Jazz, they've pulled Sanders off the case--drug bust over in Section 3. I'm still officially loaned to them but the captain would like this wrapped up. There's pressure from the top to get you off the city's payroll."

"Well, we knew that would happen," Jasper said. "Just find out for me if Edward Kucera is in Plains and if he has been in the last month. Oh, and see if he's a declared Catholic."

"The confessional?"

"Yes."

He knew it wasn't likely Kucera had declared his religion publicly since more people didn't but lawyers and politicians and public figures sometimes did to get support. A few churches called for public disclosure as a test of faith though. He didn't remember if the Catholic Church was one.

"Jazz."

He turned to find Jewel almost close enough to touch.

She slipped into his arms, her face solemn but dry. "I like the sound of your name."

"Don't wear it out," he teased and gave her a hug. "You heard?" He held out his com unit.

"Yes, you want to know where Kucera is," she said, not losing her fragile calm. "Did you know he was one of Uncle Mike's friends? His wife was a friend of my grandmother's."

"No," Jasper said, wondering how close Kucera was to Mike.

"I don't know him well but Elaine used to visit a lot. He'd come to Plains, usually with her, for our bigger Reach Out events. Our last one was about ten days ago. I don't think they've been back since but I know they were there for that one."

"And Drew was there?" Jasper asked. "Talking about his book?"

Jewel shrugged. "He was there. I avoided him. Elaine spent a little bit of time with Grandmother but she wasn't feeling well and she left early."

"Your grandmother?" Jasper asked.

"No, Elaine wasn't feeling well. Grandma was fine. She even made brownies for the event. I helped, of course."

"Of course," Jasper said. "Thanks. Let's see if the others are ready to go."

Chapter 40 - Kowalski

"We need to get going," David was saying as Jasper found him and the Kowalskis back in the reception area. "The service is at four-thirty and your train is at seven. It's the last to Cheyenne that connects with the Laramie train--if you want to be in Laramie tonight."

"We have reservations there," Ivan Kowalski said. "And it would be better for us to get away for one night before Sasha leaves."

"Yes, I understand that," David said. "Sasha, I wish you lots of luck on Mars. I'm sorry I couldn't tell Jake that."

"Thank you," Sasha said. "I'm sorry too."

"Services," Jasper said. "Let me see if the limo is here." Stepping outside the building, he quickly spotted the limo in the parking area but it was surrounded by a knot of people, including two uniformed cops. Thinking something had happened to the driver, he walked across the street to the parking area. On the way he scanned the small crowd but there was no one that looked like the Executioner. He glanced behind him to see no one but the Kowalskis and the Wests standing by the doors of police headquarters.

"What's wrong?" Jasper asked and flashed his badge at the officer he'd seen before guarding the building.

"Damnedest thing," the officer said. "A kid keyed the limo. I saw him do it but he took off running and I couldn't leave. Called it in but it was hopeless. The driver didn't even hear it happen." He motioned toward the driver who was kneeling by the car and examining the deep scratch, his face showing his dismay.

Jasper frowned, aware this was going to put them behind schedule. If there was paperwork to file, it could be an hour or more. He glanced across the street and saw David and Ivan approaching. Great. He scanned the crowd again and turned to go meet them.

"Ivan!"

"Dad!"

He heard the two cries simultaneously and saw a nightmare begin. A woman he'd ignored earlier slashed at David with what looked like a high-powered syringe. Before it connected, Ivan's arm came up and blocked it, sending the syringe flying. His leg kicked out hard, sweeping the woman off her feet. Jasper was there before the villain could scramble away, throwing his weight on top of him and pinning his arms to the ground.

The Executioner kicked, trying to free himself but then David landed on his legs. The man lay still, his breath coming fast, as he snarled up at Jasper.

"Be careful with that," Jasper snapped at the officer who leaned over to pick up the syringe. "It's deadly poison. Ivan, did he get you?"

Kowalski flexed his arm. "I think so. Might have gummed up my works if he did. I'm not supposed to get liquid in these things."

"He got your prosthetic?" Jasper asked, relieved. "Help me here," he told the second officer. "No, clear this crowd first."

"Yes sir." The Denver PD man didn't question his orders but set about removing the crowd.

"Let's get him up," the first officer said. "Who is he?"

By the time they'd got him cuffed and on his feet, Detective Evans had joined them too. "You got him?" he was incredulous. "Or is it her?" He looked over the red-skirted figure with disheveled black hair.

"Him!" Sasha Kowalski was pulling off his wig. "He walked like a man. Mom spotted him."

Jasper stared at Molly Kowalski, astonished when she grabbed the villain's skirt and pulled it right off. Before they could react, she was pointing out a second syringe and a thin knife strapped to the man's lean thighs.

"How'd you know?" Jasper demanded as the man started to struggle.

"Women have been hiding things under skirts since skirts were invented," Molly said, "but they don't walk like they got balls."

The next instant she was checking out her husband and fighting back tears. Ivan assured her and everyone else he was fine but he didn't let go of his wife.

Jasper found the driver. "Is the limo okay except for that scratch?" he demanded.

"Yes sir."

"Then forget the police report. We'll get to it later. I need you to get the Wests back to Lunarex Tower where they're safe. Got that?"

"Yes sir." He looked torn but opened the door for David.

"The girls?" David asked.

"Right here," Sasha said and they were. Jewel, Elinor, and Sasha slipped into the limo.

"I'm going to need you, sir," the Cheyenne detective said to Ivan. "Evidence."

"Right. Molly, hun, go with the girls. Jasper will look out for me." He eased his shaky wife into the car and gave her a quick kiss. "You saved me, love. I'm not leaving you now."

She gave him a tremulous smile and the car door closed.

Jasper took his real arm and felt his pulse before they walked across the street to police headquarters.

"Stop that. If he'd gotten flesh, I'd be dead by now. He got my arm," Ivan said. "I'm not even sure he got that."

"Let's find out," Jasper said and walked him across the street behind the half-nude figure of the hitman. "Good move."

"I didn't think," Ivan said. "Just luck I threw the right arm up." He finally looked shaken. "God, if he'd gotten West with me right there, I couldn't have lived with myself."

Jasper understood that sentiment and he wondered if the second syringe had been intended for Jewel. Damn him. He felt a rush of anger so intense it surprised him. That bastard had nearly gotten around him--had gotten around him. What kind of cop was he to be fooled that easily? It took an untrained farmwoman to spot a fake in the crowd.

Well, they had him. Now they just needed his employer.

Chapter 41 - Services

The services were over. Jasper barely glanced toward the small reception room they'd reserved as his guide, an employee of the Tower, took him to the elevators. They'd had no problem getting in this time. He didn't know whether it was David's arrangements or his new notoriety but he didn't care. All he cared about was getting back to Jewel.

Ivan was not as quiet but he respected his mood. When they entered David's suite he went straight to his wife and gave her a hug and a peck on the cheek before flexing his arm. "All suctioned out. I still have to see my arm doc when we get home but I'm good to go."

The others were watching him. David and Elinor sat together on the couch, looking like they would not be parted. Another couple, he recognized Jessica West, sat at the table. Sasha and Jewel were in the overstuffed chairs. They were all looking at him.

God, how could he tell them the damned killer had alibis? They had him with syringes at this place but--how the hell could he tell them that he wasn't in Cheyenne or Plains? He still couldn't believe it. He wanted to go back--he would go back--as soon as the Kowalskis were off.

Jewel crossed the room and he gave her a hug before looking at David. "We've got him for attempted murder. The stuff in the syringe was curare--the same used on Jake."

"His name?" David asked.

"He's not talking," Jasper said. "The only thing he's said is he wants a lawyer. No ID card and we haven't got anything back on his prints yet."

"What about Jake?" Jewel had caught that omission. "And Grandmother and Uncle Mike? Why isn't he charged with murder?" Her lip trembled.

"We can't prove those yet," Jasper said. "His damned cash card doesn't put him in Plains or Cheyenne. It puts him right here in Denver at the Franklin."

"Like Jake had?" David frowned. "How the hell did he do that anyway?"

Jasper grimaced. "We haven't had time to go over surveillance tapes to see if Jake was here. Most of them were on a seven-day cycle anyway so they might be lost. My guess though is Jake hired a stand-in who had dinner at the Brown Palace then went to that damned movie for him. Ex could have done the same thing but we're going to ask the staff at the Franklin to ID him. He had to present some proper identification and his bank account card to stay there. My guess is they won't know him though."

"But he had hotel transactions on his cash card?" David frowned. "Why?"

Jasper wondered if he really was that slow. "People do it all the time. They have to present proper ID and debit card to stay there and the debit card is kept on file but if someone chooses to pay with a cash card, they can. Hell, the hotels will even take cash. They don't like to but they do."

"You looked at Jake's transactions for his hotel," Jasper said. "Nothing on there. He used his cash card but he probably had to show his debit card. It's still missing. So is his com unit but I doubt that will ever show up."

"Did he kill Jake?" the woman at the table asked. "Did he kill my son?"

Jessica West looked strained, almost worn out, and not like the star he'd always seen on the screen. Her makeup was perfect but he could see the grief beneath. Not the uncaring mother he'd imagined.

"Yes," Jasper said. "We can't prove it yet but yes." Their main hope now was a voiceprint. If they could match his voiceprint to the surveillance tape, his alibi wouldn't help him.

A ripple of relief went through the room. Molly hugged her husband again and Jewel clasped his hand in a tight squeeze. He wanted to hold her tight, he wanted to kiss her but now was not the time. He wasn't done and it had to be done tonight.

"I just came back to give you that news and deliver Ivan. I've got to get back to headquarters here and keep working on this."

"Why tonight?" David frowned. "Surely tomorrow?"

"I'm being relieved tomorrow," Jasper said. "My partner let me know that I'll probably be a private citizen by tomorrow midnight."

"Damned poor timing," David said, his jaw clenching. "They won't let you finish this?"

"What are you talking about?" Jessica demanded. "How can they relieve the best cop they have? You're on a case."

"I'm also Sensor Man," Jasper said in a flat voice. "I knew it would mean leaving the force when it came out but I never expected this case. Brown is still assigned to it. She'll just have to take over."

"Sensor Man?" Jessica looked confused.

"Sensor Man," Jewel and Sasha chorused and Jasper had to smile.

"Honestly, Jess, you haven't watched the news?" David said, his brow furrowing in irritation. "I thought you were glued to the entertainment news. What's wrong with you?"

She just waved a hand, unable to speak. Her companion glared at David as he patted her hand.

"I'll fix you a sandwich," Jewel said and headed for the kitchen. That broke the tableau.

Sasha hugged her father then hugged him and went to gather her luggage. Molly clucked over her husband one more time and joined her. Elinor produced a box full of supper for the Kowalskis and they all looked at the time.

"The limo should be downstairs in five minutes," David said. "Same limo. That driver will want to talk to you, Jasper. He's got to get that police report done too."

"He can take me back over to headquarters," Jasper said. "We'll just see the Kowalskis off first."

"Then we won't go," David said. "Do you still need

Jessica's affidavit? She brought it."

Jasper looked at the star and almost shook his head then reconsidered. She'd gone to some trouble. He should take it. "Yes, just for the records."

"Don't worry too much about his alibis," Jasper told David as he prepared to leave. "I can place our hit man at Elizabeth's funeral and I have another witness who can place him at the Catholic Church earlier that day. He got into Plains and he got out. We'll prove it."

David nodded. "I'll tell them downstairs you'll be back. I don't care when--just come back."

"Yes sir." Jasper gave him a tired smile then ushered the Kowalskis out the door.

Before they reached the elevator, Jewel raced after them with a small box dangling from one hand. She pressed it into Jasper's hands with a breathless "Eat!"

He swept her up in a hug and their lips met with surprising urgency. He kissed her with sudden hunger, his mouth hard then tender. She responded whole-heartedly, opening her lips to his until the ding of the elevator and a chuckle brought them both back to their senses.

Jewel's color was bright red but she was smiling when she squirmed free. "Eat!" she admonished as she retreated down the hall.

Jasper didn't look at anyone after they entered the elevator, knowing he was flushed. He shifted, uncomfortably aware of the heat in his loins.

"I bet she'll cook for you more often," Ivan said.

Jasper stole a quick look and cleared his throat. Damn.

Ivan burst out laughing, his wife joining in even as she told her husband not to laugh. Only Sasha was quiet. She didn't look at him till they were seated in the limousine. Had he reminded her too much of Jake?

After an awkward moment, Ivan smoothly took over the conversation, peeling back fake skin and showing his wife where the department had probed and suctioned his arm. His wife listened, trying to draw Jasper into the conversation.

He told them about the initial interview. There wasn't much. The man had demanded a lawyer and had been strip searched and fingerprinted.

"Did he ask for a specific lawyer?" Ivan asked. "Didn't you say you had one under suspicion?"

"Jake's old lawyer," Jasper said. "Edward Kucera. No, he wanted a list. No mention of him."

"Cool guy," Ivan said. "He must think he'll beat the system."

"It was only Molly that stopped him," Jasper said. "Those high speed syringes are flawless, fast, and darn near painless. David might not have even felt it before Ex was away again. He could have grabbed the second one through a slit pocket in the skirt and gotten Jewel too."

He'd been lucky, he knew. He'd pinned the man's hands and body before Ex could reach that pocket. If he'd been the least bit lax, Ex would have gotten it and killed again.

"It was certified curare," Jasper added. "Practically pure and in the same concentration the euthanasia shops use. One thing we know is he has to have some contact in that industry."

"Or a veterinarian," Ivan said. "They can get the stuff. Don't ignore that."

Jasper looked at him, aware he hadn't thought about veterinarians. "Do they have access to cyanide too? How about passion flower?"

"Sasha?" Ivan turned to his silent daughter. "What about it?"

"I never heard of passion flower," she quietly said. "Not cyanide. It can't be used on animals. It's illegal."

"Thanks," Jasper said. "Are you going to be okay? Is this too much for you?"

"I have to be okay," she said, wiping away a tear. "But I miss him. I know he's guilty as hell but I loved him and now-- damn it, I'm going to miss the wedding!'

"Wedding?" Jasper stared at her, caught off guard. Thinking she meant David and Elinor, he was caught out when her parents laughed and Sasha's strained sob turned to laughter. Jasper flushed. His wedding? Finally he grinned. "I guess you will. Your parents will just have to come and send you video. You'll stay in touch with us?"

Sasha nodded. She was smiling now and just in time as the limo was pulling into the VIP stop at the train station. A valet was waiting so unloading was quick.

"I'm glad I met you," Jasper said to all of them. "It's the one good thing about this weekend."

"It was a pleasure meeting you too. When you and Jewel are free, come visit. I promise no assassins--just a lot of hard work and some pesky kids," Ivan said.

"We'll talk about it," Jasper said then turned to Sasha. He hugged her and quietly said, "You'll live. It may take a while to get over him but you'll live. I know."

She looked up at him with shiny blue eyes. "Yeah, I will. Jewel is sure lucky though." She gave him a quick peck on the cheek.

Jasper saw them into the station then climbed into the seat next to the driver. Time to get back to work.

Chapter 42 – The Franklin

Jasper waited patiently while three Franklin employees were escorted into the small office they'd been given. Jameson had rejoined the case, called back after the attempt on David but was looking bored. Detective Evans shared his boredom. Well, so was he. They'd already looked at the surveillance tapes and were just waiting for the warrant they needed for Room 401.

The three employees were from different areas of the hotel. One was obviously a desk clerk and a second a waiter. He wasn't familiar with the third. Her outfit looked almost medical.

"Rebecca North, front desk, Eddy Jones, Four Seasons restaurant, and this is Clara Alexander, one of our VIP masseuses," the hotel supervisor said. "Will these do, Lieutenant?"

"Yes, thank you." With a look at the others, he took lead. "Lieutenant Jasper Stone. I just want you to identify a person. Can you look at the vid screen please?" He threw up a photo of their suspect.

The employees smiled uncertainly.

"Why that's Mr. Starling," the desk clerk said. "Has something happened to him?"

"Starling? Are you sure?"

"That's Mr. Starling," the waiter said. "Eats breakfast every day at eight and wants the table by the window. Better light. Good tips too."

"And you?" Jasper looked at the masseuse.

She shrugged. "Full body massage, no sexual stuff. Usually tipped me two hundred." She smiled, showing even white teeth. "I liked the tips. Is he gone now?"

"But his name is Starling?" Jasper couldn't believe such an innocent name hid a killer. "How long has he been at the Franklin? What's his first name?"

The desk clerk looked at her supervisor before she answered. "Samuel Starling. Two weeks. He got here just after the fourth."

"Did he check out at any time? Miss any breakfasts?" Jasper looked at the waiter.

"Not when I was here," he said. "He came in one morning at seven but he said he was going to some of the antique shops up at Estes. That's what he does. He buys antiques."

"He does photography too," the desk clerk volunteered. "Nice guy. Really sweet."

Jasper found it hard to believe what he was hearing. Nice? Sweet? The man he'd left at headquarters didn't fit either description.

"Has something happened to Mr. Starling?" the desk clerk asked. "He's not hurt, is he?"

"Nothing too bad," Jasper said. "But he lost his ID and seemed confused as to who he was. All we knew is he stayed here. Thank you."

The three employees filed out before Jasper motioned to their supervisor. "We'll need a copy of his registration here and his bank account number then we'll need to see his room."

"Your warrant?" the supervisor asked.

"It's on its way," Jameson said. "The judge just needed his name."

"May I ask what he's suspected of?" the supervisor stiffly asked. "We don't have drug dealers at the Franklin."

"It's not drugs," Jasper said. "As for the charges, right now it's attempted murder."

"Oh, dear," the manager said. "And at the Franklin."

"We need to see his room and get his transaction information."

"Yes, yes, of course. I'll get started on it."

* * *

A half hour later they were in his room, each one of them

wearing gloves. Jasper began a careful search of the nightstand, removing drawers and checking underneath them. He'd already warned the others to beware of needles and syringes that may be hidden in the room.

The receipts they needed were in a neat pile on the dresser. He flicked through them, seeing the names of antique shops and jewelry stores and even a pawnshop or two. He didn't recognize most of them so he handed them to the Denver detective. Two boxes of small items, all antique figurines, were sitting in a corner. He carefully unpacked them and stood them up on the desk, wondering if he would find the seventh happy god in this batch. He wasn't that lucky.

After half an hour they'd caught all the likely places and were searching the unlikely. Jasper even checked the top of the curtains to make sure nothing was stashed there. The technician arrived and began work as the three detectives conferred.

"It's completely clean," the Denver detective said. "Either it's not his room or he's better than I thought."

"We'll find out with the fingerprints," Jasper said then added. "He could have a storage locker somewhere or even another hotel room."

They just looked at him and Jasper knew he was grasping at straws. "There's no sign of his tools here--not even an empty bottle. Those have to be somewhere."

"He may have disposed of them before trying for David," Evans said. "Just in case."

"He'd have to be awfully cocky to assume he'd succeed," the Denver man said. "But I'm inclined to think this isn't his room. It's too neat."

Jasper rubbed his neck and thought about it. He had to agree. They'd been led to this room but how could the employees identify him if it wasn't his. He just wasn't thinking straight.

"What time is it?" he finally asked.

"Half past one," Evans said. "And you look beat."

"I feel beat," Jasper admitted. "I need coffee."

They were true cops. Retreating to the 24-hour coffee shop, they mulled over what they'd found and what still needed to be done.

"Has Jake's hotel room been found yet?" Jasper asked. Nursing the coffee cup in his hands, he waited for it to cool. Jameson wasn't waiting but spooning ice into his to cool it down.

Evans, the Cheyenne man, checked his messages. "Not yet. Either he was paid up for more days or the hotel just didn't bother turning it in."

"He was scheduled to be in quarantine at noon tomorrow," Jasper said. "I doubt he had a room past this morning. He would have gone to Laramie tonight like Sasha."

He'd never understood the reasoning for having one of the world's four quarantine facilities in a nothing place like Elk Mountain. The altitude was high but there were higher peaks. It was located next to a major interstate but that had mostly local traffic on it now. It just didn't make sense but there it was. He supposed Wyoming had lobbied hard for it.

His mind was wandering. If he didn't solve this tonight, it wouldn't be his job but it didn't look like it could be solved tonight and he was barely holding it together. He wouldn't recognize a valid clue now if it bit him.

"We're not getting anywhere," he finally said. "And I'm pretty close to useless. Starting tomorrow this won't be my assignment either." He quietly explained the situation to them, stressing his confidence in Lori Brown.

"Tough break," Evans said and he sounded like he meant it. "This case could make careers."

"Yeah but not the one I'm headed for. I'll be happy if it keeps the Wests alive. I've gotten fond of that family."

Evans nodded. "They've been through enough."

"Aren't they related to old what's his name that designed the West-Colman reactor?" Jameson asked.

"That's what I've been told," Jasper said. "And the West

Foundation. David works for Lunar Technologies too."

Evans whistled. "I can see why someone wanted Jake's money. It wouldn't have done them much good though. In my experience, the really rich don't keep money lying around. A thief would have to be a real pro to get hold of any of it and a con man would have better luck than an assassin."

"True." Jasper sipped his coffee. "I guess I'm done. I'll brief Brown tomorrow--today."

"I think I'm done for now," the Cheyenne detective said. "Give me a lift to the train station?"

"Sure. And you to Lunarex," Jameson said to Jasper. "I'll follow up on this tomorrow. If a half dozen of those antique dealers also ID Mr. Starling, we'll know he's not the one."

Jasper nodded but didn't say anything. God, he was tired. Were the Wests waiting for a briefing? He hoped not. He toyed with just getting a room here but decided against it. It wasn't worth the trouble.

And he'd have to make the morning express. Damn.

Chapter 43 - Tuesday

Chimes. Half asleep he heard the five-note combination repeat and frowned. Who was playing them? He was still trying to puzzle it out when something comfortably warm shifted and he felt a draft. Jewel. They were on the train. He yawned.

"Wake up, sleepy," Jewel said and he smelled the aroma of the coffee she was pouring from the thermos.

"Need coffee," he said with his eyes half open. "And a warmer."

"Shameless," she said then spoiled it with a giggle. She put the coffee mug in his hands and settled back against him.

"How long have we got?" Jasper asked. He sipped the too hot coffee and felt life returning. How long had he slept? He'd gotten an hour or so at the apartment before they'd headed for the train. Had he slept through the Cheyenne stop?

"About twenty minutes," Jewel said. "Feel better?"

"Yes," he said then smiled at her. "It must have been hard for you to keep quiet."

"No, I slept with you," she said with a teasing smile. "Now you have to marry me."

"Let's not start that here," he hastily interrupted. "Too damned early."

"When?" she asked then desisted at his look. "Ok, I was tired too. Uncle David and Jessica weren't sniping at each other last night and we actually got along. It was nice but we were really late getting to bed."

"I'm glad," Jasper said. "That was better than what I was doing."

"I'm sure of that," Jewel said, pulling a sandwich out of a bag and handing it to him. "You need this. No breakfast and I doubt you had more than my sandwiches last night."

"I had coffee," he said.

"Not good enough," she retorted. "Eat. You can talk later."

He obeyed, a little bemused by this new Jewel who seemed to have taken over his life. Well, she could have her fun because he was simply too tired right now to fight it.

"They're going to the courthouse and getting the divorce finished today," Jewel said. "Aunt Jessica doesn't want anyone thinking she had anything to do with this so she told her lawyer to cut the crap and go back to what she wanted in the first place. He wasn't happy but he's a lawyer."

"That sounds sensible," he said between bites. "I didn't know I was this hungry. Are you eating?"

"In a minute," Jewel said. "More coffee?"

"Why so conscientious?" he asked, suddenly suspicious. "What are you planning?"

She looked guilty then defiant. "You'll be going back to work and I'm going back to school. I should be able to join my class at noon."

"I'd rather you didn't," he said, frowning at her. "We haven't been able to arrest Kucera."

"Edward Kucera would never get his hands dirty," Jewel said. "And we've got the hit man. I should be perfectly safe today."

He thought about it and had to agree. "Okay, one condition. You've already set me up as your boyfriend with the school. I want to join you when you go outside. What time is that?"

"Two o'clock. We're in by two forty-five."

"I'll be there. Now I think we'll have time to get to Lily Street and change the lock codes. I'll release it on one condition--you aren't to use anything that's been previously opened. I've already cleared out the groceries but I'm talking soap and bath stuff too--even toothpaste. It all goes to the incinerator."

"Yes sir."

"Don't call me sir."

"Yes, Jazz," she said with a mischievous smile. "I do like your name."

He grinned. "And I love yours. Now let's not get distracted," he said as her look changed. The warning bell for an upcoming station sounded at the same time. "Hear that, little Jewel? No time. Lily Street first."

How the hell was he going to get her to wait for the right time and place? Carol had been the shy one in his first marriage and he'd worked long and hard to get her to say yes to him. Now he was being stalked by this girl ten years his junior and he wasn't sure if it was a game or if she was serious and he didn't have time to find out. Certainly the marriage made sense but he didn't want a wife he'd have to worry about. And, if they did marry, he'd have to be doubly careful in his new role.

Well, he'd set no wedding date until he was certain. They could still live together in such a big house but he feared it would be too small if she didn't settle down.

Finishing his sandwich, he gathered up his things as he felt the deceleration begin. It was mild, no worse than an elevator, as they glided to a stop on frictionless rails. They were back in Plains.

* * *

The precinct tower of Section Five looked just the same as it had eight days ago. Jasper studied it from across the small shopping center; looking at two reporters he knew were waiting to ambush him. He hadn't bothered with the cheek pads today. From now on he had to be public and this trial in particular could no longer be avoided. For the last time he wore the conservative black suit and plain white shirt of a police detective. Tomorrow he would dress for his new role.

Taking a deep breath, he crossed to the precinct. Maybe the long wait had made the reporters less observant because he was almost there when one of them suddenly recognized him and moved to intercept.

"Lieutenant Stone?" she asked.

"Yes," he said.

"Lieutenant Stone, are you Sensor Man?" she quickly asked. "And do you have anything to say to your fans?"

He paused, looking into the camera she wore. "Yes, I am Sensor Man but today I'm still a police detective. That's going to change but for now I must stick to police business. Please respect that." He walked on without waiting for an answer.

The precinct doors behind him, he stopped at the reception desk. "Hello, Reg. Have you been having fun with them?"

"It's about time you got back," the receptionist scowled at him then laughed. "It's been a circus. We've got them tamed now. They're only outside."

"Good. Let Captain Reynolds know I'm here. When he's free, I'll be ready. I'll be in my office until then."

"Right, oh, Lieutenant Stone," she said. "They had to take your name off the door already. People were sneaking in."

"That's not surprising," he said. "Thanks for telling me why." He should have expected that. His rank gave him a private office here in his home precinct with his name on the door. The lock wasn't an imprinted one because some bureaucrats had decided that police officers shouldn't have offices that private. Except for the evidence room and the commissioner's own office, there were no imprinted locks even though they were in general use elsewhere. He did have a gun safe though and he'd have to turn in his police issue .45 today. During his eighteen-year career, he'd never actually fired it except on the practice range. In the city, a trank gun and stun grenades had always been sufficient.

Maybe he should have had it in Denver, Jasper mused. No, it was useless against Ex. If he'd been wearing it, Ex might have succeeded in grabbing it. No, the Denver cops and the Cheyenne cops had to wear their side arms in the old town but here there was no old town. In all his years here, he'd never had to deal with a smuggled handgun. There were simply too many inspection stations looking for such things.

Even disassembled parts could be stopped.

Reaching his office, he barely had time to sit down before the expected call came.

Captain Reynolds was in his own office, a step up in luxury from his. Jasper glanced around, half expecting to see Brown too but that was ridiculous. He'd just rarely been here without her since the captain liked both halves of a team to be briefed at once. He knew and the captain knew that even though he was now DEA, Brown would continue to work with him and be his liaison with the department. That had been planned since he first mentioned his plan to his superior. Well, he'd catch up with Brown later.

"Hell of a mess," his captain said as he motioned him closer. "Even I'm glad to see you go, Stone. Here's your resignation. It's involuntary as we agreed and takes effect end of today. If anyone digs into the files, they'll find out you have to a reason to be less than happy with us."

He tapped the paper. "No one liked that, by the way. The deputy mayor refused to sign off on it so they had to kick it upstairs to the mayor--he's not running for re-election. The city attorney told them you could sue and win if you tried. I had to tell them you wouldn't sue."

"Did you tell them why?" Jasper asked.

"Tell the mayor? No. The city attorney, I gave some of it. Gordon doesn't know whom you'll be working for but he knows you'll be working and it's necessary. He convinced the mayor."

"Good. I won't be making any public comment about why or even how. Sensor Man has enough money to just let it roll off his back," Jasper said as he signed the paperwork and put his thumbprint to it. "I need to brief Brown on the current case though."

"We're about done here," the captain said. "But I have some questions about that book theft. It's just too odd when you combine it with the missing tablecloths. Where do you think this professor fits in?"

"I'm not sure he is in," Jasper said. "I'm fairly sure Edward Kucera is. He was at the Reach Out event where the professor was talking about his book. He probably didn't call in the tip himself but I'm sure he had something to do with it. I'm also suspecting him in the West murders."

"How so?" The captain looked interested.

"He was Jake West's attorney and legal representative. He was also the one who secured a sponsorship for Jake to qualify for Mars. By having Jake's power-of-attorney, he basically had control of his money--and there's a lot there. If Jake had turned thirty, it would have been sixty million. It might be more than that now but I'm not sure if he'd inherit from the others."

His captain looked really interested now. "And Jake on Mars and unable to come back?" He understood. "He would have had sole control."

"Yes. It might have taken a few years of legal battles between him and the other family lawyers but if Jake had been the last one standing, he eventually would have won."

"So why is Jake dead?"

"I think he got cold feet," Jasper said. "He was forced to play a part in it. I'm not sure why they did that unless they meant to keep him in line with blackmail. Anyway, he went into hiding so they eliminated him. Maybe he was thinking of talking."

"That could be," the captain said. "It was too bad he didn't. So do you want to bring Kucera in or see if he leads you to the drug smuggling operation?"

"He's a danger to the remaining Wests," Jasper said. "If we can bring him in and question him about that, it might save Jewel's life and I'm going to marry her."

The captain blinked. "Say again?"

"I'm going to marry Jewel West."

"Damn it, Jazz, you're assigned to that case," Captain Reynolds exploded. "You can't do that."

"Put it in my file as the reason for the involuntary

separation. I'm going to marry her."

The captain stared at him. "Damn it, does the girl even know what she's getting into? How could you use her that way?"

"I'm not using her," Jasper quietly said. "I'm protecting her from the likes of Kucera. I'll make sure she stays out of the DEA stuff. She'll just be the wife of Sensor Man."

"I don't like it," his captain said.

"Then you don't have to come to the wedding," Jasper responded. "Knowing her it's going to be a long and drawn out celebration and I'm not looking forward to it. Did you know her aunt is Jessica West?"

"No. You've already proposed to her?" The captain looked sharp. "Or is this still in the works?"

"No, I haven't proposed but it's pretty much a done deal. I think I'd have to go to Mars to get out of it."

Reynolds caught that and suddenly grinned. "Damn, you've been busy. How the hell are you going to explain this to your daughter?"

"I'm not thinking about that now. I'm thinking about Kucera," Jasper said. "I'm trying to think of some way to get him interrogated. He was Jake's lawyer and Jake revoked the assignment and now Jake is dead. Do you think that will fly?"

"Yes," Reynolds said. "I want your reports. Can you get them done this afternoon?"

"I'll try. You'll have them tomorrow morning if not. I'll siphon them through Brown."

"Good enough. Well, I don't like this wedding idea but I guess it's going to be. Just don't go doing it this month. It would look bad for the department."

"We've got some things to iron out first," Jasper said. "You'll get the invite when the date is set."

"Thanks and good luck."

Chapter 44 - Termination

Back in his office, Jasper busied himself with packing. He didn't have much here that he valued. His spare suit he'd donate to the station's wardrobe and he planned to add two more and the one he was wearing over the next week. He didn't want to look like a police detective or wear the uniform white shirts again. Now he could spend more for what Sensor Man should wear. He knew he'd never go flashy but he looked forward to being able to choose his own style.

Adding Carol's photo frame to his box, he cleared items from his desktop. The thing that would take the longest was his com unit. The department issued one he had turned in years ago since he found it inadequate. The one he used was his personal property but the department techs would have to go over its settings to confirm he was really locked out of the police net. Once that was done, he could arrange a meeting with Carlson and get some new settings installed. It couldn't be done before without the tech guys possibly finding his access.

He had to get that done but he'd wait until after he met Jewel. She came before department bureaucracy now.

The in-office intercom flashed and he hit the button, wondering who wanted him. He expected Brown for a final briefing but they'd scheduled that for 3:30.

"Lieutenant Stone, there's an incoming call from the Colonial Authority," the switchboard operator said. "About the Wests."

"Ok, let me have it." Jasper threw the call onto the vid screen and waited.

"Lieutenant Stone? Yes, I see you are. I have some questions about the Wests." The man looked like a bureaucrat with his white shirt and the rust red jacket of the Colonial Authority. His hair was almost as short as a spacer's cut but Jasper doubted the man had ever been off Earth. Colonial

Authority bureaucrats never got to Mars.

"And you are?" Jasper asked in a crisp voice.

"Oh, sorry. I'm Ronald Jeffers, first assistant in Reproductive Affairs, Colonial Authority." He barely paused before getting down to it. "Lieutenant Stone, we need to know about the Wests. First is Sasha West under suspicion in her husband's murder?"

"No." It came out flat and uncompromising. "Next question."

"We saw there was an APB out for Jake West and it pertained to the deaths of other family members. Was he guilty of.... murder?"

Jasper had his answer ready. "The APB was because Jake had gone missing and we feared for his safety. As it was, we were right but too late. He was already dead."

"Oh, I'm sorry to hear that," the official said. "But was he guilty of murder?"

"What is this about?" Jasper asked, irritated. "Are you going to bump Sasha because Jake died?"

"No, no, of course not. It's just that," the man took a deep breath, "Mrs. West wants to exercise her right to have her husband's children. We cannot allow the genes of a murderer into the Martian gene pool."

Jasper stared at him. Did he know how bigoted he sounded? Could they even legally do that? No, Jake had not been charged and he hadn't been tried and this idiot was judging him when only the law had that right. It was outrageous and illegal.

"Jake West was not charged. He was a person of interest. If I hear that you have dumped his sperm for any reason, I will call for an investigation of the Colonial Authority and your decision for a violation of reproductive rights. Is that clear?"

"Yes sir." The man looked relieved. "I will enter that into the official record. He was not a murderer. Thank you."

Jasper stared at the blank screen for a long moment,

knowing he had stretched the truth. It was pretty certain that Jake had intended murder but why punish Sasha and her unborn children? And that damned bureaucrat actually seemed relieved he'd stood up to him. Maybe he wasn't as bigoted as he sounded. Maybe it was his unpleasant duty to ask--a task given to an assistant because someone higher up didn't have the guts.

He saved the call in his com unit and forwarded it to Sasha with a note to keep it. He wasn't too surprised that Sasha was exercising her right or that Jake had sperm in the colony banks. Reproductive rights were carefully guarded and it wasn't uncommon for both men and women to have genetic material stored in their twenties so they could have healthier children at a later age.

David might want to know about this but he probably wouldn't hamper it. By law children conceived after a death could not inherit without the agreement of all beneficiaries. Unless the West family agreed any children Sasha bore would inherit from her alone. Well, she'd have enough. Every dollar of Jake's money she invested in Mars would be hers. The fruits of her investments would belong to her children.

He glanced at the time again. One twenty. He'd have to leave soon to meet Jewel at the school. He'd come back after to finish up.

Brown came in followed by the Cheyenne detective. "Jasper, you've got to hear this," Brown said. "Detective Evans, Cheyenne P.D."

"Hello again," Jasper said, wondering how long this would take but curious. Ex was in custody. What could this be?

"I'm glad we caught you. We found Jake West's hotel room," the detective said. "And there was this addressed to you." He held up a flasher. "We've copied it and you need to see it."

Without asking, he plugged it into the computer slot and threw the image onto the vid screen. Jasper found himself looking at an agitated Jake West.

"If you're seeing this, I'm dead. Hell, I know I'm dead," Jake wrung his hands in his lap and there were clear signs of grief and fear on his face. "If they catch me before I enter quarantine, I'm dead. He'll kill me for sure."

"My only hope is getting into quarantine but I'm pretty sure I won't make it. I know just enough to hurt them. Well, if they're going to kill me, there's no reason to keep quiet about any of it."

"Lieutenant Stone, I admit to killing my Grandma, Elizabeth West. Well, almost. I gave her some poison but it didn't work. She tasted it. I was desperate so I hit her but she was still alive. When Smith got there, I was told to get out. I left by the upper door, took father's car and headed back to Denver."

"I didn't do anything to Uncle Mike," he said. "Nothing! I didn't even know that was planned. I guess I was naive. I thought it was just going to be Grandma but... " He took a deep breath. "They wanted me in Denver. They needed me to get Smith into Lunarex Tower and Dad's apartment. That's why I left the funeral but...I... couldn't do it." He rested his head in his hands and didn't look up.

"I didn't plan this. Hell, when I took the sponsorship, I had no idea they'd ask me to do this. Ed said I'd have to work to prove my loyalty but.... damn him! He said Centrax was thinking of pulling my sponsorship. I was less than a month away from leaving this fuckin' planet and he talked about killing my only chance. I couldn't let it happen. I couldn't."

"It's Kucera--Edward Kucera," Jake said and Jasper's jaw tightened. "He got me the sponsorship with Centrax. Then he hired Smith to help me kill Grandma. There's a second man too by the name of Jones. Hell, he even gave me the valium for Uncle Mike."

"I dumped all my texts from him on to this flasher. There's no vid. Lieutenant Stone, save Jewel and Dad. I know he wants the damned house but I think there's more to it than that. Tomorrow I'm going to an attorney and getting him locked out of my trust. That's all I can do to help."

"I'm done. I should have gone to Dad when this started but I didn't. I'm as big a fool as Dad thought I was. Worse. I killed Grandma."

The confession abruptly ended and Jasper stared, his mind racing over what he said. "Starling is Smith? Or is he Jones? Two of them? Jewel!"

"Jewel?" Brown asked but Jasper was already moving. He slapped his hand on to the face of his gun safe and punched the four-digit combination to open it. Grabbing his police special, he raced out the door, com unit in hand.

Evans raced after him, cramming into the elevator with him.

"Emergency exit, ground level, Lieutenant Jasper Stone, authorization ten eighteen alpha tango," he snapped into his com unit.

"Jasper, is that?"

"DO IT!" Jasper shut the operator up. "Just do it." He glanced at the time and saw it was 1:55. She would be getting ready to leave.

The door had an inspection station and it sent off alarms as the two armed men rushed by. He didn't care. Plowing to a stop, he looked once for the school and cursed. They were on the wrong side of the tower. He ran.

Evans didn't ask questions but kept pace, his gun still holstered. They rounded the tower and Jasper sprinted toward the Peak. Two subbies crossed his path with a basket of produce and he plowed through them without stopping. He had to get to Jewel.

There it was just fifty yards away. Even as he spied the red brick of the school, the side door opened and students spilled out. Jewel followed them, herding the slower children out the door. Another teacher followed.

"Jewel, go back," he shouted then stumbled on the uneven path and fell. Evans leaped past him but he wasn't heading for

Jewel. There was a subby heading for her--a subby with Starling's face!

He lurched to his feet and dashed. Jewel had heard him but she was gathering the children up. Uncomprehending children weren't moving fast enough.

"Just get inside, damn it," Jasper yelled as he crossed the last feet. "You, not the kids. He's not after them."

Evans had reached the killer, tackling him as the man turned toward him. It was only the killer who got up. Evans tried but collapsed.

Jasper saw Starling rise, pull Evans's gun from his holster and aim. He tackled Jewel, taking her to the ground just as the bullet tore into his back. The impact slammed him into the ground and his gun fell from his loosened grip.

Jewel, he tried to say but Jewel was holding his gun. He looked up as his precious Jewel leveled it like a pro and fired once then a second time. Gasping for air, he passed out.

When he could see again Brown was there, pressing down on his wound. "You're damned lucky, Stone," she snapped at him. "You'll live. Jewel, hands here," she ordered and Jewel's hands replaced hers.

Jasper struggled to move but Jewel held him down. "Is he dead?" he gasped the words.

"Yes," Jewel said. "How'd he get away?"

"He didn't," Jasper said. "Jake said... two."

"Don't you pass out again," Jewel shrieked at him. "You stay with me, Jazz Stone."

"Didn't know you could shoot." He struggled to stay conscious but lost.

When he came back again, paramedics were there. Jewel clung tightly to his hand until he was loaded into the ambulance. She was alive. He clung to that. He saved her.

Chapter 45 ~ Wednesday, 20 July 2179

Jasper blinked then shut his eyes against bright lights. Sighing, he winced as pain shot through his chest. Memory flooded back of the killer and the kids and Jewel--Jewel shot him? His Jewel? Someone said he was dead. Yeah, he was dead.

Where was Jewel? He had a hazy memory of the hospital and doctors but where was Jewel? He opened his eyes and the room seemed dimmer. God, was he losing it?

"I turned down the lights," Jewel said as she bent over him, "and called the nurse. Do you need anything?"

He croaked and his precious, precious Jewel was there with water and a straw. His eyes teared and he clutched her hand before going back to sleep.

The second time he woke Brown was there. He moved his lips then quit when she put a brown hand lightly on them.

"Jewel's sleeping," she said. "You start talking and she'll be crying over you again." She calmly held water and straw for him. "She's a hell of a shot. She plugged that guy dead center and it was a good thing too. He killed Evans."

Jasper struggled to put that together, his mind fuzzy with painkillers.

"As far as we know, it's over. Kucera is in custody in Denver." She set the water down.

"Mel?" he croaked.

"She's been here and would have stayed but she's got a midterm at eight. She'll be back after," Brown said. "I told her she could miss it but she's your daughter and, no, she isn't telling anyone you're her dad. She's got guts."

He smiled, closed his eyes, and faded back into sleep.

When he woke the third time Brown was gone and it was Jewel who held the water cup. She repeated to him that

Starling was dead and they were safe like it was a litany. Had she been repeating that all night? He didn't know.

Moving one hand, he caught hers in his grip. "What all did they do to me?" he asked in a stronger voice.

"Operated," she said. "Your lung collapsed--I don't know the medical terms. Bullet nicked a lung. They messed up your left pec fixing it."

"Oh," he said and felt some relief. It could have been worse.

"You'll be all right," she said. "And I'll get a nurse and get you home to Lily Street."

"No nurse," he managed to say. "Just you."

She leaned over and kissed him lightly, tenderly. It was brief but enough for now.

"I'm hungry," he said.

Jewel laughed but fetched a bowl of broth from a hospital tray then helped him sit up in the bed. "I love feeding you," she said and he allowed it, too weak to fight as she spooned warm broth into his mouth. "You lost a lot of blood. They gave you more but you're supposed to take it easy. It's a good thing the department doesn't need you."

"Oh, and I met Mel. She's a lot older than I expected but pretty. For some reason I was thinking she was about fourteen. Sasha looks younger than her sometimes." She prattled on but he was content to lie there and accept the broth. God, he must be weaker than he thought. The broth tasted good.

He finally croaked "Enough" and she put it down.

"Do you want to sleep now? More water? Or do you need a nurse?"

He shook his head and lay back. "Hand."

She gave it to him and they just sat there in silence, her warm fingers clasped in his, her thumb slowly stroking his hand. His eyes closed but he hadn't drifted off yet when he heard voices in the hall. Opening his eyes, he saw his partner and daughter enter together.

"Dad." Mel rushed to his side, almost hugging him before she remembered.

"Mel," he said. "Exam?"

"Oh, I aced it. Calculus. No big deal."

"Jewel," he said and pointed toward her without raising his hand.

"Yeah, we met," Mel said with a puzzled expression, "but I thought she was old."

Brown laughed.

Jewel looked at him accusingly.

How had Mel got that idea? He didn't know.

"Not that old," Jewel said. "I'll be twenty-seven."

"Oh." Mel looked embarrassed. "Sorry, he said he was protecting someone and showed me a picture of you and an old lady. I thought he meant her."

"That was my grandmother," Jewel said. "She's gone." Her tone was flat, matter-of-fact, and Jasper knew the hurt was still too deep.

"I'm sorry," Mel said. "I just misunderstood."

"It happens. Now is your full name Melanie?"

"Melody," his daughter said. "Just Melody. My friends call me Mel."

Jewel stared at her in disbelief then turned on him. "Jazz Stone, you named her Melody? Are you going to name our children after music?"

"Children?" Mel shrieked. "Dad!"

Hastily, he closed his eyes and made his face relax. With an effort he made his breathing even while Mel said something else then abruptly cut off. A hand brushed his cheek and he let it, not giving any resistance at all.

"He's asleep," Brown said with a low laugh. "I'll get the nurse. You'd better save it, Mel, till he can stay awake."

Jewel was still clutching his hand. When Mel tried to talk, she shushed her. God, the only thing he could do was feign sleep. He hadn't wanted Mel to find out this way. How could he explain when he hadn't even known Jewel ten days ago?

His act was edging toward real sleep when he heard a new voice, one he didn't know, talking. A cool hand felt his pulse and his forehead.

"Just sleep," the nurse said. "You'd better go. He's had enough excitement today."

Jewel released his hand with a soft pat and he felt her leave but couldn't muster up the energy to open his eyes.

"Now, lieutenant, go to sleep," the nurse said in a quiet voice. "No more visitors till you are really rested." She lowered his bed. "You have a good partner. Now go to sleep."

He opened his eyes long enough to see the nurse leave the room then sank into slumber.

It was afternoon when he woke again. No Jewel, he thought. He was trying to reach the call button when a male hand pushed it for him. He smiled at his captain and croaked a hello.

"Water, I take it," the captain said. "I'm just here for a bit, Jazz. They said you'll be better tomorrow. You just lost a lot of blood and collapsed a lung. Got it fixed now."

He stepped away when the nurse came in and waited while things were done to make him more comfortable.

"This room isn't secure so I won't say much," Captain Reynolds said. "You just picked a hell of a time to get shot. They were ready to go with the announcement that you'd left the service when that happened. Now Legal is going to make you take a pension. If you don't, the union will scream bloody murder. I don't care what it does to your plans--you'll have to take it. A cop cannot get shot in this day and age and not get one."

Jasper managed a nod. His mind was too fuzzy to think it through but it sounded right.

"I've met the girl," his captain said, "And I can't say I blame you for wanting her even if your timing stinks. She's a beauty and a sure shot too. I saw the body and she plugged him a lot better than he did you--the two bullets weren't more than a couple of fingers apart. Fine shooting."

He paused. "She might not have told you yet but the school fired her. They just couldn't have a teacher that endangered the kids even if it wasn't her fault. Tread a little easy on that, Jazz."

Jasper cleared his throat. "I will."

"You should keep talking. It'll help," his captain said. "The two hitmen were almost identical from what I hear. One's dead and the other is still locked up. Ed Kucera is sitting in jail down in Denver. He's asked for an attorney so you may be on your feet before they get around to questioning him."

Reynolds stopped to offer him the cup of water again. "I'm going to talk to the mayor about letting you continue on this one case."

"Thanks," Jasper said. "I need to see it done."

"Better," his captain said. "You'll get through this. Just don't have that wedding night too soon. From the looks of her, you'll need to be a hell of a lot stronger." He chuckled. "Ok, I've got to go. I'll send your love back in."

Chapter 46 ~ Thursday, 22 July 2179

"We're here with the people of the hour, Lieutenant Jasper Stone, and the woman who saved his life. Jewel West, isn't it?" Rex Allen thrust his microphone at her. "How did you become such a good shot?"

"My grandfather," Jewel said from her perch on the hospital bed. "When I was young, we'd go target shooting together."

"Your grandfather? Was that Benjamin West, one of the founders of Plains?"

"Yes, that's right." Jewel clutched Jasper's hand tighter. "We were very close."

"I'm sure you were," Rex said. "And it's good he taught you to shoot. Lieutenant Stone, is it true that the shooter was a professional hitman known as the Executioner?"

"Yes," Jasper said, his voice stronger today. "But he was only half of the Executioner. There were two of them--Smith and Jones. Between the two, they are credited with at least eight murders and there might be more than thirty."

"Where is the other one?" Rex asked without missing a beat even though he hadn't known that. "Is he still at large?"

"No, Smith is locked up down in Denver. Jones was the one shot here." He held Jewel's hand tightly, knowing what would come next. "They were after the West family. Smith has been charged with the murder of Jake West and attempted murder of David West."

"And Elizabeth and Michael West?" Rex asked.

"We aren't sure which of them did it," Jasper said. "It could have been either one. They weren't twins but they were still so identical witnesses have not been able to tell them apart. Brothers or cousins, we think."

"But they've been stopped? The people of Plains aren't

likely to see any more of them?" Rex asked.

"That's right. No more killings," Jasper said. "People can rest easy on that score."

Rex nodded and turned away to do a short recap of what had happened. He was good, not giving out the real names of the men but sticking to the aliases the killers themselves had used. By law neither the actual names or pictures of killers could be aired on public channels unless they were still at large.

Jewel clasped Jasper's hand tightly and looked at him, not the camera, as the description went on. Jasper listened, hearing how a fine upstanding police detective from Cheyenne had given his life in at attempt to stop the Executioner. He'd only glimpsed Evans's death himself but he wasn't surprised to hear Starling got him with curare. It was Evans's gun he used.

Brown had told him of a road car in the parking lot too. Starling had bought it outright then drove it up from Denver in the early morning hours. Once here, he'd changed into subby clothing and simply joined the pickers. He hadn't gone through any inspection stations and no one had noticed another subby. He'd simply waited for Jewel to come out with her class. If Jasper had been slower, he would have found a way to inject her and disappeared in the confusion.

His hand tightened on Jewel's before he forced himself to lighten his grip. Starling was dead. Kucera was in custody. It wasn't going to happen again.

"So what's next for you, Lieutenant?" Rex was asking. "Will you stay on the force or be Sensor Man?"

"I am Sensor Man," Jasper said. "Since I can't do police work effectively with that notoriety, I have no choice but to leave the force. Music will be my life now."

"And you, Miss West?" Rex looked at her. "What are your plans?"

"I'm his bodyguard," Jewel said. "If anyone wants to mess with Sensor Man, they need to know I'm a dead shot."

Rex laughed. "Folks, you have it there. The woman who saved his life is now his bodyguard. Will there be something more? Tune in to Plains TV2 to find out."

The cameraman signaled he was off camera and Rex turned back to them. "Great line, Ms. West. I'm sure we can milk it. Jasper, I'm glad you'll be ok. Will you call me when you're ready to do a full interview?"

"You bet," Jasper said. "And thanks for not asking too much about the Wests."

Rex shrugged. "They aren't the real story here--you and Jewel are and that Executioner," he said. "And I can't do too much with the Executioner. Did I tell you the syndicates have bought this story?"

"Yeah," Jasper said. "I'm glad I could help out."

"No need to get shot," Rex said. "I would have been just as happy with the Sensor Man interview. You were damned lucky, you know."

"I know." Jasper said and suddenly felt tired. "I wish Evans had been too."

Jewel sensed his change of mood. "It's time you left, Mr. Allen. He needs to rest."

"Right." Rex motioned to his cameraman then turned back. "When do you get out of here, Lieutenant?"

"Jasper," he corrected without opening his eyes. "Maybe tomorrow. Maybe not." He heard him leave then forced his eyes open again. "Come here, Jewel."

She was beside him in a moment, her slender fingers slipping into his lax hand.

"Forget that," he said. "Kiss me."

After a slight hesitation, she obeyed, lightly brushing his lips in a quick kiss.

"That's the best you can do?" he teased.

She took the challenge, lips pressed against his in a kiss he couldn't help returning. She tasted him, teasing him with her tongue. When she would have pulled away, he held her head closer with his good hand and slowly took his turn. She was almost as breathless as he was when he was done.

"Damn," she said and he laughed then coughed.

She was instantly all concern and solicitude but he managed to jerk the call button away from her. "Don't," he said. "Water." They'd just taken the monitors off him before the interview and he had no intention of having them on again. He took a long drink and pushed the dull ache of his chest to the back of his mind. He'd never been good about taking painkillers and he didn't want to start now--not even Bliss.

Jewel watched him carefully till he smiled at her. "Swallowed wrong," he lied.

"Uh-huh."

"Are you ready to sneak me out of here?" he asked. Carefully he swung his legs onto the floor and eased himself up. Jewel looked ready to support him but he waved her away. He was still weak but he could walk.

"I am not sneaking you out," Jewel said. "If the doctor releases you, I'll take you home in a hired car. And you will go to bed and stay there another day." She folded her arms and her chin jutted out like she was ready for a fight. "And I got a nurse. Live with it."

Jasper grimaced but didn't protest. No privacy. If they could get him up to the third floor bedroom at all, he'd probably be stuck there for the duration. He'd prefer being closer to the kitchen.

"Did you get any shopping done?" he asked. "Is there real food in the house?"

"I asked Linda to do it," Jewel said. "She used to pick up stuff for grandmother all the time."

"Right." He'd forgotten about the maid. "Did you dump the lotions and soaps and stuff?"

"Done," Jewel said. "I haven't got new yet but I still have what I took to Denver--and I'm going to take some stuff from here. You got that?"

"Yes, ma'am." Jasper grinned. "Hospital stuff."

"Better than nothing," she said. "Live with it."

He laughed and managed not to cough this time. "You'd better not get too bossy," he said. "When this chest heals, you'll regret it."

"Oh, no," Jewel said in mock dismay and laughed too.

"Well, that sounds better," a male voice said and Jewel turned to see the doctor in his white uniform coat. "I heard someone was trying to escape."

Jewel pointed to him.

"Traitor," Jasper muttered under his breath but was relieved when Jewel left the room. "This won't take long," the doctor said and examined his incision then the actual bullet hole. "Yes, healing nicely. It can still re-open though. Is it tender here?"

"No," Jasper quickly said. When the doctor waited, he changed his statement. "Not much."

"That's better," the doctor said. "No signs of infection. You should be good to go tomorrow."

"Tomorrow?" Jasper frowned.

"Tomorrow unless I have your word that you'll avoid any strenuous activity. No push-ups and no chasing after anyone younger than you," the doctor said.

"No push-ups?" Jasper asked, confused.

"You heard me. For ten days. No push-ups and no pressure on that side of your chest. Find another way to do it." The doctor signed his chart. "I'll get someone in here to help you dress if you insist on going now. Do I have your word?"

Jasper understood finally. "Yes sir. No push-ups and no pressure. No running around."

"After anyone younger than you," the doctor finished with a grin. "Take it easy. It'll be worth the wait."

Right, Jasper thought as the doctor left. Wait. Well, he could wait but would Jewel? She'd just have to. Suddenly glad of the nurse and the maid, he waited for what would come.

Chapter 47 ~ Sunday, 25 July 2179

It was a perfect summer day. The sun was westering and the shadows of the trees were starting to creep across the ground. The sky was a deep blue with only one lonely cloud to mar it. Laramie Peak itself was tree-covered and, at this season, without snow.

He sipped his coffee and studied the peak and wondered if anyone ever climbed it anymore--something he had never wondered before. He didn't want to do it himself but he wondered. He also wondered what it looked like snow-covered. Had he ever been outside in the winter? Not in the line of duty, he decided. Yes, he had taken Mel out when she was three to play in the snow. His lips twitched at the memory of how she'd screamed when he sat her down in the cold, wet snow. Until then he'd believed all kids would be fascinated by snow because he'd liked it once. Maybe now he would go out again since Jewel liked the outside.

It had taken two days for him to get up the stairs and out of the first floor bedroom. He'd had to since the movers showed up and started unloading his music equipment on this floor. Some of his furniture was still in storage but not a lot because Jewel had cleaned house. The living room downstairs had new carpet and the Japanese figurines were packed away. She'd even sent the remaining white furniture to an auction house since she didn't want to think about it again.

The black leather furniture he'd once seen on the first floor had been moved back there and his own living room furniture installed in the upstairs. Only the second floor looked untouched by the shifting and moving and that was deceiving. He knew Mel's bedroom had been recreated in one of the bedrooms so she would feel at home here.

Mel had promised to bring her boyfriend by to set up his music equipment but he was fairly sure he'd get to it first. David would be here tonight and he was sure the lunatech could do the shifting he still wasn't allowed to do. He was itching to play and knew it was because he was so idle. It had been almost two years since he'd had so many days off in a row and he itched to do something, anything, to distract him from Jewel.

She wasn't going to wait much longer but he still couldn't do her justice. He wanted to be fit and completely able when he took her to bed. No push-ups. He snorted. What the hell did that doctor know about push-ups?

He took his arm out of its sling and slowly stretched, careful not to take it past the point of pain. No, not yet. He could feel the pulling of his muscles and the tenderness. Hearing the squawk of the intercom, he started then remembered Jewel was out. She hadn't seen him.

"What is it, Linda?" he asked.

"Sir, Detective Brown is here. She's on her way up," the maid said even as Brown appeared at the head of the stairs and strode across the room.

"He's dead," she said without preamble, her clipped words barely concealing her anger. "Killed himself two days ago and they just now got this to me." She looked around for the computer slot, found it by the vid screen and plugged a flasher in.

"Who? Kucera?" Jasper bit off his exclamation, his boredom forgotten in a rush of anger. "How the hell did that happen?"

"Can she hear us up here?" Brown asked, motioning toward the stairs. "Blitzen."

What the hell? Jasper looked at his partner then turned the intercom on. "Linda, how do I blank the windows up here?"

"There's a control by the doors, sir. It's red. Would you like me to do it?"

"No, we'll get it. Don't come up. We're going to be looking

at some police business."

"Yes sir. I'll stay down here."

"Thanks, you're a treasure," Jasper said and he meant it. The maid had proved to be more helpful than Jewel in his convalescence. Jewel was just too distracting.

"What's up? Why Blitzen?" he asked as he shut the intercom off.

"He had a visitor before he did it," Brown said. "Someone we know. Since he's not a lawyer, the jailor left his cell camera on and recording. Watch."

Jasper turned to the vid screen and his eyes widened as a bearded and spectacled figure appeared. "The professor?"

Andrew Nugent was just entering the cell and it was clear the two knew each other but there was no overture of friendship. They stood well apart.

Edward Kucera had lost his professional polish, his street clothes having been changed for the coveralls all prisoners wore. His profile was haggard as he greeted his visitor.

"Drew? Why you?" he demanded then cleared his throat. "Why did you come?" His hand made a quick motion and the professor turned toward the camera.

"Is it on?" the professor asked.

"Probably," Kucera said. "I'm on suicide watch." He barked laughter. "Fools."

"I see," the professor said. "Well, you should be. I just found out you'd been arrested. What the hell were you doing? The West family..."

"What are you talking about?" Kucera quickly interrupted. "Jake was my client. I would have to be insane to have anything to do with his murder. He was worth too damned much to me. You know how hard I worked to get him that sponsorship."

The professor peered at him, his hand stroking his bearded chin. "Well, in 23 hours it'll be over. The judge waits."

"23?" Kucera froze, his face visibly pale. "23 hours?"

"That's what I'm told," Drew said without moving. "23

hours. You have an appointment."

"Why you?" Kucera was sitting on his bunk now, his back to the camera. "Why you?"

"My book," Drew said and his face hardened. "You know how I hate scandal but you used me and my book. I was questioned." He stood implacable. "I can't forgive that."

"It wasn't me," Kucera said. "I swear it wasn't."

"Then who?" the professor asked, his hesitation almost unnoticeable. "Give me a name."

"I can't," Kucera said.

"No, you can't," the professor repeated. "23 hours."

"Elaine will stand by you," the professor said. "She doesn't know."

Kucera cleared his throat. "Drew, I'm not guilty. You must know that. Mike, Elizabeth..."

"I don't know what to believe," the professor said. "Jake named you. They'll find out and they must not know."

"Damn you," Kucera said in a voice so low that the microphone nearly didn't pick it up.

The professor either didn't hear or ignored it. "I'll look after Barry. He's got a head for history."

Kucera stood up. "Thank you for coming. I'll think of you every time I pick up a book."

"Do that." The professor turned and called out to the guard. An instant later he was gone and Kucera was back on his bunk, his head in his hands.

"That's the end of it," Brown said as she froze the image. "After that he asked for some paper and a pen and started writing. There's a handwritten confession, notes to his wife, and a couple of other things. They've got all that."

"So how did he do it?" Jasper asked, his mind still racing over what the professor said. "And what is this 23 hours business? He repeated that."

"No one is sure but we think it was a code. If so, the professor is in this up to his eyeballs. We can't ignore him."

"No but we can't bring him in, either. After last time he'll scream for a lawyer every time. So how did Kucera do it?" He waved at the screen. "He was under suicide watch."

"He got ready for bed as usual. The only thing different was he asked for a bliss tab. The guard got him one from the usual supply. Kucera laid down on his bunk, chewed his tab and went to sleep. The room sensors didn't recognize his death for over an hour. They think he was brain dead long before that."

"How?" Jasper stared at her. "From Bliss?"

"They confiscated the jail supply and they're testing it. The guard swore he took one at random and it was no different than any of the others. He handed out four that night and there were no other reactions. Full autopsy."

"Damn."

"We've lost Kucera," Brown said. "But I think the professor might be a hell of a lot more useful. We know he's a link now and he doesn't know we know."

"Hell, he said that in front of an active camera," Jasper said. "That doesn't strike me as smart."

"So maybe he's an errand boy," Brown said. "One thing we know for sure is Kucera was not at the top of it. He took an order to commit suicide and he got it from the professor. It hasn't really stopped."

"Jewel?" He considered it then shook his head. "No, if they make another move against the Wests, they tip their hand. If they leave the family alone then the suspicion dies with Kucera. Did you get his confession?"

"No, his lawyer promptly made a move to suppress it. It's locked up, everything's locked up, in the Denver DA's office. I heard he admits guilt. That's all I know."

"You're kidding." Jasper rubbed his hand through his thick, brown hair.

"No," Brown said. "The only motive we have is he was Jake's lawyer and could have ended up managing all the West money if Jake was on Mars and the rest of the family was gone. Killing Jake though doesn't fit."

"I agree," Jasper said. That couldn't have been a neater plan but for some reason they didn't do it. Why had Kucera involved Jake? It didn't make sense. Surely they could have gotten to every one of the Wests in time. "So what we've got is Jake's confession before his murder and Kucera's confession before his suicide. They almost balance out."

"Almost," Brown agreed. "Murder still trumps suicide. The judge will have to rule that way eventually."

"True," he said. "But I'd like to read that confession. How long do you think they'll take?"

"It could be months or even years," Brown said. "If Kucera is found guilty of murder, his widow could lose almost everything to the Wests. She'll block it as long as she can."

"True," Jasper said but he couldn't see either David or Jewel filing a civil suit against Kucera's estate. They didn't need the money and Jewel had already mentioned a friendship between Kucera's wife and her grandmother. "Can I keep that flasher?"

"Yes," Brown said. "You'd better password it though. You've been locked out of the police net, you know."

"Yeah," Jasper said. "Well, with Kucera dead, I can't say I'm still working on the West case. It's over."

"Right," Brown said. "But I'll keep you informed. The tenth of the month is coming up soon and they'll try to get another shipment of Blissex in. We'll see if they try the tablecloth trick again."

"Good. Anything more on the Starlings?"

"Samuel Starling had been hauled in twice and questioned on other murders. The second time he was let go when another murder happened while he was in custody. Apparently that's what John was trying to do when he came up here--provide proof that his brother was not the Executioner. He must not have known we got Samuel with a full syringe of curare."

"And where did they get the stuff?" Jasper asked.

"A quick search of their family showed family members

employed by both hospitals and euthanasia shops. Any one of them could have supplied the curare. Cyanide has industrial uses so it could have come from anywhere."

"Are they investigating the relatives?" Jasper asked.

"It's going to take time," Brown said. "We aren't talking one or two businesses. They have relatives all over Illinois and Michigan and their primary career field seems to be the euthanasia system. At least fifteen stores are going to have to be inventoried."

"It might not do any good," Jasper said. "I've thought of a way they could accumulate curare without it being on the books."

"How?" Brown asked.

"I was there when they injected Carol. She was already asleep from the Valium so there was no pain for her. I watched." He forced himself to recall that scene. "They injected her with fifty ccs of curare. The attendant told me forty were needed for a woman of her body weight but they always went ten over to ensure it worked. If a clinic was supposed to use fifty but only used forty, there would be ten ccs available for other uses--and not on the books."

"Damn." Brown looked at him in shock. "Can I confirm this?"

"I've already called the director at Soma and asked her if it was possible," Jasper said. "She was shocked. She said it was and she would personally take steps to verify that did not happen at her clinic."

"I'll bet. Jasper, I'll pass that on to the right people. Thanks." She hesitated. "I wish that hadn't happened to you or Carol."

"I know but it's time to move on," he said and he no longer felt even a twinge of guilt. "Carol would be happy I found someone like Jewel." His com unit buzzed and he answered it.

"Is it ok to come up?" Jewel asked. "Linda said police business."

"Yes, we're done. Did you collect the company?" He knew

she'd gone to meet David and Elinor at the train station.

Brown was busy blanking the vid screen and unblanking the windows. She handed him the flasher and smoothly took the com unit from his hand. "Sling," she muttered then spoke cheerfully into the unit. "Jewel, when are you going to marry this guy?"

Chapter 48 - Plans

They both heard Jewel's laughter as she appeared on the stairs, David and Elinor behind her. "I'm trying but--" She shrugged, her blue eyes on Jasper.

"Too eager," Jasper said. "When the time is right." How could he tell her here in public that he wanted to give her his best? He couldn't do that till he was healed up.

"Look at you," Elinor said, taking in his black round-necked shirt and star locket. "Really rad as the kids say. I love the star."

"Not cop-like for sure," David said with a nod of greeting to Brown. "Isn't that the Futura Project's star?"

Jasper laughed. "No, it's a compass star--sometimes called a compass rose. Futura uses one like it but it goes back over a thousand years. I don't mind being connected with them though. I'm a minor stockholder."

"Even we're minor," David said. "The FTL project is the most popular place to throw away money. So what's the occasion?"

"Just a new look," Jasper said and folded his arms. "The new cover photo looks like this." He struck his pose. He knew he looked good with his dark brown hair and brown eyes. The black shirt and star helped bring out his strength and confidence. The photographer had even called him sexy when she took the shot months ago. She hadn't known he was Sensor Man, of course.

They admired him. Brown had a wide smile on her face. He knew he looked way too serious and way too classical for today's tastes but he'd deliberately chosen that. If he was going to have to be public, he was going to stand out in the crowd.

"I like it," Elinor said. "I'd buy it just for the picture. You are one handsome man, you know." That got an amused look from David.

"Yeah, I think a lot of women will buy a copy but I'm going to have the original," Jewel said and stepped closer, wrapping his arm around her. "So hands off."

That brought laughter.

"It'll work," David said. "Who made the shirt? It's not as heavy as it looks is it?" He fingered the material approvingly.

"No," Jasper said. "Made by Rex." He'd ditched the sling for the pose but couldn't do that long without his chest aching. Letting Jewel go, he put his sling back on.

"So did we interrupt something?" David looked at Brown questioningly.

"We were done," Jasper said. "Lori brought news for us though. Kucera is dead."

"Dead?" David's eyes shifted from him to Brown. "How?"

"Suicide," Brown said. "We don't have the details yet but he left a confession."

David took a deep breath and held Elinor close to his side. Jewel just waited, almost not breathing till her uncle spoke again. "So maybe it's really done."

"I think it is," Jasper said. "If there was anyone behind him, they've got nothing to gain and a lot to lose by striking again. I'm fairly sure it won't happen."

"Good." David hugged his soon-to-be bride. "But we didn't come to discuss that. Let's talk of weddings, not the past."

Brown smiled at him then turned to Jasper. "And that's my cue to get out before I catch the wedding bug. Jewel, take care of him." Without waiting for an answer, she headed down the stairs. Her quick departure raised David's eyebrows.

"Been bitten once," Jasper said by way of explanation. "She's happy for us but won't do it again." He was used to his partner's quirk.

"Understandable," David said. "I didn't think I would do it twice." He smiled down at his petite bride.

"I thought I would," Jasper said, "but years down the road. I didn't expect to get tripped up by the girl I first saw with curlers in her hair."

Jewel turned to look up at him with those beautiful blue eyes. "You remembered." Her tone was half-accusing, half-laughing and her luscious lips radiated a smile.

"I never forgot." Jasper's smile widened. "You ducked so fast and those--they were curlers, weren't they--looked so ridiculous no one could forget them." He'd just found out today from Linda what the damn things were called.

"When was this?" David asked.

"I was fourteen," Jewel said. "Grandmother had me in curlers and he came in to check the lock--just another cop. Of course, I ducked." She gave Jasper a wicked smile. "But I watched him eat her brownies and I listened and thought he was sexy. I was so disappointed when grandmother told me you were married."

"At fourteen? Shameless."

"Hey, I learned to cook because of it. And now..." She pulled his head down and gave him a quick kiss.

"Good idea," David said and gave his Elinor a deeper one. When he would have done it again, Elinor put a hand across his lips.

"Linda is going to catch us up here smooching like college kids," Elinor said. "And she's nearly got dinner ready."

"Right." David let her go then strode over to look at the Peak. He frowned down at the police bar still on the door then turned to Jasper. "Are you going to leave that?"

"No sir. I'm looking for an improved lock that will sound an alarm through the house systems if someone comes in or jams the lock. I also want a security camera outside that we own."

"Because of your fans?" David asked.

"Well, I don't think Jewel would be happy if a bunch of rabid female fans tried to ravish me," Jasper said in a light tone. "But I just like good security."

"Butler," Jewel said, not rising to the bait. "We need Butler."

"Butler?" Jasper asked, puzzled. "That automated doorbell?"

"Oh, no, he's more than that," Jewel said. "Uncle Mike designed him. He's the newest model."

"What series is he?" David asked.

"MW-17," Jewel said then corrected it at Jasper's questioning look, "the Butler MW-17."

David frowned. "I thought he could notify police of unauthorized entries."

"He was only half-installed when Uncle Mike had his accident," Jewel explained, "so the old door lock was still there. I made a couple more connections the night I stayed there so he'd recognize me. Nothing else has been done."

She warmed to her subject. "Uncle Mike did help me design a system for this house. Grandmother wouldn't let us install one but we spent a few nights figuring it out. I want Butler to do more than just unlock doors and tell me whose here. Access to the music library, for instance."

"Hold on," Jasper said with a frown. "Are you telling me that this butler can unlock doors?"

"Of course," David said. "All the Butler models can do that. I have one at the Tower."

"Why didn't I hear it?" Jasper asked. He'd assumed Michael's automated servant was just another product of Butler, Incorporated. They were known to be a bit better than the Jeeves model he once talked Carol out of getting.

"Silent mode," David said. "Another feature. I don't like canned voices."

Jasper turned back to Jewel. "You can change the system?"

"Of course," she said. "He's a prototype. Uncle Mike wasn't done tweaking him."

Jasper stared at her. He had a prototype of a Butler model? Custom designed for the Wests or...

"You didn't think Uncle Mike was just a city engineer?" Jewel asked her indignation tempered by laughter.

Jasper took a deep breath. "Owner of Butler Systems, Inc."

He hazarded a guess. "And you're a sharpshooter," he said then turned to David. "And what secret did you hold back?"

David grinned. "Not much. I'm an inventor, yes but little stuff. My hobby is helping new inventors and investing in their products. They usually make money."

"You realize how many blind alleys I could have gone down if I'd known any of this? We did question whether Mike was the intended target and Elizabeth an extra."

David's smile faded. "But you're sure now?"

"Fairly sure," Jasper said. "It looks like Kucera wanted control of the West money and possibly this house too." He studied David. "If you haven't got it set up already that the house will go to charity, leave it."

"I intend to," David said. "There will be more Wests and when they're gone, I want the house to die too. Agreed?"

"Jewel?" Jasper looked at her, wanting to agree with David but knowing this had to be her decision.

She looked around, her blue eyes taking in the room and that glorious view of the peak before she spoke. "Not before we're dead and gone, right?"

"Not before our children are dead and gone--or their children but right."

She sighed. "Then yes. No one else should have it."

Chapter 49 – The Future

Over a leisurely dinner, David West began telling Jasper about the family--their history and current investments. Jasper wasn't surprised to learn the sixty million figure Jake had thrown out was actually just a fraction of the total. Between the West-Colman Reactor technology, part ownership in several major companies, and a fair-sized chunk of Lunarex itself, the West Foundation had billions in assets. The sixty million figure Jake had used was simply what would be allocated to him at thirty. Every member of the West family had that much under their personal control at that age but the real wealth was tied up in the West Foundation.

His fortune, which was by no means small, was tiny by comparison. He didn't care. Having lived with his own, he knew better than to count such money as a blessing. Of course, his had grown partly because he lived frugally. He suspected the same was true of generations of Wests.

"My father was the last of the Wests when he married Elizabeth Sullivan," David was saying. "It looked like the family line was back before New Wave happened." His face was bleak as he recalled that event. "Six dead. If my parents hadn't had Jewel and I hadn't had Jake to raise, it might have been the end of us. It was only the kids that kept us going. Now Jake is gone too."

A black mood started to settle on him but Elinor's touch helped him shake it off. He smiled at Jewel. "We have a duty to keep the name alive. We'll both have to do it."

Jasper cleared his throat.

"Do you have a problem with that?" David asked him one eyebrow raised.

"No," Jasper said. "Our first child at least will be a West but," he debated telling them another time then decided this was the right moment, "did you know Sasha is going to exercise her rights?"

Jewel understood first, her eyes flying to her uncle. Elinor was next.

David's set expression gave no clue to what he was thinking but he finally nodded. "Wests on Mars after all. I wasn't sure if Jake had done that. She has the right."

Jasper's respect grew. David wouldn't deny his daughter-in-law even with so much money at stake.

"I'm not sure I would have said that last week," David admitted. "Her first impression on the family was pretty misleading. Now--well, I think we'd better hold on to all the family we can."

He made no mention of Ivan's actions but that didn't matter. Sasha's future and his debt to Ivan were different subjects. Jasper knew he wouldn't forget Ivan Kowalski.

"Let's talk weddings before babies," Elinor suddenly said, her brown eyes flashing. "I'm not having one without the other."

"Yes, let's," Jewel seconded her. "I want to get it done."

David grinned. "The impatience of the young," he said his eyes going to Jasper. "Are you still holding out?"

Jewel's exasperated exclamation was answer enough and he laughed.

"Patience, Jewel. It's like Christmas. You have to wait until the day," David teased.

"You didn't wait," Jewel pointed out.

Jasper felt himself reddening as he became the package they discussed but he was smiling too. David had put it right.

"Elinor needed me then and there," David said, his hand clasping hers. "To give her the gumption to live."

"Yes," Elinor said and raised their clasped hands for a light kiss on his. "The pain was," she shuddered. "David was... incredible," she finally finished.

"In bed?" Jasper asked and watched as the color rose into her cheeks.

"And out!" Elinor said and then they were all laughing, David looking both pleased and embarrassed as hell.

"So is everything all set for your wedding?" Jasper asked. "The arrangements are all made?"

"Yes, yes, it's next Saturday," David said. "Will you stand up with me? I'd like it."

Jasper nodded. "It's an honor."

"Let's make it a double wedding," Jewel suggested. "We'll all be there. Why not just get it all done at once?"

"That's an idea," David said, looking to Elinor for her approval. "If we can keep the press out of it," he added with a look at Jasper. "That's not the best place to have reporters poking in."

"No invitations to ours," Jewel said. "We can alert our friends but no formal statements. They won't know until too late."

"No," Jasper said.

"No?" David looked at him. "No on what?"

"No, we don't combine weddings," Jasper said and he didn't dare look at Jewel. Laying his fork down, he continued. "This is Jewel's first and only wedding and it has to be done right. I know it'll take time but I have to insist."

God, he hated to see the disappointment in her face. How could he tell her it was necessary? She needed the big wedding, torturous as it was, and Sensor Man wouldn't quietly get married in a senior care facility. Now that he'd gone public, he had to do it in a big way. He had to be the kind of star that would attract the wrong people. He was acutely aware of the locket on his chest and what it contained.

"He's right," Elinor said. "Jewel, you should have the white dress and everything."

"I will not wear white," Jewel responded, "and I won't wait." Throwing her napkin on her plate, she fled the table.

Jasper started to rise but she'd already disappeared down the stairs. He sat down again, not sure he could catch her.

"You're going to have a handful if this takes long," David said. "Are you going to need a wedding organizer?"

"I thought I would ask Jessica to plan it," Jasper said, still thinking of Jewel. "She has the people."

"God." David looked at him in dismay. "She'll make it a circus."

"A media circus," Jasper agreed. "Think she'll do it?"

"She would love to," David said. "But it will take months to do properly and you're going to have enough trouble holding out till next week. Jewel is one determined girl."

"I'll take care of it," Jasper said.

David and Elinor both looked at him skeptically.

"Don't worry," Jasper said. "She'll be smiling at your wedding." Somehow he'd manage it.

"Good," David finally said. "You're a lot stronger than I am but no one can hold out forever."

Elinor looked like she wanted to follow Jewel downstairs but David had her hand. "Let's go back to the Grand," he said. "I'm beginning to enjoy that place."

"But we have to go down unless you plan to walk to the nearest public entrance."

Jasper and David exchanged looks and this time Jasper smiled, appreciating the problem. How does he get by a probably angry, possibly crying niece with a fiancé who would most likely give her comfort.

"She's probably in her rooms," David tentatively said. "Elinor, do not talk to her. She'll cry on your shoulder and we'll never get out of here."

"But it's Jewel," Elinor said.

"Let me take care of it," Jasper said. "She'd much rather cry on mine."

Elinor gave him a smile but it was clear she had doubts. David was more supportive. "Make sure she cries on the good one. Should I send Linda home?"

"Please. We can manage the dishes ourselves."

"Right. Elinor, what are you doing?" he asked as she started stacking dishes.

"Just putting them in the dumb waiter, love," she said. "Jasper can't manage yet. Then on the way out, I'll put them in the sink. Much easier."

"Thanks," Jasper said. "That will save me some steps."

"You're welcome. I hope you heal up soon. Jewel will be much happier." She took the dishes to the dumb waiter and headed downstairs.

"I'd better follow," David said. "If she talks to Jewel, we won't be going anywhere tonight."

Jasper grinned. "Let me know when you get out the door."

The one thing he'd regretted about his first marriage was the courthouse wedding. He'd been twenty and Carol had just turned twenty-one when they reasonably decided to save money and do it that way. Carol had been an orphan and his mother hadn't been there and there'd been no white dress. He hadn't known for years how much Carol had missed that. There was no way to correct that for her but he didn't want Jewel thinking the same thing. That and his new image demanded they do it right.

He sat down and waited then got up and prowled through his bedroom and waited some more. After what must have been close to an hour, his com unit buzzed.

"We're out," David said. "She had to help Linda do the dishes. Linda's out too. Jewel is in the sitting area on the second floor. I don't envy you at all. Good night."

How the hell was he going to do this? Jasper only had a vague idea but he knew it was time. Slowly he descended to the second floor. Beyond the third floor, only the chandelier and the lights on the stairway remained lit, leaving the rest of the house in semi-darkness.

He paused, not knowing where the light switch was on this floor. He knew where the sitting area was though and moved slowly toward it. At first he didn't think she was there it was so quiet. Damn, had she gone to sleep? Or was she in her room after all?

"Jewel?" he murmured. Slowly his eyes made out a shadowy form reclining on the couch, her head turned away from him. He made his way there and sat down on the edge and slowly rubbed her back with his good hand. She stirred, shifting to look up at him and his hand fell away.

"What?" Jewel said, her voice husky with tears.

Had she been sleeping after all?

"I need help getting this shirt off."

Her wordless protest made him grin.

"Raise your arms," she said as she tucked his locket inside and eased his shirt up over his bandages. "Both arms, please," she repeated when he didn't. "No, wait, let me get this sling off." She lowered his shirt and removed the sling, tossing it aside. "Now both arms."

He raised his arms, letting her pull the shirt over his head. Just before it was completely free, he smoothly slid his shirt-encased arms over her head and down around her back.

"Wait a minute. I think I'm stuck," she said, looking up at him.

"I'll say you are," he responded and lowered his mouth to hers. His firm lips pressed against her luscious ones, forcing her with gentle pressure to open to him. He was in no hurry but her lips came alive under his and she began kissing him back for all she was worth. He let her have her fun then inexorably took control again, kissing her until they were both breathless.

Damn, it had been too long. Jasper felt himself harden and his pulse quickened, his breath coming harder.

Nuzzling her neck, he tasted her then nipped her so suddenly she yelped in surprise. His hands found their way under her top and stroked her ribs with sure fingers, his hands inching closer to her small breasts.

Her breath was coming fast now and she clung to him, heedless of his shoulder. When she clutched too hard, he winced.

"Sorry," she drew away, her eyes dark pools in the dim light. "We'd better stop. Your shoulder."

"Damn my shoulder," he said in a voice rough with lust. "Come here, minx."

She froze. "Here? Now?" her voice squeaked.

He laughed. Was she suddenly going to go shy on him? That he knew how to handle.

"You said," she reminded in a breathless voice, "the wedding."

"What about it?" His hands found her bra and he lifted it, freeing her nipples. Without waiting for her answer, he lowered his head to lick one sweet bud then he sucked.

Jewel groaned, arching her back. His questing hand found her other nipple and it hardened under his touch. Her shirt was gone, tossed onto the floor with his. She made soft animal cries as his lips nibbled and teased her young breasts.

"The wedding." She tried again when she could catch her breath. "You wanted to wait."

His eyes met hers in the semi-darkness and he smiled. "I never said you'd have to wait."

She froze, her eyes going wide with surprise, then she let out a whoop of delight and twisted free. His hands groped for where she'd been and he heard her laughter as she raced up the stairs.

"Minx," he bellowed and she laughed harder, her voice coming from somewhere above him.

"Come up, my sensor man, and play with me."

"Hussy," he yelled again, laughing. "I'm coming." He stalked toward the stairs, his movements swift and sure. This was going to be a night to remember.

THE END

A LOOK AHEAD

Here's a simple teaser from TO MARRY AND SUSPECT, the second Jasper Stone novel.

EDWARD KUCERA'S CONFESSION

I confess I was a fool but I had nothing to do with murder. Why would I kill my richest client? Jake West was going to Mars and I was going to represent him here on Earth. When he turned thirty he was going to the richest client in my business. I didn't kill him or order him killed.

Mike West was a good friend. I didn't order his death either.

Elizabeth West was a charming lady and a friend to my wife. She was past eighty and had taken the walk once already. Why would anyone waste time or money killing her? I certainly didn't.

I admit to some contact with the man you've called Starling. I knew him simply as Smith. He was introduced to me and I introduced him to Jake--as a favor for a friend.

Somehow I've been framed for these murders but none of them, particularly Jake's, benefited me. There are only two people they would have helped. Elizabeth's granddaughter stood to inherit everything just like Jake. You may dismiss her as just a schoolteacher but she's a West and easily the cleverest of them. She and the man she intends to marry should be questioned thoroughly. He's almost as clever as she is--not quite for I know his true role.

I'm done. Clear my name.

~~Edward Kucera

ABOUT THE AUTHOR

Ellen Anthony ran away from Wyoming in 2020, traveling through ten states and 5400 miles before the pandemic made her stop. Her characters tracked her down and continue to keep her life interesting in an undisclosed location. To find out more about the Jasper Stone series, the Syran series, and Letters Through Time, visit her author pages on Facebook (The Jasper Stone Mysteries). Your thoughts and reviews are deeply appreciated.

THE JASPER STONE SERIES

Murder is Bliss (2013) - Police Lieutenant Jasper Stone is called on to solve the most high profile case of his career when Elizabeth West is murdered. The suspects include her sons, her grandson, her granddaughter and a family friend. When one son is murdered the same day, Jasper finds himself trying to protect Jewel West as he unravels the case. To complicate matters, his secret life as a popular composer of sensa has now come out and he must dodge reporters while he does his job.

To Marry and Suspect (2013) – Former Police Lieutenant Jasper Stone a.k.a. Sensor Man marries his Jewel in a high society wedding. Afterward Jewel is implicated in her family murders then kidnapped. Jasper must cooperate with the kidnappers to get her back and re-investigate the West murders and the blissex drug ring that now seem to be connected.

Coral Crosses (2014) – A date with an orchestra in Coral Ridge, Florida turns into a plot to bomb the underwater resort city. Jasper doesn't believe for one moment the terrorists have a hydrogen bomb but when his bodyguard and another federal agent are ambushed, he's drawn into the investigation, wife and all. Why are the terrorists trying to stop the Ogaden/Somaliland conference? And who is that woman stalking him?

Between Heaven and Hell (2014) – A small investigation into Hades Syndrome unexpectedly blows up into kidnappings and murder. Jasper takes his wife and youngest son to Paradise Station to protect them then finds himself on a space-age ranch in Wyoming where they are tracked by one of the villain's lackeys. Meanwhile Kale Tunis is doing his part in rescuing one of Jewel's employees and following leads that lead him to Puerto Rico. When he joins forces with Jasper Stone, they go after a man who might be responsible for thousands of deaths from Hades—including Jasper's first wife.

Shadow Mars (2015) – Dick Mason, space cowboy and Jewel's cousin from Between, goes to Mars with two missions—protect Sasha West and uncover an illegal gold mine. When he is deliberately infected with a flu virus and inadvertently takes it straight to Sasha's boys, he falls under suspicion and now must prove his innocence as well. Sasha West won't have anything to do with a man who thinks he's cock-of-the-walk and God's gift to women but he has his orders. The hard part is not falling for the magnificent widow of Jake West.

Shadow Earth (2015) - When a space plane gets crashed by a virus, Jasper finds himself embroiled in two new investigations this time for the West Foundation. Will he uncover the source of the viruses that have plagued the Mars ships? Can he prove Kale isn't guilty of rape? And what is it with all those balls?

Webs of Deceit (2016) – Kale Tunis is sent to Africa to investigate a possible genocide while Jasper concentrates on finding out the manufacturer of the gas used. Angel Damask returns with conflicting orders. This time the CIA agent is legally investigating the West Foundation and their mission in Africa—and trying not to cross paths with Kale who knows exactly who she is.

Rebel Circuits (2020) "We will get her back." When 15-year-old Anita Spears is abducted from the West Foundation complex in Houston, Jasper Stone makes that promise to his employees and their families. He never dreamed Anita was not alone. As the case balloons, Jasper finds himself embroiled in illegal experimentation, artificial intelligence, and secrets the Foundation has kept for more than a century.

For the Future (2021) An explosion heralds a package from the future and thrusts David Wilson among the leaders of the West Foundation. Can they believe what it says and can they set the Foundation on a path to guard Earth's future? It all rests on Wilson and a child not yet born.

Light & Shadows (2023) When a simple stock manipulation case blows up, Herb Jordan gets embroiled in bribery, illegal arms sales, and a found missile. Who is his mysterious client? Who wants him dead? And how does the West Foundation fit in?

Shipwreck! (pending) Jasper Stone is back! His return trip from Mars turns into a nightmare and he must depend on his sons for rescue.

The Future Comes (pending) Events predicted in 2090 finally happen. Will the West Foundation find a way to save humanity? Or will they lose Earth?